Praise for *Magpie's Bend*

'A delight from start to end . . . don't tell Penny and Angie, but I think Lara's story might be my favourite yet!' Bookish Bron

'Beautifully written from the opening pages . . . A story about learning to love and trust again.' Tanya, @Read by the Librarian

'A ripper of a read with something on nearly every page that rang true to me—the Australianisms, the landscape, the characters and their language.' Sueanne, Done and Dusted Books

'Immersing yourself in the country characters and spirit of Bridgefield is a delight.' CWA *Ruth* Magazine

'So much delicious baking in this book you'll be ready to fire up your own oven and whip something up as soon as you finish reading. Enjoy!' Australian Romance Readers Association

'*Magpie's Bend* is a heartfelt, winsome and satisfying rural romance, a delightful read . . .' Shelleyrae, Book'd Out

'Always a joy to read Maya's rural romance stories . . . so authentic and well written.' Michelle Beesley, SheSociety

Praise for *Bottlebrush Creek*

New Idea Book of the Month
Sunday Age #3 Bestselling Romance
Top 10 Aus Fiction Bestseller
Weekend Australian #4 Bestselling Romance
Shortlisted for Favourite Australian-set Romance in the Australian
Romance Readers Association Awards

'*Bottlebrush Creek* will keep you turning pages into the early hours of the next morning.' Bestselling author Tabitha Bird

T0018506

Bestselling rural fiction author Maya Linnell gathers inspiration from her rural upbringing and the small communities she has always lived in and loved. *Magpie's Bend* is her third novel, following *Bottlebrush Creek* and *Wildflower Ridge.* A former country journalist and radio host, Maya also blogs for Romance Writers Australia, loves baking up a storm, tending to her rambling garden and raising three young bookworms. She writes to a soundtrack of magpies and chickens on a small property in country Victoria, where she lives with her family, their menagerie of farm animals and the odd tiger snake or two. For a regular slice of country living, follow Maya on social media or sign up to her monthly newsletter at mayalinnell.com.

@maya.linnell.writes

Magpie's
Bend

MAYA LINNELL

Magpie's Bend

ALLEN&UNWIN
SYDNEY · MELBOURNE · AUCKLAND · LONDON

This edition published in 2022
First published in 2021

Allen & Unwin
83 Alexander Street
Crows Nest NSW 2065
Australia
Phone: (61 2) 8425 0100
Email: info@allenandunwin.com
Web: www.allenandunwin.com

A catalogue record for this
book is available from the
National Library of Australia

ISBN 978 1 76106 707 5

Set in Sabon LT Pro by Bookhouse, Sydney
Printed in Australia by McPherson's Printing Group

10 9 8 7 6 5 4 3 2 1

The paper in this book is FSC® certified.
FSC® promotes environmentally responsible,
socially beneficial and economically viable
management of the world's forests.

For Charles, Amelia and Elizabeth.
My three littlest loves

One

Lara McIntyre charged through the front door of the Bridgefield General Store and headed straight for the postcard display.

As a kid she'd delighted in the store's one-cent lollies; through her teen years she'd posted letters to her pen pals and ordered countless hot pies and cold drinks; and she had bought more bread, milk and newspapers than she could remember—but never before had she browsed the postcard range.

In fact, Lara decided, wiping the layer of dust from the panoramas of mountains, sheep-filled paddocks and the sun setting over Bridgefield Lake, it seemed like nobody had browsed the postcard range in decades.

She chose one featuring the Grampians Mountain Range and headed to the counter, certain the memento would put a smile on her daughter Evie's face when it arrived at her fancy city boarding school.

The pie warmer glowed and cricket commentary blared from the radio, but there was no sign of the town's postmistress or her wayward nephew who helped run the shop.

Lara craned her neck to see into the back room.

'Mrs Beggs?'

Lara called out again. It still felt a little odd to not be standing on the other side of the counter serving, as she had done all through her teens. 'Mrs Beggs?'

Nothing.

She sniffed, trying to identify the strange smell. *And what was that crackling noise?*

Lara felt a prickle of apprehension. She dumped her postcard and keyring on the counter and rushed into the shop's kitchen.

A well-worn novel lay on the tea-room table, next to a half-drunk mug of tea and an empty egg carton. Eggs jumped in the now-dry saucepan, not just hard boiled but burned beyond redemption. Lara switched off the stovetop and opened a window to disperse the acrid smell.

'Mrs Beggs? Dallas?'

Sweeping into the cluttered storeroom, Lara kept her voice calm. She gulped when she spotted a black shoe beside a pile of boxes.

Her nursing instincts kicked in. She quickly assessed the situation.

If it wasn't for the arm twisted behind her, or the blood seeping from a wound on her cheek, Mrs Beggs could have been sleeping. She and Evie had both joked about being buried alive in Mrs Beggs' storeroom during their years at the shop, but the sight of those boxes resting awkwardly on the postmistress's chest wasn't the least bit funny.

Lara crouched down, gently trying to rouse her.

'Mrs Beggs, are you okay? Mrs Beggs?'

❧

Toby Paxton whistled as he locked the newspaper building. The decrepit offices of the *Bridgefield Advertiser* were a far cry from *The Ballarat Daily*'s bustling newsroom, but there was a charm to the heritage-listed building. The small farming community had a similar allure, and the 5 p.m. knock-offs were a pretty good perk of the job too.

He pulled on his bike helmet and cycled to the general store, sniffing as he opened the large glass door. The old-fashioned doorbell jangled and the strange smell grew stronger.

Maybe the pie warmer's on the fritz?

Toby grabbed a lonely bottle of soy milk from the fridge, plus a handful of bananas, and placed them on the counter, eyeing a seemingly forgotten set of car keys.

'Hello?'

Normally the shopkeeper was eager to greet each customer, the potential for local gossip quickening her movements, but not today. Mrs Beggs was too wide to hide behind the rack of birthday cards or disappear between the shelves of over-priced groceries. Her assistant, Dallas, was nowhere to be seen either. Toby scanned the bright little general store, normally pumping with customers but now eerily quiet. *Something's burning . . .*

His thoughts were interrupted as a slender woman rushed out from the back of the store. Her hair was scraped up into a high, auburn ponytail and there was a symmetry to her features that would look striking in black and white. He couldn't quite make out the logo on her monogrammed shirt, but whoever she was, she didn't look like she was here to serve pies or hand over his mail.

'Hurry, I need a hand back here,' she called, retreating without waiting for an answer. Toby automatically reached into his camera bag, then hesitated.

You're not in the city anymore.

He pulled out the Nikon anyway.

⁂

Lara cleared the boxes and pressed a tea towel against the wound on the older woman's cheek.

'Mrs Beggs, Winnie, can you hear me? It's Lara. We're going to get you to hospital,' she said as footsteps clattered down the hallway. Lara spoke over her shoulder, firing out instructions to the customer buying fancy milk.

'Do you have a mobile? I've left mine in the car. Can you call an ambulance? And flick the door sign to closed. We don't need somebody running off with the till while she's crashed out here. And a blanket if you can find one,' said Lara, checking the pulse again.

Weaker than she would have liked.

'Hang in there, Mrs Beggs,' she said, her concern growing at the postmistress's vague murmurings.

'I've got a delivery coming, Annabel . . . Christmas specials . . . Down by the lake, I said.'

Lara swept the curls off Mrs Beggs' forehead and pushed a small step-ladder aside to give her more space.

'It's Lara McIntyre, not Annabel,' she said gently. 'And Christmas has been and gone, Mrs Beggs.' Whatever box had knocked Mrs Beggs down, it had done a good job of it. Annabel McIntyre had passed away almost twenty years ago, when Lara and her sisters were in high school. Although Lara had the same pale skin, straight teeth and glossy copper-coloured hair, it was rare for anyone to mistake her for her mother, especially Mrs Beggs, who had been Annabel's best friend and a strong, warm presence in Lara's life as long as she could remember.

The man returned with a phone. He crouched down beside her, draping a tablecloth over Mrs Beggs. In the midst of the chaos, Lara noticed the gap between his shoes and his trousers: one sock was blue and the other featured colourful cartoons.

'What's happened? Should we sit her up?'

What type of idiot is this guy? Lara spun around and fixed him with a withering glare, first noticing the camera slung around his neck, then the bicycle helmet he wore, and finally the deep black eyelashes that belonged on a jersey cow, not a man.

Of all the people to walk into the general store when she needed help, did it have to be a cyclist with no idea of first aid who couldn't even match his socks? Even Mrs Beggs' inept nephew, Dallas Ruggles, would be more helpful than this bloke.

She looked at him again, placing his face. The new journalist in town. 'Brilliant, the paparazzi's here. Call the ambulance already!'

She kept one eye on him and one on Mrs Beggs, wishing he'd move a little faster. He toyed with the camera strap as he spoke with the emergency operator.

'We've got a woman injured at the Bridgefield General Store. Hmm, not sure. Hang on.' He turned back to Lara.

'Her condition?'

'Dropping in and out of consciousness. Deformed right shoulder, possibly dislocated or fractured. Pulse is weak, with an open wound to her cheek. I think she's been down for about ten minutes or so. Tell them I'm a nurse.'

He repeated the information, then added his own. 'We're in Bridgefield, western Victoria. Um . . .' He looked at Lara. 'Street number?' Then shook his head. 'It's the only shop in the main street. Stripy verandah. Old bluestone. Trust me, the ambos won't miss it.'

He bobbed his head. 'They're on their way,' he said, shoving the phone into his pocket.

Mrs Beggs groaned. 'I'm going to be sick.'

'Let's make you more comfortable,' said Lara, helping roll her onto her side. The arm dangled awkwardly. Lara couldn't leave it like that. 'This might hurt a bit,' she said, repositioning Mrs Beggs' arm and shoulder as carefully as she could.

Mrs Beggs' breathing accelerated, and she gave a sudden shudder before going limp.

'She all right?' Toby crouched down beside them.

'I think she'll be fine until the ambulance gets here, it's just the pain,' said Lara tersely.

Lara worked on autopilot, blocking out the cluttered room and the tall reporter. She splinted Mrs Beggs' arm to immobilise the shoulder, and dressed the wound on her cheek, all the while keeping an eye on her pulse and breathing. She was used to handling patients and emergencies, yet she still breathed a sigh of relief when the paramedics filed into the storeroom.

Lara followed as they stretchered Mrs Beggs out of the store. She was surprised to find the sun still high in the sky, and fluttered her shirt to get some air on her clammy skin. A crowd formed in the street, locals unashamedly jostling for a better view.

'You've done well, Mrs Beggs.' Lara gently squeezed the older woman's good hand before she was loaded into the ambulance.

A light touch on her shoulder made Lara jump. She whirled around.

It was the newspaper guy, camera still dangling around his neck, his bike helmet now sitting at a jaunty angle.

'You've done well too,' he said kindly. 'You saved her life in there.'

'Anyone with basic first-aid skills would have done exactly the same,' Lara said, dismissing the praise.

He stuck out a hand. His smile was lopsided, which added a boyish charm to his closely cropped hair and carefully pressed clothes.

No wonder Mrs Beggs was singing his praises the other week. Half of Bridgefield's divorcees probably had designs on him already.

'Toby Paxton.'

Lara shook his hand quickly but firmly.

'Lara McIntyre.'

'Pleased to meet you, Lara. I got some great photos of you in action.'

Lara's stomach dropped.

What?!? She spoke through gritted teeth. 'Delete them. Now. Every bloody one of them.'

Alarm flashed across his face as she reached for the camera. He covered the Nikon protectively.

'I wasn't going to put them in the paper or anything. Well, not unless you and Mrs Beggs give the all-clear. They're great pictures. Don't you even want to see them?'

Like hell she did. She knew firsthand that nothing good ever came from sneaky photography.

'Unless you fancy joining Mrs Beggs in the back of that ambulance, you'd better hit delete.'

A long run and a hot shower beckoned, but Lara stood her ground and waited as Toby fiddled with his camera.

'Done,' he said quietly, twisting the camera monitor to her.

She peered at the screen, still seething. *The cheek of him.*

At her terse nod, he loaded the Nikon into a padded bag and slung it over his shoulder. 'I'll see you around.'

Lara watched him cycle away, then scanned the crowd, her frown deepening as a familiar Hawaiian-shirted man made his way towards her.

Dallas Bloody Ruggles.

'Bit of action in the street, eh? What did I miss?'

The man's eagerness was almost as off-putting as the strong cologne and cheap button-up he wore.

'Your aunt's on her way to hospital, which you'd have noticed if you were actually at work.'

Dallas gaped. He whirled around to see the ambulance disappear around the corner.

'No way? What happened? Is she okay?'

She caught his guilty glance towards the pub.

Putting another flutter on, I'll bet.

Lara narrowed her eyes. 'I don't know. But I'm sure she would have appreciated your help.'

Dallas followed her into the general store.

'Guess I'll lock up, then?' he said, the note of uncertainty in his voice making it clear that he was not normally given such responsibility.

Lara collected her belongings as well as Mrs Beggs' handbag, and shrugged off the temptation to watch Dallas close the shop for the night, just to be sure. It wasn't until she was halfway home that she realised she'd left Evie's postcard on the counter. And not only that, but for the first time in months, she'd spent two whole hours without dwelling on the Evie-shaped hole in her life.

⁂

Bridgefield Lake appeared, vast and glinting in the sunlight, as Toby crested the dusty hill. The Grampians Mountain Range was mirrored in the water, along with fluffy clouds that were more for show than actual rain-delivery purposes. Windmill Track wasn't the most direct route home—it would have taken him five minutes in the car as opposed to thirty-ish minutes on the bike—and the hill was a killer on the way up, but the view across the lake and paddocks was worth it.

The old windmill at the top of the track creaked and groaned as Toby stopped to catch his breath.

The scenery was postcard perfect compared to the old commute. The streets of Ballarat and Melbourne's laneways held their own appeal, but he didn't miss the traffic fumes or crazy drivers. The past two months in his new home had instead been filled with colour and sound and wildlife of one kind or another, which suited him just fine.

He coasted down the hill, finally arriving at the cottage he leased. The lawn he'd mowed the night before looked sharp, and he could see it had flourished after last month's Weed 'n' Feed.

Parking his bike in the small shed, Toby strolled inside, pleased he'd made the effort to do a quick whip around before he'd left for work that morning. He liked it neat and tidy. Especially on the weekends his daughter, Holly, came to stay.

She'll be here within the hour, he realised, looking at his watch. He stashed Holly's soy milk in the fridge, gently placed his camera bag on the table and started fixing dinner. Before long, a bowl of pizza dough was rising on the windowsill, pizza toppings were diced and he was pouring himself a glass of Coonawarra red.

As the one-man-band running the town's weekly newspaper, every workday was different. Today's articles had taken him to the cattle sales, the primary school, a new farm-gate business, and the town's newly resurfaced netball courts all ready for the upcoming season. He loved the broad scope of his work. Small-town news stories and country articles were a nice change from front-page fatalities, although today at the shop . . .

It had been the most action he'd seen since he arrived in Bridgefield. He sipped his wine.

Lara McIntyre. The name rang a bell. Same surname as the father and daughter at the saleyards that morning. The woman buying cattle had similar features, but her smile had been quick, and she'd happily posed for a picture. Lara, on the other hand, hadn't even glanced at the photos he'd taken before ordering him to delete them. *What was with that?*

Toby was googling recovery software, trying to work out whether he could retrieve the deleted pictures—*Just for a look, then I'll format the memory card*—when a small, sleek car inched down his driveway. He strode across the kitchen, taking the front steps two at a time.

'Dad!'

Holly jumped out of the car before it was properly parked. She launched herself into his arms the way she'd done as a little girl, smelling like vanilla body spray and chewing gum and feeling taller than when he'd hugged her last. He squeezed her tight, rocking her from side to side before straightening his arms to get a good look at her. She turned away, suddenly a fifteen-year-old again.

'Hey Lollypop, how's my girl?'

'Daaa-ad,' Holly always protested at the nickname, but he knew she secretly liked it. He kissed the top of her head and slung an arm around her shoulder.

'You'd better hope the wind doesn't change, Holly,' said Petra as she leaned out the car window. Toby waved to his ex-wife, trying not to be offended by the glare she reserved just for him.

What now? Knowing Petra, it could be anything, from the blue polo shirt he wore—identical to another eight in his wardrobe—to her longstanding disappointment that he dared to cope, quite well, in fact, without her. Or, quite possibly, it was something completely new.

'How's things?'

Petra's face clouded with irritation at his cheerful greeting. 'Fine.' Her forehead hadn't creased, her eyes hadn't wrinkled, but there was no mistaking her grouchy tone.

Toby folded his arms across his chest, resisting the urge to groan aloud. There was no good response to that one. He backed away to retrieve Holly's luggage from the boot, trying not to dwell on the rapidly changing contours of his ex-wife's face. Petra might be thrilled with her new, 'improved' image but it was a far cry from the natural look he'd once fallen in love with.

Petra stayed in the car. She blew a kiss to her daughter, then fixed Toby with another icy glare. 'Make sure she does her homework, and can you please talk some sense into her about clarinet lessons? She'll never get into the school orchestra if she doesn't practise.'

Toby spotted Holly discreetly pushing the instrument case back into the car boot, and only just managed to keep a straight face.

'Nice seeing you too, Petra. I'm grand, thanks for asking. You coming in or heading straight back to Ballarat?' They all knew the answer, but he wanted Holly to see at least one of them making an effort.

Standing together, father and daughter waved until the car disappeared out of sight. 'She won't be happy when she realises you "forgot" your clarinet,' Toby said wryly.

Two

Swampy lakes dotted the paddocks, thanks to a soggy spring and damp summer, and the frogs put on their usual dusk concert as Lara ran past. Hereford cattle trotted along the barbed-wire fence.

'Evening, cows,' Lara called out.

As usual there was no response from the cows, but the thicket of roadside shrubs twitched. Out dashed Basil the kelpie, in full pursuit of a terrified rabbit. He barely slowed at Lara's whistle, only returning to her side when she reached the grass laneway dividing the neighbour's land from her own.

A flash of black-and-white feathers swooped in front of them.

'Oh sod off,' Lara snapped, breaking stride to wave her hands above her head. 'Damn magpies.'

Basil barked and leaped, but like most evenings, he failed to get within spitting distance.

The birds followed them towards Lara's big old homestead, and, much to her chagrin, settled in the flowering gum by the chook house. She could only wonder in frustration how many eggs they had pinched today.

Lara looked at the grass that needed cutting, the hedge that needed clipping. The line under the verandah flapped with washing: one pair of trousers, one work blouse, one set of running clothes, one set of underwear. The lonely sight was almost enough to make her turn around and head out for another five kilometres, but it was nearly Evie o'clock.

She dashed through the shower and rummaged in the pantry for a piece of muesli slice. It wasn't completely decadent, she told herself, savouring the sultanas and chewy oats, not like the chocolate-drizzled Florentines she was saving for dessert, but it would tide her over until dinner.

The phone rang as Lara settled on the lounge with a mug of tea.

'Hey Evie-girl, right on time!'

'Hi Mum. You won't *believe* the day I've had,' said Evie with a groan, before launching into a story about the year-nine class excursion. Lara was entertained by her daughter's dramatic recount, told with the flair and indignation only teenagers could manage.

'And I'm totally sure *all* the boarding house will be riddled with food poisoning based on the lunch they served us. It was *horrific*,' said Evie.

It was on the tip of Lara's tongue to explain that boarding-house meals were part and parcel of the life Evie had so desperately wanted and worked so hard for. The swanky private school had been Evie's idea, and as proud as Lara had been when they'd awarded her a full scholarship, she selfishly wished her precious girl had stayed in Bridgefield.

'Well, I guess you're coming home then, so I can make you hot meals and fabulous desserts every night of the week?'

'Nice try, Mum. What's happening in sleepy old Bridgefield today?'

'It's been a hive of activity, I'll have you know,' said Lara, adding her own mock indignation. 'And wait until you hear about the action at the shop.'

Just like Lara before her, Evie had worked as a casual for Mrs Beggs, learning the ins and outs of customer service, money handling and, most importantly, responsibility in the small business.

'Poor Mrs Beggs. Will she be all right?'

'We won't know more until the X-rays are back, but the fracture looked pretty rough. She'll be out of action for a few weeks at least.'

'Shall I make her a get-well card?'

Lara smiled. *That's my girl.* Kind, caring and thoughtful. She missed her even more.

✑

'Rise and shine, Lollypop,' said Toby, flinging open the spare-bedroom curtains. The lump in the middle of the single bed shifted. A moan erupted.

'Ss-too-eeeeearly.'

'Where's the kid who used to jump out of bed each morning to lace my sneakers? I've already got ten k's under my belt, had a shower and cooked brekky and you've barely stirred.'

'Justanotherhour,' Holly groaned.

'Up to you. Thought we'd head to Halls Gap after the sports photos, take some scenic shots, feed the kangaroos . . .' Toby played his trump card. 'Maybe grab some ice cream?'

Holly peeked out from under the floral quilt.

'With the homemade waffle cones?'

Bingo. Toby had known that would be the clincher.

'Absolutely.'

Toby restocked his camera bag, added sunscreen and drink bottles, and had them on the road before 8 a.m. The rock wallabies were out in force and he barely nudged the speed limit as he drove towards the mountains.

'Which camera did you pack for me, Dad? Tell me it's not the point-and-shoot one? I'll never be able to take award-winning photos like you if I don't practise with a real camera,' she said.

Toby took his eyes off the road and grinned. 'We'll take turns with mine, but keep the strap around your neck.' His camera was old compared to the latest digital models, but a replacement wasn't in the budget anytime soon.

'How's the portrait collection coming along?' Holly asked. 'You're a shoo-in to win again. I can just see you with that new top-of-the-line Nikon they're giving away.'

Toby thought of the photo he'd taken yesterday. As soon as the shutter closed, he'd known the picture would look fantastic stretched onto canvas. If he'd thought it had been hard deleting them outside the shop yesterday, it was nothing compared to looking at them on the laptop screen and *then* hitting delete.

He'd felt like a bit of a scumbag recovering the photos after he'd promised to delete them, but it had been worth it to prove to himself that the shot had been near perfect. If only Lara had looked at the photos, she would have seen herself as he had. In those pictures he'd captured a snapshot of beauty, distilled the urgency of the moment, framed her strength through the lens.

Even if he was the only one who would ever know it.

'The only thing close to award-winning is gone. I've got nothing to enter.'

'Not another transfer stuff-up?' asked Holly.

The sports club at the foot of the mountains came into view. As far as settings got, this was pretty hard to beat. Toby shook his head. 'Unhappy subject. To be fair, it was a photo I'd taken without asking during a medical emergency.'

'Cool! Blood and guts? Why didn't they like the photos? Or did the person cark it?'

Toby pulled up at the tennis courts and fixed his daughter with a stern look.

'Holly Adeline Paxton. Where's your compassion? It *wouldn't* be cool if there was blood and guts everywhere, and no, she didn't cark it.'

Toby explained the hullabaloo of last night, and how he'd called the hospital for an update before turning in for the evening.

'She's stable, but it's not something to get excited about,' he said, giving her his firmest 'dad' look.

'Don't get your back up, Dad. You're the one who was pointing a camera during a medical emergency. Shouldn't you have been, like, helping?'

Toby pocketed his car keys, straightened his collar in the rear-view mirror and tugged a baseball cap over his dark hair. Was that why Lara was so peeved? Had he been transfixed by the photo opportunity instead of the emergency? He shifted uncomfortably in his seat.

'You've got me there,' he said. Handing Holly the camera bag, Toby briefed her on the type of shots he wanted for next week's back page. 'Come on, you can help me choose an angle to make these kids look like tennis pros.'

⁂

The Bridgefield Bush Nursing Centre was even busier than usual on Saturday morning, with twice as many senior citizens milling around after Lara's Move It or Lose It exercise class.

'So, you used the defibrillating machine to get Winnie's heart started again?' said Jean.

Defibrillating machine? Lara sighed. *Chinese whispers are in full force, then.*

'I heard she was airlifted to the Royal Alfred in Melbourne. Poor Winnie. She was looking fine when I saw her at lunchtime,' added Olive.

Denise scratched her head. 'I thought it was a stroke?'

Lara knew she had to set the record straight before the rumours got out of hand.

'Mrs Beggs is sore but stable. No de-fib, no stroke, just a nasty fracture. Why don't you head to Hamilton for lunch and see how she is yourself?'

The telephone ran hot, too, and by the time Lara closed the centre at midday on Saturday, she was all peopled out. *A quick check of the shop and then home*, she told herself, looping her handbag over her shoulder and striding down Bridgefield's main thoroughfare.

She picked up her pace at the sight of a teenager knocking insistently on the general store door.

'You'll crack the glass at that rate,' she said. He jumped at her sharp voice, and as he turned towards her she recognised him as one of the high-school seniors.

'Brody.'

'Mrs Kingsley . . . ah, Miss McIntyre . . .' Lara flinched slightly at the use of her old surname. The young man's face flushed bright red and he gestured to the store. 'Mrs Beggs must have closed early? I'm supposed to collect the mail.'

'You haven't heard? Mrs Beggs is in hospital, but Dallas should've been here this morning.'

'Crap.' His grimace turned contrite. 'Sorry, I mean, no good for Mrs Beggs, but Dad's expecting a tractor part. I was supposed to pick it up after school yesterday, but I forgot. He won't be pleased if I leave town without it again today. You know what he's like.' Brody swallowed hard.

Lara softened. She *did* know what he was like. Brody's father reminded her of her ex-husband Sam.

She glanced up and down Bridgefield's Main Street. A group of young women with prams blazed a path down the opposite footpath, and a handful of utes were parked nose to kerb. She'd be mobbed from each direction if she waltzed in through the front door of the shop.

'Follow me. I wanted to check the store anyway.' Lara headed around the back.

'I was going to ask Mrs Beggs about a part-time job,' Brody said. 'I know she has Dallas and another lady sometimes, but does Evie like helping out in school holidays?'

Lara unlocked the door. She located the mail shelf and sifted through the parcels.

'She sure does, it's a good little earner for her. Especially now she's at boarding school.'

'Mrs Beggs would be a dream boss. Can't imagine her yelling,' said Brody wistfully.

Lara found the parcel. She knew all too well what it was like living with a volatile man, where a minor inconvenience could have drastic repercussions.

'Thanks, Miss McIntyre,' Brody said shyly, and then found his way out.

Lara surveyed the storeroom. Toby must have tidied the fallen boxes while she was dealing with the ambulance last night, a gesture that surprised her. *Maybe I was a bit rough to bite his head off about the stupid photo.*

But before she could continue the thought, the sound of a phone ringing came from the kitchen. Lara automatically walked towards it but her hand hovered over the phone.

Answering the call would advertise the fact she had keys.

Dallas was running this place, not her.

Lara thought of Annabel McIntyre. *Mum would have jumped in head first and sorted out the logistics later.*

She retracted her hand.

The phone stopped ringing.

Lara snuck out the back door and headed home.

ॐ

Kangaroos milled around the Halls Gap oval, unperturbed by the weekend tourists clamouring to photograph them against the mountainous backdrop.

'Hurry up, Hol. Your ice cream's melting faster than I can eat it,' Toby said, taking a lick of her ice cream as well as his own. 'Those joeys will pose for photos all day long.'

Holly relinquished her vantage point and stretched out her legs, letting the camera dangle around her neck as she retrieved her ice cream.

Wiping his hands just minutes later, Toby mounted the long-distance lens to the Nikon and passed it to her.

'Try a few shots with this one,' he said encouragingly.

'I'd love a camera for my birthday. Mum says it's too expensive, though. She said I'll like the symphony-orchestra concert more than I'll like'—Holly reached up and made air quotes with her fingers—'"a silly camera".'

Toby let out a slow breath. He was determined to show respect for Petra and her parenting—even when he didn't agree—but it wasn't always easy.

'I'll talk to your mum. Maybe you can do a few jobs for me, earn some pocket money.'

Holly's delight was immediate. 'You're the best, Dad.' The camera shutter fired away as she focused on the wildlife again.

God, how he missed having her every day of the week. Now he'd settled into his new job, and tidied up his yard so it was less of a snake-haven, he hoped there would be plenty more long weekends like this. Toby lay back on the picnic rug, tipped his hat to block out the bright day and laced his hands underneath his head.

'Tell you what, Hol. I'll give you ten dollars if you go through my sports pics and delete anything not fit for the newspaper. That'll kick off your camera savings.'

'Make it twenty bucks. We've taken at least five hundred photos today. It'll take me ages.'

She was right. Culling blurry, out-of-frame shots was his least favourite part of the job.

'Fifteen dollars if you load them onto the laptop afterwards. Wake me when you're done.' He shut his eyes, listening to the bird calls, the cicadas humming and children in the nearby playground.

He woke with a start what felt like a second later.

Holly promptly pushed the laptop under his nose.

'Look at this,' she said. Even though it was difficult to see the screen for the glare, there was a perfectly framed shot of Lara McIntyre, tending to Mrs Beggs in the back of the storeroom. *How the—*

'It's beautiful, Dad. She looks like an angel, doesn't she?'

He raised himself onto his elbows and angled the laptop screen away from the sun for a better look. The light globe at the back of the storeroom had illuminated Lara's hair, making it look like a golden halo.

'I deleted that picture,' he said drowsily. 'I deleted them all.'

'But you didn't empty the trash, did you? I know a trick or two. It's even better than the old lady helping the koala cross the highway.'

Toby studied the picture. Holly was right. His koala photo had made the front page of the Ballarat newspaper, scored him a trophy at the Country Press Australia awards night and earned his newspaper royalties when it was reprinted in

America, but it didn't have the same emotion, the same action, as this one.

Temptation swelled for a few seconds. *Lara would never know you kept it. It would be perfect for the Nikon Press Club comp.* But just as quickly, he pushed it aside. He shook his head. He already felt bad enough that he'd dragged the photo out for a look last night before deleting them again.

'Get rid of it, Lollypop. Delete them all *properly*.' With everything already resting on his conscience—the death knocks to elicit quotes from grieving families in his cadet journalist days; downplaying the corruption of politicians during his stint at the Melbourne paper; the guilt for being unable to fix his marriage—he didn't want to add deliberate deception to his tally.

Three

The KitchenAid whizzed effortlessly, whipping the egg whites into stiff, glossy peaks. Lara leaned over the mixer, pleased with the consistency.

'That'll just about do,' she said, switching it off and running a finger along the whisk attachment. The meringue was smooth between her fingertips, not a hint of gritty sugar left. She dolloped it onto the lemon curd and biscuit base and slid the pie into the extra-wide oven.

A tidy-as-you-go cook, it didn't take Lara long to put the kitchen back in order. She returned ingredients to the pantry, wiped flecks of wayward meringue off the copper splashback, and swished a damp cloth over the marble benchtops. Lara threw open the windows for good measure, but turned a blind eye to the cobwebs that danced along the exposed beams. Cob-webbing was a spring-cleaning job, and even then she did it reluctantly.

A quick stack of the dishwasher and the beautifully crafted kitchen was once again spick and span.

Lara found a calico bag and headed outside to the lemon tree. She had just about filled the bag when the magpies and crows converged on the chook-house roof, and Basil bounded across the yard in a half-hearted attempt at scaring them away.

'Waiting for dinner, aren't you, you blighters? Worse than seagulls,' she called, pitching a lemon in their direction. The birds fluttered up and then resettled. Not content with pecking at her eggs, they'd also started taking liberties with the chook food.

Shaking her head, Lara went back inside and changed into a fresh pair of jeans. She chose a blue linen shirt and fine gold earrings, pulled her straight, red hair into a ponytail and headed back into the kitchen as the oven timer pinged. The lemon meringue pie looked as good as it smelled, filling the room with a delicious lemony sweetness. *This'll go down a treat.*

Leaving Basil to guard the property, Lara got in her car, strapped a seatbelt around the basket containing their dessert, and carefully made her way to McIntyre Park. She rolled the window down when she reached the driveway. Wind whipped away the lemony aroma and in flowed the familiar smells of her childhood. With a nostalgic smile, she soaked up the ever-present scent of freshly cut grass and, as she drew to a stop, the perfume from her mother's rose garden.

Home always felt good, no matter what time of year. The peach-coloured roses stood out against the farmhouse's grey weatherboards, and bees stirred lazily as she walked between the lavender hedges.

Slipping off her sandals in the porch, Lara set her pie on the kitchen bench. They were having roast lamb, by the smell of it.

She returned to the car and collected the bag of lemons, but even after she'd emptied the contents into the fruit bowl, there was still no sign of anyone.

It was like déjà vu. *Argh, Penny, please don't be buried under a pile of boxes!*

'Hello,' Lara finally called out into the silence. 'Anybody around?'

Her hand flew to her mouth when she noticed the cane bassinet in the far corner of the kitchen. 'Oops', Lara whispered, glad she hadn't woken her niece.

Footsteps sounded on the staircase. Tim Patterson's big feet appeared first, then his rumpled jeans and shirt. A mis-buttoned shirt . . . Lara smothered a laugh as her sister Penny emerged a few steps behind him, her strawberry-blonde hair equally rumpled.

'Just catching a bit of shut-eye,' said Penny, adding a yawn for good measure.

'That what they're calling it these days?'

Penny flushed. Lara laughed and wrapped her arms around her sister.

'I'm joking, Pen. Gotta grab it when you can.'

'Lucy still asleep?' asked Tim.

Penny glanced at the bassinet. 'Amazingly, despite all the noise Lara's making.'

'Better she gets it now. It'll be like Bourke Street when the rest of the crew arrive,' said Tim, looking around the cosy kitchen that had housed McIntyres for four generations. Penny and Tim had breathed new life into the house since they'd moved in, but it still felt like her old home. The family photos and high-school portraits still hung on the walls, accompanied by new additions from the recent weddings—Penny's and Angie's—and candid shots of Tim with his brother Eddie, and the boys' grandmother, Nanna Pearl.

Lara waved as she spotted her father, Angus McIntyre, crossing the lawn between his quaint cottage and the farm-house. He ambled through the back door.

'Hey, Dad,' she said, leaning in to kiss his smooth cheek.

'How's the town hero?' Angus's smile was as broad as the Akubra he normally wore.

'Hero? Hardly. Somebody needed to do something. The guy from the newspaper wasn't much use,' said Lara.

Angus settled into his favourite chair. 'It's gone into the rumour mill, done two laps around town and been spat out the other end as open-heart surgery using barbecue implements. Think I like that version better,' he said with a wink.

Another car crunched its way down the gravel driveway, and soon Diana and Pete's three youngest sons burst into the room. They went straight for the bassinet where baby Lucy was sleeping.

Diana's eldest son, Cameron, followed, glancing around the kitchen. 'No Evie this weekend?' His feet thumped along the floorboards. Although she wasn't short, Lara felt downright petite as he wrapped her in a hug. He'd shot up since turning fifteen, quickly matching his father for height.

She shook her head. 'Nope, it's a few more weeks until she visits.'

'Bugger,' said Cameron, with a nonchalance Lara both envied and resented. Of course nobody would miss Evie like she did, she had to remind herself. It was a mum thing.

Diana's twins crowded around the bassinet, fussing over the sleeping baby until she woke up.

'Let's change her and then you can have a hold,' said Tim, herding all the children into the lounge room.

Lara turned to Penny. 'He's a keeper, Pen.'

Penny twirled a lock of hair around her finger. 'Too right. Now we need to set you up with a decent bloke and we'll all be happy.'

Lara let out a dry laugh as their eldest sister, Diana, walked in. 'What's so funny?'

'Penny's dusting off her Cupid's bow. Waste of time, sis,' said Lara.

Another car pulled up in the driveway.

'Aunty Angie! Claudia! Uncle Rob!' Young Leo raced out
from the lounge room, bounded down the steps and rushed
to open the ute's back door.

Rob Jones was the first out of the ute. He unbuckled Claudia
from her car seat and the two young cousins raced to the
trampoline, hand in hand. Angie emerged from the passenger
seat, her curls piled on top of her head, and her arms laden
with a triple-decker sponge cake. There was never a shortage
of desserts at a McIntyre family gathering.

'Hi Jonesy! Hey Angie,' said Diana, taking the elaborate
dessert from their youngest sister. 'We were trying to work out
the perfect bloke for Lara. Surely there's a few single hotties
down at Port Fairview?'

Lara groaned. It wasn't a stretch to imagine her three
sisters sitting around the dining table, making a list of eligible
bachelors. She knew they were well intentioned, and she might
have been the teensiest bit lonely since Evie left, but she wasn't
desperate.

※

Toby pulled up alongside a rustic roadside stall and handed
his wallet to Holly. Fashioned from an old wardrobe at the
entrance to a long, winding driveway, the stall was bursting
at the seams with bouquets of native flowers, pumpkins and
egg cartons.

Holly chose an impressive posy of grevilleas and proteas,
and soon afterwards a young nurse was ushering them into
Mrs Beggs' hospital room. The postmistress had never been
particularly youthful looking, but without her bright blouse
and trademark chirpy greeting, she looked much older.

'Well, aren't you the spit of your dad?' said Mrs Beggs. 'Are
you a lifesaver like your father, too?'

Toby shook his head and corrected Mrs Beggs. 'I only called the ambulance.'

'And he got a great action shot too, and that lady made him delete it,' added Holly, injustice oozing from her words.

She should be taking drama classes, not clarinet. 'Mrs Beggs mightn't have liked it either. Lara was right, I shouldn't have taken the photo in the first place.'

Mrs Beggs looked between them, and he saw the effort it took to raise her eyebrows.

'She's had a rough trot, our Lara, though you won't find a better nurse in the district. Not one to blow her own horn, either. As long as my dress wasn't riding up, or my boobs hanging out, I wouldn't have minded.'

A nurse bustled in.

'Visiting hours are nearly over, I'm afraid. Mrs Beggs needs her beauty sleep,' she said as she flicked through the medical chart. To Toby's untrained eye there seemed to be a lot of pages for someone who had only been in hospital for one day.

'When can we expect you back behind the counter?' he said.

Mrs Beggs grimaced. 'You won't, pet. This blasted shoulder won't be lifting mail bags anytime soon. I've done my dash. The shop will have to be sold,' she said, gravely. She sank back onto the pillow and Toby tried to imagine how she felt about this unexpected end of an era. Change was hard to accept at the best of times, and even more confronting when the decision was taken out of your hands.

'Sold?' he said gently. 'That's no good. Bet that wasn't in your plans.'

The nurse strode over, a sympathetic look on her face.

'That bump to your noggin's making you feel poorly too, isn't it, Winnie? Time to leave her be, folks, all this shop talk is too much.'

Toby and Holly moved to the door. Mrs Beggs' tired voice rang through the room.

'Toby, can you put an article about the shop sale in your paper? You never know what buyers might come out of the woodwork to make an offer.'

'Absolutely. I'll give it front-page billing, if you like? Shall I run the article past you first?'

Mrs Beggs closed her eyes again. 'I trust you, Toby. Haven't read an article of yours that wasn't fair and honest.'

He gave her his word. 'Leave it with me.'

॰

Lara's heart felt full as she watched Cameron pass Lucy around among the cousins. 'Hold her neck properly,' he said, sounding more grown up than ever as he rearranged Harry's grip.

Eddie Patterson bounded over to greet her, his ever-present delight clear on his face.

'Lara, Lara, Lara!' He squished her into an enthusiastic hug. Lara gently untangled herself while her ribs were still intact. Tim's brother was as gentle as a lamb with the children, particularly his new niece, though sometimes around the adults he forgot his own strength. 'Uncle Eddie!' he said, pointing a finger to his chest, beaming widely.

'She's a beauty, Eddie,' Lara agreed.

He seemed thrilled with the praise, but suddenly his face fell. 'Mrs Beggs. No good,' he said, his face creasing with concern. 'No shop.'

Lara nodded. As a young man with Down Syndrome, there weren't many job opportunities for Eddie in Bridgefield, and although he loved helping Tim on the farm, his self-confidence had skyrocketed since he started volunteering at the shop.

'Mrs Beggs will be better soon, mate,' said Lara, taking another look at the blonde cousins all lined up on the couch.

Only Evie missing, she thought wistfully. Lara caught herself. Moping around wouldn't make Evie's absence any more bearable. She had to be patient and wait for the next long weekend.

The kitchen was full of conversation and gentle jibes as the four sisters prepared the meal together. It wasn't until dessert had been cleared away, the men had finished the dishes and Annabel's treasured china returned to the hutch that the adults migrated to the back deck.

Lara nestled into the wicker chair and looked out to the Grampians.

'Reckon Dallas Ruggles will handle the shop?' Diana asked.

The rest of the family turned to look at Lara. She and Dallas had been in the same year at high school, often working the same holiday shifts at the store, and she'd picked up the slack for him on many occasions.

'Dallas couldn't organise his way out of a paper bag. I don't know why Mrs Beggs didn't sack him long ago.'

'That's family for you,' said Angie. 'What about Octavia? She's the more reliable of the casuals. Mrs Beggs could leave her in charge.'

'Hip replacement last month,' said Lara. *And cancer riddling her body again.* Like many of the health issues in the community, it wasn't Lara's secret to share. She sipped her wine instead.

'If Mum were here, she'd be holding the fort,' said Angie.

Lara knew it was true. Annabel McIntyre had always been a doer, and her four daughters prided themselves on upholding the family tradition.

'I'm sure Mrs Beggs will be back on her feet soon,' offered Lara. But even as she said the words, she wondered how many more years Mrs Beggs had planned to carry such a load. As well as selling newspapers and distributing mail, she hired teenagers during the school holidays, gave opportunities to people who needed them, including Eddie, and employed a baker on Wednesdays to make a week's worth of mouth-watering pies. *Not with a knackered shoulder, she won't be.*

Diana shrugged. 'We can't be without a shop.'

'Blokes at the stock agency reckon Dallas would sell the place out from under her if she turned her back for a minute,' said Pete. 'Nobody round here would let that happen to her, though.'

'Course they wouldn't. This is Bridgefield we're talking about,' said Tim.

Lara raised an eyebrow. 'Doesn't mean everyone's a saint, though.'

'No . . .' Tim studied his boots. He'd once been friends with Lara's ex-husband, Sam Kingsley, but when she'd finally revealed his secrets, Tim had been the first to help bring him to justice. 'No, but we look out for our own. Someone will snap up the shop the second it comes on the market.'

Diana nudged her father. 'Great retirement plan?'

Angus laughed. 'It's crossed my mind. But I'm not much use with a bung arm. And I couldn't do twelve-hour days again.' He looked out over the paddocks. 'I met your mother in that store, you know.'

The four sisters exchanged an indulgent look. They'd heard the story many times, but they still loved how Angus told it as if it were the first.

'She'd stopped for a bite to eat when I was collecting my mail. Best thing I ever picked up in that shop,' he said, nostalgia clouding his voice.

Lara tried to imagine a younger version of her father clapping eyes on the beautiful Annabel amid the shelves of groceries and newspapers.

'So, we wouldn't all be sitting here watching the sunset if it weren't for Mrs Beggs' famous pies?' Diana's tone was thoughtful.

'No two ways about it, love,' said Angus. The family fell into silence for a few moments.

'What about those community consortiums? Like they formed for St Brigid's church near Koroit, and the store in Balmoral,' Diana asked, draining her glass.

Penny lifted her chin. 'I think it's a great idea. If we hadn't bought those extra paddocks and cattle we'd consider it, but the budget won't stretch much further this season.'

'We don't even know how long Mrs Beggs is going to be away,' said Lara. 'Surely Dallas can hold the fort for a few weeks?' But Lara knew that a bustling business like the Bridgefield General Store needed more than Dallas holding the fort. In the long term, someone was going to have to step up.

⚜

It was late afternoon on Sunday when Toby drove Holly back to Ballarat. His parents' home and the little cottage he was renting in Bridgefield were of a similar era, but there was a very different vibe between the two.

Flowers spilled onto the driveway of the house he'd grown up in. Hoses were coiled by every tap and the path to the front door was neatly edged, inviting guests to enter. Maybe his place would feel a little cosier if he took a leaf out of his mother's book and added more flowers, shrubs and herbs. She was sure to be a fount of knowledge on hardy plants he might start with.

'Darlings, so lovely seeing you both,' said Alice Paxton as she met them at the end of the path. 'How are my favourites?'

'Awesome, Granny,' said Holly, gushing about ice creams and the kangaroos she'd photographed. As they stopped by the front door Holly stooped down and snapped off a sprig of flowers. She tucked it into her pocket before slipping inside.

'And you, darling?' Alice said, rubbing Toby's shoulder. 'That woman collapsing in the shop must have been a shock.'

'I stood like a stunned mullet for most of it,' he admitted, following her into the house. He still felt terrible about not knowing what to do.

'How long since you've taken a first-aid course? Maybe it's time for a refresher?' Alice was a natural at making people feel better.

It was dim inside his parents' house, and his father was perched on the couch with a paisley crocheted rug over his knee, despite the mild weather.

Eric Paxton cocked his head, eyeing the pair of them suspiciously. 'Whatever you're selling, we don't want any,' he said. 'I've got enough encyclopaedias and vacuum cleaners to last me a lifetime.' He gestured to the display cabinet, stuffed with a small portion of Alice's royal commemorative items.

Toby smiled gently and sat beside his father, inhaling the familiar scent of licorice.

'Hey, Dad.'

Holly took a seat the other side of him, helping herself to the chocolate bullets on the side table.

'Did you have a nice week, Poppa?'

The old man squirmed in his chair and stared back and forth at them incredulously. 'By heavens, this is a bit forward, isn't it? Coming into my house, pretending you're long-lost relatives. I didn't come down in the last—' The rest of his sentence hung in the air as Alice appeared, a wriggly chihuahua-cross under her arm.

Toby watched sadly as his father's face lit up.

'Oh Queenie, there you are. You little scamp! Where did you wander off to?' The tiny dog scrambled out of Alice's arms and jumped onto Eric's lap, bathing his face in kisses before finally settling down on the blanket.

Eric looked from the dog to his son, then elbowed Toby in the ribs. A fresh wave of recognition crossed his face, and for a moment Toby thought his father's memory was returning.

'You're not the travelling salesmen from yesterday,' said Eric.

Toby couldn't hide the hope in his voice.

'It's me. Toby.'

'You're the wedding celebrant, aren't you?'

Eric's gnarled hands flew to his face, checking it was clean-shaven. He smoothed down his grey shirt.

His expression was pure joy. 'We're getting married today, did you know?' he said to Holly. 'My lovely lady finally said yes, and we're getting hitched.' Eric beamed at his granddaughter. 'And I'll bet you're the florist. I can sport an artsy type a mile away. Have you got the flowers ready, then? She wanted red flowers.'

Holly picked up the geraniums she had laid down on the coffee table when she walked in, the routine as familiar as the photographs lining the walls.

'Sure have,' she said. She trailed off, but Toby still caught the quiet final word. '. . . Poppa.'

'I'll freshen up, love,' said Alice, heading into the kitchen. Toby followed his mother. She flicked the kettle on while Toby chose four cups, each featuring a different member of the royal family. The sight of their formal portraits helped ease the heaviness of these visits, he'd often thought. Each time he'd found himself wallowing about his father's lost memories, and life's random unfairnesses, he took a quick glance at Fergie's ginger bouffant and meringue-like wedding dress. Living proof that no amount of money, fame or good health could guarantee happiness. Charles's set of wingnut ears offered a similar solace.

Alice heaped sugar into the teacups.

'Don't let it get to you, my sweet. Your dad's happy as a lark. Sometimes I'm jealous that he's stuck back in the days when we were young and carefree.'

'Any news from the doctors?'

She avoided his gaze, instead leafing through the envelopes nestled in a letter holder, rubbing the stiff cream card between her fingers. She'd been a royalist since she was a little girl, and normally the letters she received from the Palace—in response to the birthday cards and wedding anniversary well wishes she sent without fail—put a smile on her dial. But not today.

Alice set the letter down with a sigh.

That bad?

She nestled a woollen tea-cosy over the teapot, turned it three times clockwise, then once in the opposite direction, before pouring the first cup.

Tea splashed out of the spout, pooling on the formica. *Worse than I thought.* Toby mopped up the spilled tea and poured the rest himself.

'Mum?' he asked quietly. Alice peered around the corner, into the lounge room. Holly was listening attentively, as if her grandfather hadn't confided his pre-wedding jitters a hundred times before.

'They keep harping on about moving him into a home. Ever since that midnight stroll, he's been a little off. Thank heavens you installed the deadbolt. I found him by the door at two this morning, desperate to polish the wedding cars in nothing but a singlet and rubber gloves.' She rubbed at a mark on the door frame. 'He'd hate it in one of those places.'

'You aren't superwoman anymore.'

Alice wrapped her arms around herself. 'He still thinks I am, bless him.'

Toby admired her resilience as she took a deep breath, and accepted the tea he proffered.

The doorbell rang as they carried the tea into the lounge room. Queenie jumped off the couch, barking as if she were ready to maul unsuspecting visitors.

'That'll be your sister,' said Alice.

'Aunty Belinda!' Holly rushed to open the door.

'Here for the wedding, are you?' Eric beamed at his daughter.

Belinda looked down at her lycra leggings and baggy pink jumper, then she handed him the Sunday papers.

'I've got your newspaper, Dad.'

Their father took the *Weekend Australian* and stared at it for a moment.

'What a mighty practical wedding gift. My boy works at one of these broadsheets, you know. Head of the whole newspaper. Couldn't be prouder,' he said, tucking the paper beside him.

Toby's heart clanged. He felt his mum pat his shoulder.

Eric looked up at them all, and gestured impatiently.

'Right then, no time for dilly-dallying. Which side are you on, bride or groom?'

Four

Even though it had been years since she'd worked at the Hamilton Base Hospital, Lara had no trouble finding room three.

A trio of women were clustered around the foot of Mrs Beggs' bed. They sprang apart as she walked in, and Lara saw the vivid bruise and large dressing on Mrs Beggs' cheek, accentuated by stiff white bed linen.

'You look like you're plotting a heist,' Lara said, shuffling vases to make room for the roses she'd plucked from her mother's garden. She wasn't a natural green-thumb like her sisters and her mum, and was happy enough to pick the occasional bunch and leave the digging, watering and endless weeding to those who enjoyed it.

'How's the patient?' She looked between the ladies.

Denise gave a sympathetic wince. 'Winnie's been dozing on and off. Poor love. We're heading to bowls in a minute. Give her our love when she wakes up next, will you?'

The room fell silent. Lara settled into the chair next to the bed and watched a blue wren serenade itself in the window's reflection. It fluttered away and she picked up the medical chart, leafing through the pages.

'Have they gone?'

Lara jumped with surprise, nearly dropping the chart. She laughed. 'I thought you were asleep?'

'If I have to listen to any more of my friends talking to me like an invalid, I'm going to jump out that blessed window,' said Mrs Beggs. 'Falling asleep is a very convenient way of hearing what they really think.' She gave a weak smile. 'Apparently I've got you to thank for getting me here in one piece.'

No thanks to Dallas.

Lara brushed away the thought and assessed Mrs Beggs. It hadn't seemed that long ago that Mrs Beggs and her mother were lugging their sewing machines into the back of an old station wagon, off for their annual craft weekend with a cask of Moselle, bulging bags of fabric and a stack of McCalls patterns. Or both tied into linen aprons, doing the dreaded end-of-financial-year stocktake at the general store while Lara and Dallas manned the front counter. Or giving a young shoplifter an ear-bashing, before allowing them to wipe the slate clean with an hour or two of service. She was a plucky old dame, no doubt about it. Maybe with some intense rehab, a speedy recovery and return to work weren't out of the question.

'You had us worried. How did you manage to get under a pile of boxes at exactly the wrong time?'

The older woman shrugged, then winced.

'Ouch, my shoulder. Even with the meds it feels like a sledgehammer driving through my bones each time I jiggle. I was trying to get a box from the top shelf, and Dallas still wasn't back from his afternoon tea break.'

Long smoko break, frowned Lara. Dallas was always lingering in the pub for extended lunches and shooting the breeze on the footpath while a steady stream of customers went in and out of the shop.

'And next thing I know,' said Mrs Beggs, 'I'm in here, hooked up with so many wires and thingamabobs I can barely move and the doctors are throwing around big words that end in *sepsis*.'

Lara scanned the medical chart. 'That fracture sounds serious. You had a pretty decent blow to the head, Mrs Beggs, and it looks like you're on antibiotics for an infection too.'

'Funnily enough, they told me I'm a lucky lady.'

'Lucky for getting knocked for six by a pile of boxes?'

Mrs Beggs exhaled slowly. 'No, it doesn't feel very lucky, but apparently the infection was already lurking. The doctor thinks it's why I fell off the ladder in the first place.'

Lara wasn't a touchy–feely person, but she reached for the hand that had passed papers, pies and postcards across the Bridgefield General Store counter for as long as she could remember. The hand that had gently guided both her and Evie through their first jobs. Lara squeezed it gently.

'You'll bounce back,' said Lara, well aware that complications from the infection could be quite serious for someone of Mrs Beggs' age, not to mention the recovery time from her fracture.

Mrs Beggs gave a dry laugh. 'The shop will be the real casualty. I can't be bothered with the hassle of leasing, and if I close it down, everyone will have to leave town for their mail. Bridgefield will never get their post office back if we let it go. I'll sell.'

Lara winced. *Sell?* 'And in the meantime?'

Mrs Beggs looked mournful. 'That's where it gets tricky. I love Dallas like my own son, but he doesn't handle pressure well.'

Lara held her tongue. Several failed business ventures didn't lie.

'Everyone who's visited has offered to help, but I'm not in much of a state to organise things. These painkillers make my brain all fuzzy. I need someone who knows what's what.'

Mrs Beggs turned to her, a question in her eyes.

Lara blinked. *Does she expect me to run the shop or prep it for sale?* The unspoken request settled like a weight on Lara's shoulders. She wanted to suggest another candidate, however with no children to shoulder the burden, Mrs Beggs had limited options. Dallas was useless, Penny had a farm and a baby, Angie lived two hours away and Diana had four boisterous boys. Lara picked at her regulation-short fingernails, pushing the cuticles back.

It's the least I can do, Lara told herself, battling against the feeling of obligation.

'I'll arrange the real-estate agent, then?' Lara tried to cover her reluctance, but even in her medicated state, Mrs Beggs was no fool. Lara tried again, with a little more pep in her voice. 'I can show him through the shop in my lunchbreak.'

The postmistress opened her mouth to say something, then closed it, giving a small sigh instead. The room fell quiet. Acutely uncomfortable, Lara decided it was time to leave. The disappointment on Mrs Beggs' face stayed with her the whole way home.

⁂

The phone was ringing when Lara shut off the shower. Hastily wrapping a towel around herself, she dripped her way along the hallway, craving a dose of Evie-style sunshine to brighten up her day.

'How's Mrs Beggs?' said Evie.

Lara relayed the latest news about the bad fracture and underlying infection. 'She might still be in hospital the next time you're home. The Easter long weekend's not far away, right?'

'Mmm, about that. I might stay in for the weekend, Mum. Hardly any of the other boarders are leaving until the school

holidays start. Another boarding school has challenged us to
a dance-off, so we're planning a group routine . . .'

Evie's change of plans landed like a blow. Lara wanted
to swear. Instead she walked across the kitchen, opened the
pantry door and stared at the calendar inside. The mid-term
break was enthusiastically circled.

'You don't mind, do you?'

Lara felt her shoulders drop as she drew a big cross through
the weekend. All that was left of the month's pressing social
engagements was her twin nephews' birthday and a visit from
the agronomist.

Lara forced enthusiasm into her reply.

'Of course not, Evie. A dance-off sounds more fun than a
boring weekend at home with your old mum. I'll be fine, I've
got friends.' She looked at the *Friends* DVD box-set Evie had
given her years ago.

A tub of ice cream, a block or two of chocolate and her
favourite sitcom would help ease the pain of another long,
lonely weekend. Perhaps she would dig out that new recipe
book Penny had given her.

A screech sounded outside Lara's window and she turned
to see a flock of pink-and-grey galahs fly past and settle in the
silver gums shading her rickety garden shed. Basil was in
hot pursuit, barking and leaping towards the sky. When the
ruckus finished, she heard the chatter of teenage girls down
the phone line.

'Lunchtime?'

'Nearly. It's probably the same barf-worthy stew as last
Sunday,' said Evie. 'Oh, and I've got a back-up plan if the
general store closes. One of my new friends has a shack at
Bells Beach. She said I could get a holiday job at her Dad's
surf school, teaching kids how to surf.'

Lara closed the pantry door and leaned against it, ignoring the way the brass handles dug into her shoulder blades. First the mid-term break and now possibly the school holidays? This conversation was going from bad to worse.

'But what about . . .' *Me?* Lara shuddered to think of Evie spending all term *and* all holidays away. 'What about our Easter egg hunt? It's a McIntyre Park tradition.'

'Oh Mum, I'm a bit old for that. I won't earn the money for the school ski trip if I sit on my bum at home all holidays,' said Evie. The phone line went muffled and Lara heard Evie talking to friends.

'But you barely know how to surf.'

'They don't know that,' said Evie with a cheeky laugh. 'I've got my bronze medallion, and if I can wrangle my cousins I can manage anything. Anyway, gotta go, Mum. Miss you!'

'Miss you too, Evie-girl,' Lara said, wrapping her arms around her waist. The damp towel provided about as much comfort as it did warmth.

Lara marched into her bedroom, flung on the first pair of jeans and shirt she laid her hands on and stormed out to the wood pile. She'd barely swung the axe before tears brimmed and the firewood blurred in front of her. It wasn't until she'd chopped a stack of red gum that she set the axe aside. Basil bounded over to her. His tail thumped against her leg and she ruffled the top of his head.

'What a sook, hey, Baz?'

Lara picked up the axe again and chopped until the loneliness was buried under a hefty layer of exhaustion.

❧

Toby flicked through last week's newspaper over breakfast, but his mind wasn't on the *Bridgefield Advertiser* this morning.

Instead of the stories he'd written and the photographs he'd taken, all he could see was his father's face.

Eric's confusion.

His affection for Queenie the dog.

His pride when he spoke about his children, completely unaware they were standing right in front of him.

Toby folded the newspaper and crossed the dining room. His bookcase was filled to the brim with paperbacks, except for two shelves—one devoted to books on photography and another to his collection of cameras. A Pentax, a box brownie, a Leica and an old Nikon that had given up the ghost years ago. His father's first camera, and Toby's first SLR. He picked up a photo frame and polished the already gleaming glass. It was taken on the day he'd been given the camera, just after his father had looped the strap around his neck. Eric stood proudly beside him in the photograph, his eyes sharp and his smile wide, with a patience Toby tried to emulate as a parent. He preferred to remember his Dad like that, instead of the absent, frail and often bewildered man he now was.

Setting the frame back on the shelf, Toby ran a finger over the cameras, checking for dust and finding none. His dad mightn't always know who he was, but his love still shone through.

I'll have the Ballarat editor's job soon, anyway, Toby reminded himself, returning to his coffee. *Two years at the Bridgefield paper and then Dad'll be proud.*

He opened his diary, scanning the to-do list for the day ahead. Photos at the local shearing shed first up, which meant his old boots and dark pants. There was something about the light filtering through the old tin, the worn sheep grates and the smell of lanolin that made him eager to get going. Maybe that's where he would snap an award-winning pic?

Toby flipped ahead to the next week, smiling when he spotted Holly's not-so-subtle nudge: '*Last chance to enter the Press Club Awards TODAY!*'

She'd written down the website for the annual award, circling it with red pen so he wouldn't miss it. He couldn't help admiring her enthusiasm.

Toby tugged on a polo shirt and the least wrinkled trousers in the closet. Brilliant blue skies heralded a clear day ahead and he packed lunch before hopping into the car.

Toby negotiated the rough driveway, then turned onto Duck Hole Flat Road. He took his attention off the road to admire the donkeys belonging to his grouchy neighbour, Clyde McCluskey, when suddenly a flock of birds swooped in front of him. Toby braked hard, but not in time to avoid the *thunk-thunk-thunk* of bodies hitting the windscreen and bonnet.

'Bugger!'

Feathers floated through the air. Toby looked at his watch and cursed again. He was officially late. Luckily he was the boss, and the receptionist only came in once a week to help with the bookwork.

He flicked on his hazard lights, then stepped out and grimaced as he assessed the damage. Four magpies lay motionless in the middle of the road. A little crow was wedged into the grill underneath the number plate. A mix of blood and feathers now decorated the Volkswagen's duco.

Toby knew he couldn't bring them back to life, but he was determined to at least minimise further damage. If he left them in the middle of the road, more curious birds would follow a similar fate. Instead, he gently carried the dead birds and nestled them in the long roadside grass.

He wiped his hands on his trousers and laid a sprig of pink gum blossoms over the birds.

When Lara drove through Main Street on Monday morning, she slowed to look at the A-Frame sign on the footpath outside the general store.

Dallas's English hadn't improved over the years.

Lara parked, sighing as she strode into the Bush Nursing Centre.

'What type of idiot puts a hyphen in the middle of mushroom?'

Cindy the receptionist set down her pen and peered through the glass double doors, where she had a clear view of the general store.

'Poor Dallas, he tries,' she said. 'Has Mrs Beggs rustled up a casual or two? I don't see anybody else beating down the door to volunteer.'

Lara's cheeks burned. She'd lain awake last night, recalling Mrs Beggs' disappointment. She still felt bad for taking the easy option, but the general store was a major ask. *Nope, not happening.*

'Hope Dallas is better at running a shop than managing a drive-in cinema.'

'Don't forget the alpaca-yarn business,' said Cindy, tapping her biro against the desk.

Lara ignored the sinking feeling in her stomach as she called the real-estate agent, Greg. He waffled on about the current state of the market and the legalities of acting on a seller's behalf, until she cut him off mid-speech.

'How soon can you come?'

She wrote the time on the back of her hand and rushed to set up for the Strong Mamas class. It was one of her pet projects, along with the Move It or Lose It seniors' class.

Surely Dallas can't bankrupt Mrs Beggs in one afternoon? She looked out the window again as the first young mothers walked through the door, followed by a heavily pregnant woman with her toddler, and another wheeling a double stroller.

The store weighed on Lara's mind as she led the ladies through their exercises. After the class was over, she strode across the street, wallet under her arm.

'Lara McIntyre, you're looking as lovely as ever,' said Greg, throwing his arms open. She'd met him briefly when she'd bought her property, but now he greeted her like a long-lost friend, as if sensing a potential commission.

She frowned, stuck out a hand and looked over his shoulder as he shook it.

'Tsk.' Lara clicked her tongue as she stared at the store's A-Frame sign and then bent down to rub an extra 'L' from the middle of the word *welcome*. 'I've only got a half-hour lunchbreak,' she told Greg. 'The quicker this is sorted, the better.'

Dallas beamed at the real-estate agent as he walked into the store.

'Roll up, roll up. We're all sold out of hot mushroom pies but I can pop one in the microwave if you like,' he said optimistically. 'Or can I tempt you with one of my homemade muffins? Pumpkin and goji berries,' he said, pulling a Tupperware container out from under the counter.

Lara gasped. It had been two years—at least—since Dallas's goji-berry farm was decimated by an exotic fungus.

This is worse than I thought. Lara stepped out from behind Greg, and immediately Dallas's mega-watt smile faltered.

'Lara, I didn't see you there!'

'Dallas Ruggles, does your aunt know you're using her store to flog your poxy old berries? The health inspector would have a coronary.'

Dallas slipped the baked goods back under the counter and retucked his tacky floral shirt into his jeans. 'Just the newspaper and mail then, Lara?'

Lara gestured to Greg. 'We're actually here for an appraisal, so Mrs Beggs can get a fair price for her business.'

Dallas's eyes boggled. 'Aunt Winnie said I could take care of it.' His pout reminded Lara of Diana's twins, when they had been told to choose between the lemon meringue pie and the sponge cake instead of sampling both.

'Mrs Beggs is selling the shop, Dallas,' Lara said firmly.

The real-estate agent shifted uncomfortably in his shiny shoes. 'I'm sure she'll take all reasonable offers into account,' he said, handing Dallas a business card.

Before she'd thought it through, Lara found herself lying through her teeth. 'Actually, I spoke to Mrs Beggs before lunch and she was delighted with my offer to arrange a volunteer roster and spread the load across the community. We can't have you wearing your fingers to the bone, can we, Dallas?'

Lara began the tour of the store, making sure to highlight every good feature the building had to offer. After a lifetime of service to the Bridgefield community, Mrs Beggs deserved to get top dollar for the business and the beautiful bluestone building housing it. Nobody was going to rip her off, not if Lara had anything to do with it.

Five

Lara returned to the Bush Nursing Centre and sank into her office chair.

What have I got myself into?

Her hands shook a little as she dialled the hospital and asked to be patched through to Mrs Beggs' room.

'Lara, dear. The real-estate agent just called. Thanks for showing him through. It's officially on the market as of 9 a.m. tomorrow. Did you have any luck with another casual? Poor Dallas will be run off his feet. Even if it's just someone to sort the post while he serves,' she said. 'I'm sure Dallas can handle the rest.'

Like hell, thought Lara, thinking of the steady stream of traffic through the general store.

'Actually, I'm arranging a team of volunteers to help out. It'll be better than paring it back to a skeleton service,' she said. *Or Dallas running it into the ground before it sells.*

'Lara, you've made my day. I must admit I was a little worried about how he'd handle it.'

A little?

Mrs Beggs thanked her so effusively that Lara felt guilty for not offering to sort it out immediately.

Lara arranged a few days off work, which was quite easy considering she had a backlog of annual leave and RDOs, but her confidence faltered when she phoned Diana and Penny. Both were busy—one with sick children and the other with lamb marking.

Penny had to yell to be heard over the cacophony of bleats. 'Sorry, Lara, next week will be okay, though. Try Nanna Pearl. Will Eddie still be able to work Wednesdays with the baker?'

Lara cringed. She'd forgotten Wednesday was pie-baking day. 'Everyone loves the pie of the day, we can't let that fall by the wayside,' Lara promised.

Tim's grandmother answered on the first ring, and Lara almost fell off her chair when she heard Pearl's busy schedule.

'Of course I'll volunteer,' said Pearl. 'Though I've got bowls on Tuesday plus cards, craft group on Thursdays, yoga Mondays and Fridays, and I deliver the Meals on Wheels to the oldies every second Friday.'

The oldies? Lara let out a snort. Nanna Pearl was over eighty herself.

'How about Wednesdays?'

'Done. And Eddie can probably help out more often too, he'd be more reliable than Dallas Ruggles.'

Lara made more calls after work, and was walking towards her Subaru when Angus phoned her back.

'I'm good for Thursday. Surely we can round up a few more helpers between us,' he said.

A whistled tune came from across the car park, and Lara spotted Toby Paxton walking down the street. With broad shoulders, tanned skin and a square jaw, he was impossible to miss. His polo shirt was tucked into his trousers, he wore a belt that matched his shoes, and she noticed a pair of sunglasses perched on his head.

Wayfarer sunnies, I bet. Was he deliberately trying to look like a Ralph Lauren model, or did he just wake up like that? She almost forgot she was on the phone until her father's voice rattled in her ear.

'Why don't you ask that chap at the newspaper? He'll write an article, I'm sure.'

Toby gave a wave and started in her direction. He was taller than she remembered. Maddeningly cheerful. And athletic, if those arms were any indication.

Lara lifted a hand in response.

'Speak of the devil. I'll ask him now. Thanks, Dad,' she said, ending the call.

Toby greeted her with an easy smile. 'Beautiful day.'

'Your ears must've been burning,' she said.

He made an exaggerated show of protecting the camera dangling around his neck. His blue eyes twinkled.

'I hate to think in what context. You don't belong to a group of anti-photography campaigners, do you?'

She shook her head. 'I don't go around smashing cameras, honestly. You just—' She looked back at him. 'You just caught me by surprise on Friday. I didn't know you were photographing me.'

Her ex-husband's sex-tape scandal had put Bridgefield in the spotlight for all the wrong reasons, and although it had been Sam Kingsley's name splashed about in the media, not hers, Lara had found the shame almost as traumatic as being secretly filmed. The online news coverage had been terrible, with vitriol from victim-shaming trolls. She could only hope that Toby hadn't read up on it before he came to town.

Lara squared her shoulders. She'd spent enough money on counselling to know she couldn't change the past. She looked down, noting Toby's socks—one navy, one striped, close enough in colour they almost matched. Her lips twitched.

'Nice socks! I was just about to ask you a favour, actually.'

He raised an eyebrow. 'I'm all ears. Am I allowed to take notes?'

Lara squinted into the late-afternoon sun, trying to work out if he was laughing with her or at her. Deciding to ignore the amusement in his expression, she inclined her head.

'I need to spread the word about a volunteer roster for the general store.'

'Volunteers? I've just filed a story for this week's paper about the shop sale. I thought Mrs Beggs' nephew was stepping up to the plate in the interim?'

Lara gave him a potted version of Dallas's entrepreneurial background, which was as colourful as the Hawaiian shirts he favoured. 'The more residents who help keep this ship sailing, the easier it'll be,' she said.

His pen raced across the notepad as she spoke.

'It's just until it sells, mind you,' said Lara. 'Should be pretty quick, seeing it's an established business. The new owners could live above it too, in that little apartment. Nobody's lived up there for ages, but it should be serviceable.'

Toby turned as she gestured to the small window above the store. 'I never even noticed it had an upstairs,' he said. 'Too busy admiring the street at ground level, I guess.' He rocked back on his heels, taking in the view.

Lara swept her gaze up and down Bridgefield's main street. The raised flower beds were nice enough, she supposed, if you liked frills and frippery, and the silver princess gums looked striking now they'd outgrown the awkward spindly stage. But to her, the beauty of Bridgefield was rooted in the sense of community, the scent of lush crops wafting across from neighbouring farms and the sound of the livestock in the nearby paddocks, not the bluestone buildings, the streetscaping or the striped verandahs.

She ran a curious eye over Toby while his attention was still on the buildings. His clothes looked preppy, especially compared to the faded work shirts, woollen jumpers and no-nonsense jeans that were standard uniform in these parts. Dark, heavy eyebrows framed his face, and his brown hair was better tended than most of the blokes she knew, with clipped sideburns and a clean-shaven jaw. A little piece of black and white caught her eye.

'You've got a feather in your hair,' she said, pointing to his ear. He tried but failed to brush it away.

'Nope, here,' Lara said, reaching up and plucking it out. He smelled good, like coffee and washing powder. *God, Lara, you really need to get out more.*

She stepped back quickly and frowned at the soft downy feather.

'Bird watcher?'

His lopsided grin faded, and she suddenly regretted her tone. She hadn't meant it to be quite so derisive.

'That'd be from the birds I hit this morning,' he said. 'Half a flock of them, poor buggers, right out the front of that beautiful old shearing shed on Duck Hole Flat Road. I'll miss their warbling in the mornings,' he said, shaking his head.

Lara's spirits soared. 'Magpies, you say? At McCluskey's shearing shed?'

He nodded slowly. 'And a crow.'

'Yes!' Lara said, punching a fist in the air. 'Those thieving bastards. I've been trying to get rid of them for months. They're driving me around the bend.'

She spotted the puzzled expression on his face and felt more than a little mean. He looked pretty cut up about it.

'Riiii-ght.' He tucked the notepad into his back pocket and stuck the pen behind his ear.

'I'm down the road from you,' she said quickly. 'Those birds have been stealing my eggs. I haven't worked out if it's the crows or the magpies or both, but either way, you've done me a big favour.'

For some reason, she felt the urge to defend herself, to tell him how many times she'd found holes pecked in egg shells, the luscious, deep-orange yolks oozing out the sides, or how the birds swooped in after feeding time, bullying the hungry hens out of their food.

'Gotta run,' said Lara. 'Let me know if you need anything for the article. And . . .' She gave a tight smile. If he hadn't thought she was odd before, he was probably convinced she was a lunatic after the bird comment. 'And thanks. For the newspaper story,' she added quickly. 'Not for killing the birds. Obviously . . .'

Not a lunatic, a raving lunatic.

'Just doing my job,' he said, raising a hand as she climbed into her car.

Lara chastised herself all the way home. It wasn't until she'd swapped her soft-soled nursing shoes for work boots and walked around the property to ensure the pumps on the water troughs were all working, that she realised something was missing from the early evening. She looked from the tall eucalyptus to the she-oak, and then across to the banksias. The finches, honey eaters and kookaburras were all present, plus the galahs and the corellas in the far corner of the yard, but their songs weren't quite the same without the cawing crows or the magpies' melodies.

Lara muscled the shop's sandwich board out onto the footpath. She had a few volunteer shifts under her belt, and had been pleased to find the routine familiar.

She looked around the shop before flipping the door sign to 'Open'. Pies were in the warmer, newspapers were sorted into alphabetical order and everything looked in place. With some luck, the morning would flow smoothly.

'Morning, Lara,' called Karen. 'Just checking if I need to bring anything special in for my first shift this arvo?'

Lara reached for her paper and mail. 'Only your good self. Thanks for pitching in.'

The doorbell rang again as Lara counted out change. Her brother-in-law Tim walked in with little Lucy strapped snugly against his chest.

'Morning, ladies. I'll have three copies of the *Advertiser*, thanks. I believe it's got a pretty special article in it today?'

Lara passed him a copy and waited for his reaction.

'Fame suits young Eddie Patterson,' Karen laughed, unfolding her edition. The full-page photograph of Nanna Pearl and Eddie making pies with the baker had come up beautifully. Eddie wore an apron and a cheesy grin, and Pearl had given her hair a purple rinse specially for the occasion.

'Their smiles couldn't get any bigger if they tried,' said Tim, clearly proud of his family.

He read the headline out loud: '*Community volunteers keep shop in business.*'

Lara had to admit the story was a charming read. Toby Paxton mightn't be able to match his socks, but he could string a sentence together while tugging at the heart strings. She studied the photo. And an eye for composition, evidently. The doorbell clanged again. Yesterday's volunteer, Denise, walked in.

'He's got a way with words, for sure,' said Tim, engrossed in the article.

'Handsome lad, too. If only we were twenty years younger, right, Denise?' said Karen, as she picked a copy off the pile and pointed to Toby's headshot.

Twenty? Lara assessed the two laughing ladies. Even if they were thirty years younger, they'd still be pushing the age difference.

'This Toby Paxton . . . I hear he's single,' said Denise. 'Won't be unattached for long in this town, not with those sky-blue eyes.'

Lara snorted, then busied herself with the mail. His eyes could be any shade of the rainbow for all she cared. Frivolous rubbish, the lot of it.

But what about his smile? asked an inner voice triumphantly. *And how good he smelled?*

Dallas walked out of the storeroom clutching the mail bag. He'd given Lara a distinctly cold shoulder the past fortnight, but it didn't bother her a bit.

'Yeah right,' said Dallas. 'I bet he's been sent out here as a demotion. Must have done something pretty bad to get banished to a one-horse town like this. Wouldn't trust him as far as I could throw him.'

That's rich, thought Lara. From the good-humoured look on Tim's face, her brother-in-law was thinking the same thing.

Tim left with Lucy and his newspapers, Dallas busied himself sorting the outgoing mail and Lara served customers.

Karen and Denise lingered, catching up on gossip.

'Did I tell you about my grandson, Lara? Real snazzy dresser *and* he cooks. He'd be a good catch.'

Lara's reply was sharp.

'Good for him. The milk'll be three dollars, Karen. Only the paper today, Denise?'

The older ladies exchanged an incredulous look. Even Dallas glanced up from the mail, his brows knitted together.

'Mrs Beggs' store has a history of friendly service,' said Karen pointedly.

Lara injected some over-the-top cheer into her tone. 'See you at midday, Karen.' The ladies chuckled as they left.

'Darn do-gooders,' said Dallas. 'They try to set me up all the time, too.'

Lara swallowed her snort of disbelief just in time. *Was he serious?* They were the same age, but with premature balding, a bad attitude and terrible dress sense, Dallas wasn't the world's most eligible bachelor. She couldn't imagine anyone wanting to inflict Dallas on their single friends or family.

'It's like a blood sport around here,' he continued, tucking his colourful shirt into his jeans. 'I'm perfectly happy by myself. In fact, I should get it tattooed on my forehead, to save everyone time and effort.'

Lara had often thought the same thing, not that she would tell him.

※

Lara stripped off as soon as she got home, pleased to be out of her pie-scented clothes. She tugged on her running tights and a singlet, but the phone rang before she'd even laced her sneakers.

'You'll never guess what I found out today.' Penny's tone carried the smile in her voice.

'Mrs Beggs has made a miraculous recovery and I can go back to cleaning leg ulcers and immunising babies full time?'

Penny chuckled. 'Ha, smarty pants. I was going to tell you there's another runner in town and he happens to be six-foot, brown-haired, blue-eyed and hunky.'

Toby's a runner?

'He's also got a daughter about the same age as Evie. She probably goes to the same boarding school and everything.'

Did he now . . .

'And that's important to me because . . . ?' Lara peered out the window, annoyed at the tiny spark of interest Penny's news ignited.

'Geez, I discover the only other marathon fanatic in town, and you can't even manage a thank you? I thought you'd like a running buddy,' she said, attempting to sound indignant.

Not this again.

The mobile rang again immediately after she'd finished talking to Penny.

'Hey, Mum. How was the shop?'

Lara's grouchy frown turned upside down at the sound of her daughter's voice. 'Hi honey. Not bad for my first month. It hasn't changed much since I used to work there,' she admitted.

Lara moved into the kitchen as they spoke. It was her favourite room in the house, the one that reminded her the most of Evie. They'd planned the renovation together, and both rolled up their sleeves and made a mighty mess pulling the shabby old kitchen to pieces. Every fitting, every cupboard and every appliance had been a joint decision, from the navy cabinetry to the stone benchtops. The new kitchen hadn't been cheap, even with her brother-in-law Rob providing mates' rates, but Lara had allowed them the luxury. It was her reward for so many years spent fighting for a say in the money she earned and the life she lived.

'I knew you'd get back into it. Any buyers yet?'

'This is Bridgefield we're talking about, not Daylesford or Dunkeld. The real-estate guy's bringing someone through tomorrow.'

Fluffy clouds had threatened all day, and they gathered as Evie filled her in on the comings and goings of school. She loved that Evie still told her everything and hoped it would always stay that way.

Through the window, Lara watched Basil dash for his kennel. Moments later, a clap of thunder came from nowhere. The mountain ranges disappeared behind sheets of rain, which pelted the dusty glass. A burst of lightning illuminated the sky. *No running tonight.*

'Miss you. Basil's missing you too, Evie.'

'At least you've got him to keep you company, Mum.'

Lara thought about it long after Evie had signed off. The dog drove her nuts sometimes, but he was as loyal as they came, quick to alert her if a car ventured down their driveway, and officially the main man in her life. Exactly how she liked it.

Toby set up the camera-cleaning station on his dining table, and began his weekly ritual of cleaning the tools of his trade, slowly and fastidiously eradicating the dust that could make the difference between a 'meh' photo and an award-winning shot.

The Nikon had cost a month's wages years ago. Although he'd told Holly there was nothing wrong with it, the upgrades on the top-of-the-line model had been beckoning to him for quite some time. It was worth the effort to at least attempt an award-winning entry in the national photography contest.

The upcoming full moon was sure to attract the young fox he'd spotted skulking around the shearing shed on his early-morning runs. If the wind was blowing from the south, Toby could find a spot downwind to frame the animal against the old shed and, if the skies stayed clear, silhouette the Grampians in the background.

Lara's email came through as he was repacking his camera bag. It was short and to the point, much like the woman herself. '*Thank you for the article. Volunteer roster almost full. Much appreciated. Lara*'

He walked through the house, switching off lights with a spring in his step. She was different to any other woman he knew, there was no doubt about it, and he wanted to find out more. She was a little socially awkward too, compared to her sister Penny, who had dropped into the newspaper office that afternoon to order an enlargement of Eddie and Pearl's photo.

He hadn't known Lara was a runner until then, but now Penny had mentioned it, there was something in her gait that made it obvious.

'Maybe you'll bump into Lara when you're running,' Penny had said, smiling as she paid for her print. Toby put his sports watch on charge, ready for the next morning and slid into bed.

Maybe I will, he thought as he drifted off to sleep.

Six

The sky was clear the following day and Lara dressed quickly, eager to hit the road. She paused to lock the door and slip the key into its hiding place. It might be the only house in the district locked on a daily basis, but the peace of mind was invaluable. Basil sat in his kennel, alert and awaiting her command.

'One paw out of place and you'll be tied up for the rest of the week,' she told him sternly. Basil cocked his head to the side, his tail thumping. 'Seriously. Best behaviour, right? No buggering off like last time. We can't chase the first thing that smells good, can we?'

Suddenly, Toby crept into her mind. She blinked away the image. Her judgement of men was obviously flawed. Even if he *was* single, and *did* have handsome written all over his face, she didn't have time for any more drama in her life.

Lara planned her day out as she ran, racking her brain for volunteers to fill the final gaps in the general store roster. The sun was a few inches off the horizon when she emerged from the tree-lined avenue of honour, planted to remember soldiers who hadn't returned from war, but there was no sign of Basil in the yard.

If he's chasing those damn donkeys around McCluskey's paddock . . .

The landline started to ring when she was unlocking her front door, and she nearly did a hamstring in her attempt to catch the call.

'Hello,' she said, sweat pouring down her midriff. But instead of a shop volunteer, like she'd hoped, it was McCluskey.

'Your dog's on the loose again,' he grumbled, slurping coffee.

'Sorry, Clyde. He was with me five minutes ago.'

'He was harassing my donkeys four minutes ago. If you can't keep him under control, you should keep him on the chain,' he said before hanging up abruptly.

No wonder he'd won the unofficial award for Bridgefield's grouchiest hobby farmer for the past three decades. How many times had his sheep squeezed through the saggy fences and into Lara's pasture? He refused to go halves in replacing the boundary fences, and she didn't have the money to fork out the entire cost. And he never remembered to get his steers de-horned, meaning they were not only annoying, but dangerous, every time they jumped into the paddock with Lara's cows.

Lara made a face and talked to the dial tone. 'No worries, Clyde. You have a fabulous day too.'

As she retraced her footsteps down the driveway she thought about taking him a plate of biscuits tonight to smooth things over. She was considering which recipe might work best when she spotted Basil in the long grass on the other side of the road. Four black-and-tan paws pointed skywards as the kelpie rolled from side to side, his tongue hanging out in delight.

'Basil, you grommit! C'mon,' she said, clipping a lead onto his collar. 'Phewee!' The rancid smell made her stomach flip, but the present he dropped at her feet was even worse.

Blowflies clustered around the half-decomposed magpie. Basil stood at her feet, waiting to be lavished with praise.

'Gross,' she said, dragging him away.

McCluskey's ute rumbled down the driveway on the other side of her fence. She lifted a hand to wave. Her neighbour's response was a slow, distinctly ticked-off shake of his head.

Seriously? No biscuits for you, misery-guts, Lara decided. As she walked, her gaze shifted a few paddocks over.

In the early morning half-light, a tall figure loped along the track. *Her* running track.

Toby Paxton?

Penny had been right. Not only was he a runner, but he was an early bird. And as she headed back inside, Lara begrudgingly conceded those two qualities meant a heck of a lot more in her books than a handsome face.

❦

Toby collected the empty coffee mugs that had somehow multiplied on his desk and pushed the clutter of newspapers, magazines and notepads into something resembling a pile. He hadn't been there long enough to get a filing system together, and with the poor state of the business, tidiness had been the least of his worries.

He dumped the coffee mugs in the tearoom sink, gave them a half-hearted scrub and passed the rest of the dishes through the soapy water while he was at it. Working in a small newspaper meant that his position as editor incorporated news gathering, advertising, sales, photography and—he examined a cup rimmed with the receptionist's pink lipstick—it seemed he was also chief bottle washer.

Bide your time and you can slide into the top job in Ballarat, Toby reminded himself, loading a backpack with his camera, a sandwich he'd brought from home and a cold bottle of water.

It wouldn't take him long to ride out to Bridgefield Lake, and in the middle of the day, exercise was always a welcome respite from arse-in-seat syndrome.

Toby buckled his bike helmet, already picturing his lunchtime vista. The lake was a great spot to eat, and if he happened to get a few nice photos between mouthfuls, it was worth the short ride.

'Hold on, Cadel Evans,' the receptionist called out. 'You've got a phone call from the big boss.'

Toby leaned his bike up against the reception counter and strode into his office, shutting the door behind him.

'Mick, what's wrong?'

Toby's boss and mentor gave a sharp laugh. 'What would you say if I told you nothing was wrong, Paxton?'

'I'd call bullshit, Mick.'

'That's my man, always on alert. Thought I'd trained you well enough to know there's no such thing as off-duty when you're a newshound. We've got a problem with one of your advertisers.'

Toby's heart sank. He'd brought a few new advertisers on board since starting at the newspaper, but not everyone had appreciated the shake-up, especially the older advertisers who were used to paying a pittance for prime ad space, when the paper was barely making a profit.

Mick talked Toby through a few suggestions to balance out the new advertisers while keeping the older ones happy. 'You've got a big job ahead of you, Paxton, but try not to get too many noses out of joint, right? You'll need to nail the balance if you want to fill my shoes when I retire.'

Toby scribbled the revised ad rates on a Post-it note and stuck it to the screen of his computer. When Mick said jump, the necessary response was, 'How high?'

'Leave it with me, I'll smooth it over,' said Toby.

'Be sure you do. What's on for the rest of the week, Paxton?'

'Nothing out of the ordinary. I'm working over the weekend, boss. And I'm about to volunteer at the general store.'

'Ah, going undercover to get the inside scoop on the general store sale? Your article was good this week, really good.'

'It'll be an easy way to immerse myself in the community.' *Purely work related*, he told himself.

Mick continued, admiration in his voice. 'I like it, Paxton. It'll be a cracking little series, and generate loads of traction on our social media. Imagine how many papers you'll sell if you sniff out any dodgy dealings or hot leads? Smart thinking.'

The buckle of the bike helmet felt tight underneath Toby's chin. He wasn't trying to trip anyone up. It wasn't like there was a huge untapped market he could infiltrate; the newspaper only covered Bridgefield and a handful of the smaller local areas. He was surprised the *Advertiser* was still in circulation. Its mantle as the longest-running country paper was its saving grace, and it had to be one of the smallest towns in Victoria to still have a weekly publication.

'While I've got you, Paxton, have you heard anything about that Kingsley bloke? Your quiet country town cropped up in yesterday's newsroom meeting. Remember the story we ran up here about a sex-tape scandal?'

Toby's ears pricked up. He hadn't been assigned to the story but he'd followed the blackmail case in the media. He'd never understood men who justified behaviour like that. His blood ran cold at the thought of Holly falling prey to such a man.

'Bastards like that give towns like this a bad name,' Toby said, shaking his head. 'Nobody's mentioned it since I arrived. Anything new happening with the case?'

Mick cleared his throat. 'Still in jail for now.'

Where he belongs.

'But keep your ear to the ground. If he lived in Bridgefield, he obviously has connections there. If we can get a sob story or two, then we might pull in a few advertising dollars to run on one of those promo days.'

Promo days? 'You've lost me, Mick.'

'You know, they've got days for everything now,' said Mick. 'Beanies for brain cancer, crazy-sock day for endangered crocodiles, that type of thing. The advertising department has been spit-balling angles. There's some good coin in it if you come up with something from one of the victims, now you're at the scene of the crime, so to speak. They could run it on White Ribbon day, or whatever awareness campaign they use for domestic violence.'

The conversation weighed on Toby's mind as he pedalled past the Bush Nursing Centre and across the bridge to the lake. Advertising dollars put food on the table, but Bridgefield was different to the city. He was working to build a rapport with the locals, and he was pretty sure they'd rescind their warm welcome if he started chasing city-style exposés or exclusives.

Investigative journalism to uncover an important issue or save people at risk? Absolutely. But for the express purpose of padding out an advertising feature? That had hairs on it.

Toby paused at the lookout. The mountains were reflected in the lake's vast surface, creating a highly Instagram-worthy panorama. And if he turned back in the direction he'd come, he had a spectacular view of the town centre and the farms surrounding it like a patchwork quilt.

Mick might be the best at his job, but his idea wasn't going to wash in a small country town. Toby would keep an ear to the ground, as requested, but he'd be the one to decide how far to go for the story.

Lara rushed through her morning at the nursing centre, and arrived at the general store to find Eddie Patterson ready for the afternoon shift.

'You're making me look bad, Eddie. Rolling up early and working late. The new owners will be delighted to hear we've got such a great team of volunteers,' she said, scrubbing her hands in the sink.

He blushed at the compliment, radiating so much happiness that Lara couldn't help but smile. She listened to the baker working with Eddie to prepare the week's worth of pies. Most small stores stuck with the bog-standard mass-produced pies, but house-made pastries had always been Bridgefield's calling card.

Lara sorted the mail with one eye on the front counter, where Dallas was serving customers, and the other on Eddie and the baker. After double-checking Eddie's ingredients, the baker gave the okay to start the industrial mixer.

'Put the guard down,' he prompted. Eddie followed the instructions to a tee and was soon pulling pastry dough from the mixer.

She hoped the new owners would continue the initiative. As well as workplace skills and social opportunities for people with a disability, the initiative brought joy to both the participants and the general store volunteers. And from the conversations she'd overheard earlier that week, it had sparked a new wave of community connections.

'I hear Jaylee's doing sewing lessons with Nanna Pearl,' she said, watching Eddie light up at the mention of his best friend, a bright young woman with cerebral palsy whose cheery nature lit up every room she entered.

'Jaylee making skirts,' he grinned. 'Pretty ones.'

Lara returned to the counter, her smile dimming slightly as Dallas sniffed.

'Waste of time if you ask me,' he said in a lowered voice. She raised an eyebrow.

'I mean, he's never going to run his own bakery, is he?' Dallas went on. 'It's all warm and fuzzy in theory, but the baker could pump out twice as many pies in half the time without Eddie slowing him down. Is it really worth it?'

'I think so,' Lara said, gripping the edge of the bench.

'Eddie,' she continued brightly, giving Dallas a pointed look as she headed into the kitchen, 'I'm whipping upstairs to air out the apartment before the real-estate agent comes. Can you keep an eye on the front counter too, please?'

She paused at the landing, flipped through the keys until she found the right one, then opened the apartment door, wrinkling her nose at the stale smell. She ran her finger along the kitchen bench. It was coated in the gritty dust that blew into every Bridgefield building on a hot, dry northerly. Cotton sheets made ghost-like shapes over the sparse furniture.

Mrs Beggs rattled around in a big old farmhouse out of town, and though Lara had a vague memory of a casual employee once living upstairs, the apartment mostly sat vacant.

Lara threw open the old sash windows overlooking Main Street in time to see Greg helping a sleek and impossibly made-up woman out of the real-estate agency car.

Lara couldn't help but wonder whether the woman had missed the memo about Bridgefield being a tiny country town three hours from Melbourne. She was as city-looking as the other two buyers who'd viewed the shop this week.

She'll probably turn tail as quickly as the other two, Lara decided as she headed downstairs and back into the shop.

The potential buyer used all the right words, explaining her passion for breathing new life into Western District businesses, and Lara almost felt she'd made a hasty judgement, right up until the woman mentioned Concongella, a tiny country town to the north.

'Lure tourists . . . Shakes and fries . . . an ode to the Deep South.'

Lara shuddered as she strode back into the kitchen. She hadn't been to Concongella since the old mechanics hall had been revamped, but from what she'd heard, every inch of the building's charm had been replaced with tacky plastic and chrome fittings to fit its new incarnation as an American hamburger joint. Locals avoided it like the plague. It was the last thing she wanted for the general store. And for her town.

Seven

The next day saw even more customers through the doors, all intent on updates as Lara replenished the pie warmer and sorted the outgoing mail. The next interested buyer came in after lunch.

The woman's accent was so thick, Greg's sales pitch was made comical by the number of times he asked her to repeat herself.

Dallas leaned in, engulfing Lara in a wave of strong cologne. 'Won't go down well, talking like that around here. Locals will be so busy trying to understand what she's saying, they'll forget what they came in to buy,' he said.

Lara slapped a handful of mail on the counter. Bridgefield wasn't exactly a thriving hub of multiculturalism, and unlike many of the regional towns, there was no migrant population. Lara's experience at the Horsham and Hamilton hospitals, where they struggled to retain staff and gratefully accepted overseas-trained doctors, had given her a healthy appreciation for varied languages, accents and the brave people who spoke them.

'What, you think your Aunt Winnie should insist that the shop only be sold to a fourth-generation Australian, like you or me?' Lara slipped an elastic band around the different mail bundles. 'A bit of cultural diversity wouldn't be a bad thing in Bridgefield.'

Dallas huffed and rearranged the sauce bottles beside the pie warmer. The buyer and the agent moved through the store before heading up the steps to the apartment.

'Well, even if they can work out what she's saying, they won't know where to look. She's plastic-fantastic. Don't know how she eats with those puffy lips,' Dallas said.

Lara almost found herself agreeing with Dallas, but before she could consider a reply, the doorbell rang and Toby strolled into the store. His crisp yellow polo shirt looked like it had been ironed. *Is he one of those guys who irons his bedsheets and handkerchiefs too?* From the corner of her eye, she saw Dallas draw himself up a little taller and move closer.

She handed Toby's mail across the counter.

'Nice out there?' she said.

'Sure is. I rode out to the lake at lunch. Pearler of a day,' he said.

Lara peered outside. Fresh air and a midday picnic sounded glorious.

Toby shuffled through his post and cringed when he got to the Ballarat College envelope.

Lara looked at the window-front, knowing it was likely to be a whopping great bill. She knew exactly how expensive private schools were, and even with Evie's scholarship, she dreaded to think how much the extras would cost overall.

'Kids, hey,' she said, giving him a compassionate look. She wasn't sure about Toby, but she would go to the end of the earth to give Evie the best life, especially after the rough start she'd endured.

Toby smiled and nodded, then leaned against the counter, his height making Dallas look even shorter. He glanced around the general store.

'How are you for volunteers? I'm happy to lend a hand,' said Toby.

'All good, mate,' said Dallas, lifting Toby's newspapers off the counter as if they were made of lead. He was the only customer who ordered *The Australian* and the Ballarat paper each day. Dallas thwacked them down on the bench.

What's got his goat today? Lara wondered. She opened the roster and ran her finger down the list.

'We'll take any helpers we can get. How does next Thursday with Karen sound? There's a morning spot that needs filling, or an afternoon shift with Olive the following Friday?'

Was it her imagination or did he look a little disappointed by those options?

Toby leaned over and tapped the next day's roster. She was supposed to be working with Jim, one of the retired farmers, whose roaring sense of humour had had her in stitches last week.

'What about this spot here? I saw Jim down the street this morning. Didn't he tell you about his dicky knee? Collapsed on him again in the cattle yards. He's not going to be dishing up meat pies or buttering bread rolls on crutches,' he said, giving her a helpful smile.

'Ah, bugger. I forgot about Jim's knee.'

'I'll be able to make it then,' Dallas said quickly.

Lara turned, cocking her head. 'I thought you had an appointment that couldn't be cancelled?'

'It's no trouble, really,' said Toby, amusement dancing across his face.

Lara looked between the two of them and huffed out a breath. It was easier to dislike Toby when she thought he was a snap-happy hack, and though she didn't want to be caught up in whatever was going on between these two, she suspected he would be much better company than Dallas.

'Toby it is,' she said, changing the roster. Toby whistled as he walked out of the store. Dallas stormed off, muttering about a lack of appreciation.

Greg closed the door behind the latest buyer, his shoulders slumping as he made his way back to the counter.

'She hated it,' he said, studying the pie warmer.

Lara couldn't help but feel offended.

The real-estate agent placed a $10 note on the counter and perked up a little as he bit into one of the freshly baked pies. 'But we've got more prospective buyers lined up for tomorrow. See you then.'

⌘

Hoping to start off on the right foot, Toby arrived early for his volunteer shift. Lara had just finished giving him a quick rundown of the cash register when the shop door opened and Clyde McCluskey ambled in. He peered into the pie warmer, the scowl on his face deepening as he pulled out his wallet.

'Howdy, Clyde,' said Toby, his tone upbeat.

McCluskey grunted.

'Still charging like a wounded bull for these pies, are they?' he said, sliding a handful of gold coins across the counter and eyeing Toby suspiciously.

'Same price they've been all year, Clyde,' Lara called from the kitchen.

'Sauce?' Toby lifted the bottle of Heinz.

The older man scrunched up his nose. 'Not that mass-produced muck. Winnie's homemade sauce. In the other fridge.'

'You mean I've been buying lunch from this shop for months now, and nobody told me there was homemade sauce on offer?

Blatant favouritism,' Toby said good naturedly. Sure enough, there was an assortment of sauces in the kitchen fridge.

'Localism, more like it,' offered Lara. 'Mrs Beggs doesn't hand her sauce out to any Tom, Dick or Harry, especially not blow-ins. You've got to earn the perks,' Lara said with shining eyes.

Toby returned to the counter with the homemade sauce.

'I've been meaning to have a word with you too,' said Clyde, turning his frown in Toby's direction. 'Can you keep the racket down on the weekends? There's laws against disturbing the peace at the crack of dawn on a Sunday morning.'

'I'd hardly call 9 a.m. the crack of dawn, Clyde.' *Lucky I'm not the kind of bloke who sleeps in, or I'd be tempted to mention your donkeys, and their early-morning hee-hawing.* 'But if it's bugging you, I'll mow the lawns later in the day.'

McCluskey ducked his head curtly and left without so much as a goodbye. Toby turned to Lara, lifting his hands in a 'What did I say?' gesture, receiving a hint of a smile in return.

'Does he get any friendlier the longer you live next door?'

Lara shook her head. 'If anything, he gets worse. And heaven help you if you have a dog that veers onto his side of the fence,' she said.

The general store was filled with a flurry of conversation as a trio of twenty-something men strolled in, all talking over the top of one another.

'Oh, isn't it *quaint*?'

'Down at the heel, but nothing a refurb wouldn't fix.'

'Get rid of those dirty old lino squares, switch out those ghastly light shades.'

'Yah, totally. New counter, new shelving.'

'Really, if it wasn't for the bluestone exterior, it'd be easier to bulldoze the lot and start from scratch, wouldn't it?' A high-pitched laugh erupted from a chap wearing the tightest jeans

Toby had ever seen on a man. The outline of the phone in his pocket was so sharp Toby almost hoped it would ring so he could see if the screen illuminated through the acid-wash denim.

Lara wiped her hands on her apron.

'I think they're wearing more cologne than Dallas,' she said under her breath. The buyers continued their assessment, lowering their volume slightly so only half the town was in earshot.

'I'm thinking smashed avo, I'm thinking vegan-friendly. Really knock the socks off this meat-and-three-veg town,' said a bloke with a man-bun and manicured beard.

'God, yes. Deconstructed gruyere bruschetta with micro-herbs,' added the final guy.

Toby caught Lara's eye. This bunch was even worse than the last buyer, and it wasn't just the silent 'h' on 'herbs'.

Lara spoke quietly. 'How can Mrs Beggs even think of selling to these people? I'd rather drive to Hamilton to collect my mail than deal with them.'

She showed Toby how to sort the envelopes and parcels, and they caught snatches of the men's conversation as they worked.

'Those pies'll be the first thing to go if we want to raise the standards,' one sniffed.

Toby shook his head. He didn't have a pie-a-day habit like some of the locals, but there was still something comforting about the option of a different handmade pie each day.

The buyers discussed target markets as the real-estate agent guided them around.

'We could open at six, catch all the yummy mummies on their way to the gym,' said one.

Gym? Yummy mummies? Toby forced himself to keep a straight face.

'Yeah, shut at two after the midday rush,' another exclaimed.

'Definitely! Make Friday open-mike night. Karaoke, baby,' said the third man.

Toby turned to Lara, ready to make a joke about the wisdom of a karaoke club in Bridgefield, but his words faded as he took in Lara's expression. She looked more insulted than amused by their comments.

'I think they've mixed up their demographics,' she said. 'I mean, who the hell's into smashed avo and karaoke around here? You're not, are you?'

Toby thought of the school concerts he'd hated as a child. His folks had driven him home from the year six performance, distraught and utterly mortified because he'd stuffed up the lines in his solo.

'Nope, not me. I've nothing against avocado, but I don't like paying big bucks for something I can make at home. And singing in public . . .' He grinned and shuddered. 'Let's just say an inland tsunami is more likely.'

Another customer came in, one Toby recognised as the cricket coach from a match he'd photographed.

'Who's that lot, then?' Kev muttered, gesturing towards the obtrusive trio.

'Prospective buyers from Melbourne. It'd almost be funny watching them try to charm the locals, you should listen to some of their ideas,' Toby said.

Kev perused a farm-machinery catalogue and Toby laughed at the sight of his face as he eavesdropped. He leaned across the counter.

'There's a limit to what we'll accept around here,' Kev said. 'I don't care how politically correct we're supposed to be these days. Those three are as gay as Christmas, and—'

Toby spoke at the same time as Lara.

'Kev—' said Lara.

'Whoa, back the truck up,' said Toby. Driven by a strange impulse—perhaps a desire to share something of himself, or curiosity to see where Lara stood on the matter—Toby held up a hand. 'Before you say anything else, know I've got a gay sister, and I voted "Yes" in the referendum.'

Two sets of eyes fixed on him. He didn't know Lara well enough to anticipate her reaction, but he hoped like hell she wasn't about to out herself as a closet homophobe. *That* would be a deal breaker.

'It got my vote too,' she said, staring down the farmer.
Phew.

Kev threw his hands up in the air. 'Calm the farm, you two. I'm not suggesting we tar and feather them . . .' The buyers had wandered outside with the agent, no doubt brainstorming new signage options and façade renovations. The cricket coach looked out the window. 'I'm just saying not everyone is as open-minded as you . . . as us,' said Kev.

'We've got a few thousand people in Bridgefield, average age's about eighty, and they might be a bit slow to warm to new owners like that,' Kev added.

Lara set her hands on her hips. 'I had a similar conversation with Dallas yesterday about a buyer's ethnicity, and I've got to say, Kev, it makes us sound like a bunch of rednecks. Surely we're not that backward?'

Toby cringed. Apart from yesterday, Dallas had been nothing but welcoming to him. It was hard to picture the odd little man making racist remarks, but, he conceded, maybe his welcome wouldn't have been as warm if his background or skin had been different.

They watched the keen buyers file inside and head through the storeroom to the staircase. Despite their criticisms, they sounded even more eager after touring the apartment.

Toby noticed the same enthusiasm from the next keen buyers, who sashayed through the door an hour later.

'I love it, darling,' said the woman within the first two minutes. 'Pop a Chesterfield and coffee table in the window, we could knock out the storeroom and put in a little tearoom. Open fireplace over there,' she said, then frowned as she pointed to the corner where the local artwork was displayed. '*Gah.* We'd get rid of all those dinky crafts.' She waved a disdainful hand at the patchwork tea cosies, the knitted scarves and small woodwork stall Mrs Beggs ran on a commission basis. They had been perfect when Toby unpacked on his first day in Bridgefield and discovered his linen was still in Ballarat. He had also acquired a liking for the lush jams sold at that stall—it would be hard to go back to the synthetic-tasting supermarket variety again.

'Knock out the storeroom? Where does she think she'll keep excess stock?' whispered Lara.

'Everything inside will need a coat of Hog Bristle White,' the woman continued. 'Timber-work, walls, trim, shelving, then I'll whitewash the floors too,' she finished, turning to her husband for approval.

Lara's face went a funny shade of red as she looked from the woman to the bluestone walls. The husband, who hadn't bothered to remove his sunglasses, shrugged blandly.

'If another little project makes you happy, then it makes me happy, sweet cheeks.'

Toby watched Lara. He could see it was on the tip of her tongue to tell them exactly what she thought of her general store being turned into 'another little project'.

He laid his hands on the counter and offered the buyer a bright smile.

'It's a lovely shop,' Toby said. 'And there's a great community initiative on the go. An all-abilities cooking program, isn't there, Eddie?' Toby hooked a thumb towards the kitchen. It wasn't pie-baking day, but Eddie had started coming in more often to lend a hand.

They all peered around the corner. Eddie waved cheerfully and the oven mitt he'd been wearing flew across the room, landing with a splash in the sink. Soapy water slopped over the floor.

'Well. Um. No.' The woman blinked rapidly. 'No, I don't think it would work with my vision. We have very high standards, you see.'

Toby's jaw dropped, and as if she could sense Toby's disapproval, the buyer looked away and linked an arm through her husband's, steering him towards the real-estate agent.

⚶

Lara locked the shop door behind the last of the day's tyre-kickers and blew the loose strands of hair from her face. *A few bobby pins wouldn't go astray right about now.* The ginger tresses, which could be considered auburn one day, dark blonde or light brown the next, depending on the sunshine, had a mind of their own after a busy day at work.

And what a day it had been. The final prospective buyers had been a family of seven.

Lara couldn't imagine dragging Evie along to a business meeting, let alone five children. She'd watched with disbelief as the younger kids ran riot around the shop while the teenagers butted in over Greg time and time again.

She strode through the store, straightening shelves as she went. 'I thought they'd never leave,' she said to Toby, who was wiping sticky fingerprints off every glass surface.

'At least that family would have the manpower to run the store. The younger ones seemed like a handful, but the teens looked old enough to be competent behind the counter,' said Toby.

Lara stared at him skeptically. 'You always a glass-half-full type of guy? They'll have a full-time job making sure those kids don't tear the place apart. I thought Diana's boys were spirited, but those girls took it to another level,' she said.

'Not afraid of making themselves heard, that's for sure,' Toby agreed.

The back door burst open and Leo, Harry and Elliot raced through the storeroom, followed closely by Diana.

'It's as if I conjured the devil,' Lara said under her breath. She heard Toby laugh, then yawn.

'Hey guys. Just grabbing the paper and post,' said Diana, looking between the two of them.

'Whoa. Rough day?'

'You betcha,' said Lara. 'You should see the crackpots keen to buy this place. I never knew there was so much wrong with our general store until today.' Lara rubbed her eyes as another yawn escaped her lips.

'I look forward to hearing all about it tomorrow,' said Diana, tucking her mail under her arm. 'See you at ours, nine sharp.'

Lara groaned. 'Oh God, is it really meat packing this weekend? My mind's like a sieve.'

Diana shook her head. 'Nope, those steers have got a few good meals left in them yet. Tomorrow's the twins' birthday party.'

Lara looked at Diana's middle sons, wincing guiltily. She was so caught up in her own world, she'd completely forgotten.

Harry and Elliot sidled up to her, their faces angelic. 'Mum said you might do the party games if we asked nicely,' said Harry, leaning into her side, fluttering lashes longer than hers.

'Can you be my partner for the three-legged race?' said Elliot shyly.

Lara glanced at her older sister. 'Last year was a one-off because you had the flu. I'm sure you'll be fine coordinating the games.'

Leo wrapped his arms around her leg. 'But you're the bestest, Aunty Lara. Mum doesn't join in the sack race like you.'

Eddie emerged from the kitchen, clapping his hands with delight. 'Sack race!'

'Yeah, you're much more fun, Aunty Lara,' Harry chimed in. 'Mum only lets us have the boring hard-boiled eggs that bounce when you drop the spoon. Evie said you always did the most awesome parties.'

Lara felt a rush of happiness. In every other part of her life, she was the serious one. The prickly one. The McIntyre who wasn't born with the natural charm, green thumb and easy-going manner of her sisters. But in her nephews' opinion, her enthusiasm for organising Evie's annual birthday parties, and one stint as their party-game host had elevated her to hero status. She would never admit it, but she enjoyed it as much as the kids.

Lara tousled the twins' curly mops, then put her hands in her pockets. 'I suppose I can clear my busy schedule.'

The boys' yahoos and cheers followed them all the way out the back door as Diana fished change from her purse. Her sister had the patience of a saint for managing a household of boys, and as much as she loved her nephews dearly, Lara knew all the noise and regular trips to the hospital emergency department would have done her head in.

Eddie wrapped Toby in a big bear hug.

'Three-legged race, Toby? Three-legged race?'

'Where are my manners?' Diana exclaimed. 'You're welcome to come too, Toby.'

Eddie released Toby, still jiggling with excitement.

Toby held his hands up. 'I don't want to intrude. It sounds like you've already got a houseful.'

Diana waved breezily. 'The more the merrier.'

Lara groaned internally. *All afternoon with Toby Paxton and now he's going to be there tomorrow too? Gah!* She knew her sisters would have their cupid's bows locked, loaded and ready to fire.

'You can help Lara with the games while I take care of the food and hand out bandaids.'

'Bandaids?'

Lara almost laughed as mild alarm crossed Toby's face. He took a dramatic step backwards.

'You'll see,' said Lara. Despite the stress of the day, and the parade of buyers, each more ridiculous than the next, Toby's shocked expression put a tiny smile on Lara's lips as she said goodbye and locked up.

She meandered down Main Street. Gentle conversations from the pub's beer garden floated on the warm breeze along with the distant rumble of cattle trucks bypassing the small town, to the backdrop of birds singing in the tall gum trees.

Lara wasn't sure which was worse: the idea of an outside investor buying the general store and modernising it beyond recognition, or the shop closing its doors for good.

Eight

Toby carried the wonkily wrapped presents to the car, along with his camera and the mud-map Diana had drawn him. Holly called as he drove, her news and recap of the school week and weekend better than a shot of caffeine.

'As soon as I've finished band practice, I'm heading to Lake Wendouree, see if I can snag a few action shots at the regatta,' she said. 'Any cool photos on the horizon for you today, Dad?'

Toby glanced at the camera kit on the passenger seat. 'Tennis and cricket shots this arvo, but I'm heading to a kids' birthday party first.'

Holly laughed. 'Wow. Totally random.'

'Yeah, one of the local families invited me along,' he said. Diana's invitation had been unexpected but he had jumped at the chance to learn more about the McIntyre family.

'What present did you get the kid?'

Toby slowed the car as a weatherboard mailbox loomed into view. A bunch of balloons were tied to its pitched tin roof, and a property name was affixed to the fence, 'Darling Downs'. When he turned into the driveway, he saw the letterbox was a miniature version of the house.

'Kids,' Toby corrected, pulling in next to various utes, four-wheel drives and the dinged-up Subaru he'd seen Lara driving. 'Twins. It was a last-minute invite, so the best I could manage were two boxes of chocolates and a Disney DVD from the general store.'

'They'll be so inundated with Lego sets and fidget spinners they probably won't even notice,' Holly said.

He whistled as walked towards the yard. The property was as pretty as the name suggested.

'Geez, Hol, this place is like something out of *Gardening Australia*. Flowers everywhere, in every colour. Your granny would be in seventh heaven.'

He signed off and strode into the party, slipping his gifts onto a decorated table. As Holly predicted, it was almost bowing under the weight of presents. He spotted Lara by one of the large sheds, ducking and looking over her shoulder. After greeting Diana and meeting her husband, Pete, Toby received high fives from their three younger boys and a handshake from their teenage son Cameron.

Toby wandered towards Lara, who was now bent over a beautifully manicured daisy bush.

He cleared his throat. 'Lost something?'

Lara straightened up and his reservations about intruding dissipated. He took in her striped linen shirt, fitted jeans and loose hair, and the smile that transformed her face. Was it the party entertainer role or the weekend casual look that suited her most? *Both,* he decided, returning her smile.

She passed him a handful of wrapped chocolates.

'Treasure hunt,' she explained, tossing two Freddo frogs into a flowerpot.

Toby could only imagine what state the plants would be in afterwards.

'And then it's your time to shine as the fun coordinator?' he said, remembering how she'd brightened at the twins' request last night.

'Something like that.' She nodded modestly, though he could tell she was pleased. He followed her around the garden and helped stash the chocolates as she ran him through the games schedule. As unexpected as the invitation had been, he was glad he'd come.

Lara wrangled the hyped-up ten-year-olds like a pro, and by the time the last prize had been awarded and the candles were blown out on the double-decker Minecraft cake, Toby felt exhausted. Holly's birthday parties had always been held at venues with quiet activities such as cupcake decorating and plaster painting. There was no way his ex-wife would have survived a party like this, yet Lara looked born for it.

'You can see she loathes getting dragged into these things, can't you,' said Diana with a wink as Lara lined up the boisterous boys in height order for a piñata.

'Hates it with a passion,' he laughed.

'Kids like her no-nonsense approach,' said Diana, assessing him with interest. 'You know what? You should come to our family meat-packing day in a few weeks. It'd be perfect for your farming feature.'

Toby glanced across the yard to Lara, wondering if she would mind him tagging along to another of her family events.

Diana followed his gaze, sensing his hesitation. 'An extra set of hands is always good.'

What's to think about? Say yes. 'Sounds great, I'd love to,' he said eventually.

The next half-hour was a whirl as children scoffed fairy bread, honey crackles and cake and fizzed around on a sugar high before they were collected. Lara was nowhere to be seen when Toby made his exit, so he thanked Diana and Pete for their hospitality, farewelled the rest of the McIntyres and headed to tennis. He found himself whistling as he went.

❧

'You *what*!?'

'I invited Toby to the meat-packing day,' Diana repeated, tossing her long honey-coloured hair over her shoulder.

Lara fished a party-popper out of a bowl of popcorn. She tossed a half-eaten quiche then a sausage roll into the chook bucket Diana held, before shooting daggers at her older sister. 'First you invite him to the birthday party, now meat-packing day?'

Penny was avoiding her eye, intent on tipping cordial dregs onto the lawn.

Diana waved a hand, casually. 'He was low on news for next month's farming feature, so I mentioned it,' she said.

'I know what you two are doing,' said Lara, jabbing a finger in Penny's direction.

A kookaburra laughed in the distance, no doubt finding the situation as amusing as her two sisters.

'What?' said Diana, the picture of innocence. 'I'm giving readers what they love. Paddock-to-plate's a feel-good story.'

Pete wandered over and plucked a sausage roll from the container in Diana's arms. He didn't seem to notice the pieces of grass stuck to them, and before anyone could tell him they'd been picked up off the lawn, he'd demolished it and reached for another.

'This birthday spread's high on the feel-good factor,' said Pete, kissing Diana's cheek.

Diana stifled a laugh. Penny covered her snort-laugh with a cough.

'And nutritious too,' said Lara, finding it hard to stay mad when her sisters were in stitches. 'Instead of meddling in my love life, you lot should put your heads together to save the shop. I can barely fathom the chaos if any of those buyers take it on.'

'Does it really matter? As long as they sell the papers, sort the mail and give our kids holiday work, then why not let it be somebody else's problem?' asked Pete. He mopped up the dregs of the homemade tomato sauce with his third sausage roll and patted his belly. 'They'd need to keep the daily pie special, of course; can't lose that tradition.'

'That's the problem,' said Lara. 'Not one of those buyers showed an ounce of interest in the current business model. One wanted to open and shut early, another wanted to whitewash the bluestone walls, and the others were adamant they could manage without any employees except their horrible children. And then there's Dallas Ruggles, but I doubt the banks would loan to him again.'

Tim and Angus wandered over from the shearing shed with Angie and Rob.

'The shop buyers?' Tim asked. 'Reckon they'll keep the all-abilities program going? Eddie loves helping out, he even made us a pie for dinner last week.'

Lara looked across at Diana's orchard, where Eddie was combing the ground for missed chocolates.

'Greg asked me not to mention the all-abilities program,' she said, gently. 'Toby tried to pitch it to one of the buyers when the agent was distracted, but it went down like a lead balloon. Sorry.'

Lara felt Angus's gaze on her. He rubbed his chin, making the bristles rasp.

'Sounds like you've got two options, love,' he said.

Lara guessed what he was going to say. 'Put up or shut up, right?'

A gentle wind picked up, and a weeping mulberry tree, identical to the tree at McIntyre Park that their mother had planted, waved in the breeze, as if Annabel were adding her support.

Lara looked around at her family. All eyes were on her.

'I've been thinking we could pool together to try to buy the shop,' Lara said. 'Cast the hat around the district, that type of thing.'

'You didn't even want to volunteer—now you want to buy the place?' said Pete.

'Better than the other options,' said Lara, crossing her arms.

'Like a community fundraiser? You need to sell a lot of cakes or raffle tickets to buy a shop,' Rob added dubiously.

'If Lara thinks it'll work, then we'll make it work,' Angie said.

Penny murmured her agreement.

Diana set the party-food leftovers back on the table. 'Where do we start?'

☙

Lara tugged on the town hall's heavy doors and threw up the double-sash windows until fresh air breezed into the stale room. She made her way to the hall kitchen. A portrait of Queen Elizabeth II stared at her from above the sink as she filled the urn with rainwater. Someone had Blu-Tacked a moustache to the glass. *Poor Queen Lizzie.* It kept her smiling as she ferried milk, tea bags and coffee from the car.

'Biscuit delivery,' called a familiar voice. Penny came in, juggling Tupperware containers brimming with biscuits.

'Anzacs and yo-yos in here. Diana's bringing jelly slice and lamingtons,' Penny said, pressing a kiss onto Lara's cheek. 'I almost brought wine too, to soften everyone up.' Penny placed the biscuits beside the mugs and saucers.

'I could do with a stiff drink right about now.' Public speaking wasn't Lara's favourite pastime, but the thought of letting the general store fall into the wrong hands was even worse. 'Hopefully we'll get bums on all those seats,' she added, straightening the rows of chairs she'd set out. They'd been busy the past few days, messaging everyone they could think of. Toby's offer to write an article in the paper had been welcome, too.

Angus and Diana breezed through the door.

'If nothing else, it'll be a nice supper,' said Angus, sneaking a biscuit.

Lara's nerves grew as the room filled and she overheard snatches of conversation.

'A city investor's offered three hundred grand.'

'Codswallop, that old building's worth twice as much.'

'Heritage-listed bluestone, they don't make 'em like that anymore.'

'I heard it's being turned into a diner.'

'Who wants to work thirteen hours a day?'

Lara made her way to the stage. Toby waved to her from the front row and she paused by his chair.

'You don't mess around, do you?' he said. 'I had no idea you were planning to try to buy the store. When did all this come about?'

She shook her head, still not sure if it was a good idea or not. 'Somewhere between those ghastly buyers on Friday and the game of pass-the-parcel,' she admitted. 'I'm not sure what the reaction will be tonight, but the thought of those buyers . . .'

She trailed off, wondering why she was explaining herself to him, a reporter of all people.

'I think it's a great idea, shows a lot of community spirit,' he said. 'Unless something astronomical happens, I'll run this article as another front-pager.'

'Thanks,' she said, impressed with his enthusiasm. 'Even Mrs Beggs was pleased with our plan, and we'll soon find out what the rest of Bridgefield has to say.'

'Good luck,' he said. 'I'll grab a few quotes, snap a few crowd shots. Ideally I'd take a picture of you, seeing as you're the main organiser, but that didn't go down so well last time . . .' He trailed off.

Lara shrugged a shoulder. 'As long as I know about it, it's okay. Go easy on the close-ups if you want people to actually buy the next edition. The more locals who pitch in, the more chance we've got of saving the store.'

She took the steps to the stage two at a time, nerves tickling her belly.

'A bit of shush, please.'

The crowd continued chattering until Lara put two fingers in her mouth and let out a sharp, piercing whistle. The room fell silent. She took a deep breath and remembered why she was there. The general store had been the hub of the community for 145 years. Without a shop, there was no financial incentive for Evie to return home in the holidays, nowhere locally for Eddie and his friends to gain experience, important skills and a sense of purpose, nowhere for the craft group to sell their products, no easy access to mail, newspapers and local news. Lara pushed aside her nerves. *You have to make this work*, she told herself. *You have to.*

⚘

Toby lifted his Nikon, peered through the viewfinder and rattled off a dozen photos of Lara on stage.

'It's just an idea at this point, folks, and I'd welcome alternative suggestions, but I propose we acquire the general store for the community. One way to do this is for people to purchase shares in the shop. Each share costs five thousand dollars, and you can buy as many shares as you want. We'll fundraise to make up the shortfall, and if we're still not close enough, we could apply for a mortgage,' Lara said, her clear voice echoing through the hall.

Toby watched as her passion for the town came through in her address to the hundred or so locals. Just as she'd managed Mrs Beggs' medical dilemma in a cool, calm manner, she responded to questions confidently. He could imagine her in the theatre ward, or a triage station, addressing emergencies in an assured manner. Even the doubters didn't seem to unsettle her.

Toby lowered his camera to write notes. He'd reported on company takeovers, hostile boardroom decisions and used the best of his shorthand to transcribe courtroom proceedings, but there was a different energy to this hall; everyone in the room sounded invested. He caught a whiff of stale sweat as Clyde McCluskey lifted his arm two seats over.

'Who's going to get the profits for the day's trading, then? I'm as happy to pitch in as the next Joe, but it doesn't sound right if we're all putting in money and then someone scoops the cream off the top,' McCluskey said.

Lara went to answer, but a voice from behind cut in.

'What about the time Edna was crook, Clyde? Nobody thought twice about helping you for a few weeks. Didn't see you writing cheques to those helpers then, or the ones who fed your dogs and checked your water troughs while she had treatment in the city. Your wife would turn in her grave to hear you now,' came the stern reply from the back of the hall. The old man harrumphed, slouched back down and tucked his chin into his hairy chest.

'Everyone's budgets are tight, I understand,' said Lara. 'And we might not even reach the target, in which case all the shares will be refunded. I'm suggesting we run it on a volunteer basis for now, and then if we buy the store, we can appoint a paid manager and the profits can go back into the community.

'And we're looking for a few key fundraising events to attract some outside money, so it's not such a drain on the local economy,' Lara continued. 'Come and see me if you want to be involved in the committee, we're open to suggestions.'

Toby slipped out of his seat and reeled off a few crowd shots as Lara answered the last questions. It would make a good front-pager, especially if he managed to capture the determination on Lara's face. Kids' party guru, bush nurse, runner and now taking the lead on the town shop campaign. Was there anything Lara McIntyre wouldn't have a crack at?

꩜

Lara drove home from the meeting feeling triumphant. Her mobile vibrated with text messages of support the whole way home, and Mrs Beggs' face flashed onto the screen as she pulled up outside her homestead. She parked and answered the call.

'My shoulder surgery went smoothly, Lara, so we'll cancel the coffin for now. How did your meeting go?'

Lara felt proud as she described the warm response.

Mrs Beggs was touched. 'It's a lovely community. I wish I could donate the shop back to Bridgefield, but it's not possible, I'm afraid.'

'Course not, and nobody expects you to. We'll give it our best shot,' Lara said. 'And from the interest I saw over the past few days, there'll be a buyer for it in some shape or form.' She didn't add the ghastly plans the prospective buyers had outlined. No need to give Mrs Beggs a heart attack.

'And Dallas was in last night, said you two have been working quite closely together,' Mrs Beggs said, approval in her voice.

Lara grimaced. 'Not as close as he'd like,' she said under her breath.

'You know, I always thought you two might get together, back when you both worked at the shop in high school. He was always such a sweet boy.'

Sweet?

Dallas Ruggles was slack, sulky and more than a head shorter than Lara. But before she could assure Mrs Beggs that there was never, *ever* going to be anything between her and Dallas, Mrs Beggs continued. 'It's a shame he's changed his mind about taking over the shop, but this crypto-currency investment he's been researching sounds like a much more viable investment.'

Lara felt like unbuckling her seatbelt and dancing in the rain. He hadn't mentioned anything to her, but that was the best news she'd heard all day.

'Oh, and the doctor said I'll be home soon,' said Mrs Beggs. The rain was still hammering down when she'd finished the phone call, and Lara dashed from the car to the house.

What a great way to cap off the night, she thought, shaking off the rain and unlocking her front door. They had enough people to form a strong committee, nobody had laughed her off stage, donations were already flooding in, Dallas was out of the shop-buying race and Evie would be home in a few short days. And then there was Toby Paxton, whose easy smile and helpful nature had stirred something in her that she hadn't felt in a long time. She finished off the night with an episode of *Friends* and for the first time in ages, Lara slept solidly.

She woke with a smile on her face and headed out for her run feeling upbeat. Basil loped along beside her, tail wagging, thrilled to be invited along. Lara sucked in the fresh air, reliving the highlights of the previous evening.

Her cattle followed her down the driveway, softly calling, their tails swishing.

'Morning, cows,' she said.

The sound of music floated on the breeze as they passed McCluskey's shearing shed.

Who would've though the grouchy old bugger had a soft spot, Lara mused. *Complains about the price of pies, yet he keeps the radio running night and day for his donkeys.*

Basil's ears pricked up.

'Basil,' she growled, watching the dog veer towards them.

The donkeys brayed.

The kelpie stuck by her side as she turned onto the sealed road and headed towards the lake. It wasn't until she was almost at the crossroads that she realised he'd given her the slip.

'Basil? *Basil!*'

Lara spun around. A rabbit hopped across the road, further evidence the kelpie was long gone.

'You mangy, good-for-nothing . . . Ugh!' Lara kicked at the gravel, cursing the dog. *To continue or not?* She had a fair idea where Basil would be heading, and if she cut across the windmill track, she might be able to get back to the shearing shed before he reached the donkeys.

❧

Toby's sports watch beeped as he hit the ten-kilometre mark. He paused at an intersection. To his left, the unsealed road dipped down between leafy crops and was swallowed up by a twisting canopy of trees. There was a slight incline to the right and paddocks of well-grazed cattle all around him. He ran on the spot, trying to make up his mind when something wet touched his hand. Toby jumped in the opposite direction, then laughed when he saw a kelpie looking up at him, tongue dangling out the side of his mouth. His body quivered and before Toby could step away, the dog shook, spraying him with foul-smelling swamp water.

'Thanks for the shower, mate,' Toby said. 'Scared the crap out of me.' The dog nuzzled his hand again, angling for a pat. Toby paused his watch and let the animal sniff his hand.

'Happy pooch, aren't you?' The dog had obviously been taught manners. It looked like the kelpie he'd seen sniffing around in McCluskey's paddocks the previous week.

A shrill whistle split the air. Toby turned to see a figure charging through the trees.

Lara.

His smile faltered as he took in her expression. She didn't look particularly happy to see either of them.

Nine

Lara squinted against the golden glare, feeling like a tornado as she barrelled down the normally deserted road. There was Basil, with one ear up and one down, making friends with the only other person in Bridgefield who would be out running at this hour: Toby.

She clenched her jaw and ascended the hill, cursing herself for Basil's poor discipline.

'Thanks for catching him,' she said.

'Fine-looking dog,' said Toby.

Lara blew out an exasperated breath and shook her head. 'He's a pain in the bum, that's what he is.' She grabbed the piece of baling twine she'd picked up from the roadside and threaded it though Basil's collar. The kelpie would hate the makeshift lead as much as she would hate holding it, but she couldn't risk him nicking off again.

'Friendly guy,' said Toby, scratching the spot between Basil's ears that always turned him to putty.

Lara snuck a look at Toby's socks. Matching today.

She held out the dog's makeshift lead.

'All yours if you want him.'

Toby laughed at her dry tone, and she felt her anger dim a little.

If the sweat stains on his chest were any indication, he would also catch a chill if he didn't start moving soon.

'No fences at my rental, otherwise I'd consider it. Surely he's not that bad?' He stroked Basil's ears.

'He has his moments.' Lara tugged on the baling twine. 'Look, thanks for finding him. I'll leave you to it,' she said, jogging away.

To her surprise, Toby fell into step with her, his tall frame taking up all of her peripheral vision.

'He found me, actually. I hadn't decided which way to head next,' he said.

Lara remained quiet, still struggling to find her rhythm with Basil on one side and Toby on the other.

A tumbling of hooves and a chorus of mooing came from the laneway. She went to call out her usual greeting before remembering she had company. *Bugger it*, she thought. *Do I really care what Toby Paxton thinks of me?* She ignored the inner voice telling her that yes, she most certainly did, then cleared her throat and called out to the Limousin heifers: 'Morning, cows.'

The apricot-coloured livestock followed them along the fence line, clearly captivated by the sight of not one but two runners and a dog on their quiet country lane. They reached the corner of the Curradarra Stud boundary before returning to graze along the creek banks.

Toby laughed.

'They usually talk back?'

'Most mornings.'

'Nothing better than getting a few k's under your belt when most people are still in bed, right?'

'Especially on a morning like this,' Lara agreed. She snuck a look at him. From the shape of his calves, he looked like an all-weather exerciser too, not one of those half-hearted athletes who only ran in perfect conditions. 'Training for anything?'

'Yeah, I'm doing Three Bays in Portland later this year.'

Lara was impressed. Not only had she heard of it, she'd run it twice. Renowned for being one of the toughest marathon courses in Victoria, the picturesque track was not for the fainthearted.

'My sister lives down near Port Fairview. Scathing course with all those hills. But what do you do when you're not reporting and running? Trivia-night whiz? Bird watching?'

'I love photography, don't mind a good crime novel, and I make a pretty good pizza, homemade base and all, even if I do say so myself.'

'Sing out if you need a taste-tester,' she said, picturing him with his shirt sleeves rolled up, elbow deep in pizza dough. The visual made her smile and she changed the subject before she invited herself around to watch.

They came to another crossroads and Lara wondered whether she should cut her run short and head home.

And settle for four measly k's when you factored in time for twelve? Pfft.

She dismissed the notion and put on an extra burst of speed, throwing a challenge over her shoulder as the windmill came into view.

'Last one there's a rotten egg,' she called, leaning into the steep incline.

Toby's footfall quickened and before she knew it, they were neck and neck.

She stretched her lead a few metres, feeling a steady burn in the back of her calves and a hammering in her chest. *It's the incline,* she told herself, *nothing to do with the man on your tail*. Her mind raced almost as fast as her legs and the baling twine cut into her hand as Basil pulled her even further ahead.

Lara's smartwatch vibrated wildly, telling her she needed to back down before her heartbeat went through the roof.

Maybe it had nothing to do with Toby. Or maybe, just maybe, her body was telling her to live a little. The thought made her run even faster.

⚬

Toby couldn't help but admire Lara as she sprinted up the hill. She was fast. And strong. And sexy as hell.

He could see her smashing out a marathon and then pulling a night shift at the hospital without raising a fuss. His ex-wife had all but hailed an air ambulance to collect her from the finish line of her first and only 5-kilometre fun run, back at the start of their relationship when they'd both been eager to please.

The thought of Petra was like a bucket of cold water. He pushed harder, leaning into the hill and focusing on the path directly in front of his feet, only realising his mistake when he looked up and his vision was filled with the sight of Lara. She was bent double at the base of the windmill, hands on her knees, drawing in ragged mouthfuls of air. Toby pulled up beside her and tried his best not to notice how her shorts moulded to her butt when she bent over like that.

He patted Basil's head then stretched his arms out long.

'It's . . . a . . . beautiful . . . view,' gasped Lara. She straightened and gestured to the rural panorama.

Toby turned abruptly, pretending to study the rich jigsaw of Western District paddocks.

Darn good view, indeed.

⚬

Lara noticed Toby's face burning as he spun away from her. *Was he checking me out?* She couldn't decide if she was annoyed or flattered. Or annoyed with herself for feeling flattered.

Contradictions spun in her mind as she tried to work out her next move.

Only a bloody fool would go back for seconds after being so badly burned.

Only a bloody fool would ignore this spark.

Lara leaned against the windmill stand, her shoulder brushing his. She could feel the warmth radiating from his body. She raised a hand and pointed out into the distance.

'See those paddocks at the base of the mountain range?'

Toby stared out at the horizon. Did he too understand the fragility of the spell they were weaving, and knew it could only be nurtured by quiet, gentle actions?

'With the big sheds?'

She took his hand and extended it, recalibrating his line of sight.

'No, over here. With all the red gums. That's McIntyre Park, where I grew up.'

The movement brought their bodies closer.

Several galahs flew past, squawking and screeching, but instead of distracting them, the noise only intensified the electric atmosphere. A thrill ricocheted through her.

What on earth are you doing?

'Nice property.'

His proximity was hypnotic. Lara's head was buzzing, and she struggled to think of a good reply. The heart-rate monitor on her wrist vibrated again.

Walk.

Away.

Now.

Lara closed her eyes, blocking out the nervous chatter inside her head.

Kiss him already.

She leaned in a fraction.

Have you completely lost your mind?

Before she could decide one way or another, Lara's arm felt like it was ripped from her shoulder.

Basil barked and tugged harder on the make-shift lead.

Lara turned to scold the dog, but the words froze on her lips when she saw what had caught Basil's attention.

❧

Toby turned away and ran a hand through his hair, grateful for the breeze cooling his body and sending the windmill spinning. Of all the weeks he'd watched out for her on morning runs, he had no idea their first run together would be like this. But it was good to know she'd noticed the zing between them too.

He felt a goofy expression spread across his face and a heat that had nothing to do with exercise. *Would've liked to see where that was heading.*

The big metal windmill creaked and whirred as another gust of wind blew across the land. He almost didn't hear Lara's words.

'Snake! Don't move!'

He stiffened at Lara's tense tone. He turned back to her and Basil, spotting the striped reptile in a silent stand-off with the kelpie. Its head was raised off the ground, exposing a yellow underbelly. Every nerve in his body screamed 'run' but he stood rock still, assessing the danger.

Basil growled, deep and low, then lunged at the snake.

Lara jumped backward, trying to drag the kelpie away, but Basil ducked and skipped sideways, then leaped forward again. The baling twine snapped and the dog dashed towards the snake.

Lara's face blanched and Toby saw she was shaking.

Fear?

Rage?

He had to do something.

And fast.

❦

Lara willed her legs to move, cursing her shaking arms for not reaching out and grabbing Basil's collar before it was too late, but she couldn't make her body shift a centimetre closer to the snake. Fear magnetised her sneakers to the dirt.

The last time she'd spotted a snake, she'd had the benefit of a shotgun and six feet of distance before she blew its head off. Now the proximity to the damn thing had her quivering like a city girl, transfixed by its deadly dance.

Basil's barking rose in pitch.

Toby looked around. 'I'll get that stick,' he said.

Lara swore and grabbed his arm.

'Don't be an idiot. Basil might be dumb enough to take on a snake, but don't risk your neck too.'

Toby twisted out of her grip, reached down and pulled a forked branch from a fallen limb.

Lara gasped as the snake struck out. Basil lunged, retreated, then lunged, retreated again, barking and snapping.

Oh God. Fear turned to dread as she watched their dangerous game.

'Basil,' she hissed, wishing she were game enough to step in herself. But the writhing reptile, now furious and in full defence mode, made her flinch with every strike. The panic increased ten-fold as Toby moved closer.

A sharp howl ripped through the air. Basil darted away. Toby anchored the branch under the snake's body and sent it flying through the air, as if he were an old hand at wrangling reptiles.

It landed with a soft thwack on the dirt and slithered away into the long dry grass. Only then did Lara's feet move.

'You idiot, Basil.'

She sank down next to the kelpie, grabbing his collar in case he was stupid enough to chase the snake. Basil shook his head. He rubbed a paw back and forth over his muzzle, whimpering.

'He's been bitten,' said Toby, squatting down to look.

Lara's sarcastic default clicked into place before she could filter it.

'No shit, Sherlock. That's what happens when you take on a snake. Lucky you didn't get bitten too.'

He shook his head sharply. 'You stay here. I'll race home and grab my car. Call the vet.' Toby charged down the hill without waiting for a reply, leaving her a little stunned by the whole thing.

She was normally good in a crisis. *What the hell just happened?*

Lara kneeled in the dirt. Stupid, sweet Basil. She swore, stroking the kelpie's soft ears. He wagged his tail, as if he knew he was all she had; the one living creature who noticed and cared whether or not she made it home at night.

Her voice shook as she called her friend Amy, who ran the veterinary clinic in Hamilton and told her to expect them.

Toby's little buzz box roared up the hill. He sprang out and lifted Basil, placing him on Lara's lap in the passenger seat.

The windmill creaked as they set off.

'Even if we get him to the vet in time and he survives the antivenom, he'll probably be soft in the head. I've seen it at the farm,' said Lara.

'Optimist, aren't you? We'll have him there in good time at least.' Toby gave her a gentler smile. 'Basil looks like a tough bloke. Bet he's a natural with the livestock,' he said, clearly trying to distract her.

Lara shook her head. 'Dumb as a box of hammers. And if he miraculously pulls through, you'll be able to see the butterflies floating around behind his eyeballs.'

She knew she probably sounded cruel. Heartless even. But she was damned if she was going to cry in front of a virtual stranger. Each word was another nail in the fence of self-protection.

Lara shot a sideways glance at Toby as they drove towards Hamilton. If he thought she was a heartless bitch, he was pretty good at keeping his opinion to himself. Sam would have blamed her for the whole thing. Told her exactly what she'd done wrong, said wrong or thought wrong to bring this on herself.

She counted to ten as she let out a long, silent breath, remembering the night Basil had come into her life. The very same night she thought Sam had taken Evie for good. The same night her ex-husband had finally got what he deserved. Her eyes prickled. She forced the memories aside, striving for clinical detachment.

Blubbering wasn't going to get them there any faster, and from the way Basil's tail had stopped wagging, and Toby's pace had quickened, she needed to focus now more than ever.

Ten

Toby's body cooled quickly and he felt gooseflesh puckering his skin as they drove towards Hamilton. Basil barely stirred now. It didn't look good.

Despite Lara's earlier bluster, Toby had known her flippant words were a bluff. The rolling green paddocks and massive red gum trees were a blur as he tried to think of the right thing to say.

He pulled up next to the veterinary clinic and hurried around to Lara's side of the car. She too had goosebumps on top of goosebumps. *Extra layers wouldn't go astray right about now*, he thought, planning to check the boot for spare jumpers as soon as Basil was seen to.

Basil barely stirred as Toby picked him up. Only a faint wag of his tail resonated through his limp body.

Lara strode ahead to the clinic, nearly tearing the door off its hinges as she wrenched it open for Toby.

The vet led them down a sterile-looking hallway and instructed Toby to put Basil on the stainless-steel table. He lowered him gently.

Vulnerability was written in the grip of Lara's arms around her torso, her fingertips pressing white orbs into her upper arms. He stood beside her. He wanted to draw her into him and rub her back, but something told him it wouldn't go down well.

'Tell me straight, Amy. What are his chances?'

The vet shone a torch into Basil's eyes and pushed a stethoscope against the kelpie's chest. Her 'tsk' reverberated through the room.

'Well, you're a nurse, so there's no hiding the fact it'll be touch and go, Lara. And it was a tiger snake, right?'

Lara and Toby concurred. There had been no mistaking the stripes on the snake's back, or the yellow belly.

'We'll use a multivalent antivenom anyway, covers all types of snakes. You happy to go ahead?' asked the vet gently. Lara shoved her hands in her pockets, giving a silent but emphatic nod that was at odds with her earlier words. As he jogged back to the car and checked the boot, Toby wondered what other contradictions lingered underneath Lara McIntyre's brusque exterior.

He was in luck. Two jumpers were folded neatly beside a wide-brimmed hat and a picnic rug. Toby tugged on an old rugby jumper, saving the nicer fleecy one for Lara, and walked briskly back into the clinic. Amy had shaved Basil's leg and was putting a cannula into the front of his shin.

The jumper was big on Lara, but even with the extra layer, he could see her shivering. *Shock?*

'I can stay, fetch some brekky from the bakery and then drive you home?'

She shook her head, her gaze locked onto her dog. 'I'll stay a while. Diana will pick me up. You've got a newspaper to put together.'

It pained him to leave her like this, but she was right. He'd taken a morning off for the shop, he couldn't afford to skip more work. He hesitated and scribbled his number down on a piece of paper. She gave hers in return. 'Call me if you need me,' he said, hoping she understood that he could—and would—be there for her.

&

Lara still shivered as she sank into the passenger seat of Diana's car. The leather was cold on her bare legs, and even the four-wheel drive's heaters couldn't shift the chill in her bones.

The morning had gone from bad to worse after Toby left. Lara was accustomed to medical emergencies, but she'd felt completely useless when Basil's heart rate had slowed, and he began vomiting all over the examination table. Recognising the signs of cardiac arrest hadn't made it any easier to watch, and she was grateful for Amy's rapid response.

'An anaphylactic reaction to the antivenom,' Amy had explained, after she'd revived and stabilised Basil.

Lara stared out the car window. The houses gave way to paddocks.

'So, it's still touch and go?' Diana's gentle probing brought Lara back to the present.

'Yep,' said Lara, turning to her sister. 'They've pumped him full of adrenaline, now it's just a waiting game.'

Diana grimaced.

'If he's anything like you, he's a fighter, Lars.'

They were silent for a moment.

'Thanks for collecting me,' Lara said.

'Don't be silly.' Diana took her attention off the road again to give Lara another concerned look. She eyed the fleecy jumper Lara wore. 'So, you're running with Toby now?'

Lara shook her head. 'No, I bumped into him.'

Even through her pain, Lara knew if she closed her eyes, she would be able to picture the two of them at the windmill, shoulder to shoulder. If she'd turned ever so slightly, her lips would have brushed his. And the worst thing was, she'd wanted them to.

She swallowed the thought down. She couldn't think of that. Not now.

'And was Toby much use, or was it like when Mrs Beggs collapsed?'

Lara bit her lip, shaking her head again at Diana's question. 'No, not at all. He was great.'

As the words left her mouth, she realised how useful he'd been. Calm, decisive and resourceful. She'd been the one frozen by fear.

Damn snakes.

Diana kept up a steady stream of conversation as she drove them back to Bridgefield. On any other morning, Lara would have laughed at the titbits of information from Diana's busy household, been amused by little Leo offering their poddy calves toast for breakfast or sympathised over Pete's latest dramas with his stock agency staff. On a normal morning, she would have quizzed Diana on fundraising ideas for the general store, or what she needed to bring to meat-packing day, but Lara couldn't think beyond the vet's final words.

Rough night ahead.

Not out of the woods.

Better than no chance.

Before long Diana had driven down Whitfield Lane, veered around Magpie's Bend, and turned onto Duck Hole Flat Road. They were home already. The sight of Basil's empty kennel hurt more than she expected.

Diana tapped the steering wheel.

'Maybe you should call in sick? Give yourself a day off for once?'

Lara flopped back against the car seat. 'What, and stare at the phone all day, waiting for Amy to call? I'd rather be working,' she said. 'It's seniors' exercise class today anyway, there'd be a mass protest if I cancelled.' She climbed out of the car. 'Thanks for the lift, Diana.'

'No worries.' Her sister gave her a sympathetic smile and conducted a seventy-three point turn. 'Let me know when you hear from the vet.'

Lara's feet felt heavy on the steps. She lifted the lavender pot, slipped the key from its hiding place and into the heavy lock and went inside to wash away the morning.

⚶

Yoga mats criss-crossed the carpet in the nursing centre's multi-purpose room, with soft instrumental music holding the beat for the final routine in the Move It or Lose It class.

Lara broke her warrior pose at the front of the class to check her notes.

Downward Dog or Peaceful Warrior?

With her mind spinning between Basil, the general store and Toby, this morning she was struggling to remember the routine.

The snake was an omen, she decided. Lara's cheeks burned as she recalled how right it had felt to be tucked in close to Toby, knowing she would have kissed him if the snake hadn't intervened. The list of exercise moves blurred in front of her. She looked at the sea of expectant faces awaiting her instructions.

'Righto, let's move into a squat and see how long we can hold it for,' she said.

The crowd murmured and she heard a quiet 'pffft' noise as the class lowered their weight and shifted into position.

There was a snigger. Giggles rippled across the room.

'Better turn that music up to drown out the sound effects,' came a dry voice. Lara turned to see an older man receive an elbow in the ribs from his red-faced wife.

Lara's phone illuminated as she upped the stereo's volume. It took every scrap of professionalism to ignore the incoming call and finish the class.

She whipped around the room afterwards, rolling up yoga mats, stuffing exercise bands back into the cupboard and moving the hand-weights to the side of the room.

She decided on just a peek at her mobile, but a hand landed on her arm as she reached the equipment table. Lara sprang backwards, knocking a tower of CDs to the ground.

'Gosh, you spook easily today, Lara,' said Denise. 'Now, I didn't realise until I got home, but we had some of the Bowerings' mail mixed in with ours this morning.' Denise pulled two envelopes from her handbag.

Lara took the letters. 'Sorry.'

Her phone vibrated and flashed on the benchtop again, but before Lara could snatch it up, the older woman leaned in closer, lowering her voice.

'We're all set to buy three shares for the general store too. Silent partners, mind you. Jim doesn't want people to think we're flashing cash about. How is Mrs Beggs, by the way? Surely she'll be home soon?'

'She's doing okay,' said Lara, wishing she could frog-march the kind lady out the door. 'Look, I don't have my shop note-book here,' she inched towards the door as she spoke, 'but I'll add your name to the list, Denise. Thanks.'

Lara's phone flashed again. She herded the last of the stragglers outside and waved.

Three missed calls, two from Hamilton area codes and one from a mobile. Amy the vet was first up.

'No news, just touching base to say Basil's still hanging in there,' she said. The update was a relief after the drama of the morning.

Lara blew out a shaky breath as the next message came through.

Mrs Beggs sounded more like her usual self.

'Howdy, Lara. Greg called, and we've got some serious interest in the shop. The family from Warrnambool. How good is that? I'm home from hospital, how about you rustle up some of those bikkies I love and I'll give you the low-down in person.' Lara's shoulders sank further at the thought of the rowdy family taking over. It was definitely worth a batch of sultana-and-oat crunchies to get the inside scoop.

Lara felt her face grow warm as she listened to the final message.

'Hey Lara, this is Toby. I know I could walk over and ask this question, but I . . .' He paused. 'Just checking to see how Basil's doing. I meant what I said, call me if I can do anything to help.'

Lara locked the phone and slipped it into her pocket. She remembered how far she'd come on her own. The last thing she needed was to throw away her independence and rely on somebody else, no matter how genuine he seemed or the attraction she felt.

She closed her eyes and pinched the bridge of her nose.

Totally, definitely not a good idea.

⸙

Toby hit the delete button and watched an entire paragraph disappear in a brief second. He normally smashed out 500-word articles over a cup of coffee, but no matter what he did, this current article was worse than a dog's breakfast.

Primary-school students could write smoother sentences than this, he thought. He cracked his knuckles but again his fingers hovered over the keyboard, unable to find the right words. It was an update on the Save the Shop campaign, outlining the new committee Lara had formed after the town meeting. The story's premise had punch, and there was a bubbling energy among the people he had interviewed so far. Everyone except his neighbour seemed to think it was a good idea.

He stared at his computer. Was it the story, or the woman at the centre of it that had him fumbling over his words? He looked down at the mobile phone—no missed calls—and then out the glass-fronted office window.

If he wheeled his desk chair a little closer to the glass, he could see the corner of the Bush Nursing Centre. A group of sporty-looking seniors had filed out a few hours ago and the foot traffic in and out those automatic sliding doors was consistent.

A runner, a mother, a nurse, a volunteer and a farmer. She didn't seem like the type of woman to be impressed by a delivery of flowers, even if there had been a florist nearby. Chewing on the end of a pen, Toby realised he looked forward to seeing more of Lara McIntyre.

Eleven

The next few days flew past, with Lara blazing a path between Bridgefield and Hamilton for regular visits to see Basil. His recovery hadn't been as smooth as Amy the vet, or Lara, would have liked. Only Evie's imminent arrival remained a shining light on the horizon. Friday afternoon's volunteer shift felt like it was over in the blink of an eye, such was the flow of customers through the general store. Another prospective buyer swanned around pointing out faults and deliberating on unnecessary changes; there were trays of salad sandwiches to be made for an impromptu luncheon of the town's Stitch and Bitch sewing club; and more than a dozen new shareholders for the general store meant they were well on their way to the asking price.

Lara walked through the shop, switching off appliances and turning out lights. Every bone in her body campaigned for a hot bath, even though that wouldn't happen until after she'd been to see Basil, but something made her pause at the foot of the staircase.

Lara dashed up the stairs, an idea forming as she walked around the small flat, trying to formulate a way to capitalise on the vacant property. Hadn't a couple along the Great Ocean Road raffled off their cafe, selling tickets for $10 and raising well in excess of the market value? She recalled the news articles and even the international attention it had attracted. By the time Lara pulled up outside the vet surgery, the idea had become a fully formed concept.

Lara's enthusiastic knocking set off a chorus of barks and meows from the patients.

Amy opened the back door, her blue scrubs covered in animal fur.

'Hey Lara, thought you were going to stand me up. You look perkier than yesterday,' she said, shutting the door behind Lara and fixing her with a wicked look. 'Did you get lucky?'

Lara narrowed her eyes. 'Seriously? Thought you'd know me better after all these years, Ames.'

Amy shrugged. 'You're not dead, you know.'

Lara ignored her friend's pointed look. 'I've had a brainwave for the general store fundraiser, and I'm pretty sure it'll generate some statewide interest. Fancy buying a raffle ticket to rent the upstairs apartment for a year? Close to work, quiet setting . . .' Lara watched the vet carefully to see her response.

Amy's enthusiasm was encouraging. 'Heck yeah. We're always looking for affordable housing for our vet nurses and locums. How much would you sell tickets for?'

Lara considered it as they walked down the hallway.

'Maybe fifty dollars each? We'd need to make it affordable, but still worthwhile.'

'Well, at that rate, I'd pitch in two hundred at least, and I wouldn't be the only one. Imagine! Two hundred bucks for a year's rent? Amazing.'

Lara's smile broadened. It was exactly the response she'd wanted, and she could only hope that it would be as well received by the rest of the committee.

'Of course we'd have to give a full refund if we didn't raise enough to buy the shop, plus the tenant would need to take care of their own utilities, but it's an idea.'

'It's genius, that's what it is, Lara.'

Lara walked past the crates of canine patients, pausing at the black-and-tan kelpie in the back corner.

Basil wagged his tail as Lara opened the cage door.

'Still a bit flat,' she said, stroking his soft brown ears. 'Any sign of kidney failure?'

'We're pumping as many fluids through him as possible to hopefully avoid that. He's hanging in there. See that?' The vet pointed to Basil's mouth. 'The venom works in funny ways. It's too early to tell whether it's a permanent paralysis, but he might always have a droopy lip.'

Lara looked at the spot where he'd been bitten. It clearly drooped lower than the opposite side, giving him a goofy, lopsided expression.

'Kinda suits him, the daft bugger. In fact, now's probably a good time to give me a heads-up on how much this is going to cost me. Hit me while I'm smiling,' Lara said.

The vet scratched her head, quietly doing the sums. The lengthy pause made Lara nervous.

'Brace yourself, it's not cheap.'

Lara bit her lip as she waited. As disobedient as he was, at times Basil felt like her only friend. Whatever it cost, she would pay it. Still, it didn't stop her cringing as she heard the figure.

'That's the ballpark, but if you budget between four and six grand, you'll be about right,' said Amy.

Lara made a show of fanning her face. 'There goes my next tropical holiday,' she joked.

Amy laughed. 'You can pay in instalments, Lars. Plenty of people do.'

Lara thought of the cutbacks at the Bush Nursing Centre and how her bank account was already stretched to capacity with the mortgage repayments. The extra funds she had invested into her cattle weren't likely to pay dividends for at least another few seasons either.

She patted Basil and pushed money to the back of her mind. She would find a way, she always did.

જ

Toby's phone rang just as he cycled out of Bridgefield's 80-kilometre zone. He kept pedalling and reached into his pocket, cursing when the phone slipped out of his sweaty hands and into the long grass.

'Bugger!'

He reefed on the brakes, his back wheel skidding in the loose dirt as he came to an abrupt stop on a sharp rock. He kept the bike upright, but before he had a chance to turn around, he heard a hiss.

'Great. Just great,' he said as he watched the back tyre deflate. He looked at his watch. Holly's bus would be pulling into Hamilton shortly. He wheeled the bike back to the spot where he'd dropped the phone. A buzz and the tinny theme song made it easy to find. Toby scanned the grass before reaching in. The last thing he wanted to pull out was a handful of angry snake.

'Mum,' he said, pressing the redial button.

'Hi darl, I wanted to see how you're doing.'

Toby pushed the bike in the direction of his house. 'Good. At least, I *was* until I blew a tyre on my bike. Holly's bus is due in half an hour.'

'Want me to call and tell her you'll be late?'

Toby gratefully accepted her assistance, signed off and picked up his pace. It would take 30 minutes to walk home, two minutes to duck through the shower and another half an hour to drive to Hamilton. The idea of Holly waiting around the bus stop didn't sit well, but he was hardly in a position to change it.

A stock truck rumbled past, the exhaust brakes squealing as the driver slowed for Magpie's Bend. The pungent aroma of cattle lingered long after, and instead of dwelling on how long his little girl would be stranded at the bus stop, Toby thought about tomorrow's meat-packing day with the McIntyre family.

Would he turn squeamish at the sight of hanging meat or big carcasses splayed across a chopping board? He hoped not. Would home-butchered meat taste different to the stuff he bought from the supermarket? He had a sneaking suspicion it would.

Should be some great photo ops too. The thought put an extra spring in Toby's step. Then he caught himself and laughed.

Four months ago, he was filing stories on trade-union battles, court cases and city-council budget blowouts. Now he was in Bridgefield, where an exciting week involved sheep sales, butchering home-grown meat and avoiding snake bites. Somehow, he had a feeling none of his Ballarat colleagues would understand how refreshing it was.

⁂

By the time Lara had flung her groceries into the back of the Subaru and torn across town to the bus stop, Evie was waiting under the shelter with a group of girls.

Lara's heart swelled at the sight of her daughter. She quickly swiped at her prickling eyes, taking in Evie's thick hair and the legs and arms that still seemed too long for her scrawny body. Was it possible for hair and limbs to grow so much in such a short time?

Lara lifted the handbrake, hoping she wasn't about to embarrass herself and Evie by gushing all over her. To her delight, Evie broke away from the group and raced towards her as soon as she spotted the car.

'Mum!'

Lara wrapped her arms around Evie, hugging her tight, relishing the smell of her.

'God, I missed you.'

Everything felt right with the world again. She gave Evie another squeeze.

'You too, Mum. How's Basil, are we going to see him tonight?'

Lara looked back at her watch. 'No, Amy's off on a date tonight, but she said we can call in tomorrow morning, before we head to the farm for the meat-packing day. Or Sunday morning. Sound good?'

Evie beamed at her and glanced over her shoulder. 'Hey, I almost forgot. I was sitting next to the girl over there on the bus, she said something about meat packing. Apparently she's coming too?'

Lara looked over at the group of teenagers standing by their luggage, recognising the dark-haired girl with glasses and an easy smile. It could only be Toby's daughter, Holly.

'She nice?' Lara hoisted Evie's suitcase into the back of the car.

'Yeah, super nice. She goes to the all-girls school down the road from me. I'll say bye and we'll head off, yeah?'

Lara watched her daughter join the other girls. She recognised a few from Evie's primary school and pre-school years. They all had long, glossy hair, some with braces, others with acne, and an effervescence that seemed exclusive to teenage girls. Evie hugged two of the girls goodbye, then walked back with Holly.

'Mum, this is Holly. Holly, this is Mum . . . ah, Lara.'

Holly gave a little wave.

'I know your Dad,' Lara said with a smile.

Holly lifted her phone, frowning at the screen. 'He's gone and blown a bicycle tyre on the way home from work. I've got to wait here for him to walk home and then drive in.'

Evie piped up. 'I told her we'll give her a lift home.'

'Righto. Let your dad know, then.' Lara reopened the boot and Evie took the suitcase while Holly tapped out a message.

Lara pushed the groceries to one side, curious to get a feel for Toby's daughter. If she was a spoiled brat, it would be a major red flag, and could save Lara a hell of a lot of time. Evie took the front seat, twisting around as Lara navigated the car park.

'It'll be good to have more helpers for meat-packing day tomorrow. It's all hands on deck, everyone gets roped into service,' Evie told Holly.

Though Lara was dying to pepper Evie with questions about her school, yesterday's test, the other boarders and Mrs Neilson, the dragon-like house matron, she was interested to hear the conversation between the girls. It was like a whole other world, learning about the television shows they watched, the books they liked, the mutual links between their friendship circles.

The conversation shifted so rapidly, Lara had trouble keeping up. She looked in the rearview mirror as Holly spoke about her grandmother. The teenager's face lit up.

'And she gets these letters from the royals. Not from Princess Mary herself, obviously, just her peeps, but it's kinda awesome.' Holly shrugged, then giggled. 'In a daggy Granny-ish way, you know?'

Lara glanced at her daughter before looking back at the road. Evie had never had the pleasure of a doting grandmother, although Lara felt that void more keenly than Evie. The chatter continued, jumping from princesses to pets to extra-curriculars. Holly seemed pretty similar to Evie, a bright, switched-on kid. Lara thought of the teenagers Evie used to play netball with, whose warm-up conversations had centred around Insta-influencers, make-up and You Tubers, and the boarding school mates who were crazy about reality TV shows. She much preferred this line of discussion.

The half-hour drive between Hamilton and Bridgefield went quickly, and soon Lara was driving past McCluskey's shearing shed and then turning into Toby's driveway.

'Is your house seriously right next door to us? Awesome,' said Evie, spinning in her seat again and pointing out their house to Holly. The Subaru shuddered along the driveway, stopping short of the rusty three-bar gate.

'No wonder he got a flat tyre,' said Lara as Evie climbed out to open it. 'It's lucky those pot holes haven't swallowed him whole. And it's not quite next door. Clyde's property is in between.'

There wasn't anything fancy about the front yard, but it was neat and well-tended. Small garden beds flanked the front steps, weed-free and bursting with the same cheery flowers featured in the driveway roundabout.

Another green thumb. Penny, Angie and Diana would be even more impressed.

Lara glanced at the cottage, wondering what it was like inside. Was he the type of guy who kept every single appliance on the benchtop, along with a sink full of dishes, or was his living room clinically clean, bland like a random hotel suite instead of a home? At a guess, she imagined he sat somewhere in between. If his garden was anything to go by, it'd probably be tidy.

Does it even matter? This weekend was about Evie.

Lara and Evie helped Holly pull her luggage from the boot. The shed door creaked open. Music blared across the backyard as Toby stepped out.

Lara scanned her memory to identify the music. *Classical? What type of guy repairs bicycle tyres to Beethoven or Debussy?* For reasons she couldn't articulate, a smile crept across her lips.

❦

The sunny sky was bright after the dim shed, and Toby squinted across the lawn. He waved to Lara and the girls, catching a whiff of something nasty in the process. The smell stopped him in his tracks. Why did bicycle tyre inners always smell like rancid belly button lint?

'Just a sec,' Toby said, ducking down by the closest tap.

The water spluttered, spraying his shoes and legs as well as his hands. Toby scrubbed his fingers and dried them on his shirt before greeting his guests.

'How's my girl?' Holly bounded over, and he pulled her into a bear hug.

'Great, Dad. I'm going to show Evie around, okay?'

She bounded off without waiting for an answer.

'Hi Holly's dad, nice to meet you,' said Evie with a wave, following Holly inside.

Lara had one hand on the car door and the other lifted to block out the late-afternoon sun. She gestured to the teenagers disappearing inside the house.

'I thought they only did that in primary school, springing playdates on you at the school gate so you look like a grump for saying no,' she said.

Toby laughed. 'Apparently not. Coffee? Beer?' He'd discovered a few local farmgate businesses the previous weekend, and there were plenty of nibbles he could pull together to go with drinks.

Cashews, big juicy kalamatas from Mount Zero Olive Farm, quince paste from Pomonal and dukkah that'd go perfectly with a cold ale. Just thinking about it made his stomach rumble.

He bent and picked up Holly's suitcase, letting Lara make up her mind without pressure. He wasn't surprised when she shook her head.

'No, I've got some baking to do for tomorrow. Everyone always works up an appetite at meat-packing day. Holly sounded like she was looking forward to it too.'

Toby smiled at the surprised expression on her face. 'When in Rome, right? It was really nice of Diana to invite us. The old *Farming Focus* liftout has been a bit light on for content.'

He pulled open the front door, called for the girls and turned back to see Lara looking down the hallway.

'Nice place?' she asked.

He spread his hands and shrugged. 'It's not the Ritz, but it's cosy enough. How's Basil?'

Footsteps clattered down the hallway.

'Still touch and go. The vet's flushing out the toxins with an IV so his organs don't have to work as hard.'

'He sounds like a tough dog,' Toby said. 'Thanks again for bringing Holly home.'

Lara rounded up Evie and set off, giving the colourful roundabout a generous berth.

Holly waved them off and leaned down to smell the bright geraniums.

'Nice flowers,' Holly said admiringly, walking around the circle to get the full effect. Toby had planted alternating colours and was pretty chuffed with the charm it added to the front entrance. She paused, then pointed to a stunted white geranium. 'What happened here?'

Toby grimaced at the odd-shaped bush. 'McCluskey's livestock paid me a visit the other day.' Keen to avoid an encore performance, he'd started shutting the gate regularly. It was in dire need of re-hanging, and he was already sick of dragging the stubborn thing open and shut twice a day. His inner-city houses had never needed much maintenance, but a few months in this place and already he was noticing his lack of handyman skills. He skull-dragged the gate shut, then turned to Holly.

'Ready for a full country weekend?'

'Totally!' Holly stretched and scanned the yard.

'What's new in the 'hood?'

Toby led her to a new section of the garden, showing off the improvements he'd made since her last visit. They paused by the prolific tomato bushes, still producing long after their normal season. He plucked one off the bush, passed it to Holly and found himself glancing over the paddocks again.

In the distance, he saw Lara had emerged from the car. She drew her daughter into the same type of hug he'd given Holly. The hug of a single parent, soaking up every missed moment.

Holly popped another cherry tomato into her mouth and followed his gaze. 'Neighbours seem nice.'

Toby nodded his agreement. He liked seeing Holly and Evie hitting it off.

Although he didn't know Evie, Holly's instant rapport with her was a good endorsement. And as for Lara . . . she was every bit as intriguing as she was attractive. Tomorrow couldn't come quickly enough.

Twelve

'Don't let me touch another piece,' Lara said, sliding the tray of pizza towards Evie. 'I'll burst if I eat any more.'

Evie shuffled across the couch, piling another slice of potato and rosemary pizza onto her plate. 'Better than the greasy stuff they serve at the boarding house.'

'Perhaps when you come home in the holidays we can have a pizza special at the shop—it could be Evie's Pizza of the Day. You'd make a mint,' said Lara, lowering the television volume.

Anne of Green Gables had been Evie's choice—the Megan Follows version of course—and they'd watched it enough times to know every scene, even with the volume turned down. Lara had introduced Evie to the books years ago, buying her the whole collection for her seventh birthday and reading them aloud each night before bed. The collection had been packed for boarding school. Knowing that Anne Shirley, Matthew and Marilla Cuthbert and Diana Barry were sharing Evie's dorm room made the transition a little easier for them both.

'If the general store's not sold by then,' said Evie. 'Any more offers? What's your fundraising tally up to?'

'Getting closer every day. And there're a few fundraisers in the pipeline.'

Evie wiped the back of her hand across her mouth. 'Oh yep, Cameron told me. Apparently Aunty Diana and Aunty Pen are planning a singles ball.'

'Like a B&S ball?' Lara frowned. 'First I've heard of it. I think we're aiming for an older demographic.' Her mind went straight to the rowdy B&S balls she'd attended in her teens. Rum cans, bottles of food colouring tossed across the room until everyone was a multi-coloured mess, and waking up in strange swags, horrified at what had seemed such a good idea the night before.

'Might be fun? You could meet someone nice, Mum. Although . . .' Evie wriggled across the couch, almost upsetting the glass of wine Lara had balanced on her thigh. She poked Lara's leg playfully. 'Holly did mention your name had cropped up in a few conversations when she's phoned home. Are you sure there isn't something between you and our new neighbour?'

A rogue pizza crumb somehow materialised in the back of Lara's throat. She gulped her wine to wash it down.

'I barely know the guy.'

'Only one way to fix that, Mum. It'd be cool to have a step-sister. We could be bosom buddies, just like Anne and Diana,' said Evie, affecting a Canadian accent as she gestured to the television, where the movie characters headed off to a concert in Avonlea, all braids and puff-sleeved dresses.

Lara stood up with the pizza tray. 'Righto, I'm cutting off your supply of pizza. Those carbs have gone straight to your head.'

Evie clasped her hands to her heart dramatically.

'Maybe there'll be romance over the butcher's block tomorrow. Nothing like a fresh carcass to inspire a little love story, right?'

'This is the problem with boarding school, Evie. All that junk TV will rot your brain.'

Lara filled a sink with soapy water and as she shoved the greasy trays in, she wondered what Toby had told Holly about her. And what on earth had made Evie think like that? It was the first time she'd ever mentioned romance and her mother in the same sentence. *The Bachelor, Love Island* and *Married at First Sight* had a lot to answer for.

'You'll never, never know if you never, never go, Mum,' Evie chanted as Lara drained her wine glass and dunked it in the water. 'You don't want to be stuck out here by yourself for the rest of your life, do you?'

Lara grabbed the tea towel from the oven door and flicked Evie on the backside.

'Nick off, Cupid. I've got you, I've got Basil, I've got work.'

'That's pretty depressing, Mum. I'll be off travelling the world in a few years and Basil isn't going to keep you warm at night,' said Evie, rubbing the spot where the tea towel had snapped against her.

'I've got the nursing centre, all the patients rely on me. And then there's the shop.' Lara folded her arms across her chest, feeling deflated by Evie's bleak summary of her life.

'Mum, they're coming into the centre to get their gross leg ulcers dressed, not for company, and everyone knows the shop's all about the gossip and the pies.'

Is that really how she sees things?

'I'm perfectly fine out here by myself. One day . . .'

The sentence stuck in Lara's mouth. How much had that phrase pained her as a kid?

Evie huffed. She reached into the freezer, pulling out the tub of hokey pokey ice cream. 'My favourite! Thanks, Mum,' she said, landing a kiss on Lara's cheek and returning to the lounge room with two spoons, not a bowl in sight.

Sermon over? Lara lifted her fingertips to her cheek, where Evie's kiss had landed. A peck from a child, a hug from a family member and the hand of a patient seeking support and comfort as she tended their wounds and ailments. That was the extent of her physical contact these days. How long had it been since she'd let someone's fingers trail along her skin with the sole purpose of pleasure? Had she become one of the lonely masses she'd read about in the medical journals, craving human contact? Skin hungry, that's what they'd called it.

Lara crossed her arms, dismissing the notion. *Ridiculous.*

One day she'll understand, Lara reassured herself. Life wasn't a big fairy tale with frogs, princes and princesses waiting for knights in shining armour.

Joining Evie on the couch, she pressed play on the movie again.

'What did you think of Toby's fun-run idea, Mum?'

Lara paused, a spoon full of ice cream halfway to her mouth. *Fun run?* She didn't like feeling behind the eight-ball, especially not twice in one night. *How many other fundraisers were being planned without my knowledge?*

'Holly was telling me,' said Evie, not noticing Lara's perplexed look. 'Apparently fun runs are the new tourism trend, people are happy to pay for a race weekend away. Especially the newbie runners,' she said, crunching a toffee piece.

How does Evie know more about this than me?

'I'm sure we'll get all the details at the next committee meeting. There'll be lots of different fundraisers needed to get this shop sale sorted.'

'Or tomorrow,' said Evie, shovelling in another mouthful of ice cream. 'Don't forget we'll be seeing them tomorrow.'

Lara twirled her spoon in the ice cream. As if she could forget.

A ceiling of stars twinkled against a denim-blue sky, with the sliver of moon doing little to illuminate the road or highlight the pot holes. Lara relied on memory as she headed out for her morning run, sticking to the centre of the road to avoid the loose rocks.

She hugged the shoulder of the road as she approached Magpie's Bend. A neighbour's tractor had lost a wheel years earlier and the divots from where the front axle speared the road was an ankle reconstruction waiting to happen. As with the long roadside grass that created blind corners and badly needed slashing, the council didn't seem in any hurry to repair the damaged road. The bigger towns continued to suck out the majority of funding while ratepayers in the smaller outlying areas had to make do with the bare necessities.

Lara looked up in time to see a shooting star sprint across the horizon. *Don't get those in the city*, she thought as the star streaked a glittering path across the sky.

A gentle lowing came from the north.

'Morning, cows,' called Lara. She couldn't see them, but she welcomed their company in the sound of the shuffling grass.

It was probably lucky Evie hadn't joined her. Talking to cows would surely be right up there on Evie's list of 'Mum's Sad, Sad Life'.

Lara headed towards the lake, relishing the fresh morning air pumping through her body. Running had been akin to therapy for more years than she could count, the problems rolling around in her mind over the long kilometres until they met with a suitable solution. And if not a solution, at least a way forward.

And then there was the sense of pride, knowing she was the only person at 5 a.m. in the back blocks of Bridgefield, getting it done. *Well, almost the only person*, she conceded.

Without a torch or full moon, she wouldn't know whether Toby was running the same route as her unless he was within earshot. A little devil parked on her shoulder and whispered, *So that's why you've stopped wearing your headphones in the dark mornings?*

Lara picked up the pace, deflecting the issue like she'd dismissed Evie's gentle probe last night. *Course not, it's just safer*, she told herself, sidestepping to avoid the bumpy track by a roadside sign, where tree roots were trying to recapture their territory. Another thing the council was yet to fix, despite regular requests.

She turned when she got to the lake, bracing herself for the winding uphill track, urged on by the carolling magpies and their dawn chorus. The sky was lightening by the time she reached the main road, with the first strains of pink-and-purple sky reflected on the lake's surface below. *Spectacular.*

Lara fixed her mind on the general store as she headed for home, trying to come up with something to counter the hare-brained singles ball idea Diana and Penny were concocting. A charity auction? A bake sale? Sausage roll and pastie drive? They were a lot of effort for little return. She thought about the apartment over the store. Amy had liked the raffle idea, and Lara hoped it would go down as well with the rest of her family, who made up three-quarters of the fundraising committee. For what seemed like the zillionth time, Toby popped into her mind. In the hubbub of the week, Lara had forgotten his request to join the committee, yet despite this, he was still planning a major fundraiser.

⁂

Toby slowed the Volkswagen as the tree-lined driveway came into view.

'McIntyre Park Merino Stud,' read Holly. They rattled over a cattle grid and turned onto the gravel track. 'Penny McIntyre and Tim Patterson. Which sister's that?' said Holly, pushing her glasses back on her nose. 'The one with all the boys? Evie said she has heaps of cousins.'

Toby laughed at the wistful tone in his daughter's voice.

'Penny's got the baby, Diana's got the boys. You'll have a cousin soon enough. Is Aunty Belinda beginning to pop yet?' Toby said.

'Nah, you can't even tell she's pregnant. I wish Aunty Belinda had thought about IVF when you and Mum had me, so at least we'd be the same age.'

Toby opened his mouth and then shut it. Holly had been as excited as him about Belinda's decision to create a rainbow family and seemed pretty au fait with the whole LGBTI+ concept, but she was too young to understand that fifteen years ago, when he and Petra were blissfully deluded newlyweds, Belinda hadn't even told their parents about her sexuality, let alone considered asking a gay friend for sperm.

A trio of sheepdogs raced out of their kennels by a machinery shed, straining at their chains as they barked at the car.

A weatherboard farmhouse took pride of place at the end of the driveway, surrounded by extensive rose bushes and clipped lavender hedges. There was more than one green thumb in the family, and it was clear where the inspiration for Diana McIntyre's garden had come from.

'It's like a *Country Style* magazine,' said Holly, her voice laced with awe. 'If they're so loaded, why do they cut up their own meat?'

'Holly!'

'Just saying . . .' Holly muttered.

Toby pulled up beside a pair of utes. Lara's battered station-wagon looked even more weathered next to the immaculately restored WB Holdens. He didn't have to be a rev-head to appreciate their restoration.

'They've even got a fountain in the middle of the driveway,' Holly pointed out as she unbuckled her seatbelt.

Toby had been so busy admiring the classic utes he hadn't noticed the water feature. 'Mind your manners, Hol. And don't forget your—' Toby tried and failed to catch Holly's attention. He followed her gaze up to the deck. Evie was standing by the back door, waving. But that wasn't who had caught her eye, Toby realised as Holly smoothed her ponytail, clambered out of the car and straightened her T-shirt. It might have something to do with the six-foot blonde teenage boy who emerged after Evie.

'. . . camera,' said Toby wryly, trying to recall Diana's eldest son's name. The scent of flowers hit him as he emerged from the car and pulled the camera bags off the back seat. More children spilled out the doorway, followed by the McIntyre adults. Harry, Elliot, Leo and . . . The name came to him as Angus greeted them in a blue-and-white striped apron.

Cameron, that's it.

'Morning, folks,' said Angus. 'Hope you're ready for a big day?'

Toby tucked his notepad into his back pocket and returned Angus's hearty handshake with a smile. Diana's younger boys jostled their way to the front of the crowd.

'Hey Toby, want to try a three-legged race again? I bet I'll beat Harry and Elliot if I've got you as my partner,' said little Leo. Toby kneeled down on the lush lawn. Leo was only a little tacker. The poor guy had been in tears at the twins' party, coming mid-pack in most of the party games, trying but never managing to match his older brothers and their friends.

'Think we've got some work to do first, but maybe when we break for lunch, okay mate?'

The answer seemed to satisfy Leo, who followed him through the lavender hedges towards the house. Lara emerged from the side of the garage, a bucket of bleach and dripping broom in her hand. She smelled like an indoor swimming pool.

'Looks like you've made a friend,' Lara said, looking from him to Leo, who had grabbed his hand and was now leading the way inside.

Toby smiled. He didn't mention that he'd always wanted a brother for Holly, or the way Petra had taken the decision out of his hands by getting her tubes tied shortly after Holly's first birthday. He'd made his peace with it more than a decade ago, although young Leo seemed to have snuck into his soft spot.

He wondered if Lara had wanted only one child, or if like him, other factors had kept it that way. A rowdy bunch of nephews would be the next best thing, he supposed, watching Lara ruffle Leo's hair on the way in.

While the exterior of the house was magazine perfect, Toby was surprised to find the inside cluttered, cosy and instantly welcoming. Winter coats and Driza-Bone jackets took up a wall in the laundry; old-fashioned Pears soap paintings hung over the wash trough; and rows of Blundstone boots lined the skirting boards.

Evie made the introductions for Holly as they walked in.

They added their boots to the neat collection, and Toby looked down at his socks: one was striped, the other was plain, but at least they were hole-free.

Commercial chopping boards and two knife blocks sat in the middle of the huge island bench, with a chequered butcher's block butted up against it. There were no overhead cabinets, instead the panoramic kitchen windows framed the majestic mountain range to the north.

'Bet no one complains about doing dishes with that view,' said Toby, setting his camera bag on the countertop. The kitchen overlooked a wide verandah, then a neat backyard with a trampoline and more extensive rose gardens. The paddocks beyond were studded with sheep right to the foot of the Grampians.

Angus laughed. 'You'd think, wouldn't you? Now, when you said you wanted a hands-on story, what were you thinking? Watching and photographing, or proper hands-on?'

Toby definitely liked the latter option. 'It'll give the story more depth if I'm having a crack. Load me up with whatever jobs you normally do on meat-packing day. Holly can take some photos of us in action, then I'll get my own shots later.'

Penny passed him an apron.

'Better whack this on, then. You can help Pete carry in the first quarter,' she said.

Toby unfolded the apron and slipped it over his head. Lara's lips twitched. Penny and Diana hooted with laughter. Holly and Evie giggled.

Angus looked Toby up and down. 'That's my favourite apron,' Angus said.

Toby glanced down and saw the apron wasn't blue-and-white striped like most of the others, or floral like Penny's. It was a cartoon man, with bulging muscles, budgie-smuggler Speedos and a chest hairy enough to make Tom Selleck proud. He caught Holly's eye and flexed his arms to imitate the man on the apron, minus the muscles.

Her face flushed. 'Daaa-ad.' She looked scandalised.

Lara shook her head and turned away, but not before he saw a hint of a smile on her lips.

⸙

The mobile cool room ticked and whirred, and a puddle had formed on the ground underneath the large air-conditioning unit. Lara stepped over the power cord and checked the temperature gauge. A steady four degrees. Perfect.

Three fair heads bobbed up and down on the trampoline by the chook shed and the boys called out while she waited for Pete and Toby.

'Watch me backflip, Aunty Lara.'

'And me front flip!'

'No! Me!' added little Leo, determined to keep up with his older brothers.

'Nice one, Harry. Nailed it, Elliot. You'll have to show Evie when she's out next. Mind this extension cord, boys,' she reminded them. Last year's meat had almost been spoiled when one of the kids tripped over the power cord and unplugged the air-conditioner. Luckily Penny had been checking twice a day or thousands of dollars' worth of top-quality meat would have spoiled.

'Yes, Aunty Lara,' they chorused, resuming their flips.

She waited at the cool-room door until Pete and Toby were both beside her.

'So,' Pete said, turning to Toby, 'we'll start with the forequarter closest to the door and work our way backwards. I'll lift the meat off the hooks and we'll carry it together once I'm down the steps.'

Lara watched Toby. *Has he ever seen inside a cool room? Will he freak out when he spots the hanging carcasses?*

'Ready?'

Chilled air flooded out as Lara opened the door. Her skin goose bumped. Rows of red-and-white striped ribcages swung in the air-conditioned breeze and the underlying hint of bleach was still there from that morning's clean. Pete grunted as he took the bulk of the weight and staggered back down the steps.

Lara swung the door shut quickly to keep out the flies, surprised by Toby's no-fuss assistance. Sam had avoided meat-packing day like the plague. There was always an excuse—a friend moving house, a call in at work, a hangover—but Lara knew the sight made her ex-husband's stomach turn. He'd puked behind the trailer the first time she'd invited him for the family occasion, ironic considering his later penchant for inflicting pain.

Not all men are like Sam, she reminded herself. Sam wouldn't have taken Leo's three-legged race concerns seriously. Sam wouldn't have cared about Basil. Sam wouldn't have served pies at the general store out of the goodness of his heart or brainstormed fundraising ideas.

She watched Toby navigate the porch steps, careful not to brush the side of beef up against the handrail. Lara felt her heart thaw a little further as he thanked Diana for opening the door, then smiled as Holly pointed a camera in his direction and took a photo.

'How's things, love?' Angus pushed a mug of tea into her hands and gave a wink. 'What about your dog?'

'Hard to know, we'll have to wait it out,' she said. That morning's flying visit to the vet hadn't been much consolation for Evie, who'd burst into tears at the sight of Basil looking so poorly. Concerns about secondary kidney damage were keeping him at the vets longer than expected.

'He's tough as old boots.' Angus pulled plastic freezer bags out of the cupboard and handed them to Toby. 'And what about your shop shares? Reckon we'll raise enough to save the general store?'

'With a bit of luck. Which reminds me,' said Lara. 'What's this about a singles ball, Penny? Surely we've got bigger fish to fry? Those events are like a meat market. Okay if you're appealing to the cougars, the rednecks and every horny farmer in the district, but there's a fine line between sleazy and stylish.'

Penny laughed, raising her voice to be heard above the sound of the hacksaw cutting through bone.

'Pah! Don't be such a Negative Nancy. I knew we should've waited until we had a watertight game plan before we pitched it to you. Who let the cat out of the bag?'

Evie and Cameron looked up from the short ribs they were loading into bags. Their tall, lanky frames and guilty expressions made them look like siblings rather than cousins.

Diana groaned. 'Can't you keep anything a secret, Cam?' She glared at them, but Lara knew Diana was as pleased as she was that the pair were still close, despite Evie's move to Ballarat. 'Heaven forbid we ever try to organise a surprise birthday party.'

Penny and Diana had almost finished explaining their concept, and Lara was reluctantly agreeing it might work, when the screen door flew open. Little Claudia ran through, followed by Diana's boys, the former squealing with delight and the latter whooping like a footy cheer squad.

'Aunty Angie's here,' said Harry.

'Claud's here,' said Leo, chasing her around the island bench.

'Uncle Rob's brought icy poles,' added Elliot, rifling through the cutlery drawer for the scissors.

'Out, out, out,' called Diana, a fillet of beef almost flying across the kitchen as she flapped her hands.

'Evie, can you take the kids outside and be in charge of icy poles? Someone will lose an eye at this rate,' said Penny, grabbing the scissors before the twins could squabble over who was cutting the tops off. The trio of teenagers washed their hands and followed the younger children outside, when Angie and Rob came in. The noise woke Lucy, whose howls carried along the hallway.

Lara collected the scraps from the beef Toby was trimming and pushed them through the mincer.

'Welcome to the madhouse,' she said with a laugh.

Toby returned her laugh, wiping his forehead against the sleeve of his polo shirt. 'It *is* chaos,' he conceded, 'but it's a nice change from weekends covering sports.'

Angie worked her way around the kitchen, greeting her family with hugs and kisses. Lara noticed her smile had turned mischievous when she got to Toby.

'Good to see you again, Toby,' she said, waggling her eyebrows at Lara the moment he picked up his knife.

Lara ignored her little sister, but couldn't help sneaking another peek at Toby. A layer of stubble darkened his jaw, and his lips were clamped together in concentration as he sliced through the meat. Without meaning to, she found herself pondering his routine. Did he avoid shaving on weekends, or was he an evening-shower-and-shave guy? She shut down the thought quickly, before her mind wandered any further off track.

He looked up, catching her gaze. Lara blanched. Had he felt her watching him? Did he know her sisters were on the warpath? *God, how embarrassing.* She busied herself with the chopping board in front of her.

Diana leaned closer, whispering in her ear.

'You'll lose a finger at this rate,' she said.

Lara shot her a withering look, grateful when Angie waltzed back into the kitchen, jiggling baby Lucy on her hip. Angie cooed at her baby niece, pointing out the window.

'C'mon, Lucy, let's go play with the kids.'

'Thanks, Ange,' said Penny. 'Her bottle's in the fridge. Jonesy, before you get your hands dirty, can you try Tim on the two-way radio again? He and Eddie should've been back from checking the paddocks by now.'

A hush fell over the room. Lara couldn't help but look out the window at the mountain range, before glancing back at her sister. Penny's smile was suddenly tight. Angie's husband didn't need to be asked twice. Everyone was quiet as the UHF radio crackled with static.

'On channel, Tim?'

Lara went to the sink, washed her hands and flicked on the kettle. Time for a cup of tea.

'He's checking the ladies-in-waiting near the north dam. Three new calves overnight,' Angus explained to Toby, washing his hands too. Toby looked between them, evidently picking up on the sudden tension in the kitchen.

Lara heaped three generous spoons of tea into the large teapot, filled it with boiling water as the radio crackled again.

'You there, Tim? Eddie?' Rob tried again.

Lara let the mugs clatter on the bench, anything to break the silence, and breathed a sigh of relief when Eddie's voice came on the radio.

'Pulled a calf, Jonesy. The little baby is cute, cute, cute.'

The colour flooded back into Penny's face. It had been almost five years since their father's farm accident, and Penny had been the one to raise the alarm when he didn't return from routine stock work. She knew the memory of that day, and the anxiousness that ambushed Penny every time Tim was out later than he'd planned, hadn't eased with time.

Tim's voice came over the staticky line.

'The mum's in strife though, Jonesy. She's one that we scanned with twins Wanna give us a hand?'

Rob listened grimly. He grabbed his phone while Tim confirmed his location, then turned to Penny.

'Chains, Pen?'

She fetched the equipment and rounded up the teenagers to accompany Rob. Lara heard a clatter of boots in the porch, then the sound of motorbikes floated across from the shearing shed.

Lara's heart swelled with pride at the sight of Evie riding one of the ag bikes, with Holly clutching her from behind like a koala, and Cameron in close pursuit. The school results and scholarship were great—what parent wouldn't be delighted with a bright, confident, A-Grade student?—but she was equally as proud to see her daughter fit back into her natural environment so seamlessly.

Thirteen

Toby was surprised by how quickly the first quarter of beef disappeared in a flash of knives. He had snapped plenty of pictures of the butchering, and the possibility of photographing a calf's birth sounded mighty appealing too. Rob disappeared out the laundry door, clearly on a mission. *Would it be rude to ditch the meat packing and invite myself along?* Toby looked up from the roast he'd been trimming, his gaze gravitating to the camera bag.

Angus piped up from across the bench.

'You should go with Jonesy, mate. Capture both sides of the life cycle for your article. We're breaking for smoko soon anyway.'

Toby didn't need to be told twice. With a quick scrub of his hands, he was out the door in time to catch a lift with Rob.

The ute bumped its way across the paddocks and Toby found himself grasping the hand grip by his left ear more than once.

'Angel bars, they call them,' laughed Rob, slowing down for another gate.

Toby climbed out to open it, fumbling with the latch when he heard a loud roar behind him. Two motorbikes carved their way across the paddock, and though their pace was sedate, his heart skipped when he realised Holly was on the back of one.

What the—

'C'mon, mate,' called Rob. 'Haven't got all day.'

Holly gave him a thumbs-up and an exhilarated grin as they rode through the gate. The fact that she was wearing a helmet did little to ease his mind. Toby frowned as he climbed back into the ute. *At least she's with Evie,* he told himself. He wasn't quite ready to see Holly with her arms and legs wrapped around a strapping teenage boy.

Rob caught him wiping his hands nervously on his jeans. 'Don't look so worried, they've been riding since they could walk. Your daughter's safe with them,' Rob said.

'I'd feel better if it was a quad bike.'

Rob shook his head. 'Don't say that around the McIntyre girls. Angus was lucky to survive a quad-bike accident a few years back. Trust me: two wheels are a lot safer on this terrain. That or the thing Tim's using.'

A side-by-side Polaris ATV loomed into view as they passed a shelter-belt of trees and rounded the great mound of dirt beside a dam. Tim stood by a small set of cattle yards, studying the rear end of a large cow, while Eddie, in his matching green work shirt, was showing the teenagers a silky mound on the grass.

Rob pulled up and he grabbed the chains from the ute tray.

'G'day Tim,' said Toby, trying not to cringe at the slimy, blood-streaked residue that went up Tim's forearm and well past his elbow. Rob launched into action without needing any instructions, while Toby stood back, not wanting to get in the way. The cow bellowed loudly, shifting her weight from side to side

'The first twin seems fine,' said Tim, 'but I'm not sure how this one will fare. The mum's getting tired.'

'Mind if I take photos?'

'Knock yourself out,' said Tim, taking the chain Rob handed him. Toby flicked the camera's power button and walked around, assessing the lighting for the shot. *Click, click.* He wouldn't be able to capture Tim's gentle, soothing murmurs, the cow's distressed calls or the rich scent of autumn crops, but he managed a few shots before Tim's hand disappeared inside the cow, capturing the look of concentration on his tanned face, and the way his other hand gently stroked the cow's hide.

'Dad, check this out,' said Holly.

Toby crouched down beside her.

'So cute, little baby,' said Eddie.

'Hey Eddie, it's a ripper,' said Toby.

'Baby, baby, baby,' sang Eddie, slinging one arm around Evie and the other around Cameron. The teenagers leaned in for a closer look. Holly stroked the calf's damp hide.

Toby lifted his camera and took a photo of the four of them, huddled around the new arrival. It shared the same glossy black coat as its mother, with a dark nose and long eyelashes.

He turned back to the cow. The chains dangled from Tim's hands.

'I can't get a good-enough grip on the second twin's legs,' said Tim. 'You have a shot, Jonesy.' Rob took off his watch and rolled up his sleeves.

'Never this much trouble at lambing time,' said Tim, turning to Toby. 'We're mostly merino sheep here, a few hundred cattle. Handy having a brother-in-law from a dairy farm.'

'A vet would be even handier,' said Rob, wryly.

Toby raised his Nikon again, focusing as Rob worked on the stuck calf. Concern turned to triumph and soon they saw hooves emerge. Tim quickly wrapped the chains around the calf's ankles, wiping his hands on his jeans before reaching into the back of the ute and pulling out another contraption.

Toby hadn't seen anything like it before, and almost forgot to take photographs as he watched them winch the calf out.

The ankles came out a little further, then the knees, and then an almost-blue flap of skin. It wasn't until a nose followed that Toby realised the blue thing was the newborn's tongue. The mother's distressed noises sent chills down Toby's spine, as if she too knew how dire things were.

'Eddie, help keep her calm,' called Tim, gripping the chains. Eddie moved to the cow's face, speaking in the same gentle manner as his brother.

Rob worked with Tim at the opposite end, sticking his fingers in to clear the muck from the calf's large nostrils. Amniotic fluid spilled down his jeans, but neither he nor Tim faltered. *Would the calf make it?* Toby lowered his camera. The tongue hanging out the calf's mouth was more purple than blue away from the lens. It didn't look good.

❧

The clock chimed midday as Pete finished with the second side of beef. Lara and her sisters worked in unison to clear the meat, chopping boards, scraps and knives from the benches. Lara filled the laundry basket with a fresh batch of meat, all bagged, weighed and labelled, then carried it out to Angus's cottage.

'Dad's freezer's nearly full too, Pen. Hope you've cleared out the chest freezer for the next side of beef?'

Penny turned from the sink, her hands covered in suds as she scrubbed the greasy meat residue off her skin. 'Is the Pope a Catholic?' She was smiling now that she'd heard from Tim.

Angus peeled the lid off the Tupperware containers, peering at the treasure trove of treats they had baked for smoko.

'Angie's new kitchen's obviously working out well,' he said, pushing the container across the bench. Lara's mouth watered at the sight of fluffy coconut-covered lamingtons, perfectly golden jam drops and a shiny white pavlova. She shared a look with Diana. Baked goods were a great sign.

Last year, when Angie and Rob had been in the thick of renovating their cottage by the coast, baking had become a dirty word. With a mother-in-law who invaded their space, a health-kick that veered into an obsession and no kitchen of her own, Angie had been on a collision course with disaster.

Lara glanced back out the window. Angie was pushing Lucy in the baby swing while Claudia tried her hardest to keep up with her bigger cousins. It was good to see the world back on its regular axis. Kids on the trampoline, meat packing well underway, the whole family together, working towards a common goal.

Diana lined up the mugs on the bench and heaped fresh tea leaves into the pot.

'It's a dream kitchen, that's for sure. Between your kitchen, Lara's, and Angie's new one, my poor old kitchen is looking very nineties,' said Diana.

Pete snorted. 'Nothing wrong with our kitchen,' he said, turning to Lara. 'And at the rate your sister's buying rose bushes and dahlia tubers, I'll need to start a second stock agency to pay the bills.' He said it with a smile, and Lara didn't miss the wink he sent in Diana's direction as he said it.

'There's a method to my madness, Pete, and you know it. One day we'll make an income from all those gorgeous flowers, mark my words.'

Pete nabbed one of the lamingtons, and turned in her direction. 'Diana my love, you have to start *selling* those flowers instead of *giving* them all away. Maybe Lara will let you have a flower stall at the shop?'

'Sounds good to me,' said Lara. 'And it's not my shop, it's everyone's.'

'You're the softie who decided it needed saving,' said Pete kindly, picking up the kids' plate of sandwiches and taking it outside.

Lara shook her head. 'I'm the sucker who couldn't watch it slip into the hands of those out-of-town idiots. At least Dallas has given up his pursuit.'

Lara looked at the sepia wedding photo on the top of the china hutch. Penny followed her gaze, smiling at the sight of their parents, young and happy, forty years ago.

'You can pretend all you like, Lars. We know you're a sentimental soul underneath,' said Penny.

Is that what it is? Lara wondered. *Sentimentality?*

'I reckon it's bigger than that,' said Angus, draining his mug. 'You're doing it for the greater good of the community, aren't you, love? Just like your mum, you saw a void and you're filling it.'

Lara felt uncomfortable as everyone turned to her. Or was it selfishness, plain and simple, naïvely hoping a school-holiday income would keep Evie returning home for years to come?

She cleared her throat.

'Wonder if they've got those twin calves out yet? Hopefully Amy's on her way. They'll need a vet if the cow's in distress.'

Angus lifted his cup. 'I'll finish my cuppa and call them on the radio, see if there's an update.'

'With a bit of luck, a stuck calf will scare Evie and Holly off childbirth for another decade or so,' said Lara, piling jam and cream onto a scone.

'And Cam,' added Diana. 'One minute he was in nappies, now he's as tall as Pete, his cheeks are covered in peach fuzz and he's going through more tissues in his bedroom than a bloke with man-flu.' Diana cringed. 'Did you see him checking out Holly?'

'More importantly, did you see Lara checking out Holly's *dad*?' Penny's giggle matched her devilish tone. 'And Toby's a lot more subtle than our Cameron, but I saw him looking when he thought nobody was watching.'

Lara waved a dismissive hand. 'He's helping with the store campaign, that's it.'

'Doesn't have to be all, though. He's single, you're single. He likes running, you like running. He's got a teenager, you've got a teenager. I'm sensing a theme here.'

Lara desperately thought of ways to head this conversation off at the pass.

'I like being single. And if I wanted some action, I'd head up to Horsham for a big night out. Even without Mrs Beggs at the helm of the general store, news like that would spread across Bridgefield like wildfire,' she said. But even to her own ears, the excuse sounded flimsy.

Her sisters smiled at each other as they headed out for some fresh air. Lara stayed indoors and picked up her knife. She ran it back and forth over the sharpening stone until the noise drowned out the self-doubt before it started to tick off all her weaknesses, one by one. She hadn't forgotten the almost-kiss at the top of Windmill Track, but the nasty voice inside her head also wouldn't let her forget what happened the last time she let her guard down.

She looked across at Penny, cuddling Lucy under the shade of a weeping mulberry tree. She'd made a great choice with Tim. Lara spotted Angie sharing a tray of sweets among the children. Rob was as steady as a rock, and having survived a renovation, she was pretty sure they could manage anything. And then there were Diana and Pete—a perfect couple. She watched Diana gesture to the Peach Profusion roses planted by their mother. Pete dutifully leaned down to smell them before nodding and allowing himself to be dragged to another nearly identical bush.

Her sisters had made good choices. Why hadn't she?

❧

The cow gave one last almighty bellow and the second calf slipped to the ground, the chains on its ankles clinking as they fell to the grass. Even the fall didn't seem to rouse the animal.

'Evie, grab the towel from the back of the ute!'

Tim and Rob dropped to their knees and started to pump the calf's legs and rub its face, trying to encourage a response.

'The towel's not there, Uncle Tim,' said Evie, her face stricken.

Cameron tugged his flannel shirt off without hesitation and passed it to Rob.

Toby couldn't help but notice the way Holly dragged her attention away from the lifeless calf to take in the view of Cameron's bare chest. Toby nudged her with his elbow.

'Where's your camera?'

Cameron's shirt was soon covered in blood and muck as Rob scrubbed the newborn's hide, determined to rub life into its limbs. It was easy to see why this one had given its mother so much more grief than its twin: it was almost twice the size.

The sun popped out from behind a cloud, bathing the paddock in bright light. Toby's shoulders relaxed as he saw the calf's long eyelashes flicker and then open.

'That's it, nugget. That's a boy,' said Rob, backing off his vigorous massage. The calf stirred as Tim unhooked the chains from around its ankles and handed them to Eddie, who carried them to the back of the ute.

'Amy's here, Amy's here,' sang Eddie. Toby turned to see a grey ute cruising across the paddock. The same vet who had treated Basil's snakebite stepped out of the driver's side, and Angus unfolded himself from the passenger seat.

'Knew you boys would have it under control,' he said, then he winked at Toby. 'What'd you make of that, then?'

'An eye opener,' Toby admitted, raking a hand through his hair.

One look at Cameron's goosebumps had Toby wondering if the boy regretted donating his shirt. He then caught Holly's smile and frowned. *Probably not.* Toby had sent her to an all-girls school so she could concentrate on her studies, not boys, and here he was bringing her to a farming weekend and putting her in front of an eligible young farm boy. *Great one, Paxton.*

The teenagers took off on the ag bikes. Tim wiped his hands on his jeans and walked over to Toby.

'Pete'll be itching to start cutting up the next side, and I'm done out here. You ready for another few hours on the knives?'

'Sure thing,' said Toby. He'd liked the atmosphere in the farmhouse kitchen. The gentle stirring among the McIntyres, the all-hands-on-deck ethos.

He followed Tim to the all-terrain vehicle, bulkier than a quad-bike but not as enclosed as a farm ute. Eddie joined Rob in the white ute, leaving Angus and Amy behind with the cow and calves. As they drove off, Toby noticed the branding across the side of Rob's ute. *Bottlebrush Building Co.* There was a theme among the McIntyre girls—they'd all chosen handy husbands: Pete the stock agent. Tim the farmer. Rob the builder.

Toby studied his own soft hands as Tim started the side-by-side. *Would Lara even be interested in a bloke who sat at a keyboard all day?* A would-be photographer who was too busy working for someone else to think about starting his own business? The only time his hands got dirty at work was putting new toner in the office printer. Toby looked at the steering wheel. Traces of muck clung to Tim's hands; they were definitely working man's hands.

'Why the long face? You look like we lost a calf.'

Toby flicked the camera's power switch and looked at the display monitor. 'Nah, nothing. You guys did a great job of delivering both the calves safely. There'll be something I can use in the farming feature.'

'Heard you've got a knack for photos. Penny said something about an exhibition last year?'

Toby gave a modest shrug as he freed up space on the camera's memory card. The wind tugged at his shirt as Tim drove the ATV across the paddock. He held his camera equipment extra tight. 'I throw my hat in the ring. The odd photo contest here and there. The exhibition was a favour for a friend. He needed something for his gallery and convinced me to get a few of my better pics framed. I'd love to set up a photography business one day, but for now, I've got my hands full with the paper and the odd photo shoot in my spare time.' Toby thought about the photo he'd taken of Lara a month or so ago. It'd been a beauty, no doubt about it.

'I'd hate to be landed with wedding photos. All those Bridezillas and cheesy smiles,' said Tim.

Toby laughed. 'It's all in the people-wrangling. It's kinda neat, being asked to capture someone's special day.' He looked back at the camera.

'Why Bridgefield? You got family down here?'

'No. The *Bridgefield Addy* couldn't afford a photographer, so they needed an editor who knew his way around a keyboard *and* a camera. My family's all in Ballarat. And if I play my cards right at this paper, I'll snag the lead role at the *Daily* on my return.'

Tim's whistle whipped away in the breeze. 'The big cheese, eh? You'd get some pretty epic stories in a rag like that.'

Toby mulled over the stories that had advanced his career. He was proud of his writing. In a perfect world, he would have had time to verify every fact, respect all confidences and cross-check every quote, but a daily paper didn't always allow that luxury. His press photography was the same, and while he'd relished the opportunities to keep readers informed, his work had taken him to some dark and undesirable corners of the city. 'Plenty of the same issues as here really, just on a bigger scale to match the population,' he said.

Toby thought about Mick's phone call the previous week. Tim would be about the same age as that Samuel Kingsley guy.

'There's not as much emphasis on farming news, obviously,' said Toby. 'And you'd be hard-pressed to find the city residents rallying together to save the local milk bar, but the bigger issues, like domestic violence and drugs, seem to touch every town. Speaking of which, did you have anything to do with Samuel Kingsley?'

The look Toby received was enough of an answer. Tim's relaxed smile vanished, and his voice was wary.

'What about him?'

'I'm wondering, that's all. Small town, I figured you might have come across him. It was splashed across the media in Ballarat, but I haven't heard a word about it since I got here.' Toby was used to asking unpopular questions and broaching personal subjects in interviews, but here he felt like he was on especially unsteady ground.

'I knew him,' said Tim, his jaw tightly clenched. 'We all knew him. But you'd want to think twice about asking those questions around here, mate.' Tim gestured to the teenagers on the motorbikes ahead. 'He doesn't deserve a daughter like Evie, and Lara's still getting over the whole shitstorm he brought into their lives.'

Toby felt his stomach twist. *Evie's father? Lara? That bastard . . .*

'I had no idea,' said Toby. He shook his head as he tried to imagine the things Lara had dealt with at the hands of Samuel Kingsley. No wonder she was so guarded. There was no way he would touch the story with a ten-foot barge pole now. Not in a million years.

Lost in thought, Toby didn't notice Tim pulling the side-by-side up in the middle of the paddock until the engine fell silent.

Tim twisted in his seat, his gaze hard and unflinching.

'Tell me you're not here to stir trouble, Toby. If this—' Tim threw his arms in the air, gesturing to McIntyre Park, the farmhouse in the distance, the kids riding the bikes. 'If this is all some ruse to get a big story for your city paper, then tell me right now, mate, and I'll drive you straight back to Ballarat myself.'

Toby shook his head, choosing his words carefully. This was a side of Tim he hadn't seen before.

'Not at all. Even if I'd known that Lara *was* involved, which you've got my word I didn't, that's not my style of journalism, honestly.' And as soon as he got back home, he'd be telling Mick so.

Tim was quiet as he drove and parked the ATV. *Unconvinced?* Toby felt his gaze as they walked to the farmhouse. He paused at the bottom of the deck steps and turned to Tim.

'I'm not that type of bloke.'

'I sure hope that's true, mate,' said Tim, shaking Toby's outstretched hand. Toby felt the callouses rub against his smooth palms and the strength in Tim's grip, and he saw the same steely message in his expression. *Don't you dare hurt Lara.*

Toby shoved his hands in his pockets. He got it, loud and clear. Hell, if anyone even thought about doing something similar to Holly or his sister Belinda, he'd want their head on a stake too. He could only imagine the legacy that type of trauma left behind. His gaze went to Lara when he stepped inside, his respect for her growing ten-fold in light of Tim's revelation.

❦

Lara rifled through the laundry cupboards, pushing aside beach towels she'd once used at the high-school swimming carnival, the Holly Hobbie bed sheets that were so vintage they were probably back in vogue, and boxes of Fowlers preserving jars.

She found the sausage press hidden behind an array of last season's plum jam, tomato sauce and chutney.

A diesel ute idled into the driveway, along with the motorbikes, and Lara paused to check her reflection in the laundry mirror. She smoothed her hair back into its tight bun, narrowing her eyes at the little grey frizzles multiplying in the hairline by her temples. Breeding like rabbits, which was one of the reasons she avoided mirrors. *God, if I look any longer I'll find chin hairs*, she thought as she strode onto the deck to rustle up the next batch of helpers.

'Lost your shirt, Cam?' said Lara, arching an eyebrow at her nephew. Diana was right: he looked more like a man than ever. All those afternoons lugging bags of chaff and chook food at the farm had transformed Cameron's large frame from lean to strong. Cam shot a quick smile to Evie and Holly as they crossed the deck. Holly sat taller in her chair. Evie muttered something that sounded like 'oh boy'.

'Get your skates on, folks. We need all hands on deck,' Lara said.

Penny fished one of Tim's green work shirts from a pile of folded laundry and threw it to Cameron.

Lara was elbow deep in minced beef, sausage binder and soft white globs of minced pork fat when Toby emerged from the laundry, drying his hands on his jeans. His camera dangled around his neck and he lifted it, gesturing to Lara.

'Mind if I take a few more photos?'

'Sure,' said Penny, answering for them all.

Lara looked at her younger sister, vivacious as ever, the picture of good health. There had been a time when she'd resented Penny's ability to glide through life, travelling wherever she liked, living the city high life and thriving in a career she loved. Lara wasn't proud of the way she'd let the jealousy fester, almost ruining their relationship years earlier, but they had come a long way since.

'So, what's the scoop on you, Toby? Your folks nearby?'

'Ballarat, and they're soaking up the royal jewellery exhibition this weekend. Mum's a staunch royalist,' he said.

'Blimey, your father's a patient man. I'd fake gastro if Diana tried dragging me to one of those,' said Pete, pausing to sharpen his knife. 'Flowers are bad enough.'

'Dad has dementia, so it doesn't worry him,' said Toby.

Lara heard the wry sadness in his voice.

'Sorry, Toby,' she said. 'Feel free to tell my family to keep their noses out of your business.' Her arms continued to work like pistons, pumping up and down to emulsify the fat and the meat.

'It's okay, but it's tough, you know. Seeing my dad struggle, when he was always so vibrant and capable.' Toby cleared his throat. It didn't sound like a subject he spoke about often. The room went quiet for a moment, the scrape of knives against chopping boards and shuffling feet were the only sound.

Diana gave Lara a look across the bench. *More in common*, she seemed to be saying. Lara bit her lip, remembering Angus's accident. The injuries had put an end to his full-time farming days. *At least he recovered though.* Dementia was a cruel illness.

Penny broke the silence. 'So, tell me about this fun-run idea, Toby. How much money do you think it'll raise for the general store?'

They listened as he outlined his idea, the way it would draw tourists from out of town so the store wouldn't have to rely solely on local cash injections.

'We could even have it the same weekend as the singles event,' he said. The suggestion was met with wholehearted agreement from Lara's sisters.

'Come for the fun run, stay for the ball!' said Penny.

'Or vice versa,' said Angie.

'God, it sounds like a logistical nightmare,' said Pete, shaking his head. 'Do you really want to take on this amount of work?'

Diana shot her husband a look. 'You're worse than grouchy old McCluskey. What route are you thinking, Toby?'

'We could use it to showcase the local highlights, like Bridgefield Lake . . .' He trailed off and glanced at Lara. 'Maybe Windmill Track,' he said.

Windmill Track.

Feeling herself flush, Lara scraped the sausage meat off her forearms and hands, keeping an ear on the conversation as she ducked into the laundry. She needed warm soapy water—the best at shifting sticky meat—as much as she needed a bit of breathing space.

'It's the best track in town,' she heard Toby say. 'Surely McCluskey won't mind a few folks running along his laneway for one morning? It's for a great cause.'

'Love your optimism, mate, but I'm not sure Clyde will see it that way,' said Pete. 'He's the town's one-man anti-progress committee.'

Lara was drying her hands when Diana joined her in the laundry.

'Would it kill Pete to be positive for a change?'

Diana reached for the soap and scrubbed her hands so hard, Lara thought she would rupture the skin. She eyed her older sister.

'What's going on with you two today?' Lara couldn't imagine what Diana's issue was with Pete, the easy-going bloke who traded in dad jokes and ferried his boys across the countryside for cricket carnivals, cricket matches and cricket training. The bloke who always had a kind word for his wife and a shoulder for all of his mates.

Diana groaned. 'We've been arguing about the general store. I wanted to cash in our shares and invest in the shop. If we had a few major backers, we'd have a much better chance of raising the collateral. Pete still hasn't recovered from hearing about my whole flower farm idea, he can't even fathom adding the general store to the mix. I've even been giving him the cold shoulder, but that just makes him grouchier.'

Lara felt a stab of guilt, then a wave of self-doubt. She studied her socks. Pete and Diana were the golden couple of Bridgefield—she didn't want the shop to be a bone of contention between the two of them.

'Maybe Pete's right. Maybe we should let the out-of-towners buy it and save ourselves the headaches and arguments,' Lara said.

'What?' Diana nudged her gently with an elbow. 'Christ, don't let a couple of stick-in-the-muds talk you out of it. This is the best idea you've had since the all-abilities cooking program.'

Lara looked up to see her big sister's broad smile. 'If I know anything, I know you can do this, Lars. McCluskey's got to have a weak spot somewhere, and Pete's in one of his moods, that's all. You wait until the bill comes for all the bare-rooted roses I've just ordered. That'll shift his focus, quick-smart!'

Diana tapped the side of her nose, just like their Dad did when he had a secret, then shoved a hand into her pocket. She pulled out an envelope. 'Almost forgot. This was at the general store this morning. Another shareholder hopefully?'

Diana handed it to Lara and strode back into the kitchen to shoo Leo and Harry away from the Anzac biscuits.

Lara opened the envelope. It was from Brody Pilkington, the young man who'd fetched the parcel for his obnoxious father.

Hi Lara, I can't manage $5000 but can I pledge $500 for the shop? (Don't tell Dad—he reckons it's pie in the sky, but if you're half as determined as Evie, I know you'll make it happen.) And please let me know if there's any volunteer shifts left. I'd love some experience for my resume. Cheers, Brody

The letter confirmed what Diana had said. Lara wasn't the only one who wanted or needed this shop fundraiser to succeed. *Pie in the sky*, she scoffed. *Watch us!*

❦

Toby looked over towards the laundry again. Nobody else seemed to notice that Lara had been in there for quite a while. He set his camera down and picked up his notebook, scribbling down snatches of conversation and snippets of meat-packing information before he forgot.

Between Tim's revelation about Lara and Samuel Kingsley, and his mind hop-skip-jumping to conclusions about what she must have endured, he could barely remember the cuts of meat

Angus showed him five minutes before, let alone the calving rates Tim and Rob had discussed earlier in the day.

Do I tell Lara I know?

He looked back towards the laundry. How the hell did he throw that in the conversation without sounding like he'd been digging into her private life? He felt even more wretched about the photos he'd taken of her and Mrs Beggs, relieved they were properly deleted now.

Nope. If Lara ever wants to mention her ex-husband, we can discuss it then.

He put down the notepad, skirted around the kitchen bench and paused at the laundry doorway.

Lara looked up from the letter she was reading and gave him a smile.

'Having fun?' She folded the letter and stuffed it into her back pocket.

Toby gestured to the blood splatters and scraps of meat decorating the muscle-man apron. 'What's not to love about meat-packing day?'

His deadpan tone made her laugh.

'I'm learning lots, and there's plenty of great stuff for my articles too,' he continued. 'I'm really grateful to your family for throwing the doors open.' Even though Tim still looked a little wary of him, he couldn't have asked for better hospitality.

A wail of laughter erupted outside the laundry window, where Holly, Evie and Cameron were scrubbing out the big plastic mince tubs. Evie had scooped up a handful of soap bubbles and tossed them at Cameron, and a bubble-war soon erupted on the back deck. Toby watched as Holly laughed and played. It was good, old-fashioned fun. Better for the soul than any clarinet recital.

'Holly's having a great time too. It's nice for her to make friends in Bridgefield.'

'So, you're planning on sticking around a while?' Lara asked quietly, her gaze still out the window. The younger children were running to join in the fun and before long they were all saturated.

'Sure do. Two years at least, and then . . .' Toby shrugged. 'Then we'll see.'

Fourteen

Lara opened the fridge and was rewarded with the rich smell of aniseed. She pulled the tray of beef and fennel sausages onto the bench, then drew one of the neatly linked bunches to her nose and took a deep sniff.

'Blooming nicely?'

Lara started, almost dropping the sausages. She whirled around, covering her embarrassment with a cough. She'd expected Evie to sleep in after the big day on her feet yesterday, yet here she was, bright eyed and bushy tailed.

'The snags are blooming marvellously. You should get a whiff of these beauties, Evie. Think we should take some to Mrs Beggs?'

Evie reached for the orange juice, groaning.

'You're bonkers, Mum. Most people take flowers and chocolates when they visit people in hospital, not sausages.'

'She's not in hospital, she's been home for a few days now,' said Lara, putting some into a bag.

'Same, same,' said Evie, poking out her tongue. Even when she was being a smarty-bum, or picking holes in her mother's life, Lara loved having Evie back in Bridgefield. They moved around the kitchen, working in a familiar but comfortable silence before taking their breakfast to the dining table.

'Making headway on that fundraising tally, Mum?'

'Getting closer every day. Some people are making small donations, which we can roll into one share with the other small donations.'

'Eddie's been saving his money, and Brody Pilkington has too. He's hoping for some work experience at the shop. Reckon he'd be any good?'

'Yeah, I guess.' Evie shrugged. 'He always helped out at the footy club, though I think it was more because he was embarrassed his dad wrote himself off every Thursday night. You know his mum left, don't you?'

Lara had patched up Brody's mother more than once. Like everyone else at the centre, Lara had cheered when Eleanor finally left her husband, albeit without her son. *Brody had hero-worshipped his father, were the rose-coloured glasses finally coming off?*

She looped her arms around Evie's shoulders, thankful she hadn't been through a custody battle.

'Yep. But Brody seems to have his head screwed on, finishing high school and looking for work already.' She hugged Evie a little closer and hoped it was true.

Lara tested a hot sausage, savouring the unique flavours. Real meat, real seasonings, none of the saw-dust texture and synthetic additives like most of the shop-bought ones.

'Sure you don't want to try these? They'll be better after they've bloomed for a few more days, but you'll be gone by then. They won't have sausages like this back in Ballarat.'

Having finished her eggs, Evie pulled out a Tupperware container and sliced off a sneaky wedge of fruit cake, taking a bite before Lara could object.

'They don't have your fruit cake in Ballarat either,' said Evie. 'Or your yo-yos and lamingtons.'

Lara missed baking for Evie as much as she missed the quiet weekends they spent poring over recipe books together and cooking up a storm. Would the other boarding-school mums send their girls back with brimming cake tins too? Would Toby be in the same boat as her this morning, wishing the weekend was twice as long, and already dreading this afternoon's bus-stop farewell? With Basil still at the vet and Evie gone, the house would be extra quiet. Stiflingly quiet.

Determined to make the most of their day together, Lara shook off the melancholy and collected their plates.

'Let's get this show on the road, Evie-girl. You washing or drying?'

Even little chores like dishes were more enjoyable when it was the two of them.

Evie finished drying the frypan and looked at the clock. 'Maybe we could have a barbecue lunch at Wannon Falls after seeing Mrs Beggs?'

The bush setting was always a winner and the waterfalls would be flowing more than normal this year, thanks to the drizzly weather.

'Sure thing. And Amy gave me the security code for the vet clinic, so we can visit Basil anytime we like. When's your bus leaving?'

'At three, but Holly said I can catch a ride home with her dad. He's driving back to Ballarat later in the afternoon.'

Lara tapped a pen against her shop notebook. 'Right. Works out well . . .'

Evie gave her a hug. 'I knew you wouldn't mind,' she said brightly. 'That way I can quiz him in person, see if he passes the Evie McIntyre litmus test.'

'Don't you dare,' said Lara, snapping her notebook shut.

Evie bounced out of the room, throwing an impish look over her shoulder as she pulled open the hallway door. 'Too late, Mum. I've already gone online and cancelled my bus ticket.'

Lara groaned as the hot-water system outside the kitchen rattled and the shower spluttered on. Diana, Angie and Penny had a lot to answer for with all this singles ball rubbish. But Evie was no better.

§

Toby pulled the laptop off his bedside table as soon as he woke up.

The articles he'd found last night were still on the desktop, and he took another look at the Kingsleys. The haughty Kingsley matriarch—Edwina—had been easy to find in the society pages, tilting glasses of champagne towards the camera at local charity events. *Her pearls alone would pay the deposit on the general store*, he'd noted. Toby's research showed they moved from their rural property into a Toorak McMansion a decade ago.

But it was the articles on their son, Samuel Kingsley, that had kept him awake into the wee hours of the night.

The more Toby knew about Kingsley's crimes, the angrier he felt. None of the women were named in the articles, but Toby's colleague, who covered the court reports, would have more details.

Sure enough, there was a reply waiting in his inbox. Toby skimmed the off-the-record email. It made his blood boil. As he had feared, the charges reported were only the tip of the iceberg. Lara hadn't been his only blackmail victim. Several women had retracted their statements or refused to appear.

That bastard.

He wrote back, thanking his colleague for his help, and then flicked off an email to Mick, telling him he definitely wouldn't be pursuing the sex-scandal line of enquiry. He would get a phone call, no doubt about it, but he would deal with Mick's wrath another day.

Toby's body ached in new, surprising places when he pulled his sneakers on and headed out into the inky dawn. Lugging heavy quarters of beef from the cool room to the McIntyres' kitchen hadn't been great for his lower back. He could only imagine how sore Pete would be.

Overall, it had been a good day. They'd packed two chest freezers and three eskies full of meat; his fun-run idea had been well received; the McIntyre family had welcomed him and Holly into their home; and he had taken enough notes to write three feature stories. Even after Holly culled his mediocre shots, there would be a hundred photographs to choose from, and he was keen to try the fresh meat Angus had insisted they take home with them.

But Tim's revelation had taken the shine off the day.

You can't change it, and Lara doesn't need your pity, Toby told himself. And he was pretty sure she wouldn't want it either.

The sky brightened and he filled his lungs with fresh air. Last night's showers had added a moist, earthy tang to the paddocks either side of him and he caught a whiff of soggy wool from the penned-up sheep in a nearby stock yard. He dashed along the avenue of honour, not lingering to listen to the rows of trees whisper their secrets, and gritted his teeth at the base of the Windmill Track.

Faster, Paxton.

Toby's watch beeped. Six k's down. The lush hillside turned golden under the sun's gentle ascent. He normally saved the hilly tracks for runs that didn't involve sprint sessions, but somehow his feet had led him in this direction, mapping out the proposed course for his fun run while he wrestled with the notion that Lara had been hurt by Samuel Kingsley.

The windmill was going hell for leather, creaking as it tried to keep up with the blustering southerly. Toby pressed on, maintaining his pace past the windmill and back home, only letting up when McCluskey's shearing shed came into view.

The donkeys were in the yard and as he drew closer, Toby saw Clyde was in with them.

'Morning,' said Toby, waving as he approached.

His neighbour barely paused as he ran the curry comb down the largest donkey's flanks. The sight of donkey hair flying everywhere gave Toby an idea. He pulled up at the fence.

Classical was playing—Mozart, from the sound of it. The small donkey wandered over, her welcome distinctly warmer than her owner's. She nuzzled his hand with her velvety mouth.

'Had them long?'

Clyde kept grooming. Toby was debating whether to repeat his question or leave when the older man eventually spoke over his shoulder.

'They were my wife's donkeys. Edna wasted hours teaching them to pull a cart, always fussing over their hooves. That's when she wasn't volunteering in town, for all the good it did her.'

The small donkey watched Toby with big, soft eyes. He reached out and stroked her tall ears.

'You must miss her,' Toby said quietly.

The donkeys would miss her too.

Clyde harrumphed and busied himself with cleaning the comb. The larger donkey wandered over, nudging the smaller one out of the way. Soon Toby's hand was black with dusty donkey grime.

Toby looked along the track dividing their properties. It must have been where she walked them. 'It would've been nice to see donkeys pulling a cart up Windmill Track.'

The austere man went back to his grooming, barely acknowledging Toby's farewell.

As he continued up the driveway Toby tried to get a handle on the old farmer. Pete's comments yesterday had confirmed his initial impressions, although McCluskey's gruff voice had lost its bite when he spoke of his wife. He clearly missed her. *What if they could find a way to honour Edna McCluskey and her donkeys. Something that might pave the way for the fun run.* Toby arrived home sweaty and dirty with the beginning of a plan.

⁊

Mrs Beggs' lounge room was awash with colour, with more floral fragrance than any Myer perfume counter. Evie rearranged the bouquets on the coffee table to make room for their plate of biscuits while Lara showed Mrs Beggs the sausages.

'Beef and fennel, my favourite. Even better than pork and fennel. Makes a nice change from all those sweets,' said Mrs Beggs. Lara smiled sweetly at Evie. *Told you so.*

While Evie took a seat on the tartan sofa, Lara couldn't help herself, straightening the magazines and books on the dining table, moving the TV remote so it was in reaching distance from Mrs Beggs' recliner, and topping up the water jug with fresh rainwater.

'Tea, Mrs Beggs?'

'Yes please, Lara love. And I wouldn't say no to one of those snags either if you wanted to fry them up. All this resting makes me a bit peckish.'

Lara quickly found a frypan, and moved around the kitchen, emptying the dish rack as they cooked. She carried a tray into the lounge. 'Bet it's lovely being home, though?'

Mrs Beggs tucked into a sausage. 'My word it is. Nobody waking me up late at night to take my vitals, though it seems awfully quiet here in comparison. I miss the shop too,' she said wistfully.

'Try not to think about the shop too much, Mrs Beggs,' said Lara. 'We've got it under control. You're supposed to be recuperating, remember.'

'Ah, there's good news there too, Lara. You'll be able to hang up your volunteer's hat sooner rather than later, I suspect.'

Lara maintained a neutral expression while she digested the news.

This doesn't sound good. Has Dallas miraculously conjured up the cash?

'Weren't you waiting until the new financial year to make a decision?' she said evenly.

Mrs Beggs grimaced apologetically. 'I know, dear, but I hadn't imagined there'd be so much interest in it. One of the buyers has such innovative plans. Crushed avocado, New York rolls, California subs.'

Lara didn't bother correcting Mrs Beggs' mix-up with the trendy foods. In-house baked pies were about as fancy as Mrs Beggs got, and that was the way everyone liked it.

'Not my cup of tea,' Mrs Beggs continued, 'but a change is as good as a holiday, isn't it?'

Lara's heart lurched.

'*Those* guys?' The ones who'd shamelessly criticised every inch of the shop? The postmistress's heart would break if she knew how they had spoken about her beloved store.

'We've almost got the funds raised, Mrs Beggs. Penny and Diana are planning a black-tie ball, Toby's arranging a fun run, and I'm about to release the raffle tickets for the upstairs apartment. Please, Mrs Beggs, give us a little longer.'

'I wish I could, Lara, but I can't expect all and sundry to keep volunteering at my shop in the meantime. This will be easier for everyone. The money will be enough to keep me in romance novels and perhaps a cruise or two when I'm better. Tarquin said he'd put down a deposit if I took it off the market early.'

Evie lifted a box of wilted red roses.

'The same Tarquin who sent these flowers?'

Lara drew in a breath. This Tarquin bloke sounded like a charlatan. A charlatan with bad taste in clothes *and* bad manners.

'Don't do anything rash,' said Lara. 'You ran the store for thirty-something years, you deserve to walk away with some money in your pocket. Give me a month.'

She cast her gaze around the room, desperate for something tangible to mark the time. She looked at the stack of slim-spined novels on the side table, almost high enough to topple over and suffocate Mrs Beggs in her sleep.

'By the time you've finished that stack of books, I'll have an action plan drawn up so we can judge how much money we'll raise from the three fundraisers and a firm offer for the store. Please, Mrs Beggs.'

'Those are Clare Connelly's finest works,' Mrs Beggs said with a cheerful smile. 'I'll have that pile of books done and dusted by the end of the week.'

'June. Give me until mid-June, then. Please.' Lara leaned in closer, preparing to play the last card in her deck, even though she knew it was a dirty tactic. 'Mum would've wanted me to give it my best shot, and I'll work my butt off to better his offer. I give you my word.'

Mrs Beggs' face crumpled at the mention of her best friend, but slowly she nodded, each of her chins wobbling like the middle layer of a pineapple sponge.

'Mid-June then, but not a moment more. No sense in dragging this out, dear.'

Lara and Evie were both quiet on the drive to the vet. Even a detour to Wannon Falls failed to lift their spirits. The sound of Evie packing her things and wheeling a suitcase into the hallway came all too soon.

'Holly said they'll be here to pick me up in five,' said Evie, fidgeting with her nails.

Lara looked at her watch in disbelief. It had gone too quickly and she'd squandered the last half of the day worrying about the shop.

'I'm going to miss you, Evie-girl,' she said, tucking a strand of long blonde hair behind Evie's ear.

'Mmm,' said Evie distractedly. She gnawed at her fingernails. They'd be bleeding soon, at this rate.

'Hey, what's up? You worried about the shop? Or Basil?'

'Nah. I know you'll smash it, Mum. And Baz is looking better every day. It's just . . .'

Lara's stomach dropped. Whatever was coming, she had the feeling she wasn't going to like it.

'We're doing a genealogy project next term, and I found the photo album when you were out for your run this morning. There's not many photos of . . .' Evie paused. 'I mean, I remember Dad's eye colour and things, but what about his parents? I can't even remember what they look like.'

Lara held her breath, instantly wary. She hadn't seen Karl and Edwina Kingsley since the court case several years earlier. When Sam was put behind bars, his parents had been more concerned about saving face than helping her and Evie. They had never made much of an effort to build a relationship with their granddaughter before Sam showed his true colours, but their underwhelming lack of support since then had been a kick in the guts.

She wanted to wrap her arms around Evie and reassure her it didn't matter. Having a father in jail was bad enough, Evie shouldn't have to deal with indifferent grandparents too.

Angus did his best to make up for Annabel's absence, and was more hands-on than many men of his vintage, but the Kingsleys barely even tried.

A little voice piped up inside Lara's head. *At least you don't have to share her with them, though . . .*

'It's their loss,' said Lara gently. 'Have you changed your mind about seeing them?'

Or had Evie just said that after the court case, when I was still shellshocked by the media circus that followed?

It felt like an age passed before Evie replied. Lara tried not to be alarmed by the silence.

'Not really, but . . . It's kind of sad, isn't it?'

Sad the Kingsleys knew the price of everything and the value of nothing? Lara vividly recalled the first time she visited their home, with a butler's pantry bigger than a hotel room and painfully expensive artwork featuring its own lighting schedule. Edwina with her pearls and charities; Karl more interested in the share market than his son. The frigid hug, where she'd discovered Edwina's bony frame had been even sharper than her cutting wit.

It was sad, all right. Sad that one day they would realise they'd stuffed up with Sam and completely missed out on the chance to know Evie.

My beautiful, funny, smart girl. Who wouldn't want a slice of Evie-sunshine in their life?

'It *is* sad,' Lara agreed, cautiously. When it came to love and nurturing, she knew she had Evie covered. But she would never be able to match the Kingsleys in wealth, luxury or connections.

Lara eased out a breath. 'And your father?'

Evie's reply was immediate: 'No. Definitely not. I don't ever want to see him, not after what he did.'

Feeling somewhat bolstered by relief, Lara found herself wanting to be the bigger person. 'Let me know if you want to contact your grandparents, okay? I have their address.'

She felt like kicking herself as soon as the words were out of her mouth. The feeling compounded when Evie scrambled for a pen.

They'll never respond, Lara told herself as she looked through her address book and wrote down their details. Evie put the address into her backpack, looking almost relieved at the sound of wheels crunching on gravel. She dragged her suitcase towards the door.

She's been thinking about them the entire weekend and waited until now to tell me.

It hurt more than Lara could have imagined.

Even the sight of Toby Paxton walking up her steps, a smile on his face and horribly clashing socks on his feet, couldn't stop an anguished noise slipping from her mouth.

Two minutes, Lara. You can endure anything for two minutes, anything. Hold it together.

She kissed Evie goodbye and drew her into one last hug. 'Miss you already.'

'You really don't mind, Mum?' Evie asked.

'Course not,' said Lara. The lie burned like hot bile.

'Thanks. Drive safely,' Lara said to Toby, pretending not to notice the surprised look on his face at her brusque manner.

As soon as the car had disappeared from sight, Lara took her frustration into the kitchen. Rummaging through a recipe book, she decided on a batch of hedgehog slice. After all those years as a teenager, making endless trays of the slice to sell at Mrs Beggs' shop, she could practically make it with her eyes closed. Silver mixing bowls clanged and cocoa powder went everywhere as she thumped ingredients onto the marble benchtop, clattered through the utensils drawer until she found the rolling pin and pummelled the Arrowroot biscuits into submission. It wasn't until the ingredients had melded into a gooey chocolatey mix, and she'd scraped it into a baking tin, that she felt some of the tension ease.

༄

Apart from the car stereo streaming an ear-piercing assortment of pop music, and the packet of chips Holly accidentally upended during their game of Car Colour Bingo, the drive from Bridgefield to Ballarat went smoothly.

While the girls chatted and shared highlights of the weekend, Toby spent the first leg of the drive trying to work out what or who had caused the haunted look on Lara's face.

He hadn't been expecting an embrace and a kiss on the cheek—hell, he wouldn't have knocked it back either—but the stiff set of Lara's shoulders and her sombre mood had surprised him.

Did Tim say something to her? Warn her off me?

They grabbed a quick counter meal at the Lake Bolac Hotel, the designated halfway point, and it wasn't until they were back on the road that he broached the subject with Evie.

'How's your mum? Tuckered out after yesterday's slicing and dicing?'

He looked in the rear-view mirror, glad it was just light enough to see her response, but not happy to see her sunny smile dip.

'Yeah, I guess. I mentioned something before I left . . .' Evie trailed off and chewed on her fingernails. 'I don't think she was very happy.'

'Don't tell me!' said Holly, twisting in her seat. 'Did you use all her good shampoo and conditioner when you were home?'

Evie shook her head. 'She just uses Pantene, same as me.'

'Ugh, my mum hates it when I use her good stuff. Or did you spring a really expensive camp on her? My camps always give Dad heart palpitations, don't they, Dad?'

Toby lifted a hand from the steering wheel and pretended to clutch his heart. 'Sure do. Clever clogs over here seems to have all the expensive hobbies. I never knew Woodwind Camp was even a thing.'

He was pleased to see Evie chuckle quietly. 'Nah, Mum knows about the camps. We're already saving up for those. I asked about seeing my grandparents. My dad's family.'

Toby knew he had to tread carefully here. He didn't want to pry, but who else would she talk to about it? She might be close to her aunts, but was it the type of thing she'd call them about when she got back to school?

'And you're worried you've upset her?' he asked gently.

Evie brushed away tears in the backseat.

'Did they die when you were little too? I never even got to meet my mum's folks, but Dad says it's probably not a bad thing,' said Holly, a wicked glint in her eye.

Toby laughed. Holly had inherited a sixth sense for situations where comic relief was required, and he was grateful for it at that moment.

'I *also* told you never to repeat that, Holly. Especially around your mother.'

'Nah, I don't see them,' said Evie. She paused, and he wondered if she was going to mention that her father was in jail. 'We don't have anything to do with them.'

'You can pick your nose but you can't pick your family, right?' he said. 'I'm sure your mum will come around, if it's what you really want.'

She seemed buoyed by this, which was lucky because it didn't look like she had many fingernails left to chew.

'That's exactly what my grandpa says!'

Justin Bieber came on the stereo and the girls started singing as they drove through the dusk and into the night.

He dropped Evie off at her boarding house first, then turned to Holly.

'Stretch your legs before I drop you at your mum's?'

Her face creased with delight, and they strolled down Ballarat's main street, admiring the heritage buildings at night. Although it was getting a bit nippy for ice cream, he found himself lingering over a double scoop of macadamia and mango, not quite ready to relinquish his girl.

'Good weekend, Hol?'

'Awesome, Dad. The McIntyre family's so big and noisy, but they're pretty nice. Do you think we'll see them next time I'm home? Though I bet you'll be seeing Evie's mum before then . . .' Holly grinned knowingly.

Toby lifted an eyebrow. Holly had never shown any interest in the women he'd dated before, and he wasn't even at that stage with Lara.

Yet.

He gave her a little smile. 'I hope so, Hol.'

Lara swatted at the alarm clock. The overly chirpy reminder irritated her, not because it was 5 a.m., but because she'd been awake for the past few hours and didn't need reminding. The night had passed slowly, filled with memories of Karl and Edwina supporting their son in court, their stout refusal to believe Lara's accusations, despite photos, blackmail videos and statements from other women he'd secretly filmed.

Why does Evie want to see them? Why now?

She nearly ripped the blind off its roller as she yanked it up.

After last night's electrical storm, the sky was clear and bright. Her cattle were visible under the full moon.

Tugging a singlet over her head, Lara dragged herself out for a run. With a hard-fought ten kilometres under her belt, she stretched and took her time making breakfast, steeling herself for the phone call she had to make. The day the police had carted Sam away in the back of a divvy van, she'd made a promise to always answer Evie's questions truthfully, no matter how awkward or uncomfortable they made her feel. She hadn't exactly lied to Evie yesterday, but she hadn't been truthful, and that knowledge had made her sleep like a princess with a pea under her mattress.

Evie sounded groggy when she answered.

'Mum? Is Basil okay?'

'Hey honey, he sure is. Basil's good.'

'Why you calling so early, then?' Evie's yawn came down the phone line.

'I was surprised, last night, and I probably shouldn't have pretended I was cool with it. It's a shock you want to see your grandparents, after all this time. Is there anything in particular you wanted to find out? I didn't know them well,' Lara admitted, 'but I might be able to help you with a few basics.'

Much about the Kingsleys' business exploits and agricultural investments could be found online, but she was pretty sure Evie wanted more depth. Despite being married to their son for a decade, and engaged for a few years prior, her insight into Karl and Edwina's hopes, dreams and favourite foods was as slim as her knowledge of their medical history. Their casual disinterest in their only son, and their only grandchild had seemed unfathomable at first—Sam's parents had never been like Angie's in-laws, with casual drop-ins, food deliveries and offers to babysit—but when Sam showed his true colours, and she'd finally found her feet again, Lara had told herself this distance was an advantage in the long run.

She drummed her fingers on the kitchen bench, then strode across to the kettle and flicked it on. Definitely coffee time.

'I'm not sure exactly what I want to find out,' said Evie, yawning again. 'But I feel like I *should* know more about them, you know?'

Lara grabbed a mug and heaped an extra-large spoon of coffee into it. She watched steam pour out the kettle. How many times had she moved hot cups and teapots away from the edge of the table when Evie was a toddler? How many hours had she shivered in the Hamilton swimming pool, ingesting unknown quantities of chlorine and God knows what else, until she was sure Evie could swim like a fish?

She'd done her best to shelter her—maybe this was the end of her days safeguarding Evie against pain and rejection?

'I'll get used to the idea,' Lara said, setting aside a niggle of unease.

'Yeah, Toby said that'd probably be the case.'

Did he now?

'You were talking to *Toby* about seeing your grandparents?'

'Yep. We spent three hours in the car together, and he asked if you were okay. It kind of went from there.'

Lara wondered what other information he'd gleaned on the drive back to the city, and something made her hope she had come across in a good light.

§

Tuesday, Wednesday, Thursday passed in a whirl. Lara whipped between the nursing centre and the general store, keeping herself so busy she didn't have time to dwell on the very likely possibility of losing the shop to a twit called Tarquin or losing Evie to the Kingsleys. It felt like she had already lost her daughter to boarding school—she couldn't imagine letting Karl and Edwina take their cut of the school holidays too.

And although she should have been bone tired by the time she'd locked the store, confirmed the next morning's volunteer shift and crawled into bed at the end of each day, Lara found the nights stretching. Even a double nip of gin couldn't ease her racing mind, or the herbal tea Diana swore by, which tasted more like cat's wee than the soothing, sleep-inducing brew promised on the packet. Longer runs hadn't helped either, nor the ridiculous meditation CD Penny dropped around. By Thursday afternoon, she felt tired enough to sleep for a week.

'Nuh-uh,' said Diana, barring the back door of the general store. They'd manned the shop together the past two afternoons, fine-tuning details for the fundraisers between customers. 'Hand it over,' she said, gesturing to Lara's bulging tote bag.

Lara clutched the bag with the laptop and notebook to her chest. The only upside of her newfound insomnia was the opportunity to turn the sleepless nights into something productive. Somewhere between 2 and 4 a.m. she had found herself applying for event permits, updating the list of prospective shareholders and baking enough to keep Mrs Beggs' refrigerator fully stocked.

'I need that stuff, Diana. Online donations have to be entered, and I've got shop stock that won't order itself.'

Diana gently prised the bag from her hands. 'You need a break, Lars. You'll look like Fester Addams if those circles under your eyes get any darker. Burning yourself out isn't going to save the general store,' she said. 'Mrs Beggs wouldn't want that, either. She called me this morning, worried about you.'

Lara didn't need a mirror to know her sister spoke the truth. Her mood was as dark as the clouds that had just dumped two inches of rain. She'd barked at the kids buying lollies after school, mixed up the mail more than once, and muddled the seniors' exercise class with the Strong Mamas group. She reluctantly handed over the laptop and notebook.

The storm hadn't let up all day, and the sisters were both drenched in the short time it took to lock the shop behind them and dash to their cars. Deep puddles sprayed water in every direction and Lara had the windscreen wipers working overtime just to see five feet in front of her. Her cattle would be grateful for the extra growth that would shoot after the opening rains, like all the other farmers in the district, but the downpour only added to her frustration.

Her headlights illuminated the house, and Lara groaned at the sight of the lounge-room window slightly open. It would be freezing inside the stone homestead, too, and the carpet underneath the window would be damp.

So much for saving the firewood until winter.

Feeling a lot like a drowned rat, Lara ran back and forth between the woodshed and the house, ferrying kindling and wood inside. Once the wood basket was full, she pulled a pot of soup out of the fridge and set it to heat slowly on the stovetop before jumping in the shower. The house was icy cold when she emerged.

She arranged scrunched-up paper in the fireplace, expecting the tee-pee of kindling to take straightaway, but it was too damp to catch. She blew gently, only for a plume of smoke to puff up in her face.

Her bed, with its thick flannelette sheets and extra blanket, was looking more tempting by the minute, and if it weren't for lack of mobile phone reception in the southern end of the house, she would have skipped tea and jumped straight into bed. But Lara would have to be frozen solid before she'd forgo her evening conversations with Evie.

'Catch, damn it.' She struck another match, blew impatiently and received another face-full of smoke for her efforts. One of those stinking synthetic fire-lighters would have it roaring in seconds, but she couldn't bring herself to toss them into her shopping trolley.

She set the matches aside. A bowl of soup and one of Annabel's quilted knee-rugs would have to suffice for tonight. Lara's back creaked like the old windmill as she straightened up but another sound caught her attention.

Scritch. Scratch.

She cocked her head, looking around the room as it came again. There were plenty of mouse traps lurking under cupboards and couches to keep mice at bay, but this sounded bigger. A possum in the roof, escaping from the rain?

The phone rang as she pulled a stepladder from the linen press.

'McIntyre possum exterminators. Can I help you?'

Evie's laugh echoed down the line.

'You're so weird, Mum. What if it was someone else calling? And what are you doing hunting possums at this hour? Cam said you were supposed to rest up tonight. Aren't you tired?'

Lara held the phone to her ear and angled the ladder under the manhole in the hallway.

'Drop-dead tired, but I won't get a wink of sleep if a brush-tail's in the roof again. I'm going to grab him by his big furry tail and drag him out backwards if I have to.'

Evie let out an exasperated sigh.

'Righto. Want me to call back after you've tossed him into next weekend, hammer-throw style? Or can you leave the possum in peace for two more minutes? I wanted to ask about ordering a new school jumper. Mine's gone missing.'

How can you lose clothing that's clearly labelled with your own name tag?

'You've got to be kidding? Have you checked the lost property?'

Lara ignored the scratching noise as she shifted back into the lounge room. At the price of the woollen uniforms, she wanted to exhaust every possible avenue before forking out for replacements. The possum would keep another few minutes. She settled on the couch with her bowl of soup and lap rug and brainstormed possible places Evie could have left it.

'Wear your jacket, and a thermal under your shirt until it turns up,' Lara said firmly. 'It's freezing with this cold change.'

'Any news on Basil?'

'Home tomorrow.'

'I thought you'd sound happier about that?'

Even though she was more than 200 kilometres away, there was no fooling Evie. Lara also had a suspicion she was checking in after all the talk about her grandparents.

'Mrs Beggs has had another offer on the property. Seems like there'll be a bidding war.'

Evie laughed. 'You were worried it wouldn't sell, now you've got the opposite problem. What about your fundraisers?'

Lara swallowed her spoonful of soup, welcoming the liquid warmth.

'The singles ball is almost sold out, and half the apartment raffle tickets have been snapped up, but we're still a way off matching the asking price.'

'You'll get there, Mum.'

Lara swivelled in her seat as the noise came again, like fingernails on a chalkboard. She set the soup aside and walked towards the fireplace.

'Mum?'

'Sorry Evie, it's the possum again. Stupid thing's in the chimney.'

'Gotta go, Mum. *The Bachelor*'s about to start.'

Lara clasped the fire door handle with a groan. 'You won't get those brain cells back, you know.'

'Oh Mum, you're so old fashioned. Night, night.'

Lara signed off before opening the wood burner. The scritch-scratch noise was louder. She peered into the fire box, relieved the fire hadn't caught—she didn't need roast possum on her conscience, but she did need a plan to evacuate the marsupial. The animal's movements became more agitated. She reached up to shake the flue. Each tap sent a flutter of soot and debris down into the firebox. The scratching sound slowly moved lower.

She grabbed a towel and draped it over the open door, then pulled on the welding gloves she kept in the wood box and rapped the chimney more forcefully.

As quick as a flash, she crouched down like Warnie defending the Ashes.

A puff of soot came from the top of the fire, followed by a bustling in the firebox. Slowly Lara extended her hands, pushing the towel past the pile of kindling to enclose the possum. But instead of the buzzing bundle of fur she had anticipated, her fingers closed around something small and trembling.

Baby possum? Rat? The latter thought made her skin crawl as clouds of ash rained down on the hearth. She brought the towel into the room, feeling the creature tremble through the thick welding gloves.

Lara peeled back the sooty towel. A pair of beady brown eyes peered back at her.

'Well, well, well. You're not what I expected . . .'

Fifteen

Lara dusted off an old budgie cage, removing dirt and cobwebs, but the magpie was not nearly as impressed with the cage, nor the bell and multi-level platforms, as Elmo the budgie had once been. She didn't know much about birds, but she was sure its wing wasn't supposed to sit like that. There wasn't a great deal she could do for him so late at night, so she draped a towel over the cage.

She ate breakfast quickly the next morning and carried the cage out to the car.

'Don't look at me like that, mate. You're the one who decided to skydive down my chimney,' said Lara, checking the cage door was fastened before closing the boot.

The magpie sang out a few times on the way to Hamilton and flapped as Lara placed it on the vet's lino floor.

'Here to collect a dog and drop off a bird,' she said to the receptionist. He leaned over the front counter as she lifted the towel.

The baby magpie glared at them both and scurried to the other side of the cage, its long black claws scrambling for purchase on the newspaper.

'Doesn't look good,' he said. 'The wing's at a funny angle. They'll probably put him out of his misery.'

Lara felt the bird watching her as she took a seat in one of the hard plastic waiting-room chairs. It was like he was pleading with her to steer clear of the 'green dream'.

C'mon, Amy.

But her veterinary friend confirmed the receptionist's earlier prediction.

'Sorry, Lara. I already called the local wildlife carer about an orphaned joey this morning and she said she's at capacity. Birds never manage well from shock anyway, her backyard is like a bird cemetery,' said Amy. 'If you're not keen on taking him, we'll have to euthanise.'

Fifteen minutes later, Lara found herself driving home from the clinic with not one but two patients in the back of her Subaru: a recovering snake chaser and a magpie she'd named Vegemite.

❧

By the end of the week, Toby had uncovered more information about Samuel Kingsley and the charges that had kept him in jail. But how the only son of a wealthy family had crossed paths with Lara McIntyre, he was still none the wiser.

He unfolded the latest edition of the *Bridgefield Advertiser* and re-read it over breakfast. There was always something gratifying about reading it in print, even though he'd written the articles and proofed them several times digitally before sending them off to the printing press.

Toby paused when he got to the *Farming Focus*, studying the article he'd done on the McIntyre family. The full-page photo from meat-packing day had come up even better than he'd hoped.

Lara, Penny, Diana and Angie McIntyre were gathered around the kitchen table with matching smiles. The photo was candid, with the window behind them backlighting the scene as they pressed, coiled and tied sausages. Angus was visible in the far left of the shot, his smile proud and genuine. It wasn't the type of picture to win awards, but he knew it would be something special for the family.

Print it? He studied the photo. *Be a nice way to say thanks for the hospitality . . .*

In a few short moments, Toby had opened his laptop and uploaded the picture to an online printing site. He added a timber frame to the cart and checked out. His eye caught on the order history. Holly shared the same account and he flicked through her last order, placed a few days ago. Photos of her pregnant Aunty Belinda, pictures with her school friends horsing around in their expensive uniforms, then her more serious shots: a series of panoramas of the fog rising from Ballarat's lake on a frosty morning, ice dripping off a tap in their backyard and moody rain clouds. Toby's phone pinged with a message and he shut down the internet window, feeling a bit guilty for snooping through Holly's photos.

A fire?

Toby jumped up, rereading the message.

McCluskey's?

His chair clattered to the floor. He grabbed his camera bag, shrugged on a jacket and took the front steps as fast as he could.

⚶

The baby magpie kept its beady gaze on Lara as she reached in and wrapped a gentle hand around its body. As it did every morning, the bird squawked and tried to peck her hand with its thin black beak, before conceding defeat. She wrapped a tea towel around his feathers to keep him still as she fed him.

'All right, Vegemite, meds time,' said Lara, reaching for the syringe.

The chick swivelled its head left and right, its performance reminding her of the children who came through the centre, adamant they wouldn't open their mouth for any of Nurse Lara's medicine. Instead of the jelly beans she kept in her nurse's uniform, Lara reached for a tiny worm she'd dug up that morning and dangled it in front of the bird's beak.

'Open sesame,' she said, slipping the syringe inside the bird's mouth as the worm curled itself around her fingertips.

The magpie's gentle pecks tickled her hands, and she smiled triumphantly as it plucked the worm from her grasp. The bird shook his beak. The worm went flying across the table and the syringe clattered to the floor.

Basil watched the ritual with half-hearted interest. For a dog who had once chased anything that moved and rounded up sneaky chickens when they breached the henhouse confines, he was a shadow of his former self.

At least he's still here, Lara reminded herself as she placed the bird on the dining table. Basil barely raised a hairy eyebrow as the chick fluffed up its soft downy feathers, tucked its good wing back into place and pecked at another worm.

He stayed there while Lara sorted through the pile of newspapers on the bench and replaced the soiled paper at the bottom of the cage.

'Here, back in you go, Vegemite.'

The grandfather clock in the living room chimed. *Time to get my bum into gear.*

She returned him to his perch, carried the birdcage into the laundry and added a fresh bowl of water. The magpie cocked its head to the side and studied her with a chocolate eye. Lara marvelled again at the fine, long black eyelashes. A little grey feather floated through the cage bars as the bird stretched again. The left wing touched the side of the cage but the other stayed at an awkward angle, as if the bird were doing a feathered version of 'I'm a Little Teapot'. Its thin eyelid flickered upward to close.

'See you tonight,' said Lara, closing the laundry door.

She shoved her phone into her pocket and paused as Basil's tail thumped against the floorboards. *Take him or leave him?* Therapy dogs visited the centre once a month, their calm temperaments perfect for the visitors who came to their healthy-legs clinic, but Basil had always been too boisterous and active to even consider bringing into work.

'Will you sit there quietly, and let the clients pat you?' she asked.

Basil cocked his head, just like the magpie had. The side of his lip where he'd been bitten by the snake didn't move, giving him a wonky charm. Lara thought of Toby's lopsided smile. She crouched down and clipped a lead onto Basil's collar. An orange glow at the end of her driveway and the billowing smoke caught her attention the second they stepped outside.

Fire!

Lara settled Basil in the boot and jumped into the driver's seat, gravel flicking under her wheels as she raced towards the shearing shed. The CFA truck was already there, but even their best efforts were too late for the old building. Flames licked the air and the stone walls gave a great huff, as if exhaling hundreds of years of history, and crumbled to the ground.

Clyde McCluskey stood on the boundary between their two properties, the glow of the fire shining off his bald patch. Ash and soot had settled on his jumper. Lara took in his scorched eyebrows and the hand he cradled to his chest.

'You right?'

'Such a frigging waste,' he said. She didn't disagree. The best shearing shed in the district devoured by flames would make local news, if not state news. She wasn't surprised to see Toby rock up a few minutes later.

'Your hand, though, Clyde? Does it need seeing to?' Lara reached for his hand and turned it gently. Even in the dim dawn light, with an orange glow from the fire, the blisters looked painful.

'I'll need to dress it at the centre.'

McCluskey looked down at his hand, as if seeing it for the first time. She coerced her neighbour into the car and pulled onto the road. She slowed and rolled down the window when she got to Toby.

'If anyone needs Clyde, he'll be back in half an hour.'

'Are the donkeys okay?' Toby asked.

The donkeys! She'd forgotten all about them.

Lara turned to McCluskey, who nodded gravely. 'By a whisker,' he said.

The smoke felt like it was following them into town, and by the time Lara had opened up the Bush Nursing Centre, dressed McCluskey's burns, locked up behind her again and driven her neighbour back home, she needed another shower and a fresh set of clothes.

The receptionist greeted her with an enviable perkiness when Lara finally walked Basil in to the nursing centre.

'There's the brave snake-wrangling kelpie. And you've been out toasting marshmallows, I hear.'

'Hardly. The CFA blokes had the fire sorted by the time I arrived,' said Lara. She looked down at Basil. 'I'm getting soft in my old age, but I'm sure he won't be any trouble.'

The receptionist wandered out from behind the counter and stroked Basil's ears. 'It's like he's sedated. If anyone asks we'll pretend he's our new therapy dog,' she said with a wink.

Lara gave a grateful smile and set Basil's basket up in the corner of the multipurpose room. He watched but didn't move a paw out of place as she prepped for the Move It or Lose It class.

Women began to stream into the room, yoga mats under their arms, briefly greeting Lara before returning to their discussions.

'If it was anyone else, I'd say it was arson for an insurance job.'

Lara looked up from the round yoga balls she was trying to corral.

Gossip's still faster than broadband internet around here . . .

'Such a shame. All that history gone up in smoke,' said Olive.

Karen lowered her voice. 'Clyde probably didn't even have it insured. Moths would fly out of his wallet if he ever opened it.'

'Serves him right, the old curmudgeon. I heard he wants young Toby to reroute his fun run so the runners don't upset his cattle and those darn mules.' Olive patted her silver perm.

What?

This was news to Lara.

'They're donkeys, not mules,' Karen corrected.

'Same thing. Edna McCluskey would be beside herself. She loved that little shearing shed almost as much as her donkeys,' Olive said, unrolling her yoga mat. The discussion was interrupted when another group of women walked into the room, followed by a couple, their matching lime-green tracksuits aquiver with excitement.

The pair hurried over to Lara. 'We've got a surprise for you, Lara dear. Our grandson Paul heard about the general store fundraiser, and he wants to make a sizeable donation,' said the woman. She looked around to be sure she had everyone else's attention, then raised her voice a little. 'You know, he's the one on the Gold Coast, with the big start-up. Graeme and Letty's boy. Early forties like you, I believe.'

Lara scratched her chin. Paul had been the biggest nerd in high school, and no matter how well he'd done for himself, she still couldn't reconcile her shy Bridgefield High classmate with the multinational entrepreneur he'd become.

'He wants to donate fifty thousand dollars.'

Lara's heart lifted.

The proud grandmother leaned in a little closer.

'There are a few minor conditions, of course,' she said, with a tinkling laugh. 'He'll get his lawyers to draft them up, but how do you feel about renaming it the ZingleDangle General Store? Or the ZC Store for short? He'll arrange new signage of course, and a full paint job so it matches with the green company branding.'

Lara couldn't look away from the matching tracksuits with their lurid tone. A lime-green general store sounded as bad as a Tarquin-owned general store with smashed avocado and karaoke nights.

The woman's husband pointed to the logo on his hoody, some type of abominable snowman.

'This is the company mascot. He'd send a bunch of these tracksuits over for giveaways at the grand re-opening. He might even fly his chopper over for the launch.'

Lara's heart sank. She would not allow the general store to be turned into a marketing exercise.

'Such a generous offer, we'll keep it in mind.' She tapped her watch and waved to the stragglers chatting by the door. 'We're starting, come on in,' she said, pressing play on the stereo.

⁂

Lara pulled the fundraiser flyers off the photocopier and wedged them under her arm before slinging her handbag over her shoulder. Penny had whipped up the colourful designs to promote all three fundraising events, plus a tear-off slip through which people could donate or buy a share.

Stuff the flyers in letter boxes, quick meeting, feed the animals, then bed, Lara promised herself as one yawn turned into two. If she didn't move quickly, she'd fall asleep on one of the centre's examination tables. She tidied up her nursing paperwork, pulled a jacket over her cardigan and walked into the foyer.

'See you tomorrow,' she said, heading to the glass sliding door.

'Forgetting someone?' The receptionist lifted the red dog lead.

Basil's tail thumped quietly against the carpet in the corner.

Lara cringed. 'Never thought I'd see the day he was so quiet I'd forget he was around,' she said, giving a short whistle. 'C'mon boy, home time.'

She walked across Bridgefield's main street, slower than normal to accommodate Basil's snail-pace, and let herself into the general store's back door.

Basil flopped down quietly beside the mail bag. The effort of walking across the street had obviously tuckered him out. Lara knelt down and scratched his ears.

'I know how you feel, buddy.'

Basil gave her a baleful look.

Setting the stack of flyers on the counter, Lara automatically checked the pie-warmer. It was still warm to touch, but the power light was off. Something about McCluskey's fire had set her on edge.

She slipped the flyers into the letterboxes, her mind wandering to the meeting she was hosting tonight. It shouldn't take long, a quick update on the shares sold, donations tally and everyone's fundraising ideas. Lara tugged her hair-tie out, gave her hair a quick finger comb before retying it, then straightened the collar of her uniform. *Nothing to do with the fact Toby will be at the meeting*, she told herself, checking that the front door of the shop was locked.

The streetlights had flickered on, illuminating gusts of rain drenching the footpath.

Lara called out to Basil as she grabbed her handbag: 'Brace yourself for a wet walk back to the car—' but she jerked to a stop as she walked into the storeroom.

McCluskey was framed by the doorway. Basil's tail wagged.

'Clyde, what are you doing here?'

Her neighbour shuffled in a little further, keeping a stern eye on the kelpie. 'Light's not normally on after hours, checking it's all kosher,' he said, taking a step backwards. 'Can't have thieves ransacking the shop while Winnie's unwell.'

So, he does have a heart after all.

Basil sniffed at the bandage on McCluskey's hand, which was already grotty.

McCluskey's oilskin jacket swirled out behind him as he turned to leave.

'Any word on the shearing shed?' Lara asked. 'Do they know what happened?'

He paused on the back step.

'Poxy old radio I keep on for the donkeys must've been on the fritz. Can't do much about it now, 'cept be thankful it wasn't worse.'

'That's one way to look at it,' she said. 'You're welcome to use my shearing shed and yards. I won't be needing them anytime soon.' Lara reached into her handbag and pulled out a flyer. 'And I know you're not a fan of the fundraiser, but we're making a last-ditch effort to get the funds together,' she added.

McCluskey stared at the flyer suspiciously. 'Why would we want all these people poking around our town?' he said. 'They could bring all sorts of trouble.'

'Even more reason to support the shop fundraiser, Clyde. What would you prefer: one weekend with visitors in town, bringing in outside dollars to help save the general store, or having to buy your bread, milk and newspapers off people who don't have any connection with this place? You should see the schmucks who've made offers already.' Lara tapped the flyer he was holding. 'I promise you, this is the better option.'

'I still don't want people trampling over my land,' he said, shoving the flyer into his pocket before leaving.

It'll probably end up in the bin.

Lara pulled the door shut behind them, checking the lock before huddling under an umbrella for the short walk to the town hall.

Most of the committee members were there, and she couldn't help feeling a little disappointed when Diana announced Toby was an apology. She drove home carefully after the meeting, her windscreen wipers working overtime.

She slowed even more as she approached Toby's driveway. His windows glowed brightly, well-lit from the inside. *What had kept him from the meeting? Was he ill? Snowed under with deadlines?*

If she braked now, she could drive down his sorry excuse for a driveway. The more she thought about it, the more appealing it became. Judging by the smoke coming out his chimney, Toby's place would be toasty warm. Maybe he'd have dinner cooking—she knew from Evie he was a gun at stir-fry and pasta, and he'd said he made a mean pizza. They could brainstorm the fun run with a glass of wine in hand, work out whether their neighbour would sabotage the fundraising campaign. Maybe retire to the couch for dessert . . .

Basil shifted in his basket. A strong smell wafted up from the back of the car and just like that, Lara crashed back to reality.

'Eww, gross, Basil,' said Lara, rolling down her window. Fresh air rushed in, along with sideways rain, fanning her flushed cheeks.

Lara pressed the accelerator and headed home. Her headlights picked up the burned shearing shed, or what was left of it.

For God's sake, get a grip, woman. You've got animals to feed, your own fire needs lighting, and a fridge fully stocked with food.

Hadn't she fought long and hard for independence? Why would she want to throw it all away now?

Sixteen

Sleep came easily that night, but the vivid dreams took on a life of their own. Lara murmured, half asleep, and rolled onto her back.

Toby's face swam back into her mind. She could almost feel the weight of his body shifting against hers.

Slowly.

Quietly.

Deliciously.

Toby's mouth burned a trail of kisses from her collarbone to the bottom of her ear-lobe. She arched her neck as he pulled away, his navy eyes darkening with desire at her moan. A smile tipped his lips.

How had she forgotten how good it could be? She pulled him back down to her. She wanted him closer. Needed him closer.

Why had she waited so long to rediscover this kind of delight? Lara pressed herself against him, her hand falling over the side of the bed as a wave of pleasure started to pulse through her.

The sharp pain came out of the blue, and all of a sudden Sam's face loomed in front of hers. Lara froze as passion turned to fear. Within seconds she was thrashing, her arms swinging wildly as she fought back. It never ended well, but damned if she was going to let him . . .

Confusion whirled as her flailing hands connected with soft fur, followed by a whimper. Lara's heart thudded as she sat bolt upright and looked around. Basil sat beside the timber bedside table, watching her every move.

Just a dream.

Relief and embarrassment jostled for pole position as Lara tugged the sheet up around her chest and scanned the room. If Vegemite hadn't chosen that exact moment to ruffle his feathers, she mightn't have spotted him sitting on her pile of books. Basil eased himself back onto the carpet.

'Make yourself at home there, guys.'

From now on she would shut the bedroom door and triple-check the latch on the budgie cage before she went to bed. It was disconcerting to see a captivated audience when she woke up from that type of dream.

The alarm on her mobile floated through the bedroom. Lara reached for the phone, receiving a sharp peck from the magpie. She assessed her hand. Two red dots puckered her pale skin.

'You! It was you who hijacked my dream, wasn't it,' she said crossly. It was the third consecutive night Toby had crept into her dreams, each saucier than the last, but the first time in a long time that Sam had made a nasty cameo.

The magpie eyed her as she pulled her exercise gear on. She could almost swear there was a hint of amused defiance in his expression.

Lara, you really are losing it. Blaming a hapless animal for your whacked-out dreams.

The bird fluffed his feathers again before pooping on the latest Jane Harper novel. Lara mopped up the mess and carried him into the kitchen. How he'd even climbed onto the bedside table with a broken wing was beyond her.

'No extra worms for you this morning, Vegemite.' She fastened the cage door with a peg and ushered Basil into the kitchen. He watched quietly as Lara slicked her hair into a ponytail and tugged on her Nike cap, but he stayed in his basket. Pre-snakebite, he would have danced on the end of the chain the second she walked out the back door, but he seemed to know his own diminished capabilities.

Lara turned and fixed the pair with a stern look as she laced her sneakers.

'Mind the fort, you two. Back in an hour.'

The moon was hiding behind a blanket of clouds, and Lara could barely make out her hand when she held it in front of her face.

Snail shells crunched underfoot as she loped across the dewy lawn. The sharp wind snatched at her clothes and whistled in her ears, stealing the normal soundtrack of lowing cows and humming frogs. Despite the eerie conditions, Lara felt her legs loosen as she ran. She welcomed the flow and focused on ticking topics off her mental to-do list.

Call Toby and update him on last night's meeting, quiz him on fun-run sponsors and media coverage.

She'd been quietly impressed with his two stories in the farming feature and the front-page promoting the shop fundraiser. He had a way with words, she'd give him that, and the description of the stuck calf's birth was nothing short of heart-warming.

And his photographs . . .

The scene he'd captured in the farmhouse kitchen was the first picture of herself she'd liked in years.

Lara's watch beeped and she spun on her heel.

Five k's out, five k's back and I'll have time to stretch when I get home, if I pick up the pace.

Lara's breath quickened, the sheen on her body reminding her of the sweat rolling down her cleavage when she'd woken. Her cheeks flushed in the crisp morning air.

Toby Paxton had been every bit as sexy in her dream as she'd feared.

Lara forced her legs to turn over more quickly, as if she could outrun the memory of her body melting under his touch.

General store, Lara, general store! That's the issue at hand.

Her lungs started to burn and she focused on her official to-do list, not the X-rated to-do list her mind kept returning to.

૭

Toby rolled over in bed. He tugged the flannelette sheets up a little higher and enjoyed the luxury of his warm bed for a few more moments, thankful the migraine that had floored him yesterday afternoon was gone. Judging by the light peeking in around the curtain edges, his alarm would go off any minute now.

Like most mornings, he spent the first few moments of foggy wakefulness stretching his body. He wiggled his neck left and right, flexed his legs out long and stuck his hands out, starfish style, across the bed, checking for tight spots needing attention. The alarm trilled as he finished kneading his left shoulder blade.

Toby jumped out of bed and pulled the wardrobe door open. A bundled-up shirt tumbled out as he grabbed his shorts. He held it to his nose. *That'll do,* he thought.

The wind whistled through a window he'd left open in the lounge room, and he recalculated his route to account for the south-easterly.

Instead of the loop he'd planned around the lake, Toby headed west. The morning was so dark, and his mind was so busy mapping out the day ahead, he didn't see Lara until she was within touching distance. If it hadn't been for her bright yellow singlet, he would have run straight past her.

'Hey,' he called out over the wind, falling into step beside her.

Lara's double-take was comical. 'You scared the crap out of me,' she said. 'Must have ESP.'

The comment made Toby smile to himself. 'Is that a good thing or a bad thing you're thinking of me at five-thirty in the morning?'

'Good, one less phone call to make in my lunchbreak. You missed the committee meeting.'

'Migraine. I'll go months without one and then I'll be floored by a string of them.'

She nodded sympathetically. Her matter-of-fact acceptance was a relief. Petra had always scorned the concept of migraines as a fictitious frivolity aimed at ruining other people's plans.

'I'll email you the minutes,' said Lara. 'And there's another meeting this week.'

'Perfect. Though I'm annoyed I missed my opportunity to recruit a few more fun-run helpers. I'm a little under the pump at work.'

'I'll pitch in.'

'I wasn't going to ask, seeing as you're already so loaded up with the general store stuff, and your raffle, but I won't knock back any helpers. You sure?'

'Yeah, it's either that or get roped into the singles event. Runners are my people, not the desperate and dateless.'

Toby laughed as they rounded the bend, then felt a twinge of disappointment when he saw his porch light glowing at the end of the driveway.

What is it about Lara McIntyre that makes me want to tack a few extra kilometres onto my runs?

Lara's week at the Bush Nursing Centre was even busier than usual, fielding calls from media outlets in Bendigo, Newcastle and even the Eyre Peninsula. It was flattering to know their campaign to save the shop was generating so much interest, and the 'golden apartment lottery' was every bit the unique selling point she'd hoped it would be, but the extra time she spent talking about the shop had gobbled up quite a bit of her paid workday.

'You'll be working tomorrow, then?' Lara's boss, Gretel, bailed her up in the tearoom on Friday afternoon, as Lara tipped yet another cold coffee down the drain. 'Those reports won't write themselves, and I need you holding up your end of the bargain with the grant acquittals,' she said gently but firmly. Lara didn't need a degree in psychology to understand the subtext. If the centre wasn't granted the next round of funding, they would have even less money to pay for clinic extras, such as the seniors' exercise classes, the young mums programs and the healthy-leg clinic.

'I'll only be in for the exercise class but I'll work on it at home over the weekend, I promise,' Lara said, pulling her lunch from the fridge. 'And is it still okay if I take a few days off next week? I've got to train up some new shop volunteers, and the *Sunday Herald* is coming to do a story on the all-abilities cooking program. Can you believe it's going to make the state-wide tabloids?'

Gretel stood up and rinsed her mug. She'd always been a supportive boss, though with less funding she would only be renewing contracts for staff who pulled their weight.

'I can't imagine anyone in Horsham ever caring this much about a shop. You look like you haven't slept in weeks.'

'Gee, thanks,' said Lara, through a mouthful of tuna salad. 'It'll settle down soon. I'll catch up on sleep when we've got the money raised and we're back on solid ground. We've got a meeting tonight, I think we're about two-thirds of the way there.'

'You're determined, Lara, no one would ever say you were a slacker. But remember this job needs your focus too,' she said, leaving the kitchen.

Lara spent the afternoon wading through her mountain of work at the clinic, then drove home on autopilot to type up the committee meeting agenda. Mrs Beggs was coming to this one and Lara wanted to be ultra-organised so she could show how serious they were about buying the shop.

Lara cast a look at the chock-a-block line of washing flapping under her verandah. *It'll keep till tomorrow*, she told herself, hurrying into the homestead and locking the door behind her. She dumped her handbag on the hall table, unwound her scarf, tossed it in the general direction of the hat stand and bustled into her bedroom.

Vegemite chirped cheerfully from the laundry, and even Basil got to his feet and wandered into the hallway, curious about her hurried movements. Off with the work blouse, a quick sniff of her armpits and a liberal spray of Rexona, then Lara scoured her wardrobe for a clean top.

There must be something in here, she thought, finding only work shirts, a handful of navy nursing blouses and running gear. A dash of colour caught her eye and she reached right to the back, behind her winter woollies. Ah ha—the pink blouse Evie had given her for Christmas. Baffled why anyone would design sleeves that flared out at the elbow, Lara pulled it on before she could change her mind.

The left sleeve drooped perilously close to the bowl of dog food as Lara whipped through her evening's chores, and almost copped a layer of soggy Weet-Bix as she mixed up the magpie's dinner. Fancy clothes were great for sitting in an office looking pretty, but not ideal for actually doing anything in. Heaven forbid she had to open a gate or change a tyre!

'Eat up, Vegemite. Fresh worms tomorrow, I promise,' she said, securing the door of the birdcage with a bulldog clip. *Hopefully that'll last longer than the peg.*

She was brushing her teeth with one hand and opening her mail with the other when the phone rang. Lara wedged the mail between the tap and the mirror and slid her toothbrush back into the drawer.

'Hey Evie-girl, didn't you get my message? I'm dashing out the door to a general store meeting.'

She didn't like hurrying Evie off, but she couldn't be late tonight—there was too much to get through before the second and final whole town meeting on Monday.

'Yeah, I know. I just wanted . . . I mean . . .' Evie took a deep breath.

Lara's stomach lurched as she ran through the options.

Is she upset because I postponed the weekend trip to Ballarat?

She's dropped her laptop and needs a new one pronto?

She's flunked that maths test she was worried about?

She'd been caught sexting?

Ack, that was the problem with modern teenagers, so much scope for trouble. For a moment, she hoped it was just another lost jumper.

'Spit it out, honey,' Lara said, as calmly as she could, refusing to look at her watch. 'Are you upset I can't come this weekend? I'll be there really soon, I promise. It's just work is crazy at the moment. And we're so close to buying the shop.'

'I know. Karl and Edwina are visiting me tomorrow. I got

a letter from them last week and then we spoke on the phone, so they're coming. I didn't know how to tell you,' she said after a long silence.

It was Lara's turn to take a deep breath. *Letter last week? Phone this week? Visiting tomorrow?*

'Karl and Edwina Kingsley . . .' she said finally.

The first and only time she'd ever cancelled on Evie and already her in-laws were jumping into her spot? It beggared belief that they would move so fast after years of not giving a toss.

'It's not because you cancelled,' Evie said firmly. 'They were heading down anyway.'

Yeah, and I'm a monkey's uncle, thought Lara. It was a little concession that Evie was calling them by their names. They didn't deserve the title of Gran or Pa.

'Well, have fun, then. They meeting you at the boarding house?'

'Nope, Edwina's booked a restaurant.' Lara heard the anticipation in her daughter's voice. Whatever it was, it would surely be a step-up from the counter meals Lara favoured on the rare occasions they ate out.

It's natural for her to be excited, don't rain on her parade.

'Snazzy. Make sure you wear something nice,' she said, cringing as the inane comment slipped from her tongue. But what *should* she say? Don't be surprised if you have dinner once and you never hear from them again? Don't be offended if they show more interest in the waiter than their own flesh and blood?

'Edwina said we could go shopping first, if I didn't have anything nice to wear, but I'm going to wear those new jeans you bought for my birthday. And the top Aunty Diana got me for Christmas, with the cat on it.'

It wasn't until Evie said it that Lara realised her daughter only received new clothes as gifts. Had she been dreaming of random shopping expeditions?

'Miss you, speak tomorrow night.' Evie blew her a kiss down the phone line before hanging up.

Lara leaned her elbows on the bathroom vanity and rested her head in her hands. The half-opened envelope fluttered to the floor. She took several deep breaths and felt slightly better until she recognised the neat cursive on the envelope. With shaking hands, she picked the mail off the tiled floor, opened it and unfolded the letter.

Dear Lara,

Evie told us how much the store means to your little community. In light of this, and as a gesture of goodwill, we have enclosed a $100,000 contribution towards the general store consortium. Please let us help and be part of Evie's life again.

   Edwina and Karl Kingsley

Seriously? First they try to buy my daughter and now they try to buy me?

As tempting as it was to feed the letter straight into the fireplace and watch it burn, Lara marched to the car, holding the letter as if it were steaming dog poo, and drove to the hall on autopilot.

⚬

Toby finished his Friday afternoon read-through, altering only a few typos on the forthcoming edition before emailing the print team with the revised copy. After the edition was officially 'put to bed', he finessed his list of story ideas for the following edition, locked the newspaper office and walked to the hall.

He looked skywards briefly. It was a lot milder than Ballarat's late autumn but the threat of rain was always present. Straightening his shirt, Toby pulled the neckline away from his skin. He gave a cursory sniff. Lara had crept into his mind all day, and he didn't want to waltz into the meeting stinking to high hell, especially when he was planning to ask her on a date. A real date, with a restaurant and table service, not a scrap of lycra or whiff of sweat involved.

Would she say yes? He sure hoped so.

He couldn't smell anything, but backtracked to the staff bathroom and blasted his underarms with deodorant, just to be on the safe side.

A kaleidoscope of colour emerged from a car outside the hall, bringing a smile to his face.

Pearl Patterson was looking resplendent in a paisley silk caftan, and from the purple tint in her hair, she looked like she was fresh from the hair salon. Her false teeth flashed brightly in the fading sunlight.

'Looking very swish, Pearl,' he said, reaching to open the hall door for her.

'Don't you love it? I found it in the Salvos. They had it on the fancy dress rack, but it's too pretty to save for parties, don't you think?'

Toby bit back a smile. The caftan wouldn't be out of place on a Mardi Gras float.

'Very eye-catching,' he said, twisting the door handle.

But no matter which way he turned it, the hall door wouldn't budge.

'Are we early?' Pearl looked as surprised as he felt.

There was a lot he didn't know about Lara McIntyre, but he'd been around her enough to notice her pride in organisation, punctuality and order. Another car pulled up and Amy the vet climbed out.

'Locked out?' she said, pulling dog-hair off her woollen jumper.

'Looks that way,' said Toby. 'I'll try the back door.'

Toby loped across the car park, careful not to slip on the damp oak leaves littering the ground. The back door opened with a creak and he moved cautiously through the darkened space, heading towards the light-filled foyer. The chairs were only half-unpacked. What had derailed their evening?

He spotted the McIntyre sisters in the hall kitchen, Diana with an arm around Lara, Penny's face taut with concern. Was Lara crying?

Toby made a quick decision, retreating silently to the back of the hall. He waited a few beats, then opened the back door and shut it loudly.

'Anybody in here? Lara?'

He walked down the hallway slowly, ensuring his footsteps rang out across the old timber floorboards. By the time he entered the kitchen, Penny had a tray of slice in her hands and Diana was pulling a bottle of milk from the vintage fridge. Lara kept her back to him.

'That time already?' said Diana. 'Better start setting up, I guess.' Penny thrust the platter in Toby's direction. His mouth watered over the array of delicacies.

'Isn't anyone coming?' she said, unloading a tray of tea-cups onto the trestle table.

Toby set the slice down beside the urn on his way to the front door.

'Might help if you unlock the hall,' he said with a wink, twisting the lock.

Penny's expression changed to relief as the rest of the committee flooded in.

'Colder than a witch's tit out there,' said Pearl, her arm threaded through Amy's.

He noticed Lara slip into the bathroom, her head low. The committee members helped themselves to supper and pulled their chairs into a small circle, and though Toby smiled and joined in the small talk, he kept an eye on the bathroom door.

Seventeen

Lara blinked until the sting of Diana's eye drops eased. She shoved the bottle into her pocket, ran the bathroom taps and splashed a handful of water on her face.

'You right?' Penny said as she stepped into the bathroom. 'You know you can just rip that thing up right now and nobody needs to be any the wiser,' she continued gently, taking the now-creased letter from Lara's hand. 'And you don't even know if there are strings attached, it's not explicitly outlined.'

Lara twisted her hair into a tight bun, then paused and let it fall loose again. At least she could hide a little if her hair was down.

'Oh, that's what they mean, all right. There's no such thing as a free lunch in their world. It's just the type of game Sam would play.' She took a sip from the glass of water Penny had brought with her. 'I'd rather sell my organs on the black market than accept a cent from the Kingsleys, especially if they're only doing it to impress Evie.'

Lara thought of the letter as she joined the meeting. The heater was on full tilt and Mrs Beggs was bundled up in at least six layers to ward off the chill. It was the first time she'd seen

Mrs Beggs out and about since she'd returned from hospital. All these people, including a handful of new fun-run marshals who had obviously read Toby's call-out in the newspaper, were giving up their time to raise funds, not to mention all the volunteers keeping the shop running.

I could fix this by accepting their donation.

But if she did, she knew she would feel even more obliged to share Evie with them. Although Evie was the one who had initiated contact, the thought of accepting their money made Lara sick.

Toby took the cap off his pen, flicked his notepad to a fresh page and looked up brightly. His gaze lingered on her face a little longer than normal, as if to say *'I've got this'*.

'Righto, let's get this meeting underway. Great to see some new volunteers here, we've got lots of sponsors on board and I've had a ripper idea that might just smooth the way with the infamous Clyde McCluskey.'

Lara looked up, intrigued.

'What if we name an event in honour of his late wife? I've got a feeling his grumpiness is more about loneliness. Was he always this miserable?'

Angus nodded. 'He's always been crotchety, though he is slightly *more* impossible without Edna's influence.'

'So, why don't we call it the Edna McCluskey 5K, and whack a donkey on the trophy?'

Even Lara found herself agreeing.

'If he'll let us use the easement along Windmill Track, I'll put both the darn donkeys on the trophy,' she said.

'Edna walked them up and down that track every weekend for years,' said Mrs Beggs. 'Rain, hail or shine.'

'Leave it with me,' said Toby, and Lara felt a weight lift off her shoulders.

The meeting moved to permit applications and equipment suppliers. They broke for a quick supper and Lara waited until everyone had a fresh cup of tea before she cleared her throat.

'There's a little more business we need to discuss,' she said, shifting in her seat. 'In the interest of transparency, I wanted to talk about a few donations that don't quite fit the mood. We've had two so far, one I think we can deal with easily. The other . . .'

She cleared her throat again.

'The other is less cut and dried. We received a hundred thousand dollar pledge today.'

'You ripper, that'd more than cover the shortfall,' Pearl said.

Amy leaned back in her chair and crossed her legs, watching Lara closely. 'And yet you aren't celebrating?'

Angus looked perplexed. 'What'd they want? Use of the upstairs apartment as a brothel?'

The small joke roused a tiny smile from Lara.

'It was from the Kingsleys. They want access to Evie,' she said, smoothing down a piece of paper, as if her hands could iron out the wrinkles.

Amy winced. Pearl let out a deep sigh. They both knew firsthand the struggles Lara had had with Sam, and how she felt about her in-laws.

Ex-in-laws.

'They're Evie's grandparents,' said Lara, noticing Toby's puzzled expression. 'I've spoken to a lawyer friend, Kylie. She says that as a committee, we need to decide whether we're willing to accept donations with personal stipulations or conditions attached. If the answer is no, and everyone votes on it, then their pledge is null and void. If the committee votes yes, then we're going to need to work out how to navigate this one.'

Toby chewed on the end of his pen.

'They're not seriously going to stand up in front of the whole town and bully you into accepting their donation, though, are they?' Toby cocked his head. 'I mean, they'll look like a pair of arseholes—' He caught Pearl's indignant cough. 'Pardon my French, but that doesn't make them look good.'

'The Kingsleys aren't used to hearing the word no,' said Penny, reaching for her sister's hand.

'Easy, then. I vote we don't accept donations with strings attached,' he said, lifting his hand.

Everyone else on the committee followed suit. Lara felt her shoulders lower a little.

Pearl piped up beside Lara. 'And what's the other donation?'

This time Lara's smile wasn't forced. 'Let me tell you about Paul Moyne and his brilliant ZingleDangle proposal. I'm pretty sure we won't be painting the general store lime green, but you'll get a laugh anyway.'

⁊

Toby pulled out of his driveway on Sunday morning on his way to the footy. He spied Lara's car in her driveway as he drove past and wished again that he'd caught up with her as soon as the committee meeting on Friday night had finished. But she'd slipped out while he was washing up and there had been no reply to his text message.

He returned from the match with a camera full of sports photos and a notepad jammed with volunteer suggestions, a general-store donation and enough story tips to keep him in articles for the week ahead. But still no word from Lara, despite the fact her car didn't seem to have moved all day. She was nowhere to be seen on his run the following day either, and despite his office phone ringing off the hook on Monday morning, none of the callers were Lara McIntyre.

He was glad to lock the office doors behind him to cover Bridgefield Primary School's annual baking competition.

'And you'll be our celebrity judge next year too?' the principal asked, after a delightful hour spent sampling an array of baked goods and declaring several worthy winners.

'Tough gig, but someone's gotta do it,' Toby agreed, patting his stomach with a smile. He walked back to the *Bridgefield Advertiser* with a full belly, loads of photos and a new appreciation for the local kids and their baking skills.

The phone was ringing when he walked back inside.

He shrugged his camera bag off his shoulder and caught the phone in time.

'*Bridgefield Advertiser*, Toby speaking.'

'Paxton, glad I caught you,' Mick's familiar voice came down the phone, though from the sound of road noise in the background he wasn't calling from the *Ballarat Daily* offices. 'What's the best way to get to your neck of the woods? I'm filling up at the Glenthompson roadhouse and the chap at the counter reckons I'm still an hour or so away. I was almost about to go north around your whopping big mountain range.'

Toby scanned the messy office piled high with old newspapers. Last week's mostly empty coffee mugs were acting as paperweights so his notes didn't scatter every time someone breezed through the door to buy a newspaper. He looked out his office to the vacant reception area.

Where is *Nancy?*

'Mick, I didn't know you were heading our direction. You definitely don't want to go the top way, that'll tack on an extra hour. Keep coming until Cavendish then turn north. We'll see you in about an hour.' Toby looked at his watch. The idea of Mick leaving his desk—heck, the idea of him leaving the city—for anything other than an emergency was unprecedented.

It made Toby more than a little nervous. 'I've got a meeting at six, though. Is this a social call?'

What have I stuffed up?

If anything, circulation had perked up in the past two months, so surely Mick wasn't driving down to deliver bad news in person. The cakes and biscuits Toby had eaten at the baking competition suddenly felt like cement in his belly.

He's giving the Ballarat job to someone else?

'Ramona's been reading all about your save-the-shop campaign and wants to get a feel for it,' said Mick.

Toby let out the breath he'd been holding. He heard a muffled voice in the background.

'Another hour or so, love. I know, I know, it's further than I thought too.'

Ramona was Mick's new, improved wife, and Toby owed her a debt of gratitude. As glamorous as she was young, Ramona was the reason the old newshound was finally planning his retirement.

'There's a delicate matter to discuss in person too, but we'll talk about it over a few drinks later tonight.'

Toby hung up, contemplating what Mick's delicate situation could be as he spun into action, cleaning the newspaper offices. By the time he'd emptied the sink and tidied the kitchenette, he had convinced himself the new journo from Melbourne had shoehorned his way into Mick's confidence.

The receptionist reappeared as he finished wiping the front counter.

'Nancy, you would've been useful an hour or two ago.'

'Sorry, long lunch!'

Toby looked at the clock. It was almost knock-off time. He could smell beer on her breath. Perhaps he should have laid down the law harder the last time.

'You can make it up tomorrow,' he said, ignoring her petulant look. 'The boss is on his way, and if you still want a job when he gets here, then you'd better brush your teeth. Liquid lunches aren't a good look,' he said, turning her in the direction of the bathroom. She wobbled a little as she walked.

❦

Lara set the axe down. She was getting used to the ache in her arms and shoulders, and if the mountain of freshly cut firewood was any indication, her efforts cutting wood after work were paying off. She had a quick shower, pulled on a fresh set of clothes and powered up her laptop for one last look through her notes before heading to the town meeting.

On a practical level, she was ready to give the shop campaign one last public pitch. If only she didn't feel so unsettled.

From the corner of her eye, Lara spotted the magpie sneaking across the counter. He jabbed his beak into the butter dish.

'Hey, you cheeky little bugger!'

Vegemite launched himself off the bench, flapping in the air for a moment before landing. His wing seemed in better nick now, but it wasn't perfect and he was easy to catch and ferry gently back to the cage.

'It's mince, vitamins and milk-thistle flowers for you, mate,' she said. 'Butter's not on your menu.'

She tended to Basil's dinner, and then dashed to the loo for another nervous wee.

The doorbell caught her by surprise. Lara checked her watch as she jogged down the hallway.

Maybe Toby's sick of being ignored?

She didn't blame him. She'd meant to call him back, but after Evie's animated update about the restaurant she'd gone to with her grandparents, and the outing they'd had afterwards, wood cutting was more appealing than company. And then there was the over-the-top donation from the Kingsleys.

The doorbell trilled again.

It was times like these she was grateful for the peep-hole she'd had installed, much to the local handyman's amusement. But her gratitude turned to surprise, then anger, as she looked through the hole.

What the hell are they *doing here?*

The pearls around Edwina Kingsley's neck were pale ivory, matching the glacial smile on the older woman's face. Her pale hair was sharply bobbed at her jaw, with a heavy fringe almost to her eyelashes. Lara only had to glance at Edwina's fine woollen knit to know it cost more than her entire outfit.

Karl Kingsley stood behind his wife, his khaki moleskins pressed within an inch of their life. Lara knew a small hipflask would be nestled in the inside pocket of his sports jacket, and while she'd never taken a shine to her former mother-in-law—a feeling that was completely mutual—she'd at least been able to hold a conversation with Karl.

'Edwina. Karl,' she said tightly. 'I'm on my way out.' She tugged on her boots, glad she had an excuse to side-step this unexpected visit.

Edwina's shoulders sank. 'I was hoping you'd at least see us, Lara. We've driven all this way.'

And now you expect me to drop whatever I'm doing?

'Next time you might want to call ahead and make sure I'm free. I really do have to go.' Lara looked at her watch. Damn it, she was going to be late.

'Didn't you get the letter with our donation? We can help buy your general store. We loved seeing Evie again yesterday,' said Karl.

'And we'd like to do it more often,' finished Edwina.

Lara bristled as she tugged her jumper sleeves down to cover the goosebumps on her arms. *Ironic, really.* They hadn't wanted to help a decade ago, when she'd stood in the Kingsleys' grand home. She'd lifted her sleeves then, shown them the bruises Sam had left, but they hadn't wanted to believe their son was capable of such a thing.

They were wrong then, and they're wrong now, Lara reminded herself, folding her arms tightly across her chest.

'Where were you when we needed support?' Lara felt her fingernails bite into her palms and stepped back to escape the cloying scent of Edwina's perfume. 'And if you'll excuse me, I've a meeting to get to.'

Lara went to close the door, but Karl slipped a leather loafer between the door and the doorway.

'We just thought—'

'You just thought what?' Lara's voice echoed down the hallway, drawing Basil to her side.

'We just thought we could help you, and you'd be more inclined to nudge Evie in our direction,' he said, his tone imploring. 'Those school fees can't be easy to manage, not on a nurse's wage. We could pay for them too, or instead, if you'd prefer. Please, let us help. She's our only grandchild.'

'Bit late for that,' said Lara, hating how bitter she sounded. 'Evie's a big enough girl to make her own decisions. She can see you if she wants, but I won't be bribed into playing happy families, or urging her into your arms,' she said. 'You can keep your money.'

Sam's mother winced as the words hit their intended mark. Karl shook his head and steered his wife away. She could hear him murmuring to Edwina as they retreated down the driveway.

Lara closed the door softly. Basil nudged her hand and she patted his head, taking solace in his calm presence.

Maybe she would feel differently if they'd listened when she'd come to them for help all those years ago. If they'd reached out after she left Sam and moved into that horrid rental. If they'd acknowledged her in the courtroom, instead of pretending she didn't exist. But wanting to weasel their way in now, after all those years of silence? Too little, too late.

Eighteen

Toby buffed the fingerprints off the glass doors, wishing he'd been given more notice. Even with his quick tidy and Nancy's attempt at cleaning, the premises looked a bit shabby. He gave the double doors another spritz of glass spray.

'A cleaner *and* a journalist! How novel,' said a high voice. Toby whipped around to see Ramona and Mick stepping out of a car.

Bugger, they're early.

Toby set the bottle of Windex down and lifted his hands in surrender.

'Guilty as charged.' He didn't need to remind them he was also the editor, photographer, advertising department and four-day-a-week receptionist.

'Christ, I'm paying you to edit the paper, not wash the freaking windows, Paxton. Where's the office girl?'

Toby tried to sound offhand.

'Gastro.'

He thought about the retching he'd heard from the toilets half an hour earlier, right before he'd sent her home. Nancy would have a sore head, but perhaps not until tomorrow. He put the cleaning products inside the door, grabbed his camera bag and notepad and quickly locked the office behind them.

'Eager to get to this meeting, I see,' said Ramona, pressing her cheek against Toby's and nearly deafening him with an air kiss. 'I'm loooooving these save-the-shop stories, Toby! You've like, got a little band of cheerleaders in the Ballarat office,' she said.

'Just following the news,' Toby said with a shrug. He wished Mick had factored in time for their deep and meaningful *before* the meeting, but he'd learned the hard way his boss and mentor wasn't one to be rushed.

Mick clapped him on the shoulder as they walked towards the hall. 'Let's see whether the town's ready to go the hard yards to get this shop over the line,' he said. 'How many people are you expecting tonight?'

'A fair few. And with a bit of luck, they'll have their wallets open,' Toby said.

The murmur of conversation grew louder as they neared the hall, where clusters of people gathered by the entrance, trading news and gossip.

'Good turn out,' said Ramona.

Toby watched Mick and his young wife take two seats close to the front. This was more than a social visit and he couldn't shake the unease.

He found Lara by the stage. Even with the grim look on her face, she was the best thing he'd seen all day.

'All set to knock 'em dead?'

Lara sucked in a shaky breath. 'Wish me luck.'

Toby gave her a smile, wishing he could erase the worry line between her eyebrows.

'Good luck, not that you'll need it. Everyone out there seems pretty excited about pitching in. You right for me to

take photos? And I'll do my spiel about the fun run, then your
sisters will do their plug for the singles ball, yeah?'

It was what they'd already discussed at the committee
meeting but Lara seemed distracted. He'd hate her to choke
on stage.

'Yep.' Lara turned, as if she were searching for someone
in particular. The sudden stiffness in her back indicated she'd
found them, and from the way her lips pressed tightly together,
he sensed it wasn't a long-lost lover.

He followed her gaze. Even though he'd only seen them in
photographs, it was obvious he was looking at the Kingsleys.

What had brought them to town? Was it the donation they'd
proposed? He glanced at Mick and Ramona, struck by the
coincidence of not one but two unlikely visitors in one day.

'Is it stuffy in here?' Lara asked, taking a deep breath.

Toby offered his most reassuring smile, trying to mask his
growing uncertainty.

'Hey, you'll be fine. You've got the community at heart,
that's what counts.'

❦

Lara clutched the microphone in a death grip, her gaze roving
over the sea of people seated in the hall.

She launched into the introductions, stumbling on the
Indigenous name in the welcome-to-country section, even
though she'd practised it. Chairs scraped against the floorboards and some stragglers snuck in, taking the vacant seats
right at the back.

Angus winked at her from the front of the crowd, and
Angie, who had driven up from the coast, gave her a nod. She
took reassurance from their encouraging smiles and the big
thumbs-up Mrs Beggs gave her from the front row.

Don't look at the Kingsleys.

She hadn't wanted Edwina and Karl at her house, and their unexpected presence at the meeting rattled her further. She wondered suddenly if this was what Clyde McCluskey felt every time he saw strangers in town.

They don't belong here.

Lara cleared her throat, but was thrown off her train of thought when she saw her neighbour in the crowd. And judging from the arms folded across his chest and the frown on his face, McCluskey didn't look like he'd warmed to the idea yet.

She glanced down at her notes and began.

'You're all here for an update on the general store sale, so let's not mess about. Mrs Beggs has had two firm offers from interested buyers, so we need to better the asking price,' she said. A ripple went through the crowd. 'We've got an excellent leg up with all the fundraisers planned, and the shares purchased so far, so we're optimistic we can make it, but we need to have a firm offer in by mid-June.'

The murmuring increased. McCluskey's hand shot up and he stood quickly.

'I can't fathom why you're so hell bent on outbidding them. If there's a willing buyer, then why don't we let them run the shop and everyone can still have their eggs, their milk, their mail and their papers, but we don't have to slave away volunteering, scrimping and saving for enough donations to keep it going.'

The old man looked around the hall, confident he'd captured everyone's attention, then sat back down.

Lara noticed a flush creeping up Mrs Beggs' neck. *Grumpy old coot,* thought Lara, annoyed Clyde was making Mrs Beggs uncomfortable. She crossed her arms tightly over her chest, then uncrossed them as she realised she couldn't speak into the microphone that way.

'It depends on the type of general store you want, Clyde. I can't imagine you're going to love the early opening and closing hours. If we buy the shop as a community, then we can more or less keep the status quo,' she said, buoyed by the enthusiasm sweeping through the room.

'I heard they want to ditch pie day,' called a voice from the audience.

'The cheek of them. I'll buy double the shares to stop that happening,' called out another.

Lara smiled as she identified the voice. 'For real, Bert?'

The man gave a salute. He was one of the chicken-and-leek devotees, and was quite partial to a lamb-and-rosemary pie too. Lara grinned at Penny, who pulled out her notepad, quickly writing it down.

'The newspaper's given us fantastic coverage,' she paused and smiled at Toby. 'So, you'll know we're planning many events to bridge the financial gap. At the moment we're three-quarters of the way to the asking price, so how about a round of applause for everyone who's pitched in so far, and those who've helped while Mrs Beggs was crook,' she said.

The clapping sounded like a herd of bulls en route to a paddock full of heifers. Mrs Beggs glanced around gratefully, and Lara hoped she knew Clyde McCluskey was in the minority.

'And make sure you get a copy of the Sunday paper next weekend, you'll recognise some handsome locals in there.'

Eddie and Tim Patterson beamed at her from the crowd.

'The apartment raffle has been very popular,' said Lara. 'Please, keep selling those tickets and spreading the word through your networks. As well as the *Bridgefield Advertiser*'s coverage, and the Sunday tabloids, the *Weekly Times* is printing a story in their next edition.'

Angus stood and faced the crowd.

'Not many places you can rent for fifty bucks a year, are there? Tell your cousins, tell your city friends. It's a lottery, but a darn fine one at that,' he said, smiling proudly.

A woman up the back raised her hand, waiting for Lara's approval before standing shyly.

'What happens to all the money if we don't meet the target?'

Lara waited for the woman to sit down.

'Great question. Like the donations and the shares, the raffle tickets will be refunded if we don't buy the shop, but hopefully we won't have to worry about that,' she said, feeling her confidence lift. 'We also have a few generous offers in the pipeline that might be a fall-back option if we can't raise the capital, though some of them have quite onerous conditions,' Lara told them.

A man she didn't recognise stood up. 'Mick from *The Ballarat Daily*. I'd like to ask whether all the donations and shareholders are made public? Where can the community find a list?'

Lara looked from the *Daily* bloke to the Kingsleys. Edwina was fidgeting with her scarf.

'Anyone interested can join the committee,' Lara said, keeping her voice steady. 'I should've made that clear right from the start, but we absolutely cannot accept donations with conditions attached.'

'But is the list public or not? Surely transparency is paramount?' The old hack was like a dog with a bone. Lara felt her heart hammering as a twitter floated up from the seats. The room seemed to heat up another five degrees.

'Transparency is crucial,' Lara agreed. 'The committee's keeping detailed records, and I'm happy to discuss the details with anyone who's interested. But I don't think we need to list all the donations and shareholders on stage, do we?'

She looked into the crowd again, reassured by Toby's encouraging smile.

McCluskey pushed his chair back, crossing his arms over his chest as he stood and said: 'Some of us have to work in the morning. Can we get to the bit about the fun run, and whose properties will be impacted by all these strangers galloping over our land?'

Lara felt a rare wave of appreciation for her neighbour.

A dairy farmer who lived near Windmill Track lifted her arm, not bothering to stifle her yawn.

'Will the public liability insurance cover our properties if people come a cropper on our land?' she asked. 'I don't want to be sued if a jogger slips in cow poo and goes belly-up.'

'Great question, Rissa. I'll hand over to Toby Paxton, our fun-run guru.'

Toby had already set his camera down and was waiting by the side of the stage.

Lara passed the microphone over and sat beside her sisters in the front row. She swivelled in her chair, looking from the newspaper man to the Kingsleys, and back, her mistrust intensifying.

⁂

If the handful of extra donations and the list of willing volunteers for the fundraisers were anything to go by, the community meeting had been a success. But it wasn't until the hall was almost empty that Lara finally allowed herself to digest the Kingsleys' unexpected appearance. *How dare they set the city media on me because I wasn't falling over myself to accommodate their wishes?*

Lara pushed the thought away as a local lady made a beeline for her.

'I still can't believe someone wanted to paint the shop bright green and call it the ZingleDangle Store,' said the young mum. 'It would have been worth telling that story on stage just to give everyone a laugh.'

Lara exhaled. She already regretted discussing Paul's ridiculous offer with the Strong Mamas Group at the Bush Nursing Centre. Giggling about the preposterous idea in private was one thing, but a whole town meeting wasn't the time or place.

'I don't think his grandparents would be quite so amused,' she said, sending silent apologies to Paul's family, who were still perplexed that she hadn't accepted the donation on the spot.

The young woman continued. 'I've told all my online mums' group about the apartment lottery and they're itching to go in the draw, especially since I told them about the awesome classes you've started at the centre. Of course, I want to win it myself—the money I'd save on my normal rent would almost cover a house deposit,' she said, jiggling the baby in her front pack.

Lara wished her luck and helped pack up the hall in a daze, trying to work out why the Ballarat paper was covering the meeting. Was that Toby's boss? Surely Toby wouldn't have told him about the Kingsleys' donation? She caught a glimpse of his tall frame across the room, helping Eddie with a tray of tea-cups. Nope, she discounted the idea straightaway. She looked towards the door that Edwina and Karl had stalked to as soon as the meeting closed. Coincidence? *Not likely.* It must have been Edwina stirring up trouble.

'I'll take that, missy,' said Pearl, breezing in with a waft of lavender and lifting the tray from her hands. 'You did a good job tonight.'

'Thanks,' Lara said, pulling a face. 'Bit of a wobble in the middle, but we got there.'

Pearl studied her. 'You're stronger than you realise, Lara. Though I'm surprised your in-laws are resorting to media intimidation? Surely they realise the spotlight will fall on them too?'

Lara met Pearl's concerned gaze with a grateful smile. It *wasn't* just her being paranoid and jumping to conclusions.

'Ex in-laws,' Lara corrected. She stooped to pick a stray serviette off the floor. 'It's not the way I'd go about things, but they're a rule unto themselves.'

'Don't let them get the better of you. You're doing a good thing.' Pearl looked around the room. 'Speaking of that, young Toby looks like he needs a hand.'

Pearl sounded almost mischievous as she looked to the far corner, where Toby was stacking chairs against the wall. Pearl was right, he'd be there all night at this rate. Lara fell into step with him and together they shifted the old church pews. His brown hair was ruffled and she could see he'd missed a patch under his jaw when he'd shaved. They moved the final bench, and when he fixed her with a smile, Lara decided she could either nurse her anger and annoyance at the Kingsleys, or she could focus on the future. *In for a pinch, in for a pound.*

Lara fell into step with Toby and they collected their things from the hall kitchen.

'Sorry I didn't get back to you on the weekend,' she said. 'Don't suppose you want to grab a drink tonight?'

Toby's face lit up momentarily, then fell.

'I'd love to, but my boss is in town. He's arranged dinner . . .'

Lara studied the soldiers' portraits on the wall, trying not to let her disappointment show.

'Right, of course,' she said. 'The guy from Ballarat? That was pretty random.'

'Not sure what's going on there,' Toby said, grimly. 'But I plan to find out.'

The Bridgefield Pub was doing a roaring trade for a Monday, and Toby found himself mobbed as soon as he stepped inside.

'Great meeting, Toby.'

'Top work, mate, we'll make a local out of you soon enough.'

Toby recognised half the patrons and he knew there would be many keen ears turned in their direction. It took every bit of his patience not to interrogate Mick the second he slid into the corner booth.

'Ordered you a steak, just the way you like it,' said Mick.

Ramona leaned back to let the waitress place their plates on the wobbly table.

'And can you bring us a round of scotch-and-dry too, please,' said Toby. He was going to need something to loosen him up. He studied his boss. What had made Mick leave his city office and trek out here, with Ramona no less, and act like an ambulance-chaser?

'What's the deal, Mick? Bit of a heads-up would've been nice,' said Toby, curbing his annoyance.

'Ah, the old Dorothy Dixer question, eh? Gotta love setting a cat among the pigeons,' said Mick, liberating his chips from underneath the whopping great hunk of beef. He chewed, watching Toby's reaction. 'Bit more spice for the next edition, anyway.'

Spice? Cat among the pigeons? It was almost as if Mick had enjoyed making Lara squirm. Hadn't he noticed the way her hands had clenched, or heard her sharp breath?

'You should've asked me, Mick. I'm on the committee too, I could have saved you a drive all the way out here if you wanted to know about donations and transparency.'

But would I have answered honestly, or would I have protected Lara's privacy?

'Where's the fun in that, Paxton?'

Ramona looked up from her vegetable-and-tofu stack.

'And then we wouldn't have had a night away from the daily grind,' she said, placing her hand over Mick's. 'And that cute little farm B&B is nestled in the most romantic setting,' she added with a wink.

Toby loaded his fork with steak, loath to imagine his boss's sex life, which clearly was more active than his at the moment. 'More spice? Mick, this is a small country newspaper. Front-page fatalities and political campaigns don't wash down here, you said so yourself. What made you question the donations anyway?'

'An old friend of a friend, Karl, tipped me off that there was something a bit hinky with those donations. Said the committee was being finicky about whose money they accepted. The whole save-the-shop campaign is sweet and fluffy—' Mick held up a hand as Toby protested. 'Now hang on, full credit for solid reporting, and it's a great angle if there's nothing else to report, but a controversy like this is pure media gold. Surprised you weren't all over it, Paxton,' he finished.

Toby shook his head. 'I'm not a fan of mud-raking, Mick. The committee voted against it, so there was nothing to report.'

Mick broke into a coughing fit. He accepted the napkin Ramona passed him, and thumped his chest, his coughs echoing around the pub's generous dining room.

The waitress appeared with a glass of water. Mick gulped it down.

'Jesus, Paxton. You're killing me. Don't tell me you've gone soft after a few months in the country? Blind Freddy could see it's a front-page angle. I'd print it in Ballarat without a minute's hesitation. *You* would've printed it in Ballarat without even thinking about it. And don't get me started on turning down that whole advertorial feature.'

Toby thought of Lara. 'What about the personal conditions? Conflict of interest and airing committee-meeting minutes? It's not fair to make one person dance to Kingsleys' jig, for the benefit of the whole town.'

Mick resumed eating. 'Then get off the committee. Or offer the committee equal space to tell their side of the story. Report the facts, let the good people of Bridgefield form their own conclusion about what's fair. You're the media, not the judge and jury, remember. Either way, it's news.'

Toby frowned at the blood pooling on his plate. *Medium-well done, my arse. Or has Mick's memory failed him along with his conscience?* When he looked up, Ramona was assessing him shrewdly.

'You like her, don't you?' she said. 'The one organising this whole shop thing. Lauren? Laura?'

Toby began to hack the steak off the bone. Any rarer and it'd still be mooing.

Mick snorted into his scotch and clapped a hand on Toby's shoulder.

'Paxton's a chip off the old block. Married to his job, like muggins here. Besides, that ex-wife scared him off women for good, didn't she, mate?'

A surly waiter came by, whisking away empty glasses and frowning at Toby's barely touched plate. He loitered, shamelessly eavesdropping as he wiped down the neighbouring tables. Toby lowered his voice.

'Her name's Lara. Lara McIntyre. There's nothing between us, but it doesn't make it right to outline her personal issues in the *Addy*. I'm not doing it, Mick.'

Toby set his knife and fork in the middle of his plate and pushed it away. It wasn't only the rare beef or the blood-stained chips. There was something in his mentor's dismissive laugh that had completely killed his appetite.

Nineteen

Lara gave up trying to sleep when the digital alarm clock ticked over to 4 a.m. The only consolation of such an early start was knowing she would be unlikely to bump into Toby on the road.

Her run was hard and fast, almost enough to take her mind off everything that was bothering her: the Kingsleys; the way the reporter from Ballarat had flustered her on stage; and the swirling feelings that cropped up every time she thought about Toby Paxton.

The full moon highlighted glossy snail tracks criss-crossing from one neglected garden bed to another. Lara had been looking forward to her first day off in months. *Not that I'll be relaxing at a day spa, or putting my feet up with a good book*, she thought wryly, wondering who on earth had time for those luxuries. The garden needed attention, but it too would have to stay on the back burner for a little longer.

She jogged lightly up the steps, careful of the slick layer of dew. The homestead door creaked as she unlocked and opened it, eliciting a squawk from Vegemite and the steady *thump, thump, thump* of Basil's tail on the floorboards. She tossed her sweaty running cap in the direction of the washing machine and shed her sodden singlet and shorts as she walked towards the shower. The dining table was strewn with paperwork from shop donations, raffle promotions and volunteer-wrangling timetables, items that would gobble up most of her 'day off'—but first, a hot shower and coffee.

Basil was waiting by the pantry when she padded back into the kitchen, towelling her hair. She scooped dry food into his bowl, surprised to see it empty by the time the kettle had boiled.

'On the mend, old boy?'

He cocked his head at her, and she couldn't help but smile at the sight of his droopy lip. She grabbed her phone, snapped a photo, and texted it to Evie.

> Look who's getting his appetite back. Good luck with your science test this arvo. Heading out to Nanna's memorial rock today, will call tonight. Miss you xx Mum

Basil followed as Lara carried her backpack to the door. For the first time since the snakebite, he dashed out ahead of her and did a lap around the homestead while Lara laced up her hiking boots.

'Maybe next time, buddy,' she said, chaining him up at the kennel. He turned three times clockwise, then once anticlockwise before settling down on a patch of lawn in the golden sunlight.

My life might be going to hell in a handbasket, but it's good to see someone else's is moving in an upward trajectory, she decided.

The drive to McIntyre Park was so familiar she could have done it with her eyes closed, although the stretch of ground between her family's shearing shed and the foot of the Grampians Mountain Range leading to Wildflower Ridge required her utmost attention. The Subaru bounced along the damp track. She watched the ground carefully for boggy spots that had soaked up the recent rain. Lara unlatched the same gates she'd opened and shut her entire childhood, knowing that the one in the house paddock always needed a little extra elbow-grease, and that the chain securing the east paddock had to be looped through twice to hold against the frisky, freshly shorn rams, high on the heady taste of fresh autumn grass and the weightless feeling of a clean coat.

New calves skittered away from the fence line as Lara pulled up against the McIntyre Park boundary. The mountains cast deep shadows across the paddock, the shade amplifying the cool autumn morning.

Lara zipped up her fleece jacket, looped her damp hair into a bun and nestled a baseball cap on her head. After years of running on backroads and grass tracks, the mountainside trail was a piece of cake. She soon found a steady rhythm, admiring the dimpled, lichen-covered boulders that had lain in the same mountainside spot for hundreds, probably thousands, of years.

It took an hour to climb to her mum's memorial site. Annabel's favourite vantage point was marked by a plaque on one of the biggest boulders. There was no sign of the small orchids that gave Wildflower Ridge its name, but the view always offered peace and solace. It was what she imagined church-goers found in chapels.

Lara took in the panorama of emerald paddocks, bushy shelter-belts and tiny specks of grazing stock. It took her breath away every time.

She unpacked her picnic. The wind snatched at Annabel's worn tablecloth, and a few opportunistic ants edged their way onto the blanket before Lara had even taken the lid off the banana muffins.

Leaning back against the rock, she ran her fingers across her mum's plaque.

'Hey, Mum. It's been a while.'

She breathed it in, waiting for the familiar, comforting smells to ground her. Another breath, but still her heart was heavy.

'We've almost saved the shop. You should see the list of people who've pitched in.'

The living and breathing Annabel McIntyre had always offered wise counsel, patiently listening and considering an issue before weighing in.

God, I wish you were still here. Sometimes the single vehicle accident that had taken Annabel—fracturing their teenage years—felt like a lifetime ago. Lara wasn't sure exactly when the horrid, raw loss had eased to a dull grief, but moments of uncertainty always brought back an echo of that earlier pain. Lara blinked until the tears retreated. She spoke into the wind again.

'Sam's parents are trying to weasel their way back into Evie's life. Can you believe it? As if we'd take their money.'

A butterfly floated by on the breeze and a wedge-tailed eagle soared past, its wingspan at least as wide as Lara was tall. She watched cars and machinery—no bigger than matchbox toys—shifting from farm to farm in the paddocks below, and even a crop duster on the far horizon, but the kernel of bitterness wouldn't shift.

'Mrs Beggs has given us a little longer to raise the money, but the other buyers are keen.'

She had a sudden vision of Mrs Beggs collecting offers in sealed envelopes, like a Dutch auction. Or maybe Tarquin or that dreadful family would play a game of one-upmanship, topping each other's bids.

Toby stole into her thoughts.

'What would you say about him, Mum? He's different to Sam.'

Annabel had never warmed to Sam, had never fallen for his charm.

It had been a bone of contention between them, and Lara had refused to back down. It wasn't until years later that Lara understood her mother must have glimpsed something lurking beneath Sam's charismatic façade, something she hadn't seen until much later.

Would you trust Toby, Mum? Would you be pushing us together, like Penny and Diana are? Or would you warn me to learn from my mistakes and steer well clear?

Lara finished the muffin when a wet splash landed on her arm.

'Eww,' she said with a grimace, glancing up for the culprits.

Bloody crows. The birds cackled, hovering above the picnic, before flying off. Their farewell message felt as clear as the cloudless sky.

Is that a sign?

Lara cleaned up the bird poo, dusted crumbs from her pants and glanced reluctantly at her watch.

The paperwork would keep cluttering up the dining table until she tackled it, and she had a hankering to bake. Cinnamon scrolls maybe, or fruit buns. She loaded everything into the backpack, before resting a hand on the hefty memorial stone, one last time.

'Miss you, Mum.'

Lara mulled over the decisions she needed to make as she hiked down from Wildflower Ridge. There was a lot she didn't know, but this she knew for sure: Bridgefield's General Store needed saving, and Annabel would be proud to see Lara at the forefront of the campaign.

⅋

Toby massaged the bridge of his nose the following morning, hoping that if he did it for long enough, perhaps when he reopened his eyes the front page would magically reappear with the article he'd filed and sent to the printers the night before.

He drew in a ragged breath and tentatively peeked at the desk again.

For crying out loud . . .

Still the same shocking headline. *'Friction between committee and community!'* For the first time in his journalism career, Toby felt ashamed to call himself a newspaper man.

'Bugger it!'

He thumped the desk, impotent rage fuelling the string of scathing curses for the colleague who'd whipped up the one-sided front-pager. The table quivered at the blow, making his mug jump. Stone-cold coffee splashed between the delete and return key. He made another attempt to contact the Ballarat newsroom. The dial tone was busy. *Again.*

In all his years at *The Ballarat Daily* he'd never imagined Mick would betray him like this. But the black ink didn't leave much room for misinterpretation. Somebody had changed the front page, and it wasn't Toby.

The receptionist stuck her head around the door.

'Get up on the wrong side of bed, did you? You'll scare away the early customers, Toby. And didn't you say yourself that the *Addy* couldn't afford to drop many more subscribers?'

Toby blew out an exasperated breath. This coming from a woman who got on the grog at lunchtime.

He lifted the newspaper and turned the front page towards her.

'*This!* Idiots like Dougal O'Leary writing gutter-trash articles like *this* will scare away the readers, not me ranting and raving. For God's sake, Nancy, if Mick or anyone from *The Ballarat Daily* ever try to reach me when I'm out of the office, I want you to drive over to my house and bang the door down. The *Addy* is better than this.' The sense of betrayal was overwhelming. *How could Mick do this without telling me?*

And then another, perhaps more disturbing thought: *What will Lara think?*

Toby stood up, moving with purpose. He needed to find Lara and explain before someone else did. He looked at his watch. Quarter to eight. Early enough that she'd be up, but if he was lucky, she wouldn't have left for work yet.

'You said to divert your calls last night, so I did,' Nancy said with a careless shrug. 'And you were right shitty when I phoned you the last time you had a migraine. You said—'

Her lack of initiative was mortifying.

'I would have wanted to be disturbed for something like this, Nancy. Surely you can see what a spot this puts us in?'

Toby reached into his camera bag for his keys, then swore. Of all the days to cycle to work. The morning's clear, crisp sky had been replaced by steely clouds and the threat of more rain.

He held out his hand to the receptionist.

'Car keys,' he commanded, snatching a fresh copy of the newspaper from the front bench.

'The work car's getting a service. The mechanic picked it up last night, said he'll have it back this arvo sometime. Here, borrow mine.'

Toby tried not to cringe as Nancy handed over a keyring complete with a fluffy rabbit foot.

Clouds scudded across the sky as he drove the hot-pink VW Beetle towards Lara's property. The wind blew straight through the gaps where the white convertible roof was attached to the pink metal frame, and even the galahs flew up from the roadside, terrified by either the hole in the exhaust or the garish paint job. Quite possibly both.

Light drizzle coated the windscreen as he turned into Lara's driveway and saw her Subaru parked by the steps. Basil barked a greeting from his kennel, but there was no answer when he knocked on the heavy front door.

He took in the ankle-length lawn and weeds creeping into Lara's garden—a ripple effect of all the hours she was dedicating to the shop campaign—and then looked down at the newspaper in his hands.

And this is how we've repaid her.

He stuffed the paper into his back pocket.

A series of sharp claps came from behind the corrugated-iron shearing shed.

'Hey, hey, c'moooon.'

Toby headed across the yard, narrowly avoiding an upturned wheelbarrow. Lara was standing with a trio of large cows. To Toby's untrained eye, they looked identical to the ones that trotted along her boundary fence line most mornings.

Her singlet and leggings seemed an odd choice for cattle herding.

'Get out, you buggers. Hey! Hey!'

She clapped her hands again, stepping between the steers and the small silo behind the shearing shed. A mound of golden grain was piled underneath the silo spout.

'Looks like they found the feed supply?' said Toby.

Lara whirled around at the sound of his voice.

'Exactly what I needed after a fifteen-k run. My legs are still sore from yesterday's hike too. Mind you, it would've been worse if I hadn't noticed it. Now they know where the grain lives, they'll knock it over trying to get more,' she said. Toby followed Lara's lead and together they herded the cattle back into the paddock.

She threw him a smile as she latched the gate, locking the cattle out of the shearing-shed yard.

'Thanks. You probably saved me another half-hour trying to wrangle them back in. Any longer standing around in this misty rain and I'd be frozen solid. What brings you out here?'

Toby swallowed, preparing to obliterate the goodwill they had generated.

Like ripping off a bandaid.

'Actually, you're not going to be thanking me in a minute.'

He handed her the newspaper and watched the colour drain from her face.

'You let them publish this? This . . . this *bullshit*?' She scanned the article, her face tight with fury. 'For God's sake! What type of rubbish is this?'

He waited for a pause before trying to explain.

'I didn't know they were going to print it, Lara. The newspaper looked nothing like that when I put the edition to bed last night, honestly. The Ballarat office went straight over my head.'

Toby looked at the front page again, shame enveloping him.

Lara's pale face flushed with anger.

'*You're* the editor, though, aren't you?' She flipped to the inside page and jabbed a finger at his smiling headshot beside the newspaper's contact details and social-media handles.

The cows jostled at the gate, bellowing indignantly. The drizzle segued into heavy droplets that soaked the newspaper.

Lara swiped a damp lock of hair behind her ear and, with a shaky hand, pushed the newspaper towards him. Rain ran down her face and dripped off her chin.

'I would never do that,' he said, stretching out a tentative hand. She was well within her rights to slap it away, to rip the newspaper back out of his hands and whack him over the head with it. 'I swear on my daughter's life, Lara.' Suddenly, there was nothing more important than making sure she knew he would never publish something like this. 'I wouldn't betray you like that, but I'll have a crack at nailing the bastards who did,' he said.

Lara held his gaze as silence fell between them, leaving only the sound of rain thudding against the silver tin, the cheeky cows lowing and the wind whistling through the gum trees.

Toby could almost imagine the internal battle going on inside her head. She shivered, rubbing her arms. He quickly pulled his jumper over his head and wrapped it around her icy-cold shoulders.

'There's no way the town wants you stepping down, Lara. Look how much they rely on you, how you've almost single-handedly raised the money. Are you okay?'

'Apart from freezing my butt off,' she said quietly.

They strode towards the house, skirting around newly formed puddles in Lara's driveway. He hesitated at his car, not wanting to leave her to digest the news on her own, but not wanting to presume anything, or barge into her personal space either.

She paused on the verandah steps.

'Don't think you're getting away that easily. Fill me in over coffee, yeah?' Even though her tone was gruff, the upswing on her last word hinted at both vulnerability and an attempt at trust.

The rain hammered down harder. They jogged up the steps but Lara paused at the door.

'Turn around.'

He turned around in time to catch lightning dance across the horizon, and counted as he waited for the rumble of thunder. Lara was the only person he'd met in Bridgefield who regularly locked her house.

Samuel Kingsley sure had a lot to answer for.

'Come on, then,' said Lara.

He slipped off his shoes.

Lara led him down the hallway and opened a cupboard door. The scent of soap and washing powder in the linen press was the same as the fragrance he often caught on Lara. She tossed a towel in his direction.

'Thanks,' he said, wiping his face and then towelling his hair.

'Shower's through there,' she said, opening the door directly to his left.

He took one look at the goosebumps covering her entire body. 'You go first, you look frozen solid.'

Toby could see courtesy jarring against common sense, and he was relieved when she didn't argue.

'I'll just be a minute. Kitchen's that way,' she said, pointing towards the light-filled room at the end of the hallway.

Toby padded across the floorboards slowly, pausing at the black-and-white prints lined up in mismatched frames. They were mostly of Evie, some alone and a few with Lara, as well as candid snapshots of the extended McIntyre family. The only image of Lara by herself was an action shot from a running race—a marathon, judging by the water bottles strapped around her waist and the streams of people either side of her—an expression of pained triumph written across her face.

Toby found the living area tucked away at the back of the house. Downlights illuminated the vaulted ceiling. He gravitated towards the freestanding wood fire, relishing the radiant heat and taking in the large, open-plan kitchen. With the high ceilings and large windows, he imagined it would be filled with natural light on a less gloomy day.

He'd expected it to be tidy, because everything about Lara was organised, but the bold navy cabinetry, high-end appliances and copper fittings were a surprise.

This was a statement kitchen, the colours and extra-wide oven chosen by a person who knew what they liked. And if those glass cannisters on the bench, brimming with yo-yos, rum balls and Anzac biscuits were any indication, Lara obviously put it to good use. A rustle came from behind the dining table and he turned to see a black-and-white bird in a wire cage.

A magpie?

Lara didn't like birds, though . . . Hadn't she been jumping for joy when he'd hit those birds by McCluskey's shearing shed?

He hadn't pegged Lara as the wildlife-rescuing type, but then he hadn't expected a kitchen like this either. He smiled to himself as he looked around, picking up extra little pieces of the Lara McIntyre puzzle. A boxed set of *Friends* DVDs rested on the rustic coffee table. Framed landscapes painted in bright watercolours hung on the wall. He took in the shopping list stuck to her fridge, postcards lined up neatly beside the kettle, two matching cane baskets brimming with lemons and eggs and an anaemic-looking house plant. He crossed the kitchen with purpose, and unable to help himself, stuck a finger in the soil. Dry as chips. So, there *was* something Lara wasn't brilliant at.

Easily fixed.

Toby watered the peace lily, and as the soil moistened beneath the plant's dull green leaves, he wondered what it would take to revive something that had been neglected for so long. All living things responded to gentle nurturing, surely?

❦

The rain was bucketing down when Lara unclipped the lock on the bathroom door. She dressed quickly, then carried a bathrobe into the kitchen.

Toby was practically sitting on top of the wood fire.

'This should fit,' she said. 'Toss your clothes out the bathroom door and I'll put them in the dryer while you shower.'

Toby's lips twitched. Amused or suspicious, she wasn't sure. Did he think she was going to wait until he was naked and feed his clothes into the fire? Or perhaps he thought this was her style of seduction?

'You're heading back to work afterwards, right? Go ahead and catch your death if you want, but your clothes will dry quickly on the hot setting. Faster than going back home and changing,' she said through stiff lips. 'And I want to hear exactly how that front page came about.'

Lara waited until the bathroom door closed and the shower started before she ventured down the hallway again. Tossing his damp clothes into the dryer, she returned to the kitchen to find two mugs of coffee on the island bench. She took a sip, surprised he'd remembered the way she took it. She smiled for all of a second, until she recalled the newspaper headline.

The relief of discovering Toby wasn't responsible for the article was short-lived. Everyone in Bridgefield would be talking about it, regardless of who wrote it. They couldn't drop the ball on the shop campaign now, not when they were so close to buying it.

Vegemite flapped in his cage, pecking at the bars. Lara rolled her shoulders, trying to decide which juggling ball she needed to catch first. The magpie squawked. Like the cattle, he would take matters into his own hands if she neglected him.

'Righto, Vegemite, keep your hair on,' she said, removing the bulldog clip and unlatching his cage.

He hopped out, walked along the bench to the fruit bowl and helped himself to a grape.

Feed the animals, eat breakfast, work my arse off to fix this mess, then save the shop—just a regular day, she told herself, mixing vitamins into the raw mince for the bird's breakfast. *And that's without trying to work out exactly how the Kingsleys were involved in all this mess.*

Washing her hands, she pulled last night's cinnamon scrolls from the pantry and placed two on a plate. The microwave dinged as Toby walked into the kitchen. His hairy legs looked out of place poking out beneath her bathrobe. Even though it gave more coverage than the sports gear he normally wore, there was something much more intimate about a blue fluffy belt being the difference between clothed Toby and full-frontal-nude Toby. She focused on serving up the warm scrolls.

Come off it, Lara.

She snuck another look at him as she pushed his plate across the island bench.

'Thanks,' he said catching her eye, his gentle smile nearly her undoing.

Gah.

Any minute now she'd rip the damn robe from his fine body.

'Help yourself,' she said, biting into the soft, sweet icing. The magpie hopped down from the fruit bowl and tiptoed across the bench. 'Not you, cheeky,' she said, scooping Vegemite onto her hand and placing him on her shoulder. Lara offered a morsel of cinnamon scroll to the bird.

Toby looked from her to the magpie, amusement written in the curve of his lips.

'So, how are we going to fix this?'

Twenty

The Subaru's windscreen wipers worked at full tilt as Lara drove into town.

Parking as close as possible to the general store's back door, she tugged her hooded jacket over her head and sprinted inside, only to see Karen, Denise and Pearl spring apart, as if they'd been caught snooping.

'Your ears must've been ringing, love. We were looking at this sorry excuse for a newspaper.' Pearl jabbed the latest edition with her finger.

'Now, brace yourself, dear,' came Denise's kind voice, her face crinkled with concern. 'There's a nasty story that beggars belief, but—'

Lara held up a hand. 'It's okay, I already know about it,' she said, flipping the newspaper over so it was face-down on the counter. The headline was even larger than she remembered.

'I spoke to Toby—'

The doorbell jangled and a familiar Driza-Bone-clad figure walked through the door, water beading off the jacket and pooling on the large mat. Her father removed his Akubra.

'Where's Paxton, then?' Angus growled. 'He's got a lot to answer for, the double-crossing so-and-so. I've cleaned my rifle, reckon I'll do a little target practice around his place tonight, make sure he knows how we feel about reporters stirring up trouble.' It would almost have been funny, the combination of anger and disappointment so foreign on her father's face, if he hadn't been deadly serious.

Penny and Diana came through behind him, doing their best drowned-rat impersonations. Baby Lucy popped out from underneath Penny's buttoned-up raincoat like a Jack-in-the-box, her giggle instantly lightening the mood.

'We don't want you to step down—you know that, right?' Penny looped an arm through Lara's. It had been the hardest part of the article to digest. A quote from an anonymous source implying exactly that.

'Definitely not,' chimed Pearl. 'You should sue the paper.'

'You should sue the Kingsleys or Toby more like it,' grumbled Angus.

Lara took a deep breath. She'd hoped this would be the reaction from her committee, but it was nonetheless a relief to hear their support voiced out loud.

'Holster your guns, Clint Eastwood,' Lara said, looking at her father. 'Toby said he had nothing to do with it.'

'And you believe him, love?' Angus eyed her warily, reaching for the newspaper.

'Yep,' said Lara. 'He came around early this morning, as soon as he found out.'

'It probably doesn't feel like it now, Lars, but all publicity is good publicity,' offered Penny, squeezing Lara into a hug. 'And we can sic the Press Council onto them, make an official complaint when we've got a second to scratch ourselves.' Penny looked at the calendar on the wall. Winter was not far off and the fundraising weekend was in three weeks. 'Which isn't right now. Best we can do is ignore it and hope Toby can pump our fundraisers up in the two editions between now and then. Anyone who matters is smart enough to make up their own mind.'

'It'll just make everyone even more determined to support the cause,' added Diana, ratcheting up her optimistic tone at the sight of their father's doubtful expression.

Angus jabbed a finger at the newspaper.

'But it's complete fiction. It's not the committee versus the community. We're all working together.'

'Penny's right, Dad. We've got bigger fish to fry now. Toby called head office from my kitchen. His editor is off sick but they were adamant they wouldn't issue a retraction,' she said.

'I can't understand why they'd print such tripe. Did the Kingsleys tip them off, then? Is that why they were at the meeting, to see if you could be forced into accepting their donation?' Angus looked around the room.

'It could be a coincidence,' Penny offered.

'No such thing,' said Pearl. 'Newspapers aren't what they used to be.'

'Toby said his boss was keen to add more spice to the newspaper, but this is taking it a bit far,' Lara said.

'So, you'll stay on as the head of the committee, despite this . . . this garbage?' asked Pearl.

Lara nodded. 'If you want me to.'

Everyone in the general store agreed. Lara's heart soared.

'Right, onward and upward, then. While you're all here, let's go through everything that needs doing this week. We can't afford to let this derail us, or you can say goodbye to the Bridgefield General Store and hello to man-buns, soy lattes and tofu quiche.'

Just like she'd done all those years ago, Lara mentally pallet-wrapped the Kingsley family dramas and forklifted them into a box right at the back of her mind, to be unpacked at a later date. She would give them a piece of her mind afterwards, maybe sew a few yabbies into the seams of their sumptuous dining-room drapes, but right now, she had a shop to save.

⁂

Toby stood up and stretched, feeling like a half-opened pocket knife as he did his closing sweep of the newspaper premises. It felt like an eon since he'd left home this morning. He'd copped flak all day, and though he'd been almost as livid about the front page as Lara, he hadn't expected such strong hostility from the Bridgefield residents who thought he was responsible.

'You should get a T-shirt printed saying "That front page had nothing to do with me",' Nancy had marvelled, after watching Toby explain himself to yet another customer. It hadn't mattered that he'd printed a dozen good stories about the shop campaign beforehand, or that the next edition and the one after would be resplendent with factual and optimistic articles.

A light on the office landline flashed. How had he missed that one? *Probably another indignant community member calling to give me a serve.* With a yawn, Toby sat back down into his office chair and pressed the blinking light. *At least Lara's on my side*, he reminded himself. It had made the storm a lot easier to weather.

Mick's gravelly voice came through on the voicemail.

'Got your message. I know you're pissed off, but you're there to report the news, Paxton, even if you don't agree, or it upsets the apple cart. Something else has cropped up, call me back.'

There's more?

Toby groaned and redialled his boss's number.

Ramona answered, her tinkling laugh like chalk on a blackboard.

'Toby, we were just talking about you. I'll hand you over to Mick so he can share the good news.'

Good news?

After the front-page fiasco, Toby couldn't imagine what now constituted Mick's version of good news. Exclusive scoops on car-accident victims? Slander campaigns? Football WAGS overdosing?

Mick cleared his throat when he came on the phone, then said simply: 'We're having a baby.'

Toby wasn't sure what he was expecting, but it wasn't that. He almost laughed out loud. *Is Mick nuts?* He couldn't imagine going back to nappies and toddler tantrums himself, let alone as a first-time parent with an extra twenty years on the clock. Ramona's excited chatter carried on in the background.

'Congratulations . . .' Toby drew the word out, unsure if it was the right answer.

'Cheers,' said Mick with a gruff laugh. 'Never thought it'd happen to me, but I'm going to give it all I've got. Ramona's beside herself with excitement. I wanted to tell you before she pasted it all over social media. Fancy coming back to the Ballarat office sooner rather than later? You can shadow me a few months before I take an early retirement.' Mick coughed. 'If you still want the job, that is?'

Toby leaned back in his chair. He'd planned to blast Mick about the front page, not congratulate him or stand slack-jawed and speechless. Headlights flickered through the gaps in his office blinds.

It was what he'd always wanted, wasn't it? The job his father had encouraged him to work for since high school. But now it was within his grasp, his thoughts didn't linger on the city job. He swivelled around on his chair, taking in the office plant that thrived on a diet of 10 per cent rain water and 90 per cent cold coffee dregs, the stack of newspapers with his by-line scattered throughout, the colourful thank-you cards from the Bridgefield Primary students, and the whiteboard that contained the most important info for the upcoming fun run.

'Who's going to head up the Bridgefield paper?' he said slowly.

'Christ knows, Paxton. I'm more concerned about the hair dye Ramona bought the same day the pregnancy test came back positive. She reckons it'll prevent me being mistaken for the kid's grandfather. What's it to you anyway, mate? That little posting was a stepping stone for the Ballarat job. This is your get-out-of-jail-free card. Surely you're not going to turn it down because you're still peeved about today's little front pager?'

Little front pager?

Toby's mobile buzzed. He pulled it away from his ear and saw a message from Lara.

5 a.m. at McCluskey's gate? Fun-run planning meeting while on the run? ☺

It wasn't the first text she'd sent him, but it was the first time she'd added a smiley-face emoji. He stared at the message. Murphy's Law was a bitch. Two mutually exclusive things arriving at the exact same time.

Mick was halfway through a sentence when Toby put the phone back to his ear '. . . and there's a keen reporter we might shove in the hot seat at Bridgefield. He wouldn't know a sheep from a goat, but he'll find his feet quick enough. It's hardly the *Sydney Morning Herald*, right?'

Toby raked a hand through his hair and stood up. That scenario seemed about as counterintuitive as letting three urbanites turn the general store into a juice or karaoke bar.

'I don't know what to think, Mick. Give me a week or two to get my head around it, yeah?'

He heard the incredulity in his mentor's response. 'A week? What's to think about? Don't leave it too long, Paxton. Every journo in my newsroom would give their eye teeth to take over my spot. If I'm honest with you, that little paper's a slowly-sinking ship. There's only so long we can keep propping it up.'

Toby locked the back door, and as he ran his hands along the bluestone walls, the blocks cut from the same quarry as those used to build the pub and the general store, he realised how much the small town had grown on him over the past six months. *The newspaper, the town or the people?* He asked himself, placing his camera bag in the boot of the Volkswagen.

Or maybe, just maybe, one particular person?

%

A mangy fox ran right in front of Lara as she turned out of her driveway and onto the limestone road the following week. She scrunched up her nose against the acrid smell of fox spray lingering in the air. If Basil had been there, he would have made it his mission to track down the fox and stir up McCluskey's donkeys in the process. She was grateful he remained tucked up in his kennel.

She could see Toby approaching the shearing shed—or what remained of it—a minute after her. The bones of the building had long since stopped smouldering, but the smell of ash and smoke lingered.

'East or west?'

'East, then we'll see the sun peep over the horizon,' he said.

Lara led the way and her cattle announced themselves via a stampede of hooves along the fence line.

'Morning, cows,' Lara called.

'Morning, cows,' Toby echoed, the amusement in his voice making Lara smile again.

Who even am I? Grinning like a loon because I'm no longer the only one greeting the local bovine community. Lucky it's dark. She checked herself. *And it's not a date anyway, it's just a run. A fun-run planning run, at that, just like the last two.*

'So, what loose ends need tidying up before the weekend?' she said. 'Evie has a student-free day Friday, so I've added her to the early-bird registration table.'

'Holly's keen as mustard too. That'll be perfect. I'm pretty sure it's out of the goodness of her heart, nothing to do with your nephew,' he said dryly. 'Entries keep flooding in, we're sitting at about two hundred registrations overall.'

Lara nearly stumbled. 'Two hundred runners? Last I heard, you had one-fifty?'

'I called in a few favours in the athletics industry, bartered some website copywriting, a few media releases in return for them bombarding their contact lists with the details. But, how about those raffle tickets?'

'They're coming along. Penny's virtual tour of the apartment has had over a thousand views already,' said Lara, not bothering to hide the pride in her voice. Raffling off the apartment had gone down better than she'd dared to hope. 'And as much as I hate to admit it, the "Save the Shop" campaign did pretty well out of that awful front-page article,' she said. 'Even if it was fake news.'

Toby groaned. 'Don't say that too loudly, I'm still not happy with Mick's half-hearted apology. Sorry I didn't see it coming either, I'm sure it was the last thing you needed.'

'Stop apologising, I'm relieved it at least generated more ticket sales. And we'll pump the raffle up over the weekend. Mrs Beggs is planning to draw the winning ticket on Sunday at the end of the fun run.'

They turned towards the lake and started to weave their way downhill. Lara snuck a look at her watch. They were setting a good pace.

'And what about your in-laws?' Toby asked. 'Did you confront them about the newspaper tip off? Bet it felt good telling them you'll raise the money without their help?'

Lara looked out at the shimmering lake, its rippled surface reflecting the moon, the low-hanging clouds, the soft glow of the fresh day ahead. She hadn't heard from the Kingsleys since the night of the town meeting, and though Evie hadn't mentioned any more visits, she'd texted her a photo of a beautiful new top with the caption, 'OMG look at this, Mum!' Edwina had dubbed it a late birthday present, but Lara knew exactly what it was: a bribe.

'To be honest, I've spent way too long caring what other people think, especially them,' said Lara. 'I mean, I won't stop Evie from seeing them, but I'm not going to send them a told-you-so letter to prove we could raise the money without them.'

She hesitated. It was easier to dismiss the Kingsleys' offer for the shop, but what about Karl and Edwina's budding relationship with Evie? Was showering their granddaughter with new clothes and fancy meals only the start? Would it lead to tropical getaways and overseas expeditions to far-flung places Lara could never afford? The 'what ifs' nagged at her more than she'd like to admit.

Lara looked across at Toby. Should she confide in him?

Maybe every parent felt this rush of guilt and worried they would never be able to give their child the world. Or was it a single-parent speciality?

'What's up?'

She shook her head.

'Nothing,' she said eventually. This morning was too beautiful for dwelling on fears or insecurities.

Toby changed the topic smoothly.

'You excited about the ball?'

This made her laugh. 'I was planning on avoiding it with a ten-foot barge pole. My sisters seem to think single means miserable and I wouldn't put it past them to slingshot me into the middle of the desperate and dateless punters.'

His soft chuckle made her heart beat faster. 'I think your sisters have been talking to *my* sister.'

Lara squeezed in next to him to accommodate the narrow pedestrian bridge. His arm brushed against hers, sending a delicious tingle right through her.

'I'm not big on those type of things,' she admitted.

'Me neither,' he said, a smile in his voice, and as the sun peeked over the east side of Bridgefield Lake, Lara felt something stirring deep inside her. *Hope.*

Twenty-one

Toby came home from work on Thursday afternoon, poured a glass of red wine and set his laptop on the bench.

He had the freezer open, deliberating between a frozen curry and a frozen tomato soup when the computer started to chime.

'Perfect timing, Lollypop,' he said, putting the curry into the microwave and answering the Skype call. She waved at him from the computer screen.

Toby took his glass of wine and dinner to the dining table, eating while they Skyped. Whitney Houston blared from the stereo in the background and Belinda danced into view.

'Yeah, I wanna dance with somebody,' Belinda sang, offering her wooden spoon microphone to her niece, who declined.

'Aunt Belinda's music-appreciation classes continue, I see?'

Holly shook her head. 'Tell me the DJ you've booked for next week's ball has a bigger range than just eighties and nineties music?'

Toby laughed. 'That's Penny and Diana's event, not mine. But I think they've got a band organised. You can join them on stage with your clarinet if you like?'

Holly rolled her eyes. 'Think I'll stick to waiting tables, thanks, Dad.'

Belinda reappeared in the background.

'Hey, that reminds me, Tobes. Miss Holly tells me you've got a big gig next weekend and nothing to wear.'

Toby huffed. 'Ye of little faith. I've got plenty of options.'

Their laughter echoed through the computer speakers.

'You've got to see it to believe it, Aunty Bel,' said Holly. 'Go on, Dad. Give us a virtual wardrobe tour.'

Toby left his dishes on the table and carried his laptop to the bedroom. He pulled a tan suede jacket from a dry-cleaning bag.

'There's this.'

Belinda mirrored Holly's aghast expression.

'Give Billy Ray Cyrus his jacket back and get something new. Something with a bit of style, Tobes. If you're going to be at a singles ball, you may as well stand out, right? Catch the eye of some gorgeous girl and whisk her off her feet?'

Toby laughed. There was only one woman he wanted to whisk off her feet, and he wasn't about to put the mockers on it by mentioning Lara to this pair.

'It's a classic. Pure nineties. I'm there to help, not pick up. I'll find a funky tie and call it quits, yeah?'

'Maybe a bow tie?' Holly piped up.

Belinda shook her head and made him rifle through his wardrobe.

'It's like *Fifty Shades of Grey*, but without any of the hot sex. I can guarantee you'll be celibate for another five years if you wear that number in public,' she said, pointing to the dull pinstripe suit Toby had pulled out.

He swung the door shut.

'I'll wear my chinos and a polo shirt, then, shall I? Or if it worries you that much, maybe I'll skip it altogether and rest up for the fun run on Sunday.'

'You can't let the team down, Dad. Not after all your lectures about community involvement. What about your whole "There's no 'I' in 'team'" spiel? It'd be totally hypocritical.'

Belinda snorted. 'See, this is the problem with raising smart, independent young women. If only you'd deprived her of books and a proper education, you wouldn't have this issue.'

Holly giggled and she slung an arm around her aunt's shoulders.

'Oh, you'll get your just deserts when your kid comes along,' Toby said. Belinda rubbed her pregnant belly like a genie with a lamp.

'Leave the ball outfit with us. We'll come up with something, won't we, Holly?'

Toby carried his laptop back to the lounge room as the pair chortled. Knowing that Holly and Belinda hung out regularly made him feel better about being so far away. If he took Mick's job, he could have Holly week on, week off, instead of Skype dinner dates, sporadic long weekends and school holidays. It was tempting.

'How're Granny and Pop? Queenie still hanging in there?'

Being closer to his parents would be a big bonus of shifting back, too. Alice wouldn't say it, but he knew the extra help wouldn't go astray.

'Same old, same old. Pop's cheerful enough, and Granny just got a letter from Queen Elizabeth, so she's thrilled.'

'Queen Elizabeth's lowly assistant, more like it,' said Toby, though he wouldn't dare say it to his mother.

Toby was rewarded with an eye roll and he settled in for Holly's mid-week update on all things Ballarat. Somewhere between the rowing try-outs and the clarinet teacher's body-odour issues, Toby found his attention straying to the window. *Is Lara still up?* He wondered if he should text her and suggest a nightcap. But by the time Holly had run out of news, and Belinda had given him more detail than he needed about her birthing plan, the lights across the paddock had flickered off. He looked out into the night, rinsed his wine glass and stacked the dishwasher. He'd just have to knock her socks off at the ball.

∽

As the weekend drew closer, Lara found herself even more excited than she could've imagined. The flurry of final permits came in all at once, just in the nick of time, and she was flat out trying to get the right signatures on the right dotted lines.

There were deliveries of catering supplies to arrange, trailer-loads of marshalling equipment to be collected from the athletics club in Horsham, and trophies to be picked up from the sports shop in Hamilton. Lara bounced out of bed on Friday to find the morning had dawned fresh and clear, with dew-dropped spiderwebs hanging off every twig. She smashed out five fast kilometres, grabbed a quick bowl of Weet-Bix and fed the animals before making her way into Bridgefield to help with the set-up.

'Perfect timing, we need someone nimble to scale that tree and string up a bunch of fairy lights,' said Diana, leaning a ladder against the old oak in the centre of town.

It was the type of job Cameron would have loved, but he'd gone with Pete to collect Evie from the bus stop, along with the trophies from the sports shop.

'I'll do it,' said Lara.

'Mind you don't break your neck on the way down,' called Diana from the ground, her face scrunched up with concern as Lara shimmied up. Lara did a little wiggle, laughing at the way Diana's eyebrows flew skyward. The fact that she, Penny and Angie were fully grown with children of their own hadn't made a lick of difference to Diana's mothering instinct; she was still undoubtedly the mother hen of the McIntyre family.

Lara took a moment to survey Bridgefield from her elevated vantage point. What the small town lacked in hustle and fast-food outlets, it made up for in charming buildings, dainty silver princess eucalypts along the main drag and the close-knit community. *All our hard work with the shop was worth it*, she thought, taking in a breath of fresh country air as she descended the ladder.

A peal of laughter came from across the street and the sisters looked up to see a pair of women walking down the footpath.

'Those girls arrived last night,' Diana said quietly. 'Single and ready to mingle, or so they told me.' The local B&B operators had been booked solid for weeks in advance. As well as raising money to help buy the shop, their fundraising weekend was pushing dollars into the local economy.

'You two were right, the singles ball was a drawcard,' said Lara.

'Sorry?' Diana cupped her ear for good measure. 'Little louder, thanks.'

'You were right, okay. It's a good money spinner.'

Angie strode over with a tray of takeaway cups.

'Olive opened the shop early for me,' Angie said, handing out coffee. 'She said those girls were knocking on the door before she'd even finished sorting the mail. Apparently—' Angie looked over her shoulder and leaned in a little closer. 'Tommo down at the pub said their table-top dancing kept last night's regulars glued to their bar stools for twice as long as usual. Flaming sambuca shots and everything.'

Diana groaned. 'Will his insurance foot the bill if the hotel accidentally burns to the ground? I hope they got it out of their system. We don't want tonight to be remembered for all the wrong reasons.'

'Or to spend our fundraising money on damage control,' added Penny. 'I'll have a word to Tommo and make sure he locks up the flammable spirits.'

She headed off, intent on her task.

A beeping noise rang through the morning air and Lara turned to see her father's Leyland truck inching backwards across the town green. Tim was in the driver's seat and the tray was piled high with hired dining equipment.

Lara held up her hand.

'Yep, Tim. That'll do it.'

Lara started untying the ratchet straps holding the load in place.

Tim climbed down from the truck cab and loosened the straps on the opposite side.

'Did Mac tell you she's got a waiting list for the ball tonight?' The pride in her brother-in-law's voice was almost as cute as his pet name for Penny.

'She's excelled herself. The fun run's almost at capacity too, all thanks to her marketing and Toby's coverage. Couldn't have done it without them,' she said.

'Not to mention a bucketload of work from you, Miss Modesty. I thought you'd be dead on your feet after all the hours you've put in, Lara, but you look like you're loving it. Nanna Pearl said you've already surpassed the fundraising target,' he said.

'I've got a good committee behind me,' she said. 'Though you're right, I am loving life now things are going smoothly again. Ask me again Sunday afternoon, and I might be singing from a different song sheet.'

Angie's husband Rob wandered across from the general store, Claudia on his shoulders, clutching that morning's newspaper.

He flipped it open as he walked. 'Hot off the press. The famous McIntyre girls. I'll have to get your autograph before you're mobbed,' Rob said, showing her the picture.

'He could have made it a little less prominent,' Lara said, groaning as she took in the huge front-page photo of her, Angie, Diana and Penny surrounding Mrs Beggs outside the shop, taken two days earlier when they'd officially bettered Mrs Beggs' asking price. The headline was a little more palatable this time. Toby had gone with *"Community spirit saves the day!"* and though their grins were cheesy, he'd captured the triumph and joy in their expressions.

'Thought you hated having your photo taken? This is the third time you've been in the newspaper this month.' Tim leaned in for a closer look, then cast a quizzical gaze in her direction.

'I've only got a problem if I don't know it's being taken,' Lara said. 'Obviously, I'd rather the credit went to all the committee, not just us.'

Angie pulled up outside the hall, antique milk pails and buckets of flowers brimming on the back of Rob's ute tray.

'Bunch of slackers. I'm out there picking posies for tonight's ball and you're having a good old chinwag?'

Angie laughed and thrust a milk pail full of lavender, proteas and banksias into Rob's arms. Lara recognised some of the colourful blooms and foliage from Diana's garden too.

'Perving on these cover girls,' Tim said, showing her the newspaper.

'Scrub up all right, don't we?' Angie said, turning it outwards so Diana could see too. Penny returned with a promise from the publican that he would stick to beer and wine tonight.

'There's my girls,' said Angus, joining them a moment later. Lara reached up and plucked the price tag off his new shirt, catching a whiff of something nice as he hurried off to help his sons-in-law.

'Was Dad wearing aftershave?'

'He's putting his best foot forward, that's for sure,' said Penny, waggling her eyebrows.

'Never thought I'd see the day,' mused Lara, carrying one of the tables into the hall. The idea of her father wanting romance made her head spin. He'd always said he was more than happy on his own, and she'd pulled out that same line more than once to fend off Penny's matchmaking attempts.

Inside, the hall decorating was in full swing. A wash of chatter floated towards them and Lara stepped aside to make way for the ladies from the Move It or Lose It exercise classes, who swooped in with blue linen tablecloths and little heart-shaped sequins.

'Almost as good a workout as the classes,' said Karen, hefting a miniature windmill onto the table. The table-number holders were exact replicas of the windmill overlooking the lake.

Lara moved across the room, straightening a flower that had slipped from one of Angie's antique milk pails. She sidestepped to avoid a procession of band members and marvelled at the musicians' ability to make it on stage without dropping their instruments. In the time she'd been admiring the hall's transformation, the stage had filled with an assortment of guitars, drums, amplifiers, music stands and microphones.

Volunteers from the CWA swarmed in and out of the hall kitchen, hefting containers of food and armfuls of cooking equipment. From the smell of things, the meal prep was well underway too. Lara took a deep, delicious breath. The aroma of roast lamb made her mouth water.

'Testing, testing. One, two.'

Lara covered her ears as the microphone screeched with feedback. She retreated outside, just in time to help Tim unload the final table.

'What's next on the list?' she said. 'I've got another half-hour before I'm needed at work.'

Penny glanced at her watch. 'I've got some banners that need hanging from the "Welcome to Bridgefield" sign, if you fancy a quick drive out to the sixty-k zone?'

'Too easy.'

'Thanks, Lars. See you tonight. Wear your dancing shoes.'

Lara paused at the mischievous note in her sister's voice. 'I'm not here to impress anyone.'

Penny gave a dismissive huff. 'Heaven forbid you actually enjoy yourself.'

Lara frowned at the love-heart bunting she'd helped string across the doorway of the town hall and lifted her chin.

'I'm the raffle and fun-run girl. You, Angie and Diana are on the singles ball, remember? I'm happy to help with set-up, registration and pack up, but that's about it.'

Lara heard Penny's heavy sigh as she folded her into a hug. She caught the scent of stale milk lingering in her sister's hair—a reminder that Penny was juggling an infant as well as a huge fundraising event—and knew she needed to set aside her reservations about the singles ball. Whether she liked the concept or not, Lara needed this weekend to be a success.

'Righto, which banner do you want at the southern end of town?'

※

Lara tugged on her nursing cardigan and then her jacket before stepping out into the brisk afternoon. The sun had started its slide to the horizon when Evie jogged up to the car.

'Missed you, Mum!'

'You too, Evie-girl,' said Lara, hugging her daughter a little tighter than normal.

'Hard day at work?' said Evie, jumping into the car.

'Probably less frantic than yours,' Lara said. 'I heard you and Cameron well and truly earned your pocket money.'

'We barely stopped for lunch. Napkin folding, wine glass polishing, all the little errands the CWA ladies needed running.' Evie paused for effect. 'Not sure what you would've done without us, really. This event-planning business is harder than it looks.'

Lara raised an eyebrow and grinned. 'You don't say?'

It wasn't until they were halfway home that Lara noticed Evie's clothes. The light-pink jumper and polka-dotted scarf didn't look familiar.

Irritation flared at once. Another Edwina Kingsley treat?

Fashion had never been high on Lara's radar, and items that required handwashing or ironing rarely made it into her wardrobe. She purchased most of their clothes on sale, always practical, hard-wearing garments that were tough enough for knocking around the farm, but tidy enough to wear into town. Evie had never complained, but . . .

Lara looked again at the fine knit. She knew quality when she saw it.

Merino? Cashmere?

Lara swallowed the questions, and a hint of jealousy. There was too much riding on this weekend to dwell on the Kingsleys. She filed the conversation away for another time.

Evie took the first shower as Lara threw a quiche together. They switched places and by the time Lara had scrubbed herself pink and washed her hair, Evie had the meal at one end of the dinner table and a staggering array of make-up spread across the other.

'Where'd you even get all this stuff,' Lara said, studying a tube of lip gloss between mouthfuls of food.

As well as the look and texture of glittery superglue, it had a nasty artificial scent.

'Ugh.'

'I've been saving my pocket money, and Aunty Angie sent me some for my birthday.'

Lara shuddered. 'And tell me why we're bothering with all this for an hour on the registration desk, Evie?'

Evie finished her dinner and fixed her mother with a steely look.

'Because you'll be letting the side down if you rock up in your jeans and a work shirt, Mum. Now, sit still and let me get on with it,' she said, in a voice the sounded very much like Lara's own.

She plugged in the hair-dryer and spritzed Lara's hair with product. The straightener was next.

'Is my hair supposed to sizzle like that?'

'Of course it is. Relax, Mum. I'll have you looking a million bucks in no time.'

Lara sipped her tea, wishing it was wine.

You shouldn't be nervous, you're not a guest, you're just on check-in, she reminded herself.

'I'm glad you came home for the weekend, kiddo,' she said, trying not to flinch when the straightener came scaldingly close to her scalp. 'When did you become the queen of girly stuff, anyway?'

'The girls in the boarding house taught me a few tricks. And I couldn't possibly let you go it alone. Imagine if you'd gone in with that ghastly dress you chose. The mauve wrap dress is totally prettier. I can't believe Nanna kept all her old clothes, they're bang on trend now. She must have been pretty cool,' Evie finished with a wistful sigh.

Lara reached for her hand, wishing that Annabel had had the chance to meet her grandchildren and laugh over the fashions swinging around in circles until her wardrobe of dresses, boots and floppy hats was back in vogue.

'Holly said they found the coolest outfit for her dad. He's going retro too.'

Lara chewed on her lip. She couldn't picture Toby in anything other than his smart-casual work attire or his exercise gear.

'Well, that'll be good for a laugh, then. Is he dressing to impress?'

As soon as the question left her mouth, Lara wished she hadn't said it.

'Not that I care,' she added quickly, catching the look on Evie's face.

Lame, lame, lame. Put a sock in it.

Lara stayed silent for the rest of the makeover, opening her eyes wide when Evie applied mascara, pressing her lips together when she was told and sneezing when the light mist of make-up setting spray landed on her face.

'Voilà!' Evie said, stepping back to give her mum the once-over.

Lara walked into the bathroom with a growing sense of trepidation. Letting Evie talk her into a makeover was either going to be a great idea, or downright terrible. She looked at her watch and noted with relief that there would be enough time to scrub it all off if needed. Just.

But when she looked in the mirror, the woman staring back at her wasn't at all what she expected. She was soft and feminine, and whatever Evie had done with the eyeshadow had brought out the green in her eyes. Her daughter had stuck to the 'low key' brief all except for her lips, and although they were brighter than she was used to, the rose-pink colour didn't look half bad. At least it wasn't that sticky lip balm.

Annabel's mauve wrap dress came to her knees and Lara had a feeling it would twirl a little if she spun around.

Not that there'll be any twirling.

'I'm a miracle worker, aren't I?' Evie declared, stepping into the bathroom with a silver shawl Penny had sent her from Turkey many moons ago.

'Ha! Con artist is the word that springs to mind, but it'll do.'

With a quick reload of the wood fire, a small serve of mince for the magpie and a pat for Basil, they locked the house and headed to the car.

'Bugger. This is why I don't wear high heels,' said Lara as soon as she veered off the path. She tugged her heel out of the soft ground and walked the rest of the way to the car on tiptoe.

Lara stole another look in the Subaru's rear-view mirror as she reversed out of the carport, and quickly drew the shawl a little higher around her neck.

'It looks great, Mum. *You* look great. Every bloke with a ticket will be fighting for a whirl around the dance floor,' said Evie, squirming to get comfortable in the black pencil skirt Penny had lent her for the night.

'I'll be long gone by the time the dancing starts, and I'll pick you up the second all the waitressing is finished, right?'

'But can't I stay—'

'No ifs, buts or maybes, Miss Evie. We've got a big weekend ahead, and a singles ball isn't the place for loitering teenagers. You, Cam and Holly will see plenty of each other at the bonfire tomorrow and then the fun run, I promise.'

❦

The newspaper office had been a hive of activity all Friday, with locals stopping by to shoot the breeze, a rush of stories and adverts filed in advance for next week's paper and the phone ringing off the hook with last-minute arrangements for the fun run.

'Busy morning, boss?' said Nancy, meandering in through the front door after another longer-than-allocated lunchbreak.

'Flat strap. Can you hold the calls for an hour? I've got to get this edition sorted.'

'Sure thing,' Nancy replied breezily, slowly scooping the change off the edge of the bench. She counted it and entered it into the cash register.

Not quite sure she would remember, Toby Blu-Tacked a 'DO NOT DISTURB; INTERVIEW IN PROGRESS' sign on the door of his office and put his noise-cancelling headphones on, hoping classical music would aid the few thousand words that stood between him and the deadline. Sunday afternoons were normally his front-page writing sessions, but with the ball, the bonfire and the fun run, he needed to have the article and the first inside spread nailed well before then.

With Beethoven and Chopin in his ear, Toby had the first three pages drafted and the inside content emailed to the typesetters before 4 p.m.

'Done and dusted,' he said, shrugging off the headphones and closing down his desktop computer.

Toby headed into Hamilton, arriving just as Holly's bus pulled in. He briefed her on the order of events and her volunteer duties as they drove home.

'The CWA ladies will give you instructions, but follow Evie's lead and see if you can snap a few pictures between courses, right Lollypop?'

Holly laughed, tossing her curly hair as they pulled up at his house.

'Relax, Dad. It's waitressing for a singles ball, not silver service at Buckingham Palace,' she said. 'Though Granny would completely freak out if I ever scored that type of gig.'

'You're not wrong,' Toby agreed.

He pulled together a quick dinner with fresh bread, heaping on thin slices of roasted McIntyre Park beef and locally made preserves. Once again, he was thankful the general store—and the little produce stall—were in good hands.

'Delicious,' said Holly, helping herself to another piece.

'Extra special because it's been made with love, all here in Bridgefield,' Toby said, proudly.

'We'll have to send Granny back with some of the McIntyres' sausages after the fun run.'

Toby paused, one hand on the dishwashing detergent, one on the scrubbing brush.

'They're coming on Sunday?'

Holly took the soapy plate from his hand.

'Yep, I suggested it. Granny's itching to get out of the house.'

Holly smiled brightly, pleased with herself, unable to grasp the extra layer of stress she had just added to his weekend. His father would be coming too. And Queenie, the little chihuahua papillon cross. Toby would need eyes in the back of his head to make sure nothing went awry.

He mulled over the news as he shaved. But after a quick blast of shampoo and a lather of shower gel, he realised there was nothing he could do about it. If his mum had made up her mind, there was little chance of changing it.

Toby finished in the shower and stopped in his tracks when he caught sight of the clothes laid out on his bed.

What the—

The lapels on the powder-blue suit were ridiculously over-sized, like something John Travolta had worn in *Saturday Night Fever*, with short sleeves and chunky buttons. He lifted the hem of the wide-legged pants—they were almost twice the width he normally favoured.

Not happening.

He pulled a pair of jocks on, grabbed the first two almost-matching socks he could find and flung open the wardrobe doors.

Empty coat hangers swung on the rack. He reefed open the drawers. Only sportswear remained.

You've got to be joking.

Toby refastened the towel around his waist before marching down the hallway.

'Holly! Where the hell are my clothes?'

His glare was met with a cheeky grin. Holly lifted her hands in surrender.

'It was Aunty Belinda's idea, not mine.'

'It's not a dress-up party. Where are my other suits and shirts?'

Holly looked down at her black skirt and toyed with a button on her white shirt.

'I put them all in the washing machine.'

Damn Belinda to hell.

'You did *what*? I don't have time for pranks, Holly. We need to get to the hall before everyone starts arriving.'

Despite his frustration, Toby mustered up what he hoped was an encouraging smile.

'C'mon, Lollypop. Stop joking around. We've gotta go.'

'Aunty Bel said to hide them or do something that would make them unwearable. And they're all on the gentle cycle. She said you'd be too chicken to wear the safari suit if there were other options. It's your size and everything.'

He groaned. He should probably consider himself fortunate that Belinda hadn't driven down from Ballarat, confiscated his clothes and donated them to an op shop on her way home.

'You'd better have left me something to wear tomorrow?'

Holly nodded vigorously. 'Yep, I definitely did.'

He looked at his watch. They were skating on thin ice now.

'Well, give me those and I'll go casual tonight. Quick!'

Holly squirmed and put down her hairbrush. Her face crinkled with apology.

'I put them through the wash while you were making dinner. They're already on the clothesline.'

It was like an April fool's prank gone wrong. Toby spun around and stalked back to his room. A tumble dryer would be useful right about now.

'For God's sake! I'll wear it, but Aunty Bel won't hear the end of this.'

The safari-suit looked even worse than he'd imagined. He let out an exasperated sigh, and when he breathed in, he caught a whiff of mothballs. Any thoughts he'd had of wooing Lara McIntyre went down the gurgler.

Twenty-two

Lara felt a little flutter as she pulled around the back of the general store and stepped out into the cool air.

'So, we're all straight, Evie? We're going home the second Aunty Diana says we're done?'

Evie closed the car door behind her and tucked her white shirt into her waistband.

'Loud and clear, Mum. All work, no play. I can write it on my forehead if you like?'

She flashed a cheeky smile that took the edge off her words, and then led the way down the narrow alleyway between the shop and Main Street. Her torch bounced off the solid bluestone walls and Lara heard a gasp as they rounded the corner and emerged on the footpath.

'Oh wow!' Evie beamed at the sight of the hall in all its decorated glory. Diana was right: the fairy lights woven through the oak branches were enchanting.

Despite the early winter chill, smartly dressed men and women spilled out of the hall and onto the street, clustered in little groups. The mix of satin and lace, bow ties and shiny shoes was the perfect contrast to the hall's worn weatherboard façade.

❦

Holly dashed out of the car before Toby had pulled the keys from the ignition, and rushed into the hall in a black-and-white blur. *Too embarrassed to be seen with Mr Safari Suit*, Toby decided, looking at the perfectly pressed crease down the front of his pants. He wasn't sure if it was the polyester fabric or the thought of walking into the hall in such a get-up, but he was itching and sweating lightly by the time he'd cleared the car park.

He paused at the hall door. For years, his fall-back response when fronting uncomfortable situations was to channel his mentor, Mick. The Ballarat editor was notorious for telling the junior reporters to drink a cup of concrete. It was an old joke around the office, and a phrase that ran through Toby's head anytime he hit the limit of his comfort zone. But after last month's newspaper front-page trick, even with the lure of the Ballarat promotion, Mick's advice no longer held the same gravity.

A bus pulled up in Main Street, its bright lights silhouetting his shadow—flared legs and all—against the weatherboard hall, making even more of a spectacle of his ridiculous outfit.

Thankfully, his self-consciousness took a back seat as he opened the door and surveyed the soft-blue tablecloths, flowers and windmills on each table, fairy lights hanging from the ceiling, and colourful strobes bouncing across the stage. He wasn't much into decorating, but he was impressed by the transformation.

'Magical, isn't it?'

He turned towards Lara's voice.

Stuff the hall. The word 'magical' suits Lara right down to the ground.

He'd seen her in active wear plenty of times, watched her stride in and out of the Bush Nursing Centre in a basic uniform that mirrored her brisk efficiency, and noticed the collared shirts she favoured for volunteer shifts at the general store, but never had he seen her in a dress with her hair flowing around her shoulders.

Downright sexy, yet here he was looking like a dork in a safari suit.

Toby melted a little more when she brushed a lock of hair away from her face.

'Just what I was thinking,' he said. He could almost feel the electricity spark between them.

'Snazzy suit,' she added, reaching for the sleeve. She rubbed the material between her fingers. A little fizz ran up his arm when her hand brushed his skin.

'Fabric's in good condition too. Where'd you find this beauty?'

Toby laughed. 'Nothing like the rustle of pure polyester, right? My sister found it. Long story, but safe to say I won't be employing her as my personal shopper.'

'I like it, great idea to make our guests smile. This was my mum's dress. Probably from the same era as your suit, actually.'

Lara's appraising look extinguished his annoyance at Belinda.

The band struck up a chord, testing their equipment, before the guitarist and banjo player launched into a fast rendition of 'Duelling Banjos'. Toby dragged his attention away from Lara to give the band a hearty clap. The flurry of activity in the hall stilled as everyone else followed suit, and the musicians bowed with a flourish before returning to their warm-up.

'Better get to work, I suppose,' Toby said, leading the way to a table by the front door. They squeezed behind the makeshift desk and he ran a finger down the registration list; anything to stop his eyes sweeping over the beautiful woman beside him. There was only so long he could pretend to admire the dress before she noticed he was having a good, old-fashioned perve.

Before long, the first wave of guests were walking through the door, and Toby soon learned that working alongside Lara in the hall was a whole different ballgame to their shifts together at the shop. It might have been the buzz of music or the hum of conversation as they greeted the excited singles, or the smooth flow of the evening, but Lara seemed to sparkle. They fell into an easy routine of handing out goody bags and green wristbands to the guests and reminding them about the lucky door prize. It was almost comical to watch the blokes reach for their wallets as soon as Lara mentioned the apartment raffle. At this rate, they'd have enough to buy the store, redecorate inside *and* replace the hall's weatherboards.

'I'll take a ticket too. It looks like there're plenty of reasons to hunker down in this gorgeous town for a year,' said a brunette guest, giving Toby a wink.

He handed her the raffle book and averted his eyes as she leaned on the registration desk to fill in the ticket, ensuring her generous cleavage was on full display.

'Good luck,' he said, handing over the pink bag that contained directions to tomorrow's bonfire, a flyer Penny had created to spruik the shop's fundraising campaign and a voucher for free Devonshire tea at Sunday's fun run. 'Have a great night.'

The woman's eyes darted to his bare ring finger, then lingered on his lips.

'See you on the dance floor, handsome.'

A snort came from behind him once the woman had left. He turned. Lara's eyes brimmed with amusement.

'*See you on the dance floor, handsome*,' Lara mimicked. The comment held a lot more appeal coming from her lips, even if she was being sarcastic.

'Friendly,' he said grimly.

'Friendly? That cougar wanted to drag you home and have her wicked way with you.'

He looked up, curiosity mixing with surprise as he studied Lara. Was she flirting with him? She held his gaze, and with all her attention, it felt like they were the only people in the room. How did she make him feel like this? And did she feel it too? A pair of tuxedoed men stormed through the door, breaking the moment, but not before he saw Lara take a shaky breath. She *did* feel it.

They were flat strap for another half-hour before registrations thinned out again. Toby took his first swig of beer. Warm, but ideal for soothing his parched throat. He glanced towards the dance floor, where the brunette from earlier was already surrounded by prospective dance partners.

He'd known she wouldn't be short of company for long. Toby looked back at Lara, whose hips gently swayed to a familiar theme song from a TV show.

'And to think I had you pegged as a country-music fan,' he laughed. 'You're a nineties tragic, through and through.'

Lara pretended to bristle at his words, but he saw the smile lurking underneath as she sipped champagne.

'Penny and Angie are the country fans. Diana's the cultured one, she loves classical music. Whereas me, I'll take anything catchy from the seventies to the nineties. *Friends* is my favourite sitcom. You?'

'I'm not particularly coordinated, but my sister spent our entire chicken-pox quarantine trying to teach me a few dance moves. I can manage a mean Nutbush, and a half-arsed Macarena, but that's about it.'

Lara's mouth curved into a slow smile. The noise, the music and the people bustling through the door en route to the registration desk slipped into the background as he basked in her approval. It was almost enough to make him march up to the stage and order the band to rip into their best Tina Turner impersonation.

'Is that right?'

He watched the fabric shift in the soft dress. It had three times more material than most of the dresses in the room, but it was infinitely sexier. His pulse ratcheted up a notch.

Get a grip, he told himself.

Somebody cleared their throat. Toby and Lara turned in unison to find their daughters standing before them, their eyes bright with amusement.

'Hate to interrupt, but Aunty Diana wants to know how many registrations are left,' said Evie.

'She's about to send entrees out,' added Holly.

They looked every bit the proper waitresses in their matching black-and-white outfits.

Lara and Toby both reached for the list at the same time and sprang back as their hands collided.

'You go—'

'No, you,' Toby said, stepping back with a laugh.

'OMG,' said Holly, rolling her eyes. Toby didn't miss the 'I-told-you-so' look she exchanged with Evie.

'We're only waiting on three people,' said Toby.

Lara looked at her watch. 'And they're an hour late, so tell her to start serving up. The stragglers will have to suffer through cold soup.'

Toby picked up Lara's empty champagne flute and downed the last of his beer, then pointed to the bar.

'Fancy another while we wait?'

Lara shook her head. 'I'd better whip into the kitchen and see if anyone needs a hand before I head off.'

Head off?

He'd assumed she was staying until close. That dress deserved at least one lap around the dance floor . . .

Oh boy.

Toby looked down at his shoes, noticing that the blue sock poking out from his left shoe jarred with the sock on his right.

Maybe she's not that into you, Paxton.

He pushed the thought aside. Now was not the time for doubt. Self-preservation and pride had gone out the window as soon as he slipped on the powder-blue suit.

'A roomful of single blokes who can't keep their eyes off you. You might find your Prince Charming,' he said, playfully.

A Prince Charming in a safari suit, to be specific.

❧

Lara was sweating in the tiny kitchen later that night. Cameron, Evie and Holly raced in and out with alternating armfuls of pavlova and lemon tart, while Penny, Angie and Diana helped the CWA ladies in the production line. Pete looked up from his sink full of soapy dishwater, the same spot he'd stood all night. He looked like he'd reached his limit.

'I hate dishes,' said Elliot, scowling as his twin brother Harry snapped a wet tea towel in his direction.

'I've told you two . . .' warned Pete, dumping a handful of clean cutlery onto the drying rack.

'They need a dishwasher,' said Harry.

'But they've got you two instead. The dish pig's the most important role in the kitchen,' said Lara. 'I'll pay you an extra ten dollars each if you get all these dishes dried and put away before the speeches are finished. And no more of that,' she said, confiscating Harry's wet tea towel and replacing it with a dry one.

'Thanks, Lars, you're a lifesaver.' Diana sent the last of the desserts off with Cameron before smoothing her floral dress and applying lipstick in a small hand mirror. She passed the lipstick to Penny, who touched up her lips, and then offered it to Angie. Lara slipped off a shoe and rubbed the back of her heel.

'Your turn,' said Diana encouragingly, noticing Lara's hesitation with lipstick. 'You look gorgeous tonight, may as well stick with the theme. How is it out there?'

'Everyone seems happy,' said Lara, slicking the colour across her lips. 'Meals have been a hit.'

Angus breezed through the door, followed by Toby. Lara's gaze met his and she smiled.

'All ready for the speeches, girls?'

Penny, Diana and Angie nodded in unison and headed out. Toby was waiting for Lara. 'Ready?'

'As ready as I'll ever be. Let's get this over and done with.'

They squeezed behind chairs, stopping to chat with guests on the way to the stage. If the feedback from the random cross-section of diners was any indication, they were onto a winner.

'Righto, everybody, can we have a bit of hush?' Angus tapped the microphone on stage.

Despite his request, the guests continued to murmur and cutlery chimed against plates.

Lara followed her sisters up the steps and stood between Angus and Toby. She gave a shrill whistle. The room fell silent.

'Well, that'll do it,' said Toby quietly as everyone in the room swivelled towards them.

Angus started again. 'Thanks for coming tonight, folks. In case you didn't notice the little bluestone building three doors down, this whole weekend's about raising money to buy our town's general store.'

Lara could see the pride in his eyes, and was struck by how much her mum would have loved to have been here for this special occasion.

Penny stepped up after Angus. 'And for those staying the whole weekend, don't forget the bonfire at McIntyre Park tomorrow. You can make your own way, otherwise a bus will leave from the hall at eleven a.m. sharp.'

She handed the microphone to Lara, who surveyed the crowd.

'We've also got raffle tickets for sale all weekend. The prize is a year's free rent at the studio apartment above the shop, an absolute bargain for fifty dollars a ticket. And before I pass you over to Toby for details on Sunday's fun run, I want to give a special shout out to Mrs Beggs, the owner of the Bridgefield General Store.'

Lara waited as a ripple of applause went through the room.

'There've been a lot of late nights and uncertainty as we've worked out how to save our shop, fundraising to acquire the bulk of the funds, but we really appreciate your support. It wouldn't have happened without this weekend, so a huge thanks to each and every one of you in the room, and the volunteers who made it all happen. I'm thrilled to announce that we've met our target.'

More clapping and whistles echoed through the hall.

A combination of relief and energy rushed through Lara as she handed the microphone to Toby. Angie reached out and squeezed her hands, her expression matching the way Lara felt. She looked at Diana and Penny. Broad smiles were stretched across their faces too.

We've done it. We've really done it.

The guests returned to their conversations as Toby followed the McIntyres off stage. Before long chairs were scraping across the timber floorboards as the band started up a pop number. Toby paused and looked back at the stage, waiting to catch the bass player's eye. The guitarist gave him a quick wink. Toby flicked him a thumbs-up.

Time to squeeze in some photos. He collected his camera and reeled off a few shots, trying to capture the electricity, excitement and anticipation in the room.

A woman squeezed past, flashing him a confident smile.

'Dr Livingstone, I presume? Love your suit. All you need is a pith helmet,' she said.

Toby laughed. *I'll be buggered. Belinda was right about the outfit all along.*

The woman stepped closer. The gold bangles on her arm jangled as she reached across and broke a small flower off the nearest table centrepiece. She moved to tuck the bloom into his top buttonhole, then looked up coyly, pursing her glossy lips.

Aware that most red-blooded blokes would have found the move as sexy as hell, he gave a polite smile and put some distance between them.

'Like a photo?'

'You can photograph me any which way you want,' she offered, doing the lip moistening thing again.

Toby took his quickest photo of the night and made his escape. Less than five photos later, he was hit on again.

Big brown eyes and a perfectly white smile flashed up at him. The woman reached out and adjusted the top button of his shirt, resting her hands by the lapel for a beat.

'Nothing better than a guy who isn't afraid to stand out in the crowd. Keen for a dance?'

This safari suit should come with a warning label, he thought, declining with an apologetic smile.

'I'm good, but thanks. Have a great night,' he said, scanning the room for a flash of mauve. There was a whole room of women looking for Mr Right, but there was only one that piqued his interest. And she was heading for the door.

Twenty-three

Despite her best intentions to leave, two hours later Lara was still weaving her way between tables, helping out with 'just one more' errand for Penny. Her feet ached like buggery, and she knew there would be endless blisters competing for her attention tomorrow morning.

She slipped outside, relishing the fresh air and cool breeze on her face. There were couples canoodling under the twinkling fairy lights, and laughter coming from hushed conversations in the shadows surrounding the hall.

The exhilaration of achieving their goal flooded over her again, along with a hefty spattering of goosebumps, and she beamed as she walked back inside.

The room was abuzz with conversation. The band was playing a low biding-their-time tune until the dessert dishes were cleared. Even though she didn't buy into the whole romance scam, it made her feel good to know they were bringing people together tonight. Whether it was for one night or longer was irrelevant. Right here, in this rustic town hall in the heart of western Victoria, there was happiness. She could almost taste the optimism in the air.

Lara saw a man edging through the crowd, the bald circle on the back of his head shining under the lights. The older singles had been an unexpected bonus, with their open wallets and jovial attitude. A niche market waiting to be tapped.

If the bush nursing gig goes belly-up, I could always start an over-fifties events business.

The man turned, and Lara stopped in her tracks as her eyes met his. It was McCluskey, all freshly shaven and slick-haired, wearing the ugliest brown suit she'd ever seen, heading in her direction.

She took in the skinny tie and his polished boots. He'd made an effort. A green wristband poked out from under his cream shirt sleeve, and she swallowed the question on her lips about him sneaking in.

'You're the last person I expected to see here, Clyde,' she said.

'If you can't beat 'em, join 'em, right?'

After years of feeling nothing but frustration and irritation towards her neighbour, Lara felt sorry for Clyde McCluskey. *Toby's right, he's just a lonely old bachelor.* Her mother had told them that very same thing decades earlier, when they'd baulked at her request to ride across town and deliver him a casserole or cake. In retrospect, he hadn't even been that old at the time, but to the teenage McIntyre girls, he'd seemed ancient. He'd found the love of his life, Edna, too late to have children, only to have her ripped from his side by cancer.

Everyone deserves a night out.

'We're glad to have you here.'

She wasn't sure he would find love, but perhaps it was a step in the right direction.

⚜

Lara didn't bother to hold back a yawn as she made her way towards the door. Making a good impression hadn't been on her agenda—hell, being here tonight hadn't been on her agenda either—and there were only a few kilometres between her and fresh bed sheets.

'Hey Lara, wait up. I haven't got a photo of you yet.'

She turned at the sound of her name and felt a little leap in her belly as a powder-blue suit veered her way.

It had been a long time since her body had reacted to a man, but it seemed to do all sorts of funny things around Toby.

He gestured to the bar where her sisters were enjoying a well-earned drink.

'Just a quick one?'

Lara studied the wilted sprig of flowers in his top pocket.

'One drink or one photo?'

He lifted an eyebrow. 'Both.'

Lara thought about Clyde dressed in his finest. She turned to see Angus waltzing around the dance floor with an elegant older woman and a smile wider than she'd seen in ages.

What's stopping you? How many times have you thought about this guy in the last five months, with his odd socks and goofy bike helmet?

Toby held out a hand, gave it a quick squeeze and led her towards the bar.

Why couldn't he have been born with a bulbous nose or crossed eyes? Or at least without that little dimple, she thought half-heartedly as she followed him.

Penny hurried up to them. 'You read my mind, Toby. Can't leave without evidence of my fab team of helpers,' she said, finger combing her hair until it was camera-ready.

Lara found herself being squished into a McIntyre-sister sandwich, but it wasn't hard to muster up a convincing smile.

The night had surpassed expectations, and the air of triumph among the committee had given the whole event a celebratory vibe.

Diana lifted the camera strap from around Toby's neck. 'Now, you guys too.'

Lara shuffled next to Toby.

'Closer.' Diana kept inching them together until their hips were touching.

About as subtle as a sledgehammer.

Lara's mind seesawed as Diana fussed with the camera.

It doesn't even have to be a thing. It could be a flash in the pan, one night of pleasure to get it out of my system.

She looked back at Toby, whose attention had turned to the stage. He clapped as the band finished their song.

Yeah, Lara, keep telling yourself that you'd be able to walk away after one night.

Just as she'd made up her mind to leave, the first bars of 'Nutbush City Limits' came across the loud speakers. Women launched from their chairs and a handful of men migrated from the bar and the tables onto the dance floor. Before the vocalist had even reached the first line, the dancers were divided into neat rows and shuffling in a slightly inebriated but nevertheless uniform style.

Toby raised an eyebrow, his shoulders bopping to the tune. Lara glanced at the stage.

'This your doing?'

'No idea what you mean,' he laughed, a glint in his eyes. 'But you can't seriously leave at the start of the Nutbush.'

Lara rolled her eyes and half-heartedly lifted one knee into the air, then criss-crossed her arms across her chest, laughing at the hopelessness of her rendition. She couldn't remember the last time she'd been on a dance floor, let alone attempted any choreographed moves.

'Yeah, nup. Dancing's not my jam, especially when it's a cover. Nobody should even try to match Tina. I'll leave you to it.'

Toby reached for her hand, his amusement clear.

'C'mon, I'll teach you.'

Lara wasn't sure if it was his mock puppy-dog eyes or his boyish enthusiasm, but she found herself following Toby into the crowd and flinging her arms and legs around as per his directions.

'Right, right. Left, left. Back, back, and on the left, left. Knees, kick and twist,' he called, showing off with a little criss-cross jump between the steps. Lara felt sweat trickle down her cleavage and tried to fit in a clap, like Toby had done after jumping. The distraction messed up her rhythm and she doubled over with laughter after her knee came precariously close to colliding with Toby's groin.

'Steady on there,' he laughed, gripping her hips and spinning her ninety degrees so she was in line with the rest of the group. As much as she tried, Lara couldn't get the hang of the moves, but when she caught a glimpse of the room's reflection in the hall window, even she couldn't deny she looked like someone having fun.

⁂

Toby felt a little like Fred Astaire, if Fred had worn safari suits and been alive when Tina Turner was in vogue. The Lara who was dancing with him now was so different to the focused woman who held tight control over her emotions, guarded her privacy fiercely and moved heaven and earth to save her local store; the runner who took sprint sessions more seriously than he took his tax and thought nothing of smashing out twenty kilometres before Sunday breakfast.

So busy admiring her carefree but uncoordinated dance moves, Toby missed the timing on the ninety-degree jump, which sent Lara into gales of laughter.

'You're supposed to be teaching *me*.'

'I didn't promise perfection,' he grinned. The band started to wind down. Lara wiped her forehead and eyed the dancers retreating to the bar and the restrooms.

He cursed himself for not having the foresight to request two decent songs in a row.

'Another one?'

Lara paused a beat, slowly shaking her head.

'The girls will be finished in the kitchen by now, I'd better head off,' she said. But neither of them moved.

'Yeah,' he conceded. 'Big few days ahead. But you've got to admit, that Nutbush was pretty funny.'

She agreed, her attention shifting behind him.

Lara waved across the room. 'Evie, time to hit the road.'

Toby reluctantly lifted a hand, making a similar gesture to Holly. The girls hurried in the opposite direction. It reminded him of the endless after-school play dates when Holly had avoided leaving her friend's houses.

He exchanged a 'kids, huh?' look with Lara, but he wasn't especially perturbed. Anything that kept Lara by his side a little longer was a win in his books. He followed her to the kitchen, and found the girls working alongside Cameron.

'Dad, can I stay another hour?' Holly's eyes were wide with anticipation.

'Aunty Diana will drop us all home if we help pack up,' added Evie.

'Mum said she had plenty of jobs, if it's okay with you both,' said Cameron.

Toby lifted an eyebrow and looked at Lara. He didn't really want to leave Holly at a singles ball until midnight, but if she was needed . . . And it would mean he'd be able to walk Lara to her car without the teenage chaperones.

Diana strode into the hall kitchen.

'All good? I'll be working them to the bone,' she said, with a quick look at the trio, who had made themselves suspiciously useful stacking away platters and wiping down kitchen benches.

Toby pulled his keys from his camera bag, pocketed them, and handed the camera equipment to Holly.

'Only if you grab a few more photos for next week's social pages.'

'Deal,' said Holly, clearly delighted.

Toby and Lara made their farewells and headed for the door.

'I'll dust off the moves so I'm right for next time,' said Toby, holding the door open for Lara.

'Not many dances in Bridgefield,' she said wryly, then shivered and tugged her shawl closer as the wind wrapped itself around them.

'Maybe the shop committee can diversify now that the fight to save the general store's over. How about a town progress association?' Toby said, just as he spotted a couple smooching under the big oak.

'Yeah, or another fun run to help sponsor the primary school's agriculture program or something.' Lara fished out her car keys as they walked down the laneway alongside the shop. She hugged her arms around herself and swung her head to flick her hair away. He knew it wasn't intended as a come on, but Lara's mannerisms were infinitely sexier than the blatant flirting he'd witnessed inside the hall. Toby felt his body respond. He longed to uncross those arms and warm her up the best way he knew how.

'What about a barn dance in summer?'

'I thought you were only here for two years; why do you even care?' Lara asked, looking even more beautiful in the moonlight.

'What if I stayed?'

Lara traced a finger along a bluestone brick.

'And give up the career you've always wanted?'

'I can think of a few good reasons to stay. The main one's standing right here in front of me.'

He stepped a little closer, close enough to hear her breath catch, before reaching out to brush a strand of hair from her cheek.

Slowly, slowly, Paxton.

He wanted to press his mouth to hers, slide his hands up and down her body, tug that soft fabric close to him and show her how much he wanted to stay, but he needed to be sure.

'This is the part where you give me a thumbs-up or something,' he said quietly. Nerves danced in his abdomen. He scanned her eyes, searching for a sign it was what she wanted too.

Lara's hand slipped into his.

She closed the distance between them.

'It's two thumbs-up from me,' she said, her lips brushing against his with each word.

Toby leaned in a fraction, and when her arms roped around his neck and her body melted against his, he knew there was no place he would rather be than under Lara McIntyre's delicious spell.

Twenty-four

Even an extra-early magpie alarm clock couldn't shift the smile from Lara's face. The taste of last night's gentle kiss was still on her lips when she woke, and for the first time in forever, she found herself lazing in bed for a few minutes, reliving the memory. There had been no time for nerves, no awkwardness and not a word from the self-doubt inside her head. It had felt right. Toby had been the consummate gentleman.

His fingertips had traced the scoop of her collarbone and he'd dropped one last sweet kiss on her cheek before opening the car door and seeing her off safely. It felt like she had floated home and fallen into an exhausted but luxurious sleep, not even waking when Diana dropped Evie off.

She glanced over the dark paddocks towards his house.

Did Toby wake up beaming too?

She dressed quickly, made a coffee and bustled around the yard, pulling the heads off milk-thistle plants and delivering them to Vegemite's cage before the sun was up. She found Annabel's famous scone recipe and slipped on an apron, smiling to herself as she stirred eggs and cream into flour with a knife.

Evie stumbled out of her bedroom, squinting at the bright sunshine streaming through the kitchen window.

'Your dressing gown's inside out,' Lara said as she handed her daughter a coffee and pushed a basket of warm scones across the marble bench.

'Scones? Shouldn't you be stressing about the fun run or the bonfire instead of grinning like a loon and baking?'

Lara heaped cream on top of a second scone and shook her head.

'All under control, Evie. The race registrations are up to date, half the salads are made for lunch and I've even tallied up all our additional fundraising. We're well over target!'

Evie's sleepy expression vanished. She jumped off her stool and rounded the island bench.

'Really? That's awesome, Mum. No wonder you look so pleased.'

Lara hugged her tightly.

No need to mention that exceeding their fundraising target was only half the reason behind this morning's smile.

※

Glowing embers fizzled and popped in the air as Tim tossed another red gum limb onto the bonfire. The group of women closest darted backward and Lara sidestepped quickly to avoid her platter of Caesar salad hitting the deck.

'What about bushfires? Aren't you worried those sparks will start another Black Saturday?' The woman's tone was flippant, as if she had no concept of the lives and livestock lost and the damage caused when the major bushfires had ravaged the area. Lara admired Tim's patient reply as he pointed out the water tanks on the back of the utes and swept his arms wide, encompassing the lush paddocks.

'See all that green grass around us? That paddock couldn't catch fire without being doused in diesel. We wouldn't light a heap like this up if the fire-ban was on,' he said.

Lara weaved through the crowd, stopping to chat with their guests. She met Penny at the food table.

'Your hubby's got the patience of a saint,' said Lara.

Penny finished unloading the last of the salads and looked over to Tim, who was simultaneously rocking the pram and educating their city visitors about fire danger.

'That lady's nodding her head like she understands the ins and outs of wind direction and fuel loads, but if she had half a brain she wouldn't have bothered blow-drying her hair for a bonfire. And heels? Heaven help us. We'll have to be more specific about the footwear next year.'

'Or maybe next year we do something a little different,' said Lara. She glanced from the tables piled high with lunch to the men cooking the barbecue, unable to stop herself smiling. 'Toby reckons a barn dance might be the ticket. Raise some money for a community project, or the primary school.'

'Ohhh, does he now?' said Penny, cocking an eyebrow as she followed Lara's gaze to the barbecue. Toby smiled back and waved with his tongs. Diana walked past with a tray of steaming hamburgers.

'Oh, you two are so cute,' Diana said, nudging Lara with an elbow. 'Lara and Toby sitting in the tree. K-I-S-S-I-N-G.'

Lara swatted her eldest sister with her free hand but her best glare didn't last long before turning back into a smile. 'Give it a rest, blabbermouth. I don't want everyone in Bridgefield finding out, especially Evie,' she said. 'I wish I hadn't mentioned it.'

'Mentioned it?' Diana scoffed, then snorted with laughter. 'Even if you hadn't said a word this morning, I would've worked it out. The dopey smile on your face is remarkably similar to the expression on Toby Paxton's mug when I walked Holly to the door last night. That rosy, just-been-kissed look was a dead giveaway.'

'Not to forget the pair of them on the dance floor,' Penny added.

The bonfire crackled as the flames feasted on a branch with dry leaves. Lara felt her face flush. She turned on her heel, heading for barbecue area. She wasn't sure how Toby had been landed with the chief barbecuing job, but at least they had found him a less lewd apron this time. Angus's striped-blue and white apron suited him. Before she knew it, Lara found herself adding it to her mental 'Christmas presents' file, along with Evie's frightfully expensive kikki.K stationery and the body products Penny loved.

Pull yourself together. One kiss and you're already planning potential Christmas gifts?

Lara cursed the practical side of her brain for piggybacking on the tiniest morsel of optimism and galloping away, but still she couldn't quite wipe the smile from her lips.

❦

The smell of onions engulfed Toby as he worked the barbecue. His stomach growled at the sight of the juicy sausages, knowing they tasted as good as they smelled. He dished up his own serve, then loaded the last of the meat onto a tray and covered it with a wire cloche.

After a morning taking last-minute fun-run registrations, setting up for the bonfire and now an hour flipping steaks, hamburgers and sausages, he was more than ready for his own lunch. He did a lap of the bonfire, scanning the crowd for Lara's green shirt. He found her by the food table, loading her plate with salad and meat. Filling two glasses with water, Toby waited until she'd grabbed her cutlery before gesturing to the hay bales.

'Table for two?'

With Lara sitting beside him, her leg pressed against his, the sun on their backs and the radiant heat from the bonfire warming their fronts, it was better than any fancy French restaurant.

⚶

Even when her plate was empty, Lara stayed sitting on the hay bale, enjoying Toby's company, the warmth of the bonfire and snatches of animated conversations all around them.

It hadn't just been her biased opinion as an organiser: the laughter and newly forged friendships humming around her confirmed the ball had been an all-out success.

'You hear that?' Toby's voice was hushed, and she leaned in a little closer, keeping her reply equally low.

'What?'

'That couple on your left. Sounds like they hooked up last night and he's trying to impress her.'

She glanced discreetly and smiled at the sight of a young man pretending to stretch his hamstrings.

Lara turned back to Toby.

'You think he's trying to pass himself off as a runner?'

Amusement danced in Toby's eyes. Before they knew it, the pair were standing in front of them, their expressions animated.

'You guys in charge of the fun run?'

Lara nudged Toby.

'Toby's the brains, I'm just a lackey. Are you entering?'

The woman studied the man beside her, a challenge in her expression. She looked like a runner, him less so, but his face lit up at the question.

'Sasha says she'll go to dinner with me tonight if I have a go at the five-k. Where do I sign up?' he asked eagerly.

Lara tried not to laugh.

'It's for a very good cause,' Toby said approvingly, pulling a notepad and pen from his back pocket. He took down the runner's details.

'He'll be sore tomorrow,' he said when the couple had gone. 'But who are we to stand in the way of true love?'

Toby's warm hand brushed against hers as the couple wandered off and she threaded her fingers through his. Life was about to get good.

Twenty-five

Lara helped Toby load the last of the trestle tables into the back of Diana's car and shut the boot. She rubbed her arms, feeling cold for the first time all afternoon, and knew if she moved closer to the bonfire again she would have trouble ripping herself away. They had stopped adding wood mid-afternoon and the sting had gone out of the heap by the time the last of the guests left, but it would smoulder for a few days yet.

'Sure you don't want to stay and have a celebratory whiskey round the fire? Not every day you can say you've saved a shop from ruination,' said Tim, leaning back in his camp chair.

'C'mon, Lars, it'll help you wind down. You too, Toby,' said Pete.

Lara shook her head as she yawned.

'No rest for the wicked. We've still got registrations to log. Our half of the weekend is ramping up, not winding down.'

'Please Dad,' said Holly, slipping in behind them with Evie at her side.

'Not a chance, Lollypop. Tempting as it is, we won't be celebrating until this time tomorrow night,' he said.

Lara's eyes locked on his and she had a sudden urge to wind the clocks forward and fast-track to the bit where she and Toby had ten minutes to themselves.

'But we'll be halfway back to Ballarat with Granny and Pop then,' Holly said.

'Maybe there'll be another bonfire next time you're home,' Lara suggested, liking the idea of future weekends with Toby and his family.

'We're heading off anyway,' said Diana, loading Leo into the car. 'I'll get this lot home and fall into bed. What time do you want Cam to help you with the race set-up tomorrow morning, Toby? He's always up at sparrow's fart, aren't you, mate?'

'Is six-thirty too early, Cameron?' said Toby. 'You can make sure all the drinks tables and signage are sorted while I show Pete and Jonesy where we need the finish-line barricades.'

'Want me to be on snake-hunting duty too, Aunty Lara? Mum said I can't take my slug gun, but I could bring my stock whip?' Harry offered, his boyish face hopeful.

His twin, Elliot, chimed in: 'We're getting pretty good at hitting a target.'

Another yawn snuck up on Lara, and she shook it away. There was too much to do tonight with the timing system to even think about sleep for hours yet.

'Stock whips and guns at the finish line? Not likely. The snakes should all be hibernating in winter anyway. Now, what else?' said Lara, casting a look around the group.

Toby flicked up the collar of his rugby jumper.

'I'll print out a few more copies of the course for the last-minute volunteers, if you want to register those lovebirds from lunchtime? Adam, wasn't it?'

Lara nodded. She wondered how Adam and Sasha's date would go tonight, and if Adam would be feeling quite as gallant when he'd hauled his untrained butt up Windmill Track.

'This time tomorrow it'll all be done and dusted,' added Angus. 'On Monday you'll be waltzing off to the bank with a cheque for the shop.'

Lara drove home, the buzz of their achievements keeping the weariness at bay.

'It's going great, Mum,' said Evie. 'What do we need to get done tonight?'

Lara outlined her checklist, delegating jobs to Evie as she went.

'Did we print off the last-minute raffle tickets?'

'Yep,' said Evie. 'And I found a plastic tub for the raffle in the shed. Worst-case scenario, we could scrub the wheelie bin clean and tip all the entries in there.'

Lara shuddered at the idea of shuffling raffle tickets inside a bin, no matter how well scrubbed it was.

'The plastic tub will be fine. How many volunteer briefing packs do we have in total?'

'More than enough, but I'll print a few extra spares if you like?'

Lara gave Evie a grateful look, before returning her attention to the road. The conversation shifted from the fun run to the ball and the barbecue, and Lara's mind drifted to Toby. She daydreamed the rest of the way home.

'Earth to Mum!'

Lara looked across at Evie, who was unbuckling her seatbelt, and realised they were parked in their driveway.

'Man, you seriously need some sleep. You didn't even laugh when I told you about the guy from Romsey who singed his eyebrows trying to toast a marshmallow.' Evie's gruff voice faded and she pushed the buckle on Lara's seatbelt. Her voice was gentler when she spoke again. 'I'm going to print those extra raffle tickets for you, then go to bed. You should too. Holly's dad is the main man on the fun run. Log in that couple like you promised, then trust him when he says he's got it under control.'

Lara eased herself from the car and followed Evie up the verandah steps, breathing in the smell of the sweet grass from the paddocks and wondering when her daughter had got so wise. Evie was right: it was time to trust again. And Toby Paxton might be the right man for the job.

🐦

Toby whistled as he draped clean sheets over the clothesline. The sun wasn't even up, but already he'd stripped his bed, done a couple of loads of washing, and entered an extra three overnight entries into the race-timing software. He pegged the last of the laundry onto the line and then headed back across the lawn.

He sent a quick prayer skywards to the high clouds framing a full moon, hoping they wouldn't give them any grief today. There was barely a puff of breeze, not even enough to ruffle the sheets. Perfect conditions for a winter fun run.

A groggy-eyed Holly stumbled into the kitchen as he finished a second coffee and started up the vacuum.

'What the . . . It's not even six o'clock and you're vacuuming? Don't you have a fun run to set up or something?'

Toby looked at his watch. 'Got to squeeze it in somewhere, don't want it messy for your grandparents. You sure you want to come in this early? Granny and Pop could pick you up when they come through about nine,' he yelled above the roar of the appliance, sucking up crumbs from underneath the dining table.

Holly flopped onto the couch and squinted at her phone.

He turned off the vacuum cleaner and laughed.

'Guess that means you're sticking with the early start, completely out of the goodness of your heart, nothing to do with Evie's cousin who's also volunteering?'

Holly rolled her eyes as he resumed vacuuming. She scrolled through her phone and lifted her feet as he worked his way around the lounge before turning the screen to him.

'Cleaning for Granny, huh?'

Toby peered down and saw a photo of him and Lara standing by the bonfire. Holly must have taken the shot from behind, but there was no mistaking Lara's green shirt, or the delight in his expression as he threw back his head and laughed at whatever she was saying.

Toby switched the vacuum off.

'Nice shot. You've got a good eye, Lollypop. Would it bother you if Lara and I started dating?'

'Gah, of course not.' She harrumphed her way back into the kitchen and heaped generous spoons of coffee into her mug. 'I don't want details, that's for sure, but if you're happy, I'm happy. Though happy's a bit of a stretch for this early in the morning.'

Toby did a last-minute dash around the house. It wasn't squeaky clean, but it was a darn sight neater than it had been an hour earlier.

❦

Sunlight peeked over the valley, bathing the paddocks in golden light as Toby jogged up to the windmill. The walkie talkie on his hip sprang to life and Angus McIntyre's cheerful voice burbled over the quiet conversations among the fun-run volunteers.

'You on channel, Toby?'

Toby slowed to a walk as he answered.

'Yep. Go ahead.'

'Cam and I've got the signage sorted, water tables are all in place and we're seeing the first runners roll up at the start line. The course's looking tip-top, couldn't have asked for a better morning. You heading down for the race briefing soon?'

'I'll be there as soon as I've checked in with Lara.'

Toby ducked into the marquee near the finish line and pulled the race briefing notes from a plastic folder. Despite the crisp morning, sweat trickled down his torso as he scanned his to-do list. Lara looked up from the laptop.

'Final registrations are logged in, timing system looks good to go, and the volunteers are all in position. What else can I do?' Lara smiled at him.

Toby's brain threw up all kinds of cheeky suggestions.

'You're a gem. Make sure you've got the radio ready for the countdown to the first race,' he said, turning to leave.

'Loved the trophies, by the way. Nicely played.'

Toby gave a modest smile, pleased he'd managed to convince McCluskey to let the runners use his easement, which allowed the route to incorporate Windmill Track as he'd originally planned. Renaming the shortest run 'The Edna McCluskey 5K', and featuring a pair of donkeys and a windmill on the trophies, had sweetened the deal.

A fresh wave of volunteers wandered into the marquee, and he gave a quick wave to Evie and Holly, who were unpacking the trophies. Even as he was passing, he could hear them cooing over the likeness of the donkeys.

'They're awesome—they look just like the ones down the driveway,' said Holly.

Penny called out to Toby from her station on the finish line: 'The last bus is heading to the start line. I've got everything under control here. Nanna Pearl's whisked your folks off for a quick coffee before it gets crazy busy.'

Toby looked across to the food vans and coffee trucks that had set up a mini food court by the windmill. He made out his parents in the distance, along with Tim's grandmother, who was easily identifiable with her lilac hair, and Eddie's green McIntyre Park shirt.

'You'd better go,' said Penny. 'Can't have the race director miss his own race briefing.'

Toby's guts churned as he drove under the archway of trees along the Avenue of Honour and headed towards the start line. He thought of all the half-marathoners they'd attracted to this tiny town, and wondered if they were feeling the same rush of pre-race adrenaline he normally felt as he pinned on a race number. Instead of months of training, he had invested months of organisation into this one event. He felt a stab of unease.

Can I really pull this off?

ॐ

The top of the hill had a carnival-like atmosphere, with cheers from the crowd as runners from the five-kilometre race crossed the finish line. The pop music paused and Pete's voice came over the loud speakers: 'And how's this for a finish at the inaugural Windmill Track Fun Run, folks? The Edna McCluskey 5K is done and dusted! Now we've got the first of the 10K runners coming into sight.'

Lara lifted a hand to shield her eyes as she looked into the sun. The woman in the lead was charging up the hill towards the finish line as if she still had plenty more left in the tank.

Diana stopped beside Lara, carrying a box of lime-green water bottles.

'Finish-line freebies have been a hit. I'm pretty sure Paul's ZingleDangle company will be pleased with the coverage they're getting from this promo.'

Lara laughed. 'It's much easier to stomach his logo on the side of a plastic drink bottle instead of the general store. Speaking of hits, your husband's a natural on the race commentary.'

Diana and Lara looked at Pete, microphone in hand as he introduced the runner coming across the finish line.

'I suppose it's like another day auctioneering at the saleyards. I keep waiting for him to throw a "Hup a bid, hup a bid, who's gonna give me a bid" into the mix,' Diana laughed.

Diana was right. Pete's auctioneering voice was a lot like his commentating voice.

'What a great day to be at the top of Windmill Track, folks,' Pete said with a wave across the crowd. 'We promised you action, and here we have it. Sasha from Canunda was one of our VIP weekend ticket holders, she's nabbed herself the 10K first-place trophy today. I wonder whether she was a winner on Friday night too? All for a great cause, of course!'

The crowd's cheers were boosted with laughter and clapping as the woman broke the tape across the finish line and headed straight into the arms of a dishevelled-looking man wearing a 5K race bib. It was the pair from the bonfire.

The couple hammed it up for the camera. From the hobbled gait as they walked away, and the smile on the bloke's face, it looked like he'd upheld his side of the bargain. Everywhere Lara looked, people were smiling, and it was impossible not to get swept up in their high spirits. Even the weather had come to the party, with only cockatoos and galahs in the cloudless sky.

Lara continued past the creaky windmill, which was now the star of many selfies, and narrowly avoided a collision with children playing tag, fuelled by fairy floss and sporting vibrant, glittery designs from Holly and Evie's face-painting stall.

She ducked into the organiser's marquee and added the morning's raffle tickets to the large plastic tub.

A tornado of blonde curls and tiger stripes—or were they supposed to be lions?—rushed up to Lara at warp speed as she stirred in the new tickets.

'Can I draw the raffle, Aunty Lara?' said Harry, thrusting a sticky hand towards the large plastic tub.

'Sorry, mate, Mrs Beggs will be our barrel girl as soon as the half-marathon's finished. Anyway, the tickets would stick to all that fairy floss and you'd pull out three winners, not one,' she laughed.

Her youngest nephew piped up. 'Not a single snake, Aunty Lara.' Leo's voice dripped with disappointment. 'We've been looking everywhere.'

'Glad to hear it, mate,' she said as the boys ran out of the marquee.

She was putting the lid on the tub of raffle tickets when a clash of palm trees and hibiscus flowers loomed into view. Lara squinted at the ghastly Hawaiian shirt. Dallas's taste in clothing hadn't improved in the weeks since his last shift at the general store. His new venture into Bitcoin investment obviously hadn't netted him a fortune.

'Just the lady I'm looking for,' he said, hurrying in her direction. His hair was slicked back, car salesman style, and he was almost quivering with excitement.

'I've got a business proposal for you, Lara . . .'

Oh boy . . .

Maybe it was the success of the weekend, or the inner triumph at having exceeded their fundraising target, but Lara found herself indulging Dallas's animated sales pitch.

'. . . and these colour runs are the hottest thing since sliced bread. I know a guy who knows a guy that gets the colour powder for mates rates, so we'd have low overheads and . . .'

She nodded and took the rainbow-coloured business card he pressed into her hand, even though she already had his contact details.

'Thanks Dallas, I'll think about it when all this is over,' she said, gesturing to the marquee full of trophies, spot prizes and race-day merchandise, and then the crowd beyond.

'Don't leave it too late, Lara. It's the perfect spin-off event and you already know we make a great team.'

We do?

In too good a mood to disagree, Lara waved Dallas off with a promise to keep it in mind.

Toby dashed in a moment later, his hi-vis Race Director vest flapping.

'Found you! First half-marathoner's on his way. He's passed the final water station,' Toby said, holding out a hand.

Lara took it, treasuring the warmth on the clear but cool day, and didn't let go until they were standing by the windmill with a bird's-eye view of the track. Lara remembered the last time they'd stood there together. How many months ago had it been? Toby squeezed her hand and she couldn't help but smile up at him, pretty sure he was remembering it too.

A voice from behind them broke the moment.

'Look, here he comes!'

Lara squinted into the sun. Sure enough, there was a small figure ploughing up the bottom of the hill, wearing the bright yellow bib that distinguished the half-marathon distance.

Pete's commentary reached fever pitch when he realised the runner was a former local.

'It's one of our very own, Bridgefield-born athlete and all round great guy Charlie O'Brien. He's been living in the city but we won't hold that against him, he's going to take out first place, this is a great moment, folks . . .'

Lara caught a glimpse of Diana in the crowd, shaking her head indulgently.

'Reckon Pete thinks he's calling the Melbourne Cup?' she said.

'Imagine him with a karaoke microphone,' said Toby.

'We sure dodged a bullet there,' Lara said with a laugh.

A breeze kicked up, making the windmill spin and promo banners flap. The smell of paddocks, fresh and fecund, drifted across the food-stall and fairy-floss aromas, a reminder that they were in the middle of prime grazing country. She caught sight of the lake in the distance, the majestic mountain range, the patchwork of properties that made up their district, and felt more grateful than ever for the place she called home.

Toby's thumb traced a line along the back of her hand. She huddled in closer, making the most of his windbreak.

The place we *call home.*

Twenty-six

The sun had lost its warmth, but instead of thinning out as Toby had expected, the crowd at the top of Windmill Track had grown. By the time he stood near the podium, handing out trophies, there was barely a spare blade of grass on the top of the hill.

He spoke into the microphone. 'This whole weekend was organised to save our general store, and we've done it.'

Toby paused as a cheer rippled through the crowd. He thanked the sponsors, the runners, and finally the community.

The applause echoed across the valley. A flock of swans lifted off the Bridgefield Lake, and not for the first time, he itched to have his camera around his neck, documenting the day. He hoped Holly had managed to squeeze in a few shots between face painting and keeping an eye on her grandparents and little Queenie, who was rugged up in a sheepskin-trimmed dog jacket for the occasion.

And if he'd thought it was gratifying to hand out the trophies, Toby was unprepared for the thrill of watching Lara and Mrs Beggs step up to the microphone to draw their raffle.

Lara's initiative had been the most innovative of the three fundraisers, the one that had drawn the most conjecture and strongest laughter, but it had raised the most money in the end.

Lara gave the plastic tub a generous shake and spoke into the microphone.

'As you all know, the winner of this raffle gets twelve months' free rent above the general store. I can't take responsibility for any pie-eating habits developed while living above the shop, nor can I promise absolute silence from the hours of eight till five. Lord knows what type of gossip will float upstairs on a gentle breeze.' She paused as the crowd laughed. 'But I can promise a neat and tidy little apartment.'

Mrs Beggs swirled her hand through the tickets theatrically.

'And the winner is . . .'

A hush fell over the crowd.

'Brody Pilkington,' said Mrs Beggs.

The name rang a bell. From the hearty clapping, Toby realised he was the local lad who volunteered at the shop.

'Absolutely perfect,' said Lara, leaning in close enough that Toby could smell her shampoo. He shook Brody's hand and presented him with the keys to the apartment.

Toby took one last look at the gathering, trying to imprint it in his memory before he switched the microphone off. He caught sight of his parents by the windmill. They were bundled up in their winter jackets and beanies, Queenie's tail was wagging and the biggest, proudest smile was spread across his mother's face. Now all that was left to do was clean up and celebrate their success.

❦

Holly, Cameron and Evie stacked the empty Tupperware containers from the bake stall into the back of Lara's Subaru. There was a perfect square of neatly pressed grass beside the windmill where the jumping castle had been, but no other sign of the crowds, the banner-flanked finish line or the stalls that had converged on Windmill Track hours earlier.

Crickets and frogs had begun their dusk chorus and the sun had started to bathe the hill in a soft, golden glow. A mob of wallabies bounded across the paddock, watching warily as they paused to nibble at the tender shoots of native grass.

'Surely it's beer o'clock,' said Tim as he packed the last of the finish-line barricading into his ute tray and tied it down.

'My oath,' said Pete, nearly hoarse after a full day on the microphone. Diana passed him a bottle of water from the car.

'Let's get the boys dinner and settle them in front of a movie first,' she said. 'One drink and I'll be out like a light.'

'We'll head off too,' said Rob, hoisting Claudia up onto his shoulders.

Angie yawned and rested her head against Rob's chest. 'You can drive, sweetie. Claud and I'll both be fast asleep the minute the car hits the highway. Remind me why we decided to move two hours away,' she groaned.

'Because you love me, and the beach is a pretty nice spot to live,' he said, kissing the tip of Angie's nose.

'Bunch of party poopers,' said Lara. 'Toby's putting on a big spread tonight, half the committee have already put in their apologies, you can't pike out now.'

'Oh yes,' said Penny, with a teasing smile. 'It'd be *such* a shame if it was only the two of you.'

'No wonder he's taking so long to collect Holly's overnight bag. He's probably sprinkling rose petals on the bedspread and lighting candles,' added Angus, barely hiding his amusement.

'Pftttt, you guys need to get out more,' said Lara, but she knew she was smiling. Her family made their farewells, each excuse lamer than the next, and headed their separate ways. Lara had almost finished her final scout around the area when two cars rumbled up the same track the runners had huffed and puffed up earlier that day.

It wasn't until she saw the older couple in the car behind Toby's Volkswagen Golf that she realised in the hubbub of race day, she hadn't even introduced herself to his parents. And here they were collecting the girls to take them back to Ballarat.

Great manners, Lara. Way to make a good impression.

She squeezed Evie into a big hug.

'Thanks for all your help today.'

The cars pulled up, but before Lara could introduce herself, Holly had opened the back door and a small dog barrelled out.

'Queenie!' cried Holly, reaching down to scoop up the chihuahua, but the little dog wriggled out of her grip and scurried down the track.

Toby was out of his car in a flash.

'Stay here with Granny and Pop. I'll get her,' he said, loping off down the hill.

'The wallabies!'

Holly and Evie ignored his instructions and followed close behind. Cameron joined them, calling the little dog. The wallabies took one look at the procession careening down the track and bounded in the opposite direction, which only intensified Queenie's yipping.

Lara hurried to the car.

'I've never seen such a little dog move quite so fast,' she said, noticing Toby's mother had the same deep-blue eyes and warm face. 'I'm Lara. Sorry I didn't catch you earlier, I meant to come and say hi when you were at the finish line.'

'Shush, I don't expect you had much time to scratch yourself, let alone greet each and every volunteer. I'm Alice, and this is Eric. And I knew who you were the second we arrived here today. You look like you did in Toby's beautiful photo.'

'With my sisters in front of the general store? I mightn't have let Toby take it if I'd known it would be turned into a front page.'

A frown crinkled Alice's face, making her soft wrinkles even more pronounced.

'I can't say I've seen that one, though it does sound special. The photo of you saving the shop lady.'

Lara's heart skipped a beat. 'Sorry?'

'You know, the one in that award? Mrs Beggs, I think Holly said her name was? She was lucky to have you in her corner that day. You've got life-saving hands, that's for sure.'

Lara froze, and her mind replayed the scene from so many months ago. The adrenaline of saving Mrs Beggs. The anger at having her photo taken.

But Toby deleted that photo. He promised. She'd seen him hit delete.

It didn't matter that he'd taken dozens of pictures of her since, or that they'd laughed the other day about starting off on the wrong foot.

'Didn't you like the photo? I would've thought you'd be pleased.' Alice's tone had taken on a note of worry. 'Our Toby's such a talented man. Newspapers, photography, we're so proud of him.'

'Sorry, I think you've got the wrong end of the stick. What photo?'

'The big one in the Nikon Press Awards. It looks so good blown up. It's sure to win first prize.'

Lara scanned the horizon. Toby, Evie, Cameron and Holly were only small dots in the distance now, the mob of black wallabies barely visible as they headed for the scrub at the bottom of the lake. She could hear the *yip, yip, yip* of Queenie's bark, but from the way Toby was running, it looked like the dog was still in hot pursuit. Any other time, she might have laughed, might have driven down and picked them up and trailed behind the stupid dog until it tired of its fruitless chase.

He didn't delete the photo, he entered it into a goddamn competition . . . How could he?

A deep voice from the other side of the car interrupted her stupor and she turned to see Toby's father leaning across his wife.

'My boy's a darn good reporter. Did you know he's top dog at the Ballarat newspaper?'

Lara remembered Toby talking about his father's dementia. He must be confused.

'The Bridgefield paper,' she gently corrected.

'Nope, the daily paper in Ballarat. I've read it every day of my life, couldn't be prouder of him,' said Eric with a wink.

Lara looked at Alice, who patted the older man on the arm as he shifted back into his seat. She gave Lara an apologetic smile and lowered her voice.

'Don't mind Eric, dear. Gets his wires crossed. Toby hasn't officially accepted the promotion yet, but he'll have his name on the masthead soon enough. Top secret.' Alice smiled and tapped her lips.

What . . .

Lara mumbled what she hoped sounded like a polite farewell but it felt like her world had tipped upside down.

He lied to me about the photo.

He said he was staying in Bridgefield.

He didn't even tell me he'd been offered the Ballarat job.

Was the whole thing a ruse to get into my pants? A little bit on the side to pass the time until he could head back to the city?

Lara marched woodenly towards her car, casting a final glance in the direction of the man she'd thought she could trust and the daughter she'd spent her life fighting to stay strong for. If she left now, she would also give up hugging Evie for the last time until the July holidays. Lara took a deep breath. She pulled the door open and tucked herself into the driver's seat.

I should drive down there and tell Toby Paxton exactly what I think of liars.

I should stay and give Evie one last hug before she leaves for boarding school.

The deceit felt even more painful on a night when she should be celebrating.

A voice from the past whispered in her ear, low and mean: *You've never been the smartest tool in the shed though, have you, Lara?*

Lara twisted the key in her Subaru. Gravel and dirt crunched under her wheels. She blinked back the tears that threatened to break the carefully constructed walls of her self-control.

❧

'For a small dog, she's pretty fast,' Cameron panted.

Toby broke stride as he glanced across at Lara's nephew. Sweat beaded on his skin, his face was flushed, and they had a solid hundred metres on the girls, who'd slowed to a walk-jog. Toby backed off his pace a little.

'Hard to believe a chihuahua could outpace a runner and three fit teenagers. We'll just have to hope her little legs tire soon,' Toby said, squinting into the afternoon sun. The wallabies were long gone, and it was almost comical to watch the dog zigzagging across the hillside following their scent. But Queenie didn't show any signs of slowing, no matter how many times she stumbled or lost her footing on the uneven ground.

'We'll be lucky to catch her with our knees and ankles intact,' Toby said, pointing out a dip on the track ahead. They both gave it a wide berth.

'So, you're pretty keen on Aunty Lara?' said Cameron.

The comment was so out of the blue that Toby almost lost his footing.

'I am, she's great.'

Cameron coughed, then continued, his voice somehow deeper. 'You'd better be good to her, you know. Anyone who hurts her again is going to have us to answer to.'

Toby was impressed by Cam's loyalty. He toyed with the idea of quizzing Cameron on his intentions towards Holly, but before he could, the girls let out a whoop of delight.

'She's all out of puff!'

Toby shaded his eyes against the glare to see Queenie flop down in the middle of the track, letting out the occasional protest bark.

'Hard to know whether to shake her or pat her, silly thing,' said Evie when the girls caught up with them. Toby grinned. Evie was a chip off the old block, no doubt about it.

'Granny and Pop are still watching, so best not shake her,' said Holly dryly, scooping Queenie from Toby's arms and beginning the trek back. The teenagers all groaned when they reached the base of the hill.

'Last one to the top's a rotten egg,' said Toby, breaking into a slow jog. He was eager to get back to Lara and find out what the night held. 'You girls can rest your weary legs on the drive back to Ballarat. Think of poor Queenie, she'll be in twice as much pain with double the legs!'

They let out a chorus of exasperated groans. He smiled to himself as he climbed the hill. *Hard to beat a Dad joke.*

The windmill came into view and then his parents.

Concern was written across their faces.

'Queenie's fine, just knackered,' he said, keen to allay their worries.

Alice reached for his hand. Her voice trembled.

'No, it's not Queenie. Your lady friend, Lara, just left.'

Toby spun around, looking for Lara's car. It was odd that she hadn't stuck around to say goodbye to Evie. Very odd.

'She looked really upset,' his mum continued. 'Her face went white as a sheet, like a ghost walking over her grave.'

The teenagers huffed and puffed their way to the car.

Toby's stomach clenched.

'Why? What were you talking about?'

'Well, I was saying what a lovely photo you'd taken. The one for the contest.'

Toby scratched the back of his head.

'I haven't entered any contests this year, Mum.'

Alice looked at her granddaughter, puzzled.

Toby in turn looked at Holly, who bit her lip.

'It was supposed to be a surprise. I was only going to tell you after they'd done the judging. I'm sure it'll win, Dad, and imagine that new Nikon. It's top of the line, the type of prize that would really kick off your photography business.'

Toby shook his head, trying to understand.

'The Nikon Press Club comp?'

Holly studied her shoes.

Toby sucked in a sharp breath. There was only one photo he'd taken this year that was contest worthy, and he'd deleted it. *They'd* deleted it. 'You didn't . . .'

Holly scuffed her toes in the dirt, still not meeting his gaze.

Alice Paxton gave a bright smile, eager to cut through the tension.

'It was a lovely photo, darling. You should see how grand it looks in Melbourne with all the other portraits.'

No, no, no. Toby shook his head, trying to get a grip on his anger. His tone dropped a few decibels.

'Holly *Paxton!* You bloody well didn't!'

Out of the corner of his eye, he saw Evie flinch. He eased a carefully measured breath through gritted teeth and tamped down the anger. With Sam Kingsley for a father, Evie had probably seen enough aggro for one lifetime, and losing his cool wasn't going to help anyone.

'Did you, or did you not, delete Lara's photo like I asked? Or did you go behind my back and enter it into a contest?'

'Which picture are you talking about?' asked Evie, confused.

Cameron's narrowed gaze swung back and forth from Holly to Toby to Evie. Toby could almost see the boy's trust dissolving.

Holly's eyes flashed when she looked back up at him. 'The one with your mum saving Mrs Beggs.' She shot Evie an anxious look before continuing. 'It's your photo, Dad. It'll win, I know it.'

'We thought you'd be able to give the photo enlargement to Lara as a gift after the exhibition finishes, but she didn't react quite the way I was expecting,' said Toby's mother.

Toby groaned. 'It's a great photo, but that's not the point. Lara asked me to delete it, and I did.' His cheeks burned as he thought about the way he'd dragged it out of the camera's trash file to admire it on the laptop screen. 'Well, I thought I did . . . She hates having her photo taken without consent . . .'

It was Holly's turn to look confused. He hadn't mentioned anything to her about Lara's past and obviously Evie hadn't either.

Evie chewed on the end of her ponytail, a gesture that made her look about five, not fifteen.

Cameron shook his head and put an arm around his cousin.

'Is it breakfast time yet?' said Eric. 'I could eat a horse and chase the jockey.' He leaned down close to Queenie. 'Miss Queenie needs her meaty bites, too.'

Toby looked at the setting sun. Now wasn't the time or place for an explanation. He needed to find Lara and his folks needed to head off before every kangaroo between Bridgefield and Ballarat started the Russian roulette of roadside grazing.

Evie took a seat in the rear of the car, propping her backpack next to her. She looked like she would rather hitchhike home than sit beside Holly. Evie slipped her headphones in and tapped at her phone screen.

Texting her mum?

Holly gave him a final hug before slipping into the car.

'I'm sorry, Dad,' she whispered, pressing one of Alice's floral hankies to her nose. 'I wanted you to win that camera,' she added with a hiccup.

Toby pulled her in tight. 'Love you, Lollypop. Always have, always will. Even when I'm angry with you. We'll talk about it later, okay?'

Cameron didn't say a word as Toby drove him home, only a terse thanks before he hurried out the door. Diana waved from the kitchen window, and Toby wondered if she'd already heard the news. He pumped the accelerator, pushing the Volkswagen Golf as fast as he dared on the gravel road towards Lara's homestead. Her battered Subaru was parked at an awkward angle.

Toby took the steps two at a time, almost brushing a pot plant off its saucer, but no amount of knocking would bring Lara to the door.

He crouched down and lifted the flap on the old-fashioned mail slot.

'Lara, I didn't know about the photo. I swear. I only wanted to see it on the big screen and then Holly hijacked things.' *You're waffling, Paxton. Cut to the chase.* 'Anyway, I'm really sorry. Holly thought she was doing me a favour.'

A sharp pain exploded in his lower leg. Toby swore and sprang backwards as a flash of black and white launched off from the verandah. The magpie fluttered at knee height, flapping its wings. It fixed him with a beady glare, then attacked his leg again. Its sharp claws felt like little knives poking through his jeans. Another sharp pain came as the bird pecked at his hand.

'Owwww!'

Toby darted away. The magpie squawked indignantly then hopped its way across the deck. A trickle ran down the back of Toby's hand and when he looked again, he saw it was sticky with blood.

'Better than a rottweiler,' he murmured with a wince.

Footsteps echoed down the hallway, and moments later Lara opened the door. Toby had braced himself for anger, but he wasn't prepared for the anguish on her face.

'Save your excuses. If I can't trust you, Toby, if you can't stand behind your word, you're no better than my ex-husband.'

She closed the door quietly, and Toby lifted his bleeding hand to knock again, but paused.

Banging the door down wasn't going to prove exactly how different he was to Samuel Kingsley. From all he gathered, the man hadn't taken no for an answer.

You're no better than my ex-husband. The words had more bite than a mid-June frost, haunting him as he walked away.

Twenty-seven

The days merged into weeks, then months and before Lara knew it, spring was bearing down on them. Tulips from a long-ago owner were pushing their green fronds through her soil, irises were popping up along her driveway, blooming happily despite the neglect, and a hive of bees had decided the chook house roof was the perfect place to swarm, scaring the hens off the lay once again. And still, Lara hadn't replied to Toby's letter.

He'd slipped it under her door in the week following the fun run. No matter how many times she'd read it, and the letter of apology that had also arrived in the mail from Holly, she still hadn't made headway on her response.

Lara picked up the letter, now folded and creased, and re-read his apology. She couldn't fault Toby's sincerity, and yet she still couldn't find the words for her own reply. She sat it back on the bench, next to Holly's letter, and picked up her pen and notepad.

Flicking through the pages, she reviewed her latest attempt. Neat handwriting meant nothing when the words couldn't convey how she felt. She tore the lined sheet off the notepad and tossed it across the kitchen. It rebounded off the KitchenAid and landed in the chook bucket.

'Give me a break.'

With a sigh, Lara retrieved her rambling half-finished letter and tossed it in the bin. She remembered the cold horror of finding out what Sam had done with the footage he'd secretly filmed. How could she explain how it had made her feel when she'd discovered Toby's photo had been used without her permission?

It's not logical, she told herself. *Toby isn't Sam.* And yet every time she put pen to paper, trying to tell him that she *knew* his photo was nothing like Sam's video, and she *knew* Holly had used it without his permission, she couldn't explain all the emotions it had stirred up.

Trusting someone always leads to pain.

Lara huffed out a frustrated breath as she locked up behind her, refilled Basil's water bowl and topped up his dry food. She stalked across the lawn, then paused as she realised something was missing.

Now that his wing was healed, the magpie had taken to impressing her with his new and improved flying skills every time she walked outside. But today, Vegemite zipped past, paying her no attention, and landed in the tree beside another bird.

From a distance, they looked like a pair of matching bookends, both black and white, although as Lara got closer, she noticed the smaller bird had a slightly grey ruffle around its neck.

The bad mood that Lara had woken with lifted slightly. She watched the female magpie edge a little closer to Vegemite.

'So, you've finally found a mate,' she murmured, catching herself before she went gooey, or worse, felt jealous. 'Don't think I'll be feeding two of you. Or a whole magpie family.'

The magpies were the perfect excuse to call Evie on her way into work.

'Hey Evie, how's things?'

'Mum? What's wrong?'

'Can't I call to say good morning?'

'Let me guess. Brody locked himself outside the apartment again wearing only his Garfield boxer shorts?'

Lara managed a laugh as she pulled out of her driveway and onto the sealed road. The new tenant in the upstairs apartment had been embarrassed and freezing by the time she'd noticed three missed calls and driven into town with the spare key the previous week.

'Nope, though you've got to admit that was pretty funny.'

Helping Brody settle into his new home had been the only highlight of the past month, and though she felt like her personal life was in turmoil, it was satisfying to see him thrive now that he was out of his father's house. With a bit of luck, his shifts at the shop would be a stepping stone to employment when he graduated high school.

Evie's guessing game continued.

'Did Olive mix up the pie days again and nearly cause a riot by serving the chicken and leek on Monday then cheese-and-bacon on Thursday?'

'Better than that. Guess who's got himself a girlfriend?'

Evie's response was incredulous: 'What? And why do you sound happy about it?'

It was Lara's turn to be exasperated.

'It's Vegemite! The magpie. The *magpie* has a girlfriend. I thought you'd like to know.'

Lara pulled in behind the Bush Nursing Centre and killed the engine.

'Not everything in this world is about Toby Paxton,' Lara said.

Evie sighed loudly. She could almost see her daughter rolling her eyes in the boarding house.

'He's a nice guy, Mum. You liked him and he liked you, that's all.'

'Past tense, Evie-girl. That's real life, I'm afraid, not everything gets wrapped up with a pretty bow like those soppy TV shows you've been watching.'

Lara caught sight of her reflection in the rear-view mirror. The words belonged to an old shrew, not someone in her early forties, but it was easier this way.

'But you know it wasn't Toby's fault, Mum. He was as surprised as you. You need to see this article, Toby's—'

Lara winced. She couldn't sit through another pro-Toby conversation, not this morning. Whatever she thought they might have been, she was mistaken. The quicker she erased him from her mind, the better.

'Stop right there, missy. I need to go, really,' Lara said, blowing loud kisses down the phone before hanging up.

The conversation played on her mind for the rest of her shift. Even the bumper turnout at the Move It or Lose It class failed to brighten her mood.

Cindy the receptionist had left a copy of the *Bridgefield Advertiser* upside down on the lunch-room table. Lara studied the back page football coverage as she ate her sandwich, then, with a huff, she flipped over the paper and read the headline:

Bridgefield Advertiser set to close

Close?

Lara scanned the article, swallowing the lump in her throat along with the last of her sandwich. She folded the paper in half, refusing to wonder what this would mean for Toby.

Not my problem, she reminded herself, tossing the edition in the bin on her way out.

☙

Toby took the first park he could find at the saleyards, pulling up by the truck-washing bay. A horn tooted, and the pungent aroma of cow shit wafted across from a B-double truck awaiting its turn.

Toby tried to shake off his melancholy mood as he headed towards the auction arena. The cattle sales had always been a highlight, with news tips coming from the most unusual places. He would miss the upbeat feel to the day, the sense of occasion as the local farmers caught up with friends, trading stories from their paddocks. His thoughts were interrupted as a hand clapped him on the shoulder, startling him out of his gloom.

'Long time no see, mate.'

Toby greeted Pete, and looked over his shoulder to see if Cameron was there too.

Last night over the phone, Holly had confided she hadn't heard from Evie or Cam since the fun run, and the misery in her voice had been as clear as her millionth apology. He glanced around again. Pete was the only one from Lara's family there, as far as he could see.

'This month hasn't been one to write home about,' Toby admitted.

'Sorry to hear about the newspaper closing, mate. Are they really mothballing it even after all the community backlash? I thought you were on a two-year contract?'

'The board of directors *had* committed, but apparently a proud past doesn't make up for a sleepy present,' he said, repeating the weak excuse the company's directors had given him.

'It's insulting, that's what it is. After all the effort you made to get the *Addy* back on track. So, readership was up but they still closed it? Doesn't make sense.'

'Turns out elbow grease and warm, fuzzy feature stories aren't enough when the number crunchers are baying for blood.'

'Over a hundred and fifty years of local history, gone for good? Ludicrous,' said Pete, his voice laced with disgust. 'What will you do for a crust? Do you have to pack up and head for the big smoke, cap in hand at your old paper?'

Toby thought about the job Mick had offered him, and the lure of a steady income doing something he knew well. He'd known instantly that it wasn't the path he wanted to follow anymore. Not after that front-page Mick had run. He'd also toyed with the idea of starting a community newspaper but hadn't fully fleshed out the business plan yet.

He shook his head.

'I'm going freelance. I've got plenty of contacts in magazines and newspapers, plus it'll give me a chance to focus on my photography. There're enough weddings and family portraits to keep me afloat, and I can work from anywhere.' Even if it meant he had to sell one of his city investment properties, he knew he would have enough to live on and support Holly.

'Just make sure they sign permission slips, eh?'

Pete gave him a wink and laughed at his own joke. Toby grimaced. He still felt bad about Lara's photo ending up in the Nikon photography contest, and even though he'd tried to right the wrong—Holly's wrong—he knew it was too little, too late.

'Terrible joke,' said Pete, groaning. 'Can I shout you a bacon-and-egg sanga?'

Pete ran him through the day's cattle prices on the way to the saleyards canteen before moving on to the McIntyre clan. Toby listened with half an ear, his mind wandering to the McIntyre sister who had taken his heart.

Has Lara opened my letter, or did she turf it?

It was easier to fill the Lara-shaped void in his life during the day, when his head was full of newspaper stuff, but she snuck into his mind every time he headed out for a run or heard a carolling magpie. Hell, if it wasn't the radio station having a Tina Turner-a-thon, it was the television pumping out *Friends* re-runs like they were going out of fashion. She was everywhere he turned. And next week, when the newspaper closed its doors for good, he would have even more time to dwell on what could have been.

'Lara's looking as miserable as you, mate. Not that I'd dare tell her that,' said Pete with a chipper smile. A glob of yolk dribbled down the front of the stock agent's red shirt. 'She'd bite my head off and then some.'

It wasn't much consolation. Toby hated knowing he'd inadvertently drawn them both under this cloud of unhappiness.

They left the canteen and headed back to the saleyards. Pete looked over to the bidding area, where stockies and auctioneers called from the overhead platform.

'It's my turn in a minute,' he said. 'Don't stress too much, mate, I know Cam and Evie have cooled down and Diana reckons Lara'll simmer down in her own time. Never was one for being rushed, that girl.'

Toby wiped his hands with a napkin and lifted an eyebrow. 'Really?'

His wry tone made Pete chuckle. Toby made his farewell and ambled through the crowd with a slightly lighter step than he'd walked in with.

Lara threw herself into tasks that could be done on autopilot, and was restocking the shop fridge when a customer swept in.

'These are *glorious*.'

A voice came from the middle of the store, and she looked up to see a customer admiring a big bouquet of flowers. Any logical person would like the posies, studded with proteas and sprays of grevilleas and gum blossoms, but Lara could barely look at the brimming buckets, even the ones from Diana's ever-expanding patch.

Brody put down the mail he was sorting and helped the woman choose a bunch.

'They're from local farms too, grown on the outskirts of Hamilton and right here in Bridgefield,' he said enthusiastically. 'We've only just started stocking them.'

Nanna Pearl had raised the idea at the last committee meeting, and Lara had been as impressed as the rest of them until she learned it had been Toby's suggestion. Every bunch she sold reminded her of what they'd almost had.

Your choice, remember?

Lara wrapped the flowers in old newspapers, flaring the edges like Diana had shown her. She looped ribbon around them, and ran it along the blade of her scissors, but the ribbon refused to curl.

She forced a smile as she handed over the bouquet and farewelled the customer.

'They're popular,' said Brody. 'Diana said we should make a sign saying "Grown, not flown", to increase the feel-good factor. What do you think?'

Lara tried another smile. 'Knock yourself out.'

Brody's enthusiasm knew no bounds. She was glad to see him thriving in his new environment, but she felt exhausted just watching him.

The shop door flung open and a young couple ambled up to the counter, arms wrapped around one another.

Lara had to look away; the way they moved in unison was too much. Young holiday makers in Bridgefield? The wildflower season was ramping up in the Grampians, but most of those tourists were normally Angus's age, not twenty-somethings.

'We hoped we'd find you here!' The woman beamed and waved a hand in Lara's direction, as if she were auditioning for *Sale of the Century*.

Weird.

'Are you here for the pies? We've got steak and rosemary today,' Lara offered doubtfully.

The customer's face fell.

Vegan perhaps?

'Or salad rolls if you'd rather?'

The bloke gave a chuckle. He leaned in so he was cheek-to-cheek with his girlfriend.

'You don't remember us! We were at the fundraising weekend. Adam and Sasha. I was the idiot who almost had a heart attack on the 5K finish line. Sasha here breezed in with first place in the 10K.'

Lara laughed for the first time all week.

'How could I forget? You're looking very . . .' *Sickeningly happy? Smugly smitten?* Lara felt like a shrivelled-up old prune compared to this loved-up pair.

'And we're engaged!'

Lara's laughter scudded to a halt, and she felt her mouth form a perfect 'o' shape. Young, loved-up and stupid. What a heady combination.

Brody jumped in with his congratulations, thankfully making enough fuss for the both of them while Lara gathered her wits.

'Wonderful news,' she said, swallowing down the urge to caution them about heartbreak.

Sasha held out her hand again and Lara realised she was supposed to admire the chunky diamond ring. She made the appropriate noises as the pair outlined their plans to exchange vows at the top of Windmill Track next year.

Sasha and Adam buzzed with excitement as they headed off, their arms wrapped firmly around one another again.

The door jangled shut. Lara let out a sigh.

'They're happy now, but I bet you fifty bucks there won't be a wedding at Windmill Track in twelve months' time,' she said.

Brody hesitated. 'What, you mean they wouldn't get a permit to get married there? Isn't it Crown land?'

'No, I just mean that people change, infatuations wear off and half of those frilly white wedding dresses in the op shops never even made it down the altar.'

Her words hung in the air. Lara caught Brody's eye and cursed her pessimism. Just because she was miserable, she didn't have to bring everyone down with her.

'Rant over,' she said, shaking her head with a sheepish look. 'Maybe they'll be happily married for fifty years. Plenty of people seem to manage it.'

Brody's sparkle seemed to wane a little, seeing straight through her false bluster, and she felt even worse when he shook his head and agreed with her.

'Maybe you're right. It didn't happen for my parents. Or for you and Evie's dad. Maybe you're just a realist,' he said with a sigh that sounded too weary for his seventeen years.

Lara walked through to the kitchen and made them both a cup of tea. The first mouthful scalded her lips, and she took another as penance. She stared into the strong brew, searching for a way forward and finding nothing but a rogue tea leaf.

She trudged up her front steps later that night, ignoring the unruly lawn that tickled her ankles and the self-seeded poppy blossoms that had burst into bloom beside the chook house, their origin as mysterious as the irises and tulips.

Lara flicked through the TV channels, scowling at the limited options. Too trashy. Too whiney. Too cheerful. Too boring.

She was reaching for the *Friends* DVD when Basil scratched at the door. Lara let him in.

'What would Evie say, Baz? Stop moping and go for a run?' Inspiration struck as she patted the dog. 'That's it! We need a slice of Evie-sunshine, Baz. Shall we see if we can jail-break her out of boarding school?'

The more she thought about it, the better the idea sounded. Lara dialled Evie's number.

'Hi, Mum!'

Suddenly, Lara couldn't wait a moment longer to see her daughter.

'Put the kettle on, Evie girl, I'm coming your way.'

She jumped off the couch, shoving things into an overnight bag as she outlined her idea. It was the most invigorated she'd felt in weeks. 'I'll be there in a few hours, we can get Thai for dinner, head out for ice cream. You can wag school tomorrow and we can do some shopping, grab the midday movie and—'

'Mum? Mum!' Evie's voice cut over hers. Lara paused, but continued loading clothes into the bag. Why hadn't she thought of this earlier? It would be the perfect pick-me up.

'You're worried about getting into trouble, aren't you? I'll . . .' Lara cast her gaze around her bedroom, spotting the bottle of St John's wort tablets Angie had described as happiness in a bottle. 'I'll make up some bogus doctor's appointment.'

'Mum, that's not it. I'm going to the ballet at Her Majesty's Theatre with Edwina tonight,' she said softly. 'I told you, remember?'

As quickly as Lara's excitement had risen, it went again in a whoosh. She braced herself against the bed frame and sank to the mattress. *Of course Evie had plans, but why oh why did they have to be with the Kingsleys?*

'I'm sorry, Mum, I didn't know you were planning to visit.' Lara heard the worry in her daughter's voice and felt even worse. 'She arranged the tickets ages ago. Dinner too. I can cancel? Or you can come with us?'

Lara let out a shriek of laughter. Dinner and ballet with her ex-mother-in-law? But before she knew it, great big sobs came from somewhere deep inside. Warm tears welled, making her vision swim. It felt like her Jenga-tower of a life had well and truly tumbled.

I've ruined everything. I've lost Toby. I'm losing Evie. She thought of her bitter response to the happy couple earlier that day. *I've got nothing.* Something warm nudged her hand, and through her tears she saw Basil by her side. *Nothing but a snake-chasing kelpie and a chip on my shoulder.* Lara's shoulders shuddered as she tried to rein in the tears.

'Mum?' Evie's voice was kind, and more than a little concerned. 'I know you don't like Edwina and Karl, but they're never going to replace you. I wouldn't trade you for anything,' she paused, making sure Lara was listening. 'Or any*one*.'

Lara took a shaky breath. She didn't know what to say. She caught sight of herself in the wardrobe's mirrored doors and felt ashamed of her jealousy and her bitterness. How had it come to the point where her teenage daughter was consoling her?

Pushing herself up off the bed, Lara didn't stop moving until she was outside. The wind whipped away her tears and she filled her lungs with the clean, country air she loved. Lara pressed the phone to her ear again, relieved Evie was still on the line.

'I'm sorry, Evie. I've been so scared of losing you.'

'Oh, Mum.'

Evie listened quietly, as Lara shared her fears and the resentment that arose every time the Kingsley name dropped into Evie's updates.

'You don't need to worry,' Evie said eventually. 'You've been here for my whole life, encouraging and helping me every step of the way. These guys aren't going to come and steal your thunder in just a few short months,' she said, a smile in her voice.

Lara swallowed hard, taking in the maturity and percept- iveness that belied Evie's fifteen years. 'They're not bad people, Mum,' said Evie softly.

Closing her eyes, Lara nodded. 'I know.'

'And they can't cook to save themselves, so you'll always know the way to my heart.'

Lara laughed, feeling the late afternoon sun warming her skin. Was she right? Was there enough love within Evie to go round? She let her daughter change the mood with a few jokes at her teachers' expense, before enquiring after Cameron and the rest of her cousins.

They settled on a get-together the following weekend, and Lara felt a little better by the time she'd hung up. She walked around the overgrown garden, pulling out the odd thistle and throwing it into the chook pen.

The ruffled poppies swayed gently in the breeze. Lara noticed a ladybird trapped in a spiderweb that dangled between two flowers. She plucked it free and watched it climb up and down her fingers before fluttering away.

This is not about me, it's about Evie. She's got a heart the size of Uluru—who am I to regulate who she shares it with? It wasn't until Lara had crossed the garden that she spotted a black-and-red dot crawling up her arm. The same ladybird or a totally different one? The little insect lifted her spirits. Instead of pushing the resentment aside, as she normally did, Lara sat on her deck until she'd reached a decision. *I can't let the Kingsleys keep living rent-free in my brain.* There was enough love within Evie to light up the moon, of that she was sure, and while she didn't want to sit down for jam and scones with Edwina and Karl, she let herself accept that Evie wasn't comparing them, or ditching her for her grandparents.

෴

Toby woke the next morning refreshed. Three a.m. had passed without its usual wake-up-and-dwell-on-things specialty, and he treated himself to a long leisurely run. Two shooting stars, what sounded like an amorous pair of koalas and one kookaburra chorus later, he was looping back past Lara's driveway. The windows were dark, as if she'd taken a rare sleep-in. Toby found himself calling out a greeting to the cows that followed him along the roadside until Lara's property boundary ended.

He would miss this.

His phone buzzed as he passed the remains of McCluskey's shearing shed, and for a second he let himself imagine it was Lara calling to say she was done stewing and ready to talk.

But as he tugged the phone out of his shorts pocket, Holly's name flashed up on the screen. He stopped on a dime, his flow disappearing in an instant.

'What's wrong, Lollypop?'

'Good morning to you too, Dad. Can't a girl call her old man to say hi?'

Toby started to walk the short stretch towards his driveway.

'At six in the morning?'

'I'm calling with good news,' she said. He could hear her smile all the way down the phone line.

'You got a job that pays all your school fees, so your poor, nearly unemployed Dad can keep you in the luxury to which you're accustomed?'

Holly laughed. 'No silly, the Nikon awards. Your photo won! The email came through late last night after I'd gone to sleep. I knew you'd win it,' she said.

Toby carefully navigated his driveway. A recent downpour had washed away the top soil, making it even more rutted than usual.

'Doesn't make it right, Hol.'

'But think of the great photos you'll take with that new camera. You're not going to turn it down, surely?' Her voice was incredulous. 'It's the best Nikon on the market. You've lusted after it more than . . . than . . .'

Holly struggled for an analogy, as if realising she didn't want to picture her daggy old dad lusting after something. Or someone.

'More than you lusting after Cameron McIntyre?' he offered, wedging the phone between his ear and shoulder as he tried to coerce the gate into opening.

'Daaa-ad. That's gross.'

'Tell me I'm wrong.'

Holly's groan was only half-hearted. 'Well, Cam might be part of the reason I'm up early. He sent me a message this morning, first one since the fun run. He's an early bird like you.'

'How's Cameron going to react when you tell him the photo won? That's not going to score you any friends in the McIntyre clan. It means the picture will be used in the marketing for next year's awards. Evie and Lara aren't going to like that.'

Holly's enthusiasm wavered.

'I didn't think of that.'

Toby kicked at a rock on the driveway. He knew Holly felt bad about the pickle she'd got them into, but it didn't make Lara's silence any easier to bear. An idea formed as the coffee brewed. He couldn't change the outcome of the awards, but maybe he could find a way to do good with that expensive camera he'd won. By the time he'd finished the coffee and showered, Toby had come up with a plan.

Twenty-eight

Lara tore along the deserted track, legs pumping and arms swinging, focusing solely on the amount of speed she could cram into her twenty-minute run. Even the most gruelling leg-burning, chest-on-fire sessions did little to dull the hurt. The next best thing would be some torturous hill sprints up the side of Windmill Track, but she couldn't go back there. Not yet.

Lara was almost at her front gate, the ambling heifers who had followed her along the driveway fence line no match for her furious pace, when her phone buzzed inside her exercise belt. Her watch screen lit up too. *Personal best!*

She switched off the watch, barely acknowledging those two validating words that danced across the digital screen. Basil greeted her at the door, his tail wagging, and followed her down the hallway. Lara extracted her phone from the sweaty exercise belt and read the new message.

Hi Lara, could I trouble you for a cup of milk to make my porridge? No hurry, just on your way to work would be fine. Let me know if you can't make it and I'll try Dallas xx Mrs Beggs

Mrs Beggs' medication needed to be taken with food, and there was no way Lara would leave it in the hands of the eternally unreliable Dallas. She arrived at the little cottage ten minutes later, bottle of milk in hand.

'Thanks, darl. Come in,' Mrs Beggs said, beckoning Lara through the door. 'Won't keep you long, I just wanted to show you this.'

Lara followed Mrs Beggs into the cosy lounge room, wondering whether she was about to see a rash or an oozing wound, and was surprised to be handed a newspaper article.

'What's this?'

Mrs Beggs stayed silent while Lara studied the photos.

She felt her breath catch. It was from *The Ballarat Daily*. The first picture was of Holly, standing with a woman outside a modern-looking brick house. The second was the photo of her working on Mrs Beggs. *It's good*, she admitted to herself. *Really good.*

Lara's feet stayed glued to the floorboards as she read the article.

'Toby won the contest but then sold the prize?'

'And donated the money to charity,' said Mrs Beggs, sounding like a proud mother.

Not just any charity, but a women's refuge.

'The refuge helps women who have escaped abusive relationships, it says. That sounds like a very good thing, doesn't it, dear?'

Lara swallowed then re-read the article, pausing when she got to Holly's quote.

I'm so pleased for my dad. He never toots his own horn, which is why I entered his work in the contest. I was surprised he didn't keep the camera, especially seeing he's starting his own

photography business, but it makes me proud to
know it will help women who've survived trauma.

The spokesperson from the refuge centre said the money
would provide a much-needed boost to the families who used
the emergency accommodation service.

Donations like this are always gratefully received,
and I thank Mr Paxton on behalf of all the brave
women who come through our doors.

Lara reeled from the news.

Why would he part with a top-of-the-line camera?

She handed the article back to Mrs Beggs and tried to jolt
her thoughts into order.

'He's a decent bloke, Lara,' said Mrs Beggs gently.

Lara felt even more muddled by the time she'd driven home.

You once thought Sam was a decent bloke too, remember?

There was only one thing for it. Lara strode into the kitchen,
flicked on the oven and pulled an apron over her head. She
separated eggs and set the whites to whip. Just as she was sifting
flour, her mobile pinged with a text from Evie. It was a photo
of the article Mrs Beggs had shown her.

Did you read the article? I called Holly after I saw it in the
paper. She says to tell you again how sorry she is xxx Your
favourite daughter, Evie

Lara pushed the phone aside and returned to the recipe
book, wiping a drip of egg white from the well-loved sponge-
cake page. But even as she tapped the brimming sponge tins
on the benchtop to get rid of the air bubbles, she couldn't
stop thinking about what might have been if she hadn't heard
about the photo contest or the job offer, shunting her from
pure happiness to perfect misery in one fell swoop.

She slipped the sponges into the oven and set the timer, still feeling antsy.

It was too big a hurdle to get over.

Wiping her hands on her apron, she decided more baking was in order, so she tossed an extra handful of flour onto the bench and worked on a cinnamon-scroll recipe that tasted as good as it looked. The mixer would have made short work of the dough, but she felt the need to knead.

Lara turned the dough over and over.

Was Toby a good dad? Yes.

Stretching and pulling.

Did he roll up his sleeves and help save a shop because he's a nice bloke? Yes.

Pulling and stretching.

Is he tolerant of animals, and old people, and children, even Harry and Elliot? Yes, yes, yes and yes.

Slowly she felt the fibres in the dough began to loosen. She thought of Toby's powder-blue safari suit and his gentle, unhurried kiss after the ball.

The oven timer went off before she'd made up her mind. With the sponge cakes out of the oven, Lara set the dough aside to rise. Her heart ached.

Toby was the first man she'd wanted to trust in a long time, and already that fragile thread had been tested and found wanting. Lara pulled cream from the fridge and tipped it into the mixer. Even after the fridge door was closed and the beaters were coated with creamy whipped peaks, she felt a chill deep in her bones.

Don't forget what happened last time, she told herself. She never, ever wanted to give anyone that power over her again, not in this lifetime. Her brain told her that it was easier to be lonely than risk it, even if every piece of her heart disagreed.

Toby surveyed his living room, wondering where to start. He had always hated packing.

Belinda would appreciate the extra hand with her new bub, his mum would too, and maybe if he spent more time with his dad, his memory lapses might not be so vast. Being back in Ballarat would make it easier to see Holly during the week too, as well as on the weekends, and it made sense to be closer to Melbourne for his new photography business.

It's the smart thing to do.

Toby flicked the kettle on and opened the cupboard. Jars of homemade pickles lined the shelves, along with fresh rhubarb jam from Diana, and the colourful blue-and-yellow apron Nanna Pearl had whipped up in one of her sewing lessons with Eddie and Jaylee.

He stared at the local goods, feeling a prickle in the back of his throat at the love that had gone into each and every item.

How could he leave Bridgefield and the woman who'd captured his heart?

He picked up the teapot his mum had given him as a housewarming gift. It was one of her favourite pieces, commemorating the 1981 marriage of Lady Diana and Prince Charles. Alice hadn't given up on his dad for all those years, even on the days he couldn't remember his own name, the days when his eyes lit up for Queenie, but not for her or their children or grandchildren. She hadn't given up on the royals either.

His laptop dinged with the arrival of an email, illuminating the screen with his new website. Pride swelled as he watched the slideshow of his best images—the portraits, the weddings he'd shot for friends, the landscapes. He double-clicked on the photo he'd taken down by McCluskey's shearing shed, before it had all gone up in smoke. It was everything he loved about living in Bridgefield: the serenity, the early mornings, the quiet roads, the space. He'd been happy here.

Toby's gaze went to the rows of cameras lined up on the shelf by the window—the old Box Brownie, the Pentax and the retired Nikons he hadn't been able to part with, even when he'd transferred to digital.

Good things were worth saving. Good things are worth working for.

Bugger it, what's the worst Lara can say? Goodbye once and for all?

Toby headed to the door and drove across Bridgefield to Pearl Patterson's house. Music flooded out through open windows when he arrived. He could hear her singing along to Kenny Rogers, and when the door opened, the smell of baked goods rushed out the door to greet him, followed closely by Eddie.

'Toby, Toby, Toby,' said Eddie, crossing the threshold to wrap him in a hug.

'Morning, mate, is your nanna around?'

Eddie nodded gleefully. He grabbed Toby's hand and tugged him inside, where Pearl was pulling a tray of scones from the oven.

'You must've followed your nose down the laneway,' she said with a chuckle, dusting her hands on a purple flowery apron. 'Get 'em while they're hot,' she added, pushing a plate towards him.

The smell was divine. As Eddie broke open a scone, the most magnificently scented steam poured from its middle. Toby's stomach rumbled so loudly that both Eddie and his grandmother laughed.

'Nanna Pearl's best scones,' said Eddie, piling two onto Toby's plate.

'It's a crime to walk away from hot scones,' said the older woman, tapping the lids of the various jams. 'Quince jam, peach jam, rhubarb-and-banana jam, or boring old blackberry,' she said. 'Straight from the orchard.'

Toby looked at his watch.

'Thanks, maybe just one,' he said, picking up the plate. 'I was actually hoping to ask you a favour,' he said. 'I've got a surprise for Lara, and I need a couple of helpers.'

Pearl leaned in, her smile so broad he could see a smear of pink lipstick on her teeth. 'I'm all ears.'

Twenty-nine

Lara flung the tray of burned biscuits onto the lawn. It was the second batch she'd ruined in as many hours and she didn't have the patience to risk a third.

'I'd probably stuff them up too,' she muttered under her breath. Basil wandered across the yard, sniffed the smouldering biscuits and gave them a wide berth.

'Wise move, Baz,' she said, rubbing the kelpie between his ears.

If her sisters were here, they would urge her to have another shot. But Lara had knocked back their company. It was much easier to wallow when you didn't have an audience.

She slumped onto the couch and tried to muster up some enthusiasm for the latest *Country Style* magazine, but no matter how many beautiful kitchens she admired or recipes she skimmed, she couldn't get her mind off Toby.

Call him.

Call him and tell him you overreacted.

Just call him.

But as she reached for her phone, it started to trill in her hand. Lara answered on the first ring.

'Oh Lara, so glad I caught you,' said Nanna Pearl. 'Eddie missed the bus from Hamilton, and Tim's at the saleyards today. Any chance you can cover at the shop while I pick him up?'

Lara looked at the pile of magazines Penny had delivered with strict instructions to chill.

'Of course I can. Be there soon.'

Purpose was good. Purpose gave her a little window of grace before she dredged up the courage to swallow her pride and invite Toby back into her life.

Nanna Pearl was waiting at the back door of the shop when Lara pulled into the car park.

'Sorry to drag you away, pet,' said Nanna Pearl, smiling warmly. She didn't look half as harried as she'd sounded on the phone. 'Be back shortly.'

Lara waved her off and went straight into tag-teaming with Brody, serving customers and handing out mail. Two pies, three bags of mixed lollies, several newspapers later, she heard a noise coming from Main Street. Lara shielded her eyes against the afternoon sun and peered out behind the dusty postcard stand.

There in front of the shop, right beside the A-Frame board promoting the pie of the day, stood Toby.

The familiar strains of the *Friends* theme song filtered through the glass windows.

He raised a microphone.

But he hates . . . singing in public. A smile escaped, completely unbidden, as she opened the front door. The sound was even worse at full volume.

※

From the corner of his eye, Toby could see the traffic slowing. The Mums and Bubs walking group had stopped short of the

Bridgefield pub, their strollers banking up. A child cried at the sudden lack of motion and quite possibly his singing. Five seniors with yoga mats paused outside the Bush Nursing Centre.

Why did I choose rush hour?

He moved onto the chorus and it took every skerrick of his self-control not to close his eyes and block out the amused stares, giggles and most likely sniggers.

He kept his eyes fixed on Lara's, searching for a sign that this crazy idea had been worth it. He closed the gap between them with another step, studying her gold stud earrings, the strands of hair that had snuck loose from her bun, the almost invisible freckles dusting her cheekbones—anything to distract himself from the spotlight he'd stepped into.

Why in God's name had he chosen a song with so many verses?

The music swung into the third verse. He sang along, his attention veering from the printed lyrics in his hands to the walking group. Most of the children had their hands covering their ears, and even some of the parents, though at second glance he noticed one of the mums pulled a mobile from her nappy bag.

Great, now someone's filming me making a complete twit of myself.

But still he kept singing.

Toby ignored the drops of rain landing on his face. The skies could open up, but he would stand here until every last bit of fight had drained out of him. Hell, he'd even do an encore if that's what it took.

The music started to wind down, but still Lara stood with her arms folded across her chest.

It hasn't worked.

For the first time in his life, he wished the *Friends* theme song was twice as long. The small crowd outside the nursing centre started to clap as Toby stopped singing and the music cut out. The toddlers in the strollers joined in even though it was quite possibly the worst piece of street entertainment ever to be inflicted on the town of Bridgefield.

Lara raised an eyebrow. 'I'm pretty sure that violated at least ten different noise-pollution laws,' she said. 'You'd better come in before they start throwing rotten tomatoes.'

Toby followed her into the shop, closed the door behind him and flipped the sign to closed.

'But it made you smile, didn't it? I know how much you like that song.'

'There's so much you don't know about me, Toby.'

Toby heard the anguish in her voice, but even worse was the sadness in her eyes as she looked away.

⚭

Lara blinked slowly, feeling the familiar stab of uncertainty well up inside her.

A few months ago, at the top of Windmill Track, she'd wanted to kiss him.

A few weeks ago, at the top of Windmill Track, she'd wanted to slap him.

A few days ago, in the dark of the night, she'd mourned the future they almost had.

An hour ago, she realised exactly what she'd missed out on and wanted to remedy that.

And now, standing here in the Bridgefield General Store, the same place she'd first met him all those months earlier, she felt more conflicted than ever.

She fixed her gaze on the mailboxes behind the counter.

'You're right,' Toby said, 'there *are* so many things I don't know about you. But here's what I *do* know.' He smiled. 'I know you're stubborn. I know you hide your key under the purple flower pot. I know you like to try to keep up a gruff pretence but you saved Basil—you would've carried him to the vet yourself if that's what it took. I know you care more about your community than your own wellbeing, and that nobody else could've saved this shop.'

He ran a hand through his hair.

'And those magpies you hate so much? You still had a big enough heart to adopt Vegemite,' said Toby, the look on his face so hopeful that it made her heart ache. Toby continued, talking faster, as if he could see the storm of emotions and the damage they could wreak.

'And you know so much about me. How many times have you rolled your eyes at my odd socks? It was years before Petra even noticed. You know I'm pretty rusty at the Nutbush but I still give it a shot. You know I can't sing to save myself.'

He cleared his throat and fixed her with those earnest eyes.

'You know we could be good together,' he finished simply. *I'd mess it up.*

Lara shook her head. 'I *don't* know that, Toby. My judgement's completely up the creek. I didn't even know my husband was an abusive bastard until years into our marriage. I've been jealous of my in-laws—people who have a son in *jail*, for God's sake—because Evie is forming a relationship with them. If past history's anything to go by, I'm missing some vital points on the human compass.'

Shame rose from deep inside as she spoke the words aloud, and she shivered. *If she didn't let him in close, she couldn't get hurt.*

༄

Toby studied the strong set of her jaw. *How can I make her understand?*

He wanted to pull her into his arms, kiss the little mole on the underside of her jaw, smooth the wisps of chestnut hair back into her bun.

'So, you're not perfect. Me either. But I'm not planning on spending the rest of my life whipping myself for it. Holly's the best thing that ever happened to me, and I'd wager Evie's right up there on your list of achievements, yeah?'

Lara murmured her agreement.

'Hell, if you'd told me last year that I'd turn down the job I've wanted my whole career, for a woman I've known for six months, I would've laughed. But there's something about you, Lara McIntyre. And if you'll have me, I'm here . . .'

Another cheer came from outside.

What the . . .

Toby turned and looked through the shop window. The crowd was still gathered in the street. The staff from the Bush Nursing Centre was watching too. Farmers had spilled out of the pub for a stickybeak, one giving Toby a thumbs-up. He looked down at his hands, realising the microphone was still switched on. And they'd heard every word he'd uttered.

If you're gonna be a bear, you might as well be a grizzly.

He raised the microphone to his lips, ignoring the voice inside his head that reminded him he still had a slither of pride left.

He sang another few bars from the *Friends* theme, meaning every word. He wanted to be there for her, rain, hail or shine. He wanted her to feel safe with him, and fall asleep beside her knowing she was there for him too.

A loud whistle came from outside.

Lara whirled around in time to see Tim's WB Holden crawl down Main Street. Nanna Pearl's purple hair glowed from the passenger's seat.

'I thought Tim was stuck at the saleyards?' She looked back to Toby. 'How many people did you rope into this charade?'

'Only enough to make sure you'd be at the shop.'

'Did you arrange the rent-a-crowd?'

Toby held out his hands.

'You can thank Nanna Pearl and the gossip hotline for that one.'

Lara yanked the shop door open.

'Righto, everyone, show's over,' she called.

§

Lara's mind searched desperately for the courage needed to let herself be vulnerable, to be brave like Toby.

He'd made a complete fool of himself, yet here he was, standing in the Bridgefield General Store, having given one of the worst karaoke renditions she'd ever witnessed.

Damned if she didn't feel more drawn to him than ever.

'Anyone in favour of the karaoke bar is now thanking their lucky stars it didn't get off the ground,' she said.

Toby ignored her and took a step closer until he was inches away. So close she could smell the lemony hint of his laundry powder.

'I want to make it work, whatever it takes,' he said.

His words started a domino effect, little frissons of happiness that did funny things to her heartbeat, but caution kept her at bay.

Toby scanned her face.

'Tell me you don't feel the same? Tell me, hand on heart, that there's a good reason not to choose happiness?'

'I thought I'd made good choices before, but—'

She faltered. It made complete sense in her head, though as she said it out loud, it felt clear as mud. She blurted out the rest quickly, before logic deserted her. 'I've been there, done that,

Toby.' Lara drew a ragged breath. 'Sam proved how wrong I was. And if I've learned anything from that bastard, it's that nice guys are for fairy tales.'

She tore her eyes away from his, not wanting to see the sympathy that would break her resolve. The only thing more unbearable than letting Toby get close again would be watching him walk away. She looked up at him, wishing he could take a step closer so their lips were touching and she wouldn't have to make the decision.

But as much as she willed him, as much as she wanted to explain, or tell him that she cared for him so much it scared her to death, the words wouldn't form on her tongue, and her feet stayed planted to the old linoleum floor.

The gentleness in his voice was almost her undoing.

'I wish I could go back in time and catch Samuel Kingsley in a dark alley and teach him a lesson he'd never forget. I wish I could've rescued you, Lara.'

He reached for her hand, but instead she wrapped her arms around her chest.

'I'm not a hopeless princess sitting in a tower, waiting for a prince to rescue me, Toby. I should've been smart enough to rescue myself.'

Toby winced.

'Good blokes *are* out there,' he said quietly. 'Look at Tim. Look at Rob. Pete. Your dad. Sam's the odd one out, not you. Can't you see that?' His gaze was imploring, as if the choice should be obvious. She started to wring her hands, wishing she could believe him. 'I'm falling in love with you, Lara.'

The word brought the memories flooding back. There was no way he could know how much she despised the L-word.

'No.' Lara laid a finger over his lips and swallowed hard. 'Sam used the word "love" as a weapon,' she explained. 'And you're nothing like him, I know that now, but . . .'

Lara thought of young Brody, now thriving in the upstairs apartment. He'd thought he owed it to his dad to stay, but even at age seventeen he'd been braver than her and chosen his own path. She thought of the man standing before her, studying his odd socks. He'd thrown aside every scrap of dignity he had and serenaded her in the main street, for God's sake.

What more do you want, Lara?

When she looked up, Toby's eyes were on hers. He gently reached out and cupped her cheek, and she knew in that moment, that everything was going to be okay. Tears prickled her nose, her eyes grew slippery and all of a sudden her vision was blurring. All the years of holding it in, the trauma, the bravado, the fear of losing Evie, the fight to save their shop, welled up inside.

'I'm pretty well acquainted with a thesaurus,' he said, his voice filled with tenderness. Lara closed her eyes a moment, finding it hard to imagine that after everything, he was still interested.

'Well, I guess that's lucky for both of us, Toby Paxton,' she said, leaning in until her lips pressed against his.

A roar came from outside the shop, and together they turned to the raucous applause of the Bridgefield crowd.

Epilogue

Lara stared at the tools she'd laid out in the back of the Subaru.

Drill—check.

Spanner, shovel and hardware—check.

Supper for two—check.

She had everything necessary for the job, but she needed to get a wriggle on if she was going to pull off the surprise before Toby got home from his first shift as manager of the Bridgefield General Store. Basil's tail thumped on the ground, each repetition raising little puffs of dust, and his tongue lolled out the side of his mouth, waiting for her command.

'Come on, Baz,' she said, giving a quick whistle. Basil leaped into the boot and turned a couple of times before settling down on her old winter jacket.

She added her wide-brimmed hat, shut the boot, then checked the trailer's safety chain.

Yep, that'll do it. That load of gravel isn't going anywhere.

The smell of warm biscuits filled the car, and she drove slowly up her driveway, along the road fifty metres and then down Toby's driveway. Basil stayed in the boot, content to watch as she upended shovel after shovel of gravel into the ruts, inching the car and trailer forward every ten minutes or so, until the deep corrugations were barely visible.

'One job down,' she said, wincing as she swung the shovel into the empty trailer. It had been a long time since she'd emptied a trailer-load of gravel by herself, but even longer since she'd replaced a gate.

Basil jumped out of the car, giving her a slobbery lick of encouragement, before trotting off to inspect Toby's brimming flower beds.

Lara pulled the old gate off its hinges and marked the fence for the new hardware. She had a sheen of sweat, a few splinters from the treated pine post and aching shoulders, but before long a new bottom bracket was fixed into place. She looked at the twelve-foot gate lying on the ground.

Just got to lift it back on, fix the new hinge and— whammo—job done.

Basil loped back over, his tail going ten to the dozen. Lara looked up to see a bicycle at the top of the driveway.

She wiped her forehead with the back of her hand and then went to the gate. She could still get it done before he arrived. She man-handled the gate upright and almost had it in place when Toby's voice carried down the driveway, along with the sound of crunching gravel.

'Hey, wait a minute. Let me give you a hand.'

Lara shook her head, trying to line up the far corner of the gate onto the blocks she'd brought with her.

'I can do it myself,' she said.

'I know you can, but you don't have to. Tell me what to do, I'm happy to help,' he said.

Lara turned, smiling at the sight of him hanging onto one end of the gate, still wearing his bicycle helmet, awaiting her instructions. He hadn't been lying about not knowing how to swing a gate.

She got him to kick away the blocks she'd sat on the ground and lift the gate until it was the right height.

'Hold it there,' she said, grabbing the coach screws from the back of her car. She screwed the hardware on and walked back to Toby. 'Give it a go,' she said, watching his amazement as he pushed the gate and it swung freely. Basil walked over and perched himself beside Toby's feet.

'To what do I owe this honour? Mighty neighbourly,' he said, leaning down to pat the dog.

Lara stared at her work boots, and then smiled as she realised she was wearing one red-striped sock and one white ankle sock. She took a deep breath before looking up and meeting his gaze.

'I'm not very good at mending fences, but I'll have a crack at fixing your gate,' she said.

His calm expression dissolved into laughter. Basil gave a woof.

'That's got to be the cheesiest pick-up line I've ever heard.'

Heat flamed her cheeks, but she smiled.

'It was pretty bad, wasn't it?'

She gathered up her tools, returned them to the back of the car, and followed him inside with the platter she'd prepared.

'Brought you some sweet treats too.'

His eyes lit up as he took in the perfectly round yo-yos with pink filling, the coconut-covered lamingtons and the jam drops filled with Diana's latest batch of blackberry jam.

She spread a picnic rug out on the back lawn, admiring the garden beds Toby had filled with pretty, scented flowers. In the distance, she could just see the new timber frames of McCluskey's replacement shearing shed. He could never replicate the intricate stonework of the previous building, but with a few neighbourhood working bees to help clear the site, and a few yet to come, he had started the process of building a new shed. With a bit of luck it would be serviceable in time for the next round of shearing.

Toby headed inside and returned, minus the bike helmet, with a tray of mugs and a teapot that looked like it was straight out of *Antiques Roadshow.*

'Is that Princess Di?'

'Sure is, and look at young Charlie. Very dashing.'

Toby tucked into the jam drops as she shared her day at the Bush Nursing Centre and lay back on the rug while he filled her in on his day at the shop.

'And I've just had another wedding booking if you fancy a weekend away at Daylesford,' he said.

Basil's tail thumped and she smiled as Vegemite and his magpie mate flew over to join them.

'I'm pretty sure I can handle that,' she said, leaning in until her lips pressed against his. He tasted of sweet jam, and of all the good things she'd thought she never deserved. He tasted like the perfect tomorrow.

Acknowledgements

I love reading acknowledgements pages and it gives me great pleasure to again be writing them, this time for *Magpie's Bend*, my third novel.

A huge thank you to you—my readers—whether you've bought, borrowed, shared, been gifted or listened to this story or joined my newsletter community. Your kind words, enthusiasm for the McIntyre family and encouragement keep me returning to the keyboard each day. I cherish every single message, review and social-media shout-out. If you could teleport to our rural property in western Victoria, you'd know I do a little happy dance and read them all out loud to my husband/children/cat/calf/lamb/dog (whoever is closest). I also love seeing your photos of my books with your pets, in your hands, your homes and on your holidays, so please keep them coming. Word-of-mouth recommendations are the best present you can give an author, so please don't be shy about spreading the word.

To all the booksellers, librarians, bloggers, reviewers, journalists and podcasters—*mwah*! Booklovers like you keep our industry afloat, and on behalf of all Aussie authors, please know we are so grateful for your support and your superpower in getting our novels into the hands of the right readers, especially during the pandemic.

Sending big love to the fabulous team at Allen & Unwin, particularly my publisher Annette Barlow, editors Samantha and Claire and proofreader Megan, publicity and marketing gurus Isabelle, Laura, Yvette, Rebecca, Fleur and Matt, cover designer Nada, and all-round treasure, Jenn. There's a reason you guys have won Publisher of the Year fourteen times. Teamwork makes the dream work and I value your behind-the-scenes efforts to make my books shine.

There were plenty of helpers who assisted in the research stage. Thanks to Paula and Maddy Jasper for the whys and hows of keeping our local post office afloat, Sue Elms for outlining the effort to save St Brigid's Church at Crossley, Sam Carter for explaining real-estate processes, Kylie Holland for guidance on committee legalities, Bonnie Taylor for sharing her snake-bitten kelpie story last summer, Sally Watson for lending me her beautifully embossed (and very treasured) letters from the royal palace, Detective Senior Constable Jarrod Anderson and Nicholas from Australia Post for helping with a mail-fraud plot line that was unfortunately cut in the editing process.

Thanks to Amy Smoothy and Ann Miller for the veterinary insights and Kate Griffith for reading my medical scenes over a glass of rosé and a cheese platter. I think that might just be my new favourite method of fact-checking! Also, cheers to my Winter Solstice Fun Run crew for many happy miles and making fun-run planning so enjoyable that I had to include one in *Magpie's Bend*.

Many sets of eyes went over the manuscript before it hit the printing press, and I'm indebted to Julie Linnell, Pamela Linnell, Kaneana May, Karen Nancarrow, Lindy and Amber Sloan and my husband Jason for entering the not-quite-formed world of the McIntyre family, helping me with plot holes, and boosting my writerly spirits in the second and third draft stage. Again, thanks must go to my lovely neighbours, with special mentions for Karena, who dropped off the most delicious cream puffs when I was in the depths of structural edits, and Tony who ran his eagle eye over it too. Any errors are most certainly mine. Kudos to the legends at Griffin Press, SA, for filming *Bottlebrush Creek* as it came off the printing press. Possibly the coolest eight minutes of factory footage I've ever seen, head to www.mayalinnell.com/news to watch it yourself.

I also dedicate Lara's character to all the strong women who put up and shut up for too long. Ideas for this story percolated while I worked in communications for a healthcare agency, and domestic violence was one of the issues we dealt with. This flowed into my writing, along with stories from friends—beautiful, strong women—who were mentally and physically hurt by men they trusted. Sending big love your way, ladies.

Thanks to my writing buddies, especially the Scribblers Ink writing group, for advice and encouragement and friendship. Writing is a solo occupation, but I treasure our Friday morning zoom sessions.

To my close friends and family, your belief in me and my novels is amazing, and much appreciated. We didn't get to celebrate in person last year, but I'm sure we'll make up for it with *Magpie's Bend*. Thanks for cheering me on, sneaking my books into conversations with your extended networks and collecting little snippets that might come in handy for future manuscripts.

Jase—for a bloke who prefers newspapers over novels, you do a mighty fine job of braving my manuscripts, helping brainstorm plot issues, sneaking sweet post-it notes into your proofreading feedback and talking about these characters and this completely fictional world as if it were real to you too. Thanks, Jase. I couldn't do this whole author gig without your support.

Charles, Amelia and Elizabeth—your big day is finally here! You've been itching for a dedication and you sure deserve this one. Thank you for getting excited about book mail, sales milestones, new contracts, lovely reviews and book tours, for keeping quiet downstairs during (most of) my Zoom events and for being pretty good office mates during the Covid lockdown. Much of this novel was written and edited in the depths of the pandemic, with its online learning and lockdown challenges, unlike the last two books, which were mostly penned during school hours. This one's for you!

Happy reading, folks! I hope you enjoy reading Lara's story as much as I loved writing it.

Love,

Maya

PS: If you'd like a little more writing, baking and green-thumb antics in your life, come find me on Instagram or Facebook @maya.linnell.writes or sign up for my monthly newsletter at www.mayalinnell.com

Read on for the first chapter
of Maya Linnell's new novel,
Paperbark Hill

Paperbark Hill

Diana McIntyre and her four boys have had a tough eighteen months but with the love and support of her family, she believes their lives are finally back on track. Diana's dream of starting a flower farm has been the perfect diversion, with an elderly dahlia expert showing her the ropes. She won't have to do this alone.

Locum pharmacist and single dad Ned Gardiner hasn't called Victoria home for years. However his father's death forces Ned to return to the family farm, a place that holds few happy memories for him. Dealing with his estranged mother and sorting his father's affairs, he plans on leaving as soon as possible, but what will it take for Ned to put down roots?

With six children between them, can this pair juggle families, farms and an unlooked-for romance?

One

Diana McIntyre swiped a dusty sleeve across her damp forehead, tucked her trowel back into her tool belt and proudly assessed her day's work.

Six long garden beds ran the length of the paddock, two with freshly turned soil. In all her years of gardening, these were the patches she was most excited about, planted with tubers for her first commercial dahlia crop.

'Two down, four to go,' she said, fanning herself with her straw hat and trying to recall the last time they'd experienced such a spring heatwave in the western Victorian town of Bridgefield.

It wouldn't look like much to a visitor. Heck, if she hadn't spent the day on her knees, with her hands in the dirt, even she wouldn't be able to tell there were thousands of dollars worth of dahlias buried in the first two patches.

Pete will be impre . . . Diana pressed a hand to her heart. She'd lost count of the times it still caught her unawares.

She dusted her hands on her overalls, as much to remove the dirt as to shake off the sudden stab of loss. The mob of corellas that had been watching her all afternoon swooped down and began picking through the soil. Diana started towards the birds, waving her hat, covering just a few steps before her body reminded her she'd used up her quota of energy for the day.

The gate hinges creaked as she crossed from the dahlia patch into her main garden. Diana snipped a bloom from the flourishing Abraham Darby rose bush, willing the scent to distract her. The last thing she needed was the boys to arrive home from school and find her in tears again.

Fresh starts, she reminded herself, cradling the bloom as she ascended the steps to her weatherboard farmhouse. Starting a flower farm was a step in the right direction, darned if she was going to let grief swallow her now.

※

Despite the early hour, Darwin's oppressive heat had sweat trickling down Ned Gardiner's back as he squeezed the final boxes into the moving van. He took a quick look over his shoulder to see his ten-year-old daughter Willow striding outside.

'Morning, sleepyhead,' said Ned. 'Ready for adventure?'

Willow pushed her glasses back up her nose and lifted an eyebrow.

'Are you *sure* Stan's going to make it through the red centre?'

Ned turned and met Willow's doubtful stare. He crouched down, smoothed her jet-black hair behind her ears and unfolded her scrawny arms.

'Sure as eggs,' he said. 'Has Stan the Van failed us yet?'

'I'll miss the fresh mangoes,' Willow said, nestling into his embrace.

'Me too. But maybe not the neighbours,' he stage whispered.

A giggle escaped and, just as he'd hoped, Willow's face brightened.

'Mrs Neilson was a little bit mean, wasn't she?'

It was his turn to grin. That was probably the nicest thing in years that anybody from the apartment block had said about the disapproving resident in number five.

Seven-year-old Doug yawned as he ambled down the steps, his T-shirt on backwards.

'Ready to rock, Dad?'

Ned nodded, feeling his shirt sticking to his body. He wouldn't miss the Darwin humidity.

Doug jumped into the front seat while Willow farewelled the mangy tabby cat weaving between her legs.

'He'll fool someone else into feeding him before the day's out,' Ned assured her.

'Mrs Neilson might feed you if you're a good boy, Flopsy,' Willow crooned, scratching under the cat's faded flea collar.

Ned's eyes went to the twitching lace curtains. Mrs Neilson was more likely to dance naked in her front yard, but kind-hearted Willow didn't need to know that.

'What about the mango tree, Dad? Are you sure we can't take it with us?'

Her pensive gaze stayed on the tree she'd lavished with attention during their stay, just like the tabby cat and the semi-translucent geckos that frequented their balcony.

'I wish we could, Willow. How about one last water?'

Ned looked over his shoulder as he uncoiled the hose and sprayed a jet of water towards the tree.

'Dad!'

It was worth risking the wrath of the water-conservation nuts on the strata committee, just to see the children's delight. The curtain twitched even more as he finished watering, latched the van's back door, climbed inside and clicked his seatbelt on.

'Mrs Neilson saw you doing that,' said Doug, his eyes wide.

'She'll report you to the water authority. Or . . . or the police,' added Willow.

Ned gave her a wink and waved to their nosy neighbour—
former nosy neighbour—before coaxing the van into gear and
pointing it south.

❦

Diana rebraided her strawberry-blonde hair as hoots and
hollers floated down the driveway.

By the time she'd reached the window, the twins were
halfway down the gravel track. Harry was in front this time,
his curls whipping back from his face and lanky legs pumping
madly as he raced his bicycle past the hay shed.

His twin, Elliot, wasn't far behind, leaning forward like a
Melbourne Cup filly hoping to win by a nose.

Competing for sheep stations again.

Diana's eldest, Cameron, rode at the back with little Leo,
still her baby at eight years of age. Despite the large age gap, or
maybe because of it, they chatted away, leisurely cycling home.

She headed outside with a container of lamingtons, warding
off the inevitable 'I'm starving' and 'coconut on the floor'
dilemma in one swift move. Bickering over who was today's
driveway derby winner, the boys skidded to a halt at the dog
kennels.

Diana's heart felt full as they unclipped the dogs and made
a fuss over the two sheepdogs. Cam and Leo joined the fray,
covering the final stretch of the driveway as a team.

My beautiful boys.

'Hi, Muu-uum.'

'Lamingtons!'

'You should hear what Harry did at school today.'

They shoved their bikes haphazardly against the garage,
gave her a quick hug and launched themselves at the food.

'Good day, Mum?'

Diana had to reach up to tousle Cameron's fair hair. 'Sure was, buddy. Notice anything different over there?'

The teenager took a lamington and followed her gaze.

'You got all the dahlias in?'

'I'm not a machine. I was pretty darn pleased to get *two* flowerbeds planted out today.'

Cam chewed thoughtfully.

'Reckon we can do the rest over the weekend. Might even rope those ferals into service.'

He nodded towards Harry, who was balancing a lamington on his nose. Paddy, the young kelpie, was glued to the sight, just waiting for a slip. Leo and Elliot were trying to copy him, much to the delight of their elderly border collie Bonzer, who was feasting on the fallout.

Diana shook her head, biting back a grin. It was a circus, but it was *her* circus.

⚜

The road sign lit up under the glare of the van's headlights, telling them it was another 150 kilometres until the next town. Ned glanced across at his little passengers. Doug had fallen asleep two hours ago, full of roadhouse burgers and ice cream, while Willow had fought to keep her eyes open, only dropping off half an hour ago. Her hands were still curled around the paperback she'd been reading for most of the day, and her glasses had almost slipped off the end of her nose.

Ned reached across and gently removed the tortoiseshell frames that were a smaller version of his own. She stirred, murmured and settled back to sleep. They'd always been good travellers.

The phone danced on the dashboard and a photo of Ned's little brother appeared on the screen.

Bit late for Jonno . . .

He put the call on speakerphone and slipped it into his top pocket, beside Willow's specs, expecting a jet-lagged catch-up but instead hearing panic in Jonno's voice.

'Colin's in hospital.'

'What? How bad?' Ned drew in a quick breath, mentally calculating the kilometres between him and his father's property in western Victoria. Almost 3000 clicks. He automatically pressed the accelerator a little harder.

'I'm on my way there now,' said Jonno, 'but from what I've heard, it doesn't look good.'

Jonno shared what little he knew about the accident, all second hand from the nurse who'd called him. Ned listened in quiet disbelief, straining to hear as the phone conversation dipped in and out of reception.

'What the hell was he doing? Re-sheeting the roof in the middle of gale-force winds?'

'You know Colin. The roof would need to be replaced entirely before he asked for help. Apparently he was trying to fix a loose sheet of tin before it got worse.'

'Worse is an understatement from the sounds of it,' Ned murmured.

He looked at the clock on the dashboard. Time was against him. Even if he drove through the night and got the first plane out of Alice Springs tomorrow morning, there was still a four-hour drive from Melbourne to Bridgefield. At best, they'd be back in the Western Districts around sundown tomorrow.

Ned listened to the medical terms Jonno used, knuckles white against the steering wheel. His mind flew through the possibilities, but each new option required more dicking around than he had time for. What he'd gain in catching a flight, he'd lose in making arrangements for the van.

He slapped the steering wheel with his hand.

'Thought you were only back in the country for forty-eight hours?'

'I am,' said Jonno. 'The ship's all set to sail. I'll let you know how he is when I get to the hospital, but I reckon I'll cancel my trip.'

'Don't be a bloody idiot. Six months on an ice breaker doesn't come along every week. Colin will be fine. He's too stubborn to die.'

Ned called the hospital as soon as Jonno hung up, but the nurse's grave update didn't instil any faith in him.

'I'll get the doctor to call you back, he's arranging a transfer to a city hospital as we speak.'

Staring into the dark night, Ned rubbed the bridge of his nose, trying to smooth out the indent made by his glasses.

'What a bloody mess.'

A little hand wrapped around his.

'What mess, Daddy?' Willow's sleepy lilt was followed by a yawn.

Ned looked at her, glad his little girl didn't realise quite how many answers there were to that question. The mess they had found themselves in when his now ex-wife, Fleur, decided parenting was 'too hard'. The mess they lived in for a week or so each time they unloaded the van at a new rental. The mess of paperwork each new school required for the kids' short-term enrolments.

'Shhh, go back to sleep,' he said, keeping his voice low.

He drove into the bleak night, reluctantly stopping at a motel in Tennant Creek and getting an earful from the owner when he knocked on the reception door.

'You know what time it is, mate?'

Ned apologised and paid handsomely for a seedy-looking room with an op-shop aroma.

Willow stirred but Doug barely flickered an eyelid when he carried each of them into the motel and tucked them between the mothball-scented sheets. Ned didn't have the same luck. Even after a quick shower, sleep proved elusive. After a decade of avoiding trips to Victoria, he couldn't get back to his home state fast enough. Would they make it in time?